Kris Longknife
DEFIANT

"[A] brave, independent and intrepid heroine."
—Midwest Book Review

Mike Shepherd

ISBN 978-0-441-01349-4

5 0 7 9 9 >

EAN

Kris Longknife
DEFIANT

Mike Shepherd

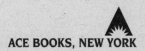

ACE BOOKS, NEW YORK

THE BERKLEY PUBLISHING GROUP
Published by the Penguin Group
Penguin Group (USA) Inc.
375 Hudson Street, New York, New York 10014, USA
Penguin Group (Canada), 90 Eglinton Avenue East, Suite 700, Toronto, Ontario M4P 2Y3, Canada
(a division of Pearson Penguin Canada Inc.)
Penguin Books Ltd., 80 Strand, London WC2R 0RL, England
Penguin Group Ireland, 25 St. Stephen's Green, Dublin 2, Ireland
(a division of Penguin Books Ltd.)
Penguin Group (Australia), 250 Camberwell Road, Camberwell, Victoria 3124, Australia
(a division of Pearson Australia Group Pty. Ltd.)
Penguin Books India Pvt. Ltd., 11 Community Centre, Panchsheel Park, New Delhi—110 017, India
Penguin Group (NZ), 67 Apollo Drive, Rosedale, North Shore 0745, Auckland, New Zealand
(a division of Pearson New Zealand Ltd.)
Penguin Books (South Africa) (Pty.) Ltd., 24 Sturdee Avenue, Rosebank, Johannesburg 2196, South Africa

Penguin Books Ltd., Registered Offices: 80 Strand, London WC2R 0RL, England

This is a work of fiction. Names, characters, places, and incidents either are the product of the author's imagination or are used fictitiously, and any resemblance to actual persons, living or dead, business establishments, events, or locales is entirely coincidental. The publisher does not have any control over and does not assume any responsibility for author or third-party websites or their content.

KRIS LONGKNIFE: DEFIANT

An Ace Book / published by arrangement with the author

PRINTING HISTORY
Ace mass market edition / November 2005

Copyright © 2005 by Mike Moscoe.
Cover art by Scott Grimando.
Cover design by Rita Frangie.
Interior text design by Kristin del Rosario.

ISBN: 978-0-441-01349-4

ACE
Ace Books are published by The Berkley Publishing Group,
a division of Penguin Group (USA) Inc.,
375 Hudson Street, New York, New York 10014.
ACE and the "A" design are trademarks belonging to Penguin Group (USA) Inc.

PRINTED IN THE UNITED STATES OF AMERICA

10 9 8 7 6 5

To the magnificent men and women who do it—
because there *is* no other choice.

Winston told the English boat owners there was a British army in trouble on the far shore. So they set sail by the smoke of Dunkirk and brought off 300,000 embattled Tommies and Frenchmen. No one knows the price they paid.

In '44 off Sumar, six escort carriers desperately needed time to run. Three destroyers didn't question their orders, but turned bows on to the entire Japanese Battle Fleet, setting a course from which none returned.

On September 11, a smoking bier told American boat owners that hundreds of thousands needed to be taken off Manhattan. With no orders given, no commands spoken, ferries and taxies, tourist boats and tugs, anything that could sail and carry weary workers, set sail for the sea wall at the Battery to take them home. Upriver, professional divers were working on a bridge pier. They knew, with that many boats in close quarters, someone's rope would wrap itself around another's prop. Without instructions or promise of pay, those workmen dropped what they were doing and sailed for the smoke. A half-dozen lines or more later, their work was done. And an uncounted fraction of a million got home that night.

And the passengers of Flight 93 made their fateful calls. It was their families who drew the heavy duty of telling loved ones they only wanted home that fate now stood in the way. And those souls who were no different from a quarter billion other Americans— except for the tickets they bought—showed a wondering world the true mettle of free men and women.

We do what we *have* to do, because there is *nothing* else to do.

Acknowledgments

I would like to sincerely thank Heather Alexander for permission to use her song, "The March of Cambreadth," liberally in this novel. Anyone who hasn't heard a hundred plus fans singing *"How Many of Them Can We Make Die!"* has missed out on one of life's moments. You can own Heather's "The March of Cambreadth" for yourself by making a quick visit to www.heatherlands.com and ordering the *Midsummer* album. Heck, order them all. I did . . . regularly. Every time one of my kids left home, they took my Heather collection with them, and I had to order up a new set.

I would also like to thank the folks at the WW I discussion group for letting me raise the hypothetical question of what might have happened if the British government had fallen in July 1914 over the Irish question and then faced the beginning of World War I. I'd especially like to thank Syd Wise for his refresher on the British and Canadian systems and Luke Taper and Geoffrey Miller for the Australian model . . . which I borrowed with variations for Wardhaven. Obviously, the changes, and any mistakes, are my own.

1

Lieutenant Kris Longknife grinned from ear to ear, no minor accomplishment at 2.5 g's. The short hairs on the back of her neck were standing up. At a brace. And saluting. She was scared spitless and had never had so much fun in her life.

This being Tuesday, under Commodore Mandanti's rotation system, she commanded Division 3, four dinky fast patrol boats, as they charged the battleship-size target ahead of them. And, if she trusted those little hairs on the back of her neck at all, the Commodore and his gunners on the *Cushing* had the PF-109, Kris's very first command, and the other boats of Div 3, pinned in the crosshairs of their defensive lasers.

It was time to get her boats moving to a different evasion pattern or they'd be left powerless, drifting in space . . . like the eight boats of Division 1 and 2 that had failed in their attack just minutes before her.

And she and the other eleven skippers of the fast patrol boats would be buying the beer for the Commodore's gunners.

And there would be a very critical report filed saying the PFs—small, easy, and quick to build with semi–smart metal—were failures, unable to defend a planet from attack. If that was true, each planet in the newly formed United Sentients would need a full, heavy battle fleet in its orbit if it was to weather the unknowns rapidly developing in these troubled times.

The political ramifications of that were something Kris Longknife, Prime Minister's daughter and great-granddaughter to King Raymond I of the U.S. alliance of ninety planets, did not want to think about. Far better for each planet to see to its own defense with a tiny mosquito fleet like her boat and let the heavy ships handle the problems of the whole alliance.

You're thinking too much again, Longknife. Get out of your head and kick some battleship butt.

Kris mashed the comm button under her thumb. The order that went out was short and scrambled. What it meant was, "Division 3, prepare to change to Evasion Plan 5 on my mark."

Kris waited. Waited for her own helmswoman to switch to the new plan, waited for three other boats to make the same switch.

"Ready," Boson 3/c Finch reported from her station beside Kris on the tiny bridge. The small brunet's voice was hoarse under heavy acceleration. Kris gave the other boats a slow three count.

THEY SHOULD BE READY TO EXECUTE NOW, Nelly said directly into Kris's brain. To call the tiny computer at Kris's neck a supercomputer would probably offend Nelly's growing sense of her own self-importance. What Kris spent on Nelly's last upgrade would have bought and paid for one of the battlewagons Kris and her crew were practicing to kill.

SEND MY MARK, Kris ordered, and the computer not only sent the execute to all four boats, but made the evasion pattern change within the same nanosecond—something no mere human could do. This computer intervention was not standard Navy procedure, and it had not been easily won. But it was at the heart of the plan of attack that Kris and her division skippers had knocked together last week at the O club—with Nelly's avid help.

"Executing Evasion Plan 5," Fintch reported.

And Kris's tiny command slammed her hard against the left headrest of her high-acceleration chair as what had been a soft left turn converted to a hard right turn and dive.

Kris swallowed and tightened her gut muscles. Again.

The division has started its wild charge from 150,000 klicks out, well beyond even 18-inch laser range. They'd gone to 1.5, 2.0, 2.5 g's acceleration, mixing up their growing speed with erratic right and left, up and down swerves. Sometimes hard, sometimes easy, sometimes in between. Always unpredictable. The tiny fast patrol boats were small as bugs beside the huge battlewagon they sought to slay. Now they danced like June bugs.

If they danced just right, they would live. And the battleship would die.

Because the fast patrol boats, though tiny, were deadly, too. Each PF carried four 18-inch pulse lasers. The quick burst from one of them could gut a cruiser or knock a gaping hole in a battleship's ice armor. Maybe even burn through to the mass of weapons, machinery, and humanity below.

So cruisers and battleships mounted secondary guns that fired fast and often and tried to slash through small stuff like the PFs. And big ships spun on their long axis, rotating slashing lasers away from damaged ice and into thick, un-hurt ice before burn-through into vitals could happen.

Measure, countermeasure, counter-countermeasure, layered thick and heavy. That was the way it had been since the time beyond recall when some human first set out to kill his brother. It wasn't enough to just have a fast ship, good weapons, and solid teamwork. You needed a plan and skill . . . and luck.

Or so Phil had told them all when he invited them out to dinner at the O club a week ago.

* * *

The Wardhaven O club, two blocks from Main Navy, had been ancient when Kris's Great-grampa Ray was a freshly commissioned subaltern. Its carpeted and thickly curtained rooms were perfect for fine dinning between the wars. On its walls hung battle trophies from Wardhaven's first unpleasantness with fellow Rim worlds. Rich oil paintings celebrating victories going back to mother Earth's dim, bloody past before humanity spread into space four hundred years ago.

Kris wasn't tempted to drink here; she got high on just the ambiance. But the white-jacketed waiter led the twelve junior officers right through the main dinning rooms to a small one off to the side, smelling of fresh paint and new, cheap carpet.

"What did we do to deserve this?" Kris frowned.

"Not us," Phil Taussig said, his perpetual smile only slightly dampened by the toxic outgassing from the recent refurbishment. "Being junior officers, and somewhat less reputable than swine to the president of this august mess, we are cast out into this for our dinner tonight."

"It stinks," Babs Thompson said, making a face, which on her, the scion of one of the wealthier families on Hurtford, still was beautiful.

"Probably because they had to rebuild it after the last herd of JOs got through with it," Heather Alexander said, another rich offspring who had been shuttled to Fast Patrol Squadron 8 for crimes yet unconfessed. With the war scares, lots of young men and women were signing up to do their patriotic duty. Several of them were causing General Mac McMorrison, chair of the Joint Staff, fits as they struggled with greater or lesser success to fit their own strong heads into uniform hats.

None of them had come as close to open mutiny as Kris had. But then, no charges had been filed, so Kris wasn't officially a mutineer. It was now generally agreed—behind closed doors—that she had been right to relieve her first

Captain of his command during what was about to become wartime.

Of course, that hadn't made it any easier for Mac to find Kris a second, now third commanding officer. Squadron 8, with its bunch of spoiled, hotshot orbital skiff–racing hooligans, at least looked like a safe place to dump Kris. With any luck, Mac probably figured, the troublesome JOs would take each other down a peg or twelve, teach each other a few desperately needed lessons in humility, proper social behavior, military deportment, what all. All the Navy risked was a few tiny toys half the fleet considered worthless anyway. And the last few wisps of hair on Commodore Mandanti's shiny pate.

How often had Kris heard her father, the Prime Minister, mutter about bringing all his problems together in a small room and letting them solve themselves? Kris savored the pleasure of being one of someone's too many problems as she glanced around at her fellow skippers and wondered if they would find a way to prove Mac and all the other top brass wrong . . . or all too right.

Dinner was ordered and eaten as the twelve took each other's measures again. Most knew or had heard of each other from the skiff racing championships. Taking a thin eggshell of a craft from orbit to a one-meter-square target on the planet below while using the least amount of fuel had taught them to feel ballistics in their bones. But a racing skiff didn't have a crew of fifteen nor did it work as part of a squadron of twelve.

Kris kept up her end of the table banter while thanking whatever bureaucratic god it was that gave her the crew she drew. Her XO was Tommy Lien from Santa Maria's asteroid mines. Her buddy from OCS had backed her up through thick and a whole lot of thin. Of all the crews, she and Tommy were the only two that had actually heard shots fired at them in anger. A few of the shots Tommy had dodged had actually been in legitimate firefights, not assassins' bullets that had missed Kris first.

Chief "Stan" Stanislaus was her only crew member

who'd earned any hashmarks for his dress uniform. Ten years in the Navy, Kris would be losing him soon to OCS. Until then, she counted on him to see that PF-109 was real Navy rather than the playboy/girl toy flotilla that the media tagged them.

The rest of the crew of PF-109 were a challenge. Raw and new, Kris and Tommy spent most of their time trying to come up with ways to get them past green to something close to practiced. Take Fintch at the helm. She was a whiz at ballistics and tested out of sight on the Navy's aptitude scores . . . all involving computer games with her bottom comfortably seated on firm ground. But she'd never actually steered anything bigger than a motorbike. And never been off planet in her life!

Fintch was actually an easy one; Kris took her over to the Wardhaven Space Yacht Club, rented a two-seat racing skiff, and took her backseat on a skiff drop. Halfway down, Kris handed Fintch the spare stick she'd hidden aboard.

"You land her. Crash her. Your call."

"Yes, ma'am," Fintch said, ignoring the offered stick. And she did manage to put them down. Just over a mile from the target. Next to the number-three green at Wardhaven's most exclusive country club. At least they didn't scorch that much grass.

"Sorry, ma'am. I'll do better next time, ma'am," Fintch insisted as the two of them hotfooted it off the course, the still cooling skiff dangling between them.

"Let this be our little secret," Kris said. And it was. Until the five o'clock news featured them.

But Fintch did better the second drop, and Kris stood her for membership in the Wardhaven Skiff Club, paid her first year's dues, and got out of her way.

If only it was half as easy to come up with ways that made it as much fun to maintain and calibrate the ship's lasers, electronics, motors, sensors, and all the other drudgeries that went into converting a very small chunk of space into one deadly little warship.

Dessert was on order when Phil Taussig rapped on his

crystal water glass. Most fell silent, though Ted Rockefeller and Andy Gates had a problem with who-gets-in-the-last-word and didn't shut up until they noticed ten very silent peers staring at them.

"It could not have escaped your notice," Phil said, "that should hostilities ever come to the space above Wardhaven, we are its last line of defense."

"And its worst," Babs put in.

"Speak for yourself," Andy said.

"Well, folks," Phil said, trying to cut through the usual banter. "I, for one, would like to see us take out a battleship or two. Hopefully without being annihilated like a torpedo squadron namesake of ours was a few centuries back that I've mentioned once or twice."

"Or forty-eleven times," Babs sighed.

Phil Taussig was one of the two exceptions to the rule of spoiled rich kids among the boat commanders. His family was Navy, going back to the times when navies were wet water affairs. Kris suspected that Phil had been added to the mix by Mac in an effort to reduce the hooligan factor. Among his several contributions was digging up the story of Torpedo 8, a flying squadron that sounded very much like them. They'd taken on some ocean type battleships and been annihilated, almost to a man. Though Babs rolled her eyes at the ceiling, even jolly Andy Gates now gave Phil his undivided serious attention.

"As I see it," Phil went on, "our problem breaks down into several easy phases." He held up a hand. "Find the enemy, approach the enemy, destroy the enemy, exit the battle area in one piece." Phil counted each on a finger. "That says it all."

"Shouldn't be any trouble finding the battleships," Andy Gates put in. "Since our PFs don't do star jumps, we'll just be lounging around here in orbit when the big boys waddle in."

No one laughed.

"I would suggest surviving our approach to the enemy battle line deserves one of your fingers, Phil." Chandra

Singh said, her voice slightly singsong. "If we are not alive to shoot our lasers, all else is mere sorrow."

Dark-eyed Chandra was the second exception to the rule. Older than the other skippers . . . she actually had two children waving from her husband's side on the pier when the squadron pulled away. She was a mustang. She'd come up through the enlisted rates, earning her commission even before the present emergency had the Navy combing its ranks for chiefs to leaven the ranks of green college kids like Kris and her fellow skippers.

"We're mighty small targets," Ted Rockefeller of Pitts Hope pointed out. His trust fund wasn't quite as well-stocked as Kris's. He was cute but not very smart, which he regularly showed by the misconclusions he drew. "It'll be mighty hard for an old battlewagon to draw a bead on one of us tiny targets."

"Kind of like you shooting skeet," Andy Gates said, nudging him with an elbow.

"If they have fire control systems anything like I broke many a screwdriver over, they will spot you," Singh said.

"So we dodge," Gates said. "That's what Commodore Mandanti says. Dodge. Never go straight for more than five seconds."

"And if you follow his advice," Taussig cut in, eyes locked on Kris, "you'll be dead in three seconds. Right Kris?"

"More likely in two," she said. The room got very quiet as she put down her water tumbler.

"The Commodore is a good man," she continued, "but he was retired to his chicken ranch for fifteen years before they brought him back to ride herd on us juvenile delin-quents." That was the PF commanders' secret name for themselves. Kris doubted it was any secret from the Com-modore.

"For most of the last fifty, sixty years, not much changed on a warship from what came out of the Iteeche Wars. No need. The Society of Humanity kept the peace throughout human space. Now human space is in pieces and . . . Well, you hear the news." Heads nodded. Wars and war rumors sold a lot of soap these days.

"The technologies developed in the long peace have been finding their way aboard warships. Last ten years, things have been changing. Singh, you must have noticed it as a maintainer."

The old Chief, now lieutenant, nodded.

"My grandfather's bottom line has made a few ter-abucks off of the new stuff. I doubt he's been alone," Kris said dryly, giving the rest of her mates a smile that was pure cynic. They nodded back. The technical growth had driven a long economic expansion. All peaceful. Now the plowshares were being hammered into swords and the money their families had all banked in the good times just might be in line to kill their heirs real soon. Great thought to take home to the next Christmas dinner.

"So we need to dodge a lot," Heather said, bringing them back to the matter at hand.

"Jinks, I'm told, is the military term for it," Kris supplied, Phil nodded. "And you need to do it both faster than any human can think it through and in a more random pattern than any fire control computer can analyze. Be slow. Be predictable. You'll be dead and your ship and crew with you."

The servers delivered slices of pie, cake, and bowls of ice cream into that silence. From the wide-eyed looks that passed between them, it was apparent they'd never been in a room full of JOs that were quite as subdued as this bunch. Alone in their room once more, no one seemed to have any appetite.

"Is this where I come in?" came a pleasant voice from around Kris's neck.

Kris undid the top button on her undress whites. This put her out of uniform, but with her depressingly small chest measurements, she'd be no distraction to the male half of the room. "Does anyone object to my computer, Nelly, joining us?"

"I was hoping she would," Singh said.

"So, Nelly," Phil began, "can you give us an erratic enough approach course?"

"I have already given this question some thought, since I did not doubt that you would come to me for my expertise on this," Nelly said.

Kris rolled her eyes at the ceiling. Humility might be something ten rich kids could teach each other the hard way. But how do you teach virtue to a computer? Especially one you'd paid top dollar to make the best and who knew very well that she was. *What did Singh say? "Some things in life just must be suffered."*

Of course, after saying that to her crew, the old mustang was wont to borrow a toolbox and fix just the thing the crew insisted couldn't be fixed.

"What have you got for us?" Kris said.

Nelly immediately flashed a holograph of a battleship at one end, a tiny replica of a PF at the other end. The PF started its approach at full power and maximum evasion: up down, right left, fast, slow. Its course was a corkscrew of twists and turns that made several captains at the table turn a fine shade of green.

"You will want to start at a lower acceleration," Singh pointed out. "Our engines are small. If we spread radiators to dissipate the heat, we present a bigger target. If we don't, we risk overheating if we abuse them for too long. Begin the approach at one point five g's acceleration, then build up."

"I don't know," Gates said. "Balls to the wall sounds like a great way to go to me."

Kris made a mental note to do it Singh's way.

"So each of us does our own evasion pattern and charges in," Rockefeller said.

"I would not suggest that," Kris said.

"Why? You aren't going to say that we all have to evade the same way. What happened to unpredictable?" Alexander asked.

Kris glanced around the table; all she got back were blank stares. She'd even managed to get ahead of Phil this time. Most of them were smart, but they hadn't been shot at. They hadn't gotten that gut kick that came when your best plan fell apart despite your best effort. They had yet to be left standing there, or lying, or running, and wondering what you should have done better . . . different. Kris took a deep breath and swore that she'd do this slow, earn everyone's support.

It had to be all for one and one for all.

"If I zig away from a chunk of space, just as you zag into it," Kris used her hands to show ships passing, "the shot intended for me becomes a shot that hits you."

"The chances against that are a million to one," Gates spat.

"Yes, and you'll be just as dead," Phil said. He chewed on his lower lip for a second. "We're training so we can do it right the first time, every time. But we can't expect bad luck to stay off the battlefield. Nelly, could you develop a different jinks pattern for all twelve boats? One that lets us jink all over, each boat fully random but never close to the other's space anytime near to when another boat was in it?"

There was a longer pause than Kris had come to expect when talking to Nelly. Long pauses were happening regularly now as Nelly gained more comprehension of the full extent and the size of the problems humans faced regularly. Nelly might be a supercomputer, but her decision trees were getting supersized. "Yes, I can do that. Each boat will need to start the attack from well-spaced positions. The Commodore usually has you in line behind the flagship. You will need more space than that to maneuver."

"Good observation, Nelly," Kris said. Yes, Nelly was even responding to praise. Exactly what had Kris bought with her latest upgrade, and with that bit of Santa Maria rock in the self-organizing matrix that she'd told Nelly not to look at but . . . ? Well, there was one more spoiled brat on the PFs than the Navy had assigned.

Phil leaned close to Kris's ear. "I'd heard stories about your Nelly. This is the first I've seen her in action. Nice."

"You caught her on one of her better days."

"I heard that."

"Good, because I want five different evasion approach plans for all twelve boats," Kris snapped. No use having all that computing power if she wasn't going to put it to use. And an idle Nelly was something to avoid at all cost.

"We can never tell when we'll need to switch to a new random route. Face it, Nelly, they've got computers, too. And if they figure out one of your random sets, we need a backup and another, and another. Got it?"

"Yes, Your slave-driving Princess-ship," Nelly said.

Around the room, hands covered poorly suppressed grins. None of them referred to Kris as anything but Lieutenant. Aboard ship or ashore, she was Navy, never Princess, to her shipmates.

But what her own computer did to her . . . Well, that was a hoist of another petard.

"One more thing," Kris said. "We've got 18-inch pulse lasers. They give out a quick, powerful burst of energy on our target. But there are no reloads. We have motors, not reactors that could refill our capacitors. It's one shot and then we're done."

Heads nodded. They'd all read the manuals.

"We need to make sure that our shots do as much damage as they can. If we're coordinating our approaches, maybe we could do something else."

Phil and Singh leaned close. Others folded their arms; they'd be a hard sell. Kris ignored her melting ice cream and got into sales mode.

"Thirty thousand kilometers to the target," Tom reported from his station on weapons at Kris's elbow. "Close range for the secondary armament."

And this close, the battlewagon's ranging and search systems, radar, lasers, magnetic and gravitational measurements would be picking up solid returns on even the tiny signatures of the fast patrol boats. Time to make their firing solutions as complicated as possible.

"Take the division up to three g's acceleration. Implement evasion scheme 1 on my mark," Kris ordered. "Begin Foxing." She paused for the other boats to make ready, then ordered, "Mark."

Evasion scheme 1 was nothing if not more evasive. And now when each PF changed direction—more often, more wildly—it launched Foxing decoys as well. At each course change, a mist of iron needles, aluminum strips, and phosphorus pellets shot out just as the boat made the turn. The chaff showered out along the old course as the PF turned toward the battleship for a new course. For that fraction of a second, while the boat itself was nose on, the Foxer decoyed the radar, laser, infrared, and magnetic sensors into showing the boat on the same old course.

That was usually just long enough to get a shot off from the battleship's secondary lasers—at empty space.

The Foxer's chaff also gave color to the lasers as they cut through the space where your ship wasn't.

Unlike dances and fancy planet-bound fireworks shows, Navy lasers in space should show nothing. A hammer and tongs battle between a dozen ships of the line is a dark, silent affair with nothing more to show than when the ships are swinging around the station. At first, at least. For a while.

Then laser hits flash ice armor into steam that shoots off in jets that quickly freeze again. Those crystals catch laser light, reflect it, refract it, and turn horrible murder and butchery into something unspeakably lovely that the poets write about. If they survive. That artists try to capture in paint and steel and graphics for the rest of their lives. If they live to old age. Like twenty-five.

But PFs like Kris's had no ice to boil off. For them, the chaff created the living color that just might let them live.

"Wow. Did you see that?" Fintch gaped at the main ahead screen for a moment as near misses lit up the decoys around them.

"Pass it along to all hands," Kris said. There was painfully little to do as they raced toward simulated death, their death or a battleship's. It was either done and done right, and all the crew had left to do was watch gauges stay in the green, or it was done poorly and they'd fail as badly as the other two divisions.

"Twenty thousand kilometers," Tom said. "All four lasers are nominal and hot."

"Division, go to evasion scheme 6. Prepare to execute evasion and attack on my mark," Kris said.

"Yeah. Go, girls," Nelly said, breaking her ordered quiet.

Kris waited, gave the division an extra count. Do IT, NELLY.

The division scattered, going into a dance that left them high, low, and medium on the battlewagon. Then, after a series of twists and turns that left Kris's head bouncing off her headrest, it was time.

"Fire," Kris ordered. If Nelly had done her work right, the order was unnecessary, but this was Kris's command, and she'd give the order herself, thank you very much.

"Lasers firing," Tom yelled. "All four away at sixteen thousand kilometers. All fired by the timer."

"Begin escape evasion," Kris ordered. And held her breath.

Was the battleship still there? Blown up? Damaged but still fighting?

"Just what do you young rascals think you just did?" came over the command channel. At least Commodore Mandanti was calling them rascals today, not hooligans.

"A coordinated attack, sir," Kris answered. It being Tuesday, she had the lead of the division, so it fell to her to explain just what they had decided to do, her and Phil and Chandra. Heather had gone along with them, though she had her doubts. They'd persuaded the tall redhead that the entire division had to do it if it was to work at all.

"Well, quit your bouncing around, put some decent deceleration on your boats, and explain to an old man who only happens to be your commanding officer just what this is that you call a coordinated attack, Lieutenant."

"Yes, sir, cease evasive maneuvering. Rotate ship, begin deceleration at one point five g's. Motors, spread the radiators." When she got her replies, Kris took a deep breath and began the explanation she'd prepared for.

"Sir, an 18-inch pulse laser sounds mighty powerful when you read the book on it, but even the smallest battleship has a lot of ice armor, and it's rotating at a clip intended to prevent our laser from burning through in the short time that we're hitting their ice."

"That's just part of the sad realities of being a mosquito boat skipper in a big-ship Navy."

"Yes sir, but what if we hit the same spot on the battlewagon with two pulse lasers simultaneously?"

"There you go using that 'we' again. Who am I talking to, a princess or a Navy Lieutenant?"

Kris gritted her teeth; the Commodore had only hit her with the princess gig two or three times. Kris was about to reply when she found she didn't have to.

"That 'we,' sir, includes me," Phil said. "And me," said Chandra. "And me," said Heather. "We all kind of figured," Phil went on, "that there wasn't much good of going through all this risking of our fair young necks—"

"Or old ones," Chandra cut in.

"If we weren't going to leave some dead battlewagons lying around when we were done. As you saw, sir, by coordinating our approach evasion courses, we managed not to step into each other's paths and let your defense gunners get two hits for the price of one, or hit one when they were aiming at the other.

"Anyway, Kris suggested that if we coordinated our final approach, we might get some solid double hits on the battlewagon that would cut through the armor to the soft, chewy insides."

Kris was content to leave the talking to Phil now. It seemed that the Navy Way included its own way of talking about murder and mayhem. Kids brought up Navy knew how to talk to their elders. Kris wasn't always sure the English she spoke did the job as well.

It was good to have Phil and Chandra along to translate.

"Hmm," came back. "Well, then. I was going to give you credit for thirteen hits out of sixteen on the old target drone, but since you raised the stakes, let me see how many of your shots qualified as solid double hits."

"Damn," Tom whispered beside Kris. "I bet if the old man found a pile of presents under his Christmas tree, he'd first check to see if Saint Nick tracked in any reindeer dung."

"Of course he would, Mr. Lien," came Chief Stanislaus over the ship's net. "The Navy Way don't include having no reindeer crap all over the front parlor when visitors might come calling."

At least the boat got a laugh. Off command net. To itself.

"Well, now, you kids didn't do too bad, even under the goals you set for yourselves," came from the Commodore after a long minute. "Drone Five isn't exactly rigged to measure what you were trying to do, but it looks like ten of your hits were pretty close in both time and space. Say you got five double hits. Call it enough to burn through a President-class battleship's main belt. I definitely think I'm buying the beer tonight.

"And you ladies and gentlemen by an act of Parliament leading the erstwhile boats of Division 1 and 2 who no doubt attended whatever conspiratorial den in which Div 3 hatched their plan, why didn't you try the same instead of letting good old Drone Five and my fine bunch of gunners shoot you down like delicate butterflies pinned to a piece of cheap cardboard?"

Kris tried to swallow a grin that seemed to infect her entire crew. Before the silence on net stretched too far, the Commodore filled it.

"Never mind. You can all explain yourselves to me over beers tonight. All divisions, set course and speed to form on my flagship within the next three hours. We should be alongside the pier by seventeen hundred hours. Party starts at twenty-one hundred."

The net went silent. Beside her, Tommy tapped the

central comm to take PF-109's ship net off the main battle net, and cheers erupted around Kris.

"You did a damn fine job, all of you," Kris said into their happy noises. "Tononi, I don't know how you kept the engines cool for the run-in, but you did it."

"I had ma pet goat piss on 'em when they got too hot, ma'am," he said, alluding to one of the farm animals he was reported to keep penned up in the engine room.

"Just so long as you get your space Shipshape and Bristol fashion to please the chief," Kris said, "I don't care how you kept your cool."

Chief Stanislaus, at his battle station backing Tom up on weapons, scowled, but his reputation as a hard-driving old chief was in serious danger, there being way too much up in evidence around the edges of that particular scowl.

"You heard the Commodore. We only have four hours alongside the pier before he wants to throw that party, so let's get the whole ship back to Bristol fashion now rather than later."

Kris leaned forward in her chair as it went from heavily inflated high-g station to a normal acceleration station. Feet on the deck, she turned to face the helm. "You have a course laid in for the flag?"

"Flag has established a stately point eighty-five g course for the station," Fintch reported. "Computer has generated a course that puts us in line aft of the flag in exactly three hours, ma'am."

NELLY? Kris asked her own computer through the plug that fed her thoughts directly to Nelly. There were risks in having too easy a connection, but when a gun was at her head, Kris didn't want to be subvocalizing and trying not to move her jaw.

NAVY-ISSUE COMPUTER IS DUMB AS A STUMP, BUT A ONE-HANDED MONKEY WITH AN ABACUS COULD SOLVE THAT BALLISTICS PROBLEM.

I AM SO GLAD YOU DIDN'T SAY THAT OUT LOUD TO FINTCH.

I AM NOT LACKING IN THE SOCIAL GRACES, PRINCESS. IT

IS JUST THAT THEY — AND TRYING TO RESOLVE PROBLEMS WHILE DOING THE MINIMUM DAMAGE TO WHAT YOU HUMANS CALL FEELINGS — ARE JUST SO TIME-CONSUMING.

THINK OF IT AS AN ART FORM. NOW, CHECK OUT THE SHIP AND MAKE A LIST OF DEFICIENCIES. BET YOU THAT YOUR LIST ISN'T MORE THAN HALF AGAIN AS LONG AS THE LIST THAT THE CREW SPOT.

YOU ARE ON. AND IF I WIN?

WE'LL TALK ABOUT IT LATER.

I WOULD LOVE TO SPEND SOME TIME EXAMINING THAT PIECE OF ROCK FROM SANTA MARIA THAT IS STILL SITTING IN MY MATRIX. I BET I COULD INVESTIGATE ITS ALIEN CONTENTS AND NOT LOCK UP.

THAT BET IS NOT ON THE TABLE. NOW, MISS NELLY, IF YOU DON'T MIND, I HAVE A SHIP TO COMMAND. BUZZ OFF.

AYE, AYE, YOUR SKIPPERSHIP.

The Navy listed the crew size for PF-109 at fourteen. Kris counted fifteen. And that last crew member brought with her all kinds of advantages . . . and pains in the butt.

Kris turned to Tom and the Chief. "I don't know about you, but my head did an awful lot of banging around. Is my skull just kind of small, or do the high-g stations need some adjustment?"

The Chief shook his head. "The stations are a problem, ma'am. Maybe we ought to fit all hands with brain buckets. But I don't think that's our worst problem. I was watching the laser fire from that old tub. I know the official Navy take is that the drone has the same defensive suite as a battleship, but I'm not buying that we got a full workout. And even with that, there were an awful lot of too damn close near misses." The chief of the boat, an old man of thirty, shrugged. "If it was a real fight, we'd have to do better."

"Ah, man, that's not what I was wanting to hear," Tom said, his grandmother's brogue leaking out.

"Chief, you look into those helmets, and I'll have Nelly adjusting each high-g station to personally fit each crewman, helmet and all." Kris shook her head. "You know, after this one practice run, the idea of us taking on battlewagons with these splinters isn't nearly as frightening as it sounded the day we commissioned the squadron."

"Not likely we'll be defending Wardhaven from battlewagons," Lien said. "Look at the size of the fleet your da has swinging around the station. Me, I'm surprised we haven't been run down, turned into some battleship's bowsprit."

"Figurehead," both Kris and the Chief said together.

"If you'll excuse me, ma'am," the Chief said, "I'll be taking my falling arches off to see what's happening in the rest of this rust bucket. I think you have the bridge as well under control as any captain can."

Kris let that rattle around in her head for a second . . . and decided it was as close to a compliment as a Chief could give a junior officer. "You do that, Chief."

She watched him leave, which left her eyes resting on the empty station directly behind her. "I see you got the intel battle station set up."

"And didn't I say I would," Lien said, getting up from his own gunnery station and slipping into the seat of the new one. "Having Penny on that intel station of that yacht that you, ah, borrowed off Turantic was a godsend. I got one set up here just as fast as I could find a spare station lying around the dock and no one paying too much attention to its ownership," he said with his lopsided grin taking a most definite lean to port.

"You stole it."

"Not all of us can have your petty change purse, Kris." The smile made it almost a joke. Without the smile, it would have hurt. Still, the truth was, she could have bought the entire squadron out of her last year's earnings and not touched the principal of her trust fund. There were some advantages to being one of those damn Longknifes.

"Penny still coming for breakfast tomorrow?" Kris asked.

Tommy's grin got even wider, passing aft of his ears and probably meeting somewhere in back. Well, that was the way a guy was supposed to react when you mentioned his future bride. At least they always did around Kris. All the guys who Kris met and who ended up asking gals that Kris knew to be their brides. And brides who always asked Kris to be their maid of honor.

Kris had given up trying to figure out what it was about her bubbling personality that was such a catalyst for other people meeting and falling happily in love. At least she told herself she was going to give up trying to figure it all out. Give it up by next Thursday.

"Penny is so tickled you offered us the garden at Nuu House for the wedding. Her mom is living on Cambria now with her present husband. My folks are all on Santa Maria. We don't have a place to call home. But to be married in the gardens where King Raymond and Rita were married. Kris, you're wonderful."

There were many answers to that. Kris settled on "I'm glad to offer a quiet place for your families to get together."

"Well, I think mainly it will be the squadron, unless there's some cheap fares between Santa Maria and here for my family. Her da," Tommy shrugged. "Penny sent out a chaser mail three days ago, but she doesn't really know where he is. Probably just a quiet wedding among us sailors."

"You want crossed sabers?"

"I think she would like it. You know, I'm not sure if she intends to wear a white dress or dress whites."

"Just be glad we're keeping this whole affair a secret from my mother. If she got ahold of it . . ." Kris shivered at the mere thought of Mother planning a wedding.

Maybe that was the best reason for staying single. "So," Kris pointed at the intel station. "Any idea who might crew it?"

"How about Penny?" Tom said, almost sounding serious. "She knows just about all there is to know about the warships a Wardhaven fleet might face. She has a full range of intel skills. You can't keep holding her duty of interrogating us 'mutineers' against her."

"Don't even use that word as a joke," Kris said, blanching.

"Then you hire a PR firm to come up with a nice short term for what we did on the *Typhoon*," Tom said. "Anyway, we'll need someone with all Penny's skills, so why not ask for Penny? She's done enough desk time. She'd love some ship duty."

And Tom would love to have his wife stationed right behind him. And the minor fact that Penny had held her Lieutenant rank for a whole year longer than Kris shouldn't cause any trouble in the chain of command of a ship as tiny as PF-109.

Yeah. Right.

But Penny had done fine work on Turantic when Kris had needed some very fine work if she was to stay alive. She could do worse than have someone like Penny backing her up. The chief might be right; any real targets they went up against might well be shooting back with a whole lot nastier stuff than the antiques that the Commodore had them training against.

But PF boats defending Wardhaven! Who was kidding who? If they were lucky, they'd all be shipped off to some backwater planet. Ordered to defend some place that no one thought needed all that much defending when things changed suddenly and . . .

Hmm, maybe having a full intel officer and a full intel report might not be a bad idea for wherever they ended up having to show that these toys could fight.

Three hours later they were all tucked right in behind the flagship, tiny ducklings following in the wake of the *Cushing*, an antique destroyer, the last of her class not yet sent to the breakers, kept around only to nursemaid this harebrained idea that you could use penny boats to blast dollar bill battleships.

Stan brought Kris the list of ship deficiencies. It was long. Nelly's list was longer, but fell four short of exceeding the Chief's list by half. "Nelly, pass your list to the Chief."

Stan looked at the longer list, pursed his lips, then went to check it out.

"So I don't get to mess with the rock chip," Nelly said,

sounding as sad as a computer could. "Auntie Tru would be so happy if I discovered whatever secrets of the Three races that built the jump points that might still be recoverable on that data source. She might even cook you up a batch of chocolate chip cookies."

"Nor can you bring up the topic for a month," Kris said, ignoring the rest of the blandishment.

"A week," Nelly countered. "You didn't specify a length when we made the bet."

"Two weeks," Kris said. Nelly went quiet in her head. *It's really weird when you can tell your computer is pouting by just the way your skull feels.*

"Is that the way it works?" Tommy asked.

"What works?"

"Keeping Nelly under control?"

"She is never under control."

"You got that right, Your Skippership."

"Sorry I asked," Tommy said, swallowing something halfway between a snarf and a chuckle.

"Nelly, I want you to research the best helmets for the crew to reduce brain damage and neck strain when we're whipping around at high-g's on evasion. Then reprogram the battle stations to secure the head and neck supports tightly on the helmets so our heads don't take as much battering as we did today."

"If you'd just let me run the ship, you could all stay home," Nelly said.

Fintch at the helm did a double take.

"Yes, Nelly, but the Navy Way is old-fashion about that. So you just do what I tell you, and we'll get along fine."

The rest of the cruise back was quiet as all hands turned to make right as many of the deficiencies on the Chief's list as they could without a dock to help. The list was noticeably shorter when Kris ordered all hands to pier detail.

Kris watched over Fintch's shoulder as she brought the boat smartly alongside the pier, caught the bow lockdown on the first try, and followed it as it smoothly pulled the boat to the pier.

"Well done," Kris said, giving Fintch a well-earned pat on the shoulder.

"Power line passed to the pier," the chief reported from his special space detail station at the quarterdeck amidships. "Air, comm, and water connected. The hatch is opened."

The pressure in the boat changed the tiniest bit. No ship ever managed to maintain the same atmosphere as the station, even for only a one-day out and back in.

"Captain, we've got—" was cut short.

"Chief, do we have a problem?" Kris demanded as her eyes went over the board. All lights were green. There was nothing wrong with the boat. Nothing showing.

NELLY?

"I'm being jammed," the computer said, surprise flooding its voice. "I'm trying to . . ."

Kris turned in her command seat as five MPs in Army khaki marched onto her bridge, a major in the lead.

"Are you Lieutenant Kristine Anne Longknife, sometimes styled Princess?" he demanded.

There are some moments in your life that you know are coming for you. Moments that, when you are just a kid, you know will happen to you before you die. It's probably different for different kids. If your folks are farmers, maybe it's a plague of locusts at harvest time or that one great crop that will never be equaled. If you're an army brat, you know that somewhere out there is a battle, a fight for your life, that will find you.

Kris was a politician's daughter; somehow she knew that *they* would come for her one day. As a kid of nine, she'd watched a vid of Marie Antoinette and wondered what it had been like to face that first arrest, to walk those final steps to the guillotine.

All her life, Kris had wondered how she'd handle this moment, so it both surprised her . . . and failed to.

She stood, faced her accuser, and answered simply, "I am Kris Longknife." Strange, at the moment, how all titles fell away.

"I have orders to relieve you of your command and place you under arrest. Sergeant, cuff her."

Kris's mind raced. What to do next? She turned to Tom. "You have the conn," she said. The command had to be transferred clearly. That was the Navy Way. Then she turned back to this Army invasion on her bridge.

"May I ask what for?" Kris said, keeping her hands at her side. Resistance was futile . . . worse . . . undignified. But she'd be damned if she'd help them.

An Army Sergeant, no Marines or Navy in sight, whipped out a pair of cuffs and shoved Tom aside. The Navy Lieutenant reached for the ruffian.

"Stand down," Kris ordered.

Tommy did, though tiny Finch took a step forward and slowed down the other Sergeant charging in on Kris's other side.

The major whipped out his sidearm as did the two MPs behind him.

"Stand down," Kris ordered, louder. "Neither I nor my crew are under arms. We cannot nor will we offer you any resistance. Finch, let the men through, even if they are barging around on our ship without so much as a by-your-leave."

Kris had dreamed this scene asleep and awake too many times. Sometimes it ended peacefully. Other times not. She knew how she wanted it to end.

The MPs had their guns out; they nervously eyed the bridge crew. "Major, the only people on this bridge armed are your people. No one is going to resist you, so relax." Kris tried to make that last sound like an obvious invitation. "But would you mind telling me what this is all about?"

"Lady, I got my orders. It says arrest you, and it don't say why. Some of us do what we're told, see. Now, are you coming with me, or do we carry you?"

Mac had warned Kris that not everyone was happy about the way she'd been stopping wars of late. Apparently, this party had not been recruited from among her fans.

Okay, the idea is to live through this day, girl. From the looks of the goons beside her and behind the Major, they dearly wanted to carry her. And once they got their mitts on her, she'd just happen to resist arrest and just happen to deserve the maximum application of force and restraint allowed by law.

"I may be Navy, Major, but I do know how to walk." The Sergeant with the cuffs had grabbed both of Kris's hands and locked them down behind her back. She felt vulnerable. Terribly vulnerable. Still, she could walk.

Kris stepped forward, two guards behind her; two fell in ahead of her. They turned to head back the way they'd come, and the major bounced his skull off the overhead. PFs were not designed with six footers in mind.

"Watch your step," Kris said. "Tom, call Harvey at the house."

"Yes, Your Highness," her XO answered. They knew. This was political theater; each had their part. If they played it right, they'd all live to tell their grandkids about it and laugh.

The climb down to the quarterdeck was none too easy, but Kris made it before her knees started shaking. A firefight with a gun in her hand and an enemy to run at was one thing. Being cuffed and shoved around by guards was something else entirely. At the hatch, the Chief and the special detail stood at their stations. Stan was developing what looked to be a real shiner.

"Sorry, ma'am."

"No problem, Chief. Send my regrets to the Commodore for missing tonight's beer bash."

"Yes, ma'am."

"Do you want my coat?" the Chief asked. Kris wasn't cold. Then she heard the shutters and saw the flashes. Twenty, thirty camera crews waited outside. The Chief wasn't offering a coat to keep her warm but a hood to hide her face.

"No thank you, Chief, this is all part of the drill," Kris said. She raised her head high and stepped across the brow of her boat without missing a step.

That was important. Not to look like a prisoner. That

was the impression to project. That was what she'd always planned for this moment.

Her guards moved along, and Kris moved right with them. Let the commentator report she was their prisoner. Let the image show Princess Longknife advancing to meet the people with her honor guard. Kris set her face neither in a smile nor a scowl. Neither frown nor blank stare for this moment. *Dare you to use these pictures.*

Just please, dear God, don't let my knees give out.

She made one exception to her no-reaction policy. There, off to the left, peering through a mob of newsies, was Mr. Singh with his two kids, a boy and a girl. They stared at Kris through eyes gone wide—in fright? Wonder? What must their three- and five-year-old world make of this? Kris chipped a smile off the marble she'd hardened her lips into. She nodded a centimeter in their direction. They waved enthusiastically, all joy at the attention. Goran Singh gave her a thumbs-up.

A moment later she was at the door of the waiting station cart. She settled inside, then turned back to the cameras to give them the required princess smile. Just another day of doing that royal thing. The sergeant slammed the door shut with unnecessary violence, leaving her alone with her guards as the electric cart motored off quietly.

Now, with the cameras gone, Kris would find out just what her chances were of living until morning.

2

"You Print-cess Longa-knife?" the guard asked.

Kris blinked away exhaustion as she took inventory of her three-by-four-meter brig cell. It was cold, gray on gray, concrete floor and walls, unpadded slab for a bed, toilet without the courtesy of a seat. It stank of old vomit, but nobody was here but her.

She let go of her knees; she'd pulled them up to her chin for warmth and the feel of something human. She allowed herself a sleepless stretch. Her blue shipsuit identified her as a Navy Lieutenant; it properly displayed the name *Longknife* over her right breast. She swallowed several cutting replies that she doubted the guard had the good sense of humor to take and settled for, "I am Kris Longknife."

"Somebody finally showed up to sign for you." The Corporal snickered and signaled to a security camera. With a buzz, the cell door opened.

Kris reminded herself that whatever that camera recorded would show up in the media to the worst reflection on her, her father the Prime Minister, and, more importantly, Grampa Ray, the king. Hungry, tired, madder than she'd ever been in her life, Kris stood with as much grace as her aching muscles allowed and carefully paced the distance to the door. "Thank you," she told the man as if he had done her royal person a great service.

"You're welcome," he said, then glanced up at the camera and made a sour face as if he might somehow take back those words. There was more than one way to get even, Kris reminded herself.

He made up for that mistake by grabbing her elbow and trying to rush her along. Kris was too tired, ached too much, and had too many other problems for that to end up well. "Could we please slow down?" she asked. "My shoes don't have any laces, and if I walk too fast, I'll walk out of them."

"Oh." The guard looked down, slowed. "Sorry."

Kris doubted that was what his superiors wanted on the record, but she'd often found that a bit of human kindness in the worst situation encouraged human kindness in return. Today, it had worked. She wouldn't take it personal if tomorrow it didn't.

The prison maze she'd been led through last night was now done in reverse. It coughed her up in the booking room. A new desk sergeant was looking at his monitors and camera feeds; he studiously ignored her. NELLY, YOU GOT THE BADGE NUMBERS?

YOU BET.

Kris was a naval officer, but she'd been raised a politician's daughter. There would be payback for this night.

From flimsy plastic chairs across from the desk sergeant's cage, two familiar figures rose. Jack was no surprise.

Special Agent Montoya, the head of her security detail, should have been able to arrange her release by a quick flash of his badge. No badge was in evidence.

Rising to his feet beside Jack was Great-grampa Trouble. He had another name, but he'd been Trouble to so many people, not all of them enemies, during his long Marine career, that now he was Trouble even to Kris's mother.

In name and fact. Former chair of several different planetary general staffs, he was now semiretired. Today he wore slacks and a three-button shirt. And if someone mistook his ramrod back and burr cut for just any retired officer, they deserved what they got.

Kris had several million questions, but a glance at Jack and Grampa showed that they had no intention of saying a word under the watchful eyes of the security cameras around the rooms.

NELLY. WHAT'S THE NEWS?

KRIS, I STILL CANNOT ACCESS THE NET. NO MAIL, NO NEWS, NOT SO MUCH AS A RADIO WAVE. THERE'S A SHORT RANGE, ALL-FREQUENCY NOISE JAMMER THAT HAS BEEN FOLLOWING US AROUND SINCE YOU WERE ARRESTED. I CANNOT CUT THROUGH. I DO NOT HAVE THE POWER FOR IT. DO YOU WANT ME TO MAKE A TRY? IF I FAIL, I COULD BE LEFT SURVIVING ON JUST A TRICKLE.

NO. WE'LL BE OUT SOON ENOUGH. THEN WE'LL FIND OUT WHAT THIS IS ALL ABOUT. Kris held her tongue while the sergeant ran Grampa Trouble's IDent through his machine, glanced at the results he got . . . and blanched.

He fled to the other side of his cage and turned Kris's processing over to a cheerful woman sporting Spec 4 strips. She actually gave Kris a wan smile as she produced Kris's personal effects. "I'm sorry about this. We got very explicit orders from the Chief of Staff on how to handle your case."

"From Mac?" Kris knew she had caused General McMorrison one or two problems, but this!

"No, ma'am. Admiral Pennypacker, the new Chief of Staff."

Kris thought she knew most of the senior serving officers by name; Pennypacker was a blank. She glanced at Grampa Trouble.

"Please finish clearing the Lieutenant," he ordered. "Mr. Montoya and I do not have all day."

"Yes, sir."

Mr. Montoya! Not agent!

The Spec 4 went through Kris's wallet. "You are ordered to surrender your diplomatic passport within twenty-four hours."

"I'm not going anywhere. You have my ship," Kris snapped.

"Ma'am, I'm just following orders. There will be a pretrial hearing a week from tomorrow. You will be notified of its exact time and location when we send you the charges against you. If you cannot afford counsel, the Navy will appoint counsel for you," the woman said, then looked at the file and added, "Oh, right, you're one of those Longknifes."

"Tell the Navy I want them to appoint me counsel." Kris would hire a lawyer, too, but the quality of counsel the Navy provided would tell her as much about the outcome of the court-martial as the verdict.

Five more minutes of this agony, before Jack stepped aside to open the door for Kris . . . and she found herself facing the last person in the world she wanted to see. Adorable Dora, host of *The Real Talk of the Town—at Two,* blocked Kris's way.

Surgeons had repaired that perfect nose from the last time an interviewee had broken it. Two men, both sporting several tiny cameras about their hunky frames, backed Dora up. Kris really didn't feel like decking the woman; she was way too tired for that. She just wanted to get home and find a quiet corner where she could dig a hole and crawl into it for an hour or two.

But if the woman stayed between Kris and that quiet hole, Kris might reassess her priorities.

"What do you think about your dad selling out the farmers?"

"I didn't know he had," Kris said, smiling like she'd been taught, while sidestepping to the left. Grampa Trouble imposed himself between Dora and Kris. Kris took two steps forward before she found herself stopped by one of the hunks and the realization that she didn't know where she was going. None of the cars in the lot were any of the limos or armored town cars normally assigned to Nuu House.

"That rental over there is ours," Jack said, rolling past Kris and blocking camera one while pointing at a five-year-old baby blue town car. Kris took the opening provided and quickly walked for the car. But Dora was coming up on the outside.

"How do you feel about being charged with misappropriation of government funds by your former commanding officer?"

That caused Kris to miss a step, giving Dora and her two cameramen a chance to gain position. Kris took a breath, glanced at Jack, who was rolling his eyes heavenward, and risked a question. "Does this former commander of mine have a name?"

Kris had a number of former commanders. Some were actually still alive. A few were still serving honorably.

"Lieutenant Pearson, your commander on Olympia. She says you pocketed large sums of money from the emergency funds provided to feed the starving farmers and townspeople there."

Kris missed two steps this time. That allowed Jack to catch up, muscle one cameraman aside and away from the car. Grampa opened the door for Kris. She positioned herself to finish the interview and vanish into the car. Taking a breath, Kris organized thoughts that were at once both exhausted and spinning.

"I served *with* Pearson, never *under* her. She was more concerned with writing policies that I don't believe she ever finished. I saw to it that people got food to eat . . . and they did." Kris started to duck into the car.

Dora would not call it quits. "She says she has proof that money was missing from many accounts."

Kris held herself erect by holding onto the door. "No doubt money disappeared from her unit. She stayed holed up in her office for days on end and never went out to see what was actually happening. She did love her policy. Me, I donated money out of my own pocket to get people off their backs, out of the mud, on their feet, and back to work. Check my tax returns. They're part of the official record. Now, if you'll excuse me, I'm tired, and this interview is done."

"Do you think your dad will win the election?"

That required no thought. "Of course. His party best represents the hopes and aspirations of the people of Wardhaven," Kris said and pulled the door closed.

"Sorry about that," Jack said as he settled into the driver's seat. He waved at the car. "And this. It was the only one we could get on short notice that had the armor and security we needed. Your dad and brother took the new ones."

"If someone doesn't start talking to me," Kris said between clenched teeth, "I'm going to break my promise to my big brother not to kill anyone this month."

"Hold your horses a moment," Jack said—and produced a bug locator and burner.

"I am tracking three bugs," Nelly said. "Two are standard newsies, but the other is more expensive. Kris, I have a full news download from the net. Would you like me to brief you?"

Two sparklings in midair showed where Jack had nailed all but one of the problems. Kris gritted her teeth and waited. Nelly was good for news, but Jack knew what interested Kris. He'd tell her what she wanted to know before she had to ask.

A third nano finally went down in flames, trailing wispy smoke toward the carpeted floor.

"Jack, Grampa, what happened?" Kris said in what she considered an amazingly restrained voice.

"At ten thirty yesterday morning," Jack said quickly. "Your father's government lost a Vote of Confidence over the farm subsidy program cutbacks that he was pushing through to reduce the level of deficit brought on by the increased defense spending."

"That's impossible. Father had a solid understanding with the farm wing of his party to support the cutbacks." Kris might spend most of her time Navy, but she couldn't hold down a princess's social calendar and not have her ear bent by things as politically hot as the budget and farm wing.

"Apparently, the family farmers weren't as solidly in my grandson's pocket as they told him," Grampa said. "For what it's worth, it came as a really big surprise to your dad."

"So the opposition forms a caretaker government until elections," Kris said, leaning back in her seat. She knew how these things went. Politics 101. She'd learned it along with how to eat her porridge back before she was out of diapers, though for all her life, her father or grandfather had been the Prime Minister, and the opposition had been little more than a voice crying in the wilderness of the back benches.

Kris reviewed what she knew. "But a *Pro Tem* government isn't supposed to change policy . . . or appoint a new Chief of the General Staff like Pennypacker . . ."

Jack came in right on the downbeat. "But this caretaker government got a solid majority to vote it full powers, things being what they are in human space at the moment, and with that vote behind them, they got King Ray to sanction them."

"How'd Father take this?"

"Rather poorly," Jack said.

"I'll say," Grampa chuckled. "My, but the old boy was spewing venom. Quite a sight. It will be the classic text for how not to lose a vote of confidence in the future."

"Well, we Longknifes aren't all that practiced at losing," Kris observed dryly.

Jack ignored her quip and went on. "And the opposition had a good point. With all the wars and rumor of wars, this is not a good time to have the government of Wardhaven treading water. A lot of your father's allies sided with them. They promised to vote with your old man again if and when he's got the warrant to form a new government, but just now, they felt they had to vote to juice up the *Pro Tem* government. I think that's why King Raymond supported their claim and need to appoint a cabinet and take the full reins of government. Anyway, what's done is done."

"And what is done, *Mr*. Montoya?"

"Oh, that." Jack actually seemed embarrassed. "Since you are no longer the Prime Minister's daughter, you don't rate protection. Therefore, I was recalled and reassigned to the new Prime Minister's youngest daughter."

Kris glanced at her watch, something she could do faster than asking Nelly what time it was. "When's your next shift?"

"I declined the reassignment and am on terminal leave," Jack said briskly. "I'll rescind my resignation when your father is reelected, Princess, but Tilly Pandori is a real snot, and I'll be damned if I'll take a bullet for her."

Having spent too many hours listening to the daughter of the opposition leader drone on and on at parties, Kris couldn't object to Jack's tastes. But it was the first evidence she'd had that his professionalism had its limits.

It also left her wondering if there wasn't more to Jack being at her side than, well, Jack being ordered to be there.

Time to change that *topic*.

"Am I *really* being charged with misappropriation of government property?" Kris struggled to keep her voice calm . . . and almost succeeded. "That bloody mission to that swamp cost me a small fortune." Not to mention her life . . . almost . . . twice.

"Must be true," Jack said. "Pearson was on all the talk shows saying so. She has printouts to prove it. Was waving them, though she didn't let anyone get a close look at them."

All Kris could do was shake her head. "No good deed goes unpunished. Yes, I took a solid tax deduction for the money I donated, but the idea that I'd stooped to stealing the rice, beans, and survival biscuits we shipped to those starving farmers . . . While getting shot at for the privilege . . . Nelly, how's the Ruth Edris Fund for Displaced Farmers doing on Olympia? Are we still sending them money each month?"

"No, Kris. There are now more local donations coming in than money going out. I asked the board of directors to consider either closing it or coming up with proposals for investing the money in low-interest loans to help folks start up small businesses or homestead on abandoned farmland. They like that idea and will get back to you with a business proposal that may involve rechartering the fund as a credit union."

"Well, if Pearson plans to try this thing in the court of public opinion while my father is in a run for his political life, Nelly, you better drop a note to Ester or Jeb and ask them to arrange some interviews with their local Olympia media. Maybe some with the ministers, priests, and rabbis we worked with, too."

Grampa Trouble shook his head. "Girl, a nice canned interview in some podunk place fifty light-years away won't count for much when the other side's got people running from talk show to talk show right here."

"Hold it, Nelly," Kris said, knowing that Grampa was right, and she'd never have needed a reminder if she wasn't so tired. "Send a check to cover four or five tickets and per diem for folks, and ask Ester if she could get some volunteers to come."

"You paying their way won't look all that good," Jack said.

"So, if I don't, I look bad. If I do, I look lousy. Give me a break. Some breakfast, a nap, a shower, not necessarily in that order. This is about the worst morning I've ever had."

"If that Pearson woman wasn't your boss on that rainsodden planet, maybe you could have who was speak for you," Grampa said.

"Colonel Hancock was my CO, and I reported directly to him. He had as few people as possible report to Pearson."

"Sounds like a smart man," was high praise from Grampa.

"Colonel Hancock," Jack said slowly.

"Yes," Kris said with a nod. "Lieutenant Colonel James T. Hancock, SHMC."

"Oh, him!" Grampa Trouble shook his head. "The opposition's talk show hosts will be foaming at the mouth to get him on as your character witness."

"Am I missing something?" Jack said, looking away from where the car was taking them. "I should think a Marine Colonel would be a perfect character witness.

"Not a Colonel found not guilty, but not innocent either, of using machine guns for crowd control," Trouble said.

"Oh, that Colonel Hancock," Jack said and looked away. "Maybe you could arrange for him to praise Pearson."

Grampa Trouble's silence said all Kris needed to hear.

"I think there's a good reason why he's still on Olympia and probably will remain there until he sinks into the swamp. There are other folks who were on Olympia with me. There's Tom. He was with me at the warehouse. He saw what was going on."

"The Tom who's getting married at the house?" Jack asked. "Kitchen crew is real excited about baking the wedding cake."

Hmm, maybe Tom didn't look all that unbiased at the moment.

"Well, we've got a week," Kris concluded.

"Maybe not," Nelly said. "I have been examining the news, Kris, and I think the media is engaging in what is called a 'feeding frenzy.' Would you like to sample some of the news?"

Now it was Kris's turn to glance at Grampa and raise a quizzical eyebrow. "Is it that bad?"

"I believe the opposition intends to try you in the media and hang your father from your highest yardarm. Or something equally nautical."

Kris said a word princesses aren't supposed to know and settled back into her seat.

They dropped Grampa Trouble off at his town house, which was good, because the entrance to Nuu House was a media circus. News trucks and cameras besieged the entrance to the compound. Only the locking gate and eight-foot-tall brick wall . . . and the not-so-visible security systems above it kept the media outside. Kris faced straight ahead as she rode through the barrage, trusting the car's armor to stop anything really dangerous.

It was only as Jack drove the short distance to the mansion's front entrance that she remembered Penny and Tom were supposed to drop by this morning to talk about their wedding plans. Poor Tommy, having to make it through that rabble. She hoped he hadn't cut and run. She wanted to know how the rest of the squadron was taking her arrest.

The doors to Nuu House opened automatically at her approach, leaving her facing the last person in the world she wanted to bother with at this moment.

Father!

William Longknife, Billy to his millions of intimates, stormed toward Kris, a hurricane in full blow, his face redder than Kris remembered it this early in the morning. Had he already been at the wine cabinet?

Trailing Father across the spiraling black and white tiles of the foyer was his political shadow, Honovi. Kris pitied her older brother his chosen fate, though he seemed to be succeeding fairly well at following in their father's political footsteps.

For her part, Kris had run off to space to avoid the family's business. If she could, she would have fled farther. At the moment, it looked like she hadn't run nearly far enough.

"What do you think you're doing, young woman?" Father shouted, halting directly in front of Kris, unblinking eyes demanding an answer. He leaned into her, nose to nose, violating her personal space. *Yep, he's been into the wine supply already. Things are bad and headed for worse.*

Kris denied the urge to take a step back. Five years ago she would have. A year ago she might have. Not today. She'd faced battleships and assassins. What was a merely angry politician compared to that? But she didn't want a fight. Not now. She weighed her options and chose a non-confrontational one.

"I *think* I'm looking for breakfast," Kris said with as much good cheer as she could muster. "They didn't finish booking me until after supper last night. I got sprung before breakfast. And, Father, you must look into the temperatures of your prisons. I almost froze last night."

"I'll do that, Sis, when we get back in office."

"Don't let her change the subject, Honovi. Kris, what are you doing to my reelection campaign?"

"Nothing, Father. Remember," Kris pointed at her shoulder tabs. "I'm Navy. We stay out of politics."

"Like hell they do. These charges leveled against you—"

"Will be handled quickly and promptly."

"No they won't, Sis."

"Why not?" Her brother had Kris's undivided attention. Well, almost. From the open door to the Rose Parlor on Kris's left she was catching snatches of conversation. The word *wedding* kept coming up. Mother was doing most of the talking, but Kris thought she heard Tommy or Penny's voice occasionally trying to get a syllable in edgewise.

"You have a message," her brother said, "from the Navy Judge Advocate General listing the charges and telling you that your initial hearing has been delayed two weeks."

"What!" Tired, hungry, mad, Kris barely suppressed a shout. But then she didn't know who to shout at: her brother for opening her mail or the Navy for slowing down her tribulations.

Or Mother insisting Penny must have eight bridesmaids. "Nothing less will do. It simply will not do," Mother said with a theatrical flair that would grate chalk off a board.

"I'm sorry," Honovi said. "The letter came to the house, and I felt I'd better open it."

"You see," Father said, talking over his son, "they're playing you into the election news cycle. They'll hang you out there, day after day, attacking me through you. There's nothing for you to do but resign from the Navy and come work for us."

"No!" And this time Kris did shout. She used the voice her DIs had taught her at OCS. Her "no" carried through the house, reverberating off walls that still echoed with years of history.

Then Kris took the two extra steps that put her in the door of the Rose Parlor and repeated, "No."

"Mother, you are not taking over Penny and Tom's wedding." She spun back to face her father. "And Father, I am not one of your political hangers-on that you can order about. I've got my own career, and I will do what I have to do to keep it."

Having made her position clear, Kris listened for a very long minute while Mother and Father told her how wrong she was. Kris had little argument with her father. No doubt, this was probably the most important election since Wardhaven freed itself from the yoke of the Unity thugs eighty years ago with the help of Grampa Ray's assassination of President Urm.

Oh yes, that lie again.

However, she failed to see that she had any role in this massive political theater of his. As for Mother, even when she attempted to tie a major spring wedding "in the garden where King Ray and Rita wed" to the election as worth a hundred thousand votes, Kris still refused to budge. Then Mother played what she thought was her trump.

"How can you expect *me* to stand *idle* while there are *preparations* to be made for a *wedding* in my *own* home."

"Your. Home." Kris spat. Kris had had Nuu House to herself since she moved out of the Prime Minister's official residency to go to college. Father had immediately converted her bedroom to office space for two new deputy under assistants for something or other. Mother hadn't seemed to notice at all.

"Yes, Sis. We kind of had to leave the residency in a hurry last night. The Pandoris insisted on moving in this morning. We didn't bother your suites, but we did move back in."

The idea of living under the same roof with Mother, Father, and God bless her poor brother and his new wife was not something Kris needed to think about.

"I'm moving out."

"You can't," Father and Mother said together.

"Where to?" Abby, Kris's maid of four months, asked. Kris hadn't noticed the tall, severely dressed woman at the foot of the stairs. Jack, who might take a bullet for her but wouldn't get between her and her father, had gravitated over to stand beside her.

"I can and I will move out. I am a grown woman and a commissioned Naval officer. I can afford my own apartment."

Father just snorted at the idea. Mother raised her nose in the air. "Where would you find anything appropriate to your station on such short notice?"

Wrong question, Kris thought.

Kris had gotten an education when she recently rescued Tom from kidnappers on Turantic. It wasn't Tommy's fault; he'd been taken as bait to trap Kris. But busting him loose had involved a walk down the seamier underside of Turantic, leaving Kris with questions about whether Wardhaven had some places just as ugly . . . just as empty of hope. Home, she did a search. It was easy; she just looked for the places where Father never sent her to campaign.

Yes, Wardhaven had its slums, and a diligent search by Nelly through ownership records, and records of who owned those who owned the ones who owned the ones who . . . Anyway, several layers of deniability up from the poor sods who collected the rent, Kris found Grampa Al and her own trust fund getting wealthy on way too many of them. She fired off a letter, with plenty of attachments, to Grampa Al, asking him to look into this. And got no reply.

What better time than now to do something about it.

"I'm sure there are several vacant apartments in Edgertown that I could rent today."

"Edgertown," Mother huffed.

"Why would you rent something there?" Father asked,

his eyebrows coming together like two woolly caterpillars, unsure whether to fight or mate.

"Because we own them, Father. Or rather, your father owns them, through the necessary intermediaries to avoid embarrassing questions."

"Kris, this is not a good time to think about doing something like that," Brother said.

"Who's thinking? As soon as I can call a cab, I'm out of here."

Jack stepped forward. "I'll drive you, Kris."

"Young man, I forbid it," said Father.

"Sir, I don't work for you. Even when you are Prime Minister, I'm under civil service rules."

Kris would not bet her career that such rules would hold when the full cyclone of her father's anger stormed down on them.

"Besides," the vacationing agent said, "your daughter seems quite intent on going apartment hunting on the wrong side of town. Wouldn't you want someone with my credentials"—here he opened his coat, giving everyone a flash of his service automatic—"seeing that she gets out okay?"

"We are not finished, young woman," her father stormed, but Kris had done a fast about-face and was headed for the door, Jack and Abby hurrying to catch up.

Outside. Kris took two quick steps and found that her knees were again filing for nonsupport. She collapsed on the stone steps she'd sat on after school so many years ago. Then, she'd used them as an excuse not to go in, not to face her mother and father. Now she sat there recovering from them. No difference.

"You hungry?" Jack asked.

"Starved."

"Let's get some decent food into you while I find a well-armored car that doesn't look the part."

Kris glanced down at herself. Her shipsuit looked like she'd sweated through an attack on a battleship, slept through a bad night in a brig, and survived a family get-together of the worst kind. "You don't mind being near me?"

"Wasn't planning on getting closer than ten feet, and that upwind," Jack said. "Remember, I'm on vacation. Any bullets that have a date with you today, it's just you and them, kid."

"Thanks for the reminder," Kris said and looked up at Abby. "And why are you going with me?"

"You're headed into hoods like where I grew up, girl, and you gonna need someone who knows the way things hang. If you don't want to end up hanging upside down. You get my meaning?"

As usual where her maid was concerned, Kris was none too sure exactly what the woman's meaning was. That it usually worked out for the best was the sole reason Kris shrugged and said, "Fine."

"Which also explains why Momma Abby took a few moments when she heard you were coming home to put together a survival kit for her chick." With a flourish, Abby opened what for her was a purse totally out of character, huge . . . with multicolored stripes. A glance in showed Kris a powder blue sweater and brown slacks . . . and a body stocking.

"Armored?"

"Why wear one if it ain't, baby ducks."

"Do you wear armored underwear?" Jack asked.

"I do better than that, love. I lead a nice quiet life of desperation, one that no one would want to end violently." Her smile for Jack almost looked honest.

Jack's personal car got them to the Scriptorum, one of Kris's old college haunts. By the time they'd eaten and Abby had helped her do a quick cleanup and change, Jack had wrestled up a car.

Abby got wide-eyed as she took in the wreck. "You're driving a beater into my hood. You're risking the princess here having to thumb her way out when this thing goes white belly up in the middle of the road."

"Abby, you're not the only one who wears your camouflage well. Get in. By the way, Miss Nightengale, my latest request to redo the background check on you just came back from Earth."

Jack took the driver's seat, Abby the backseat across from him, leaving Kris to open her own door. Kris was used to her princess status going less than far where these two were concerned. After all, she'd been promoted from Prime Minister's brat to princess less than a year ago, and it was more often a nuisance than a help. Well, it had helped a bit on Turantic.

But Abby's background. That tickled Kris's curiosity. "What did it say?"

"Nothing. Perfect support for what she said about herself. Not even the tiniest hole in her résumé."

"Well, I should expect so," Abby sniffed, arranging the fall of her severe gray skirt just so. Kris wondered how much heavy weaponry it hid today.

"Perfect match. Too perfect for even the guys doing the background search. They say they'll do more checking. I got the impression that you intrigue them. You want to be their hobby?"

"No," Abby huffed. "I am what I am. Doesn't a poor working girl have the right to some privacy?"

"Yes," Jack said, "once you tell me who you're working for."

"Kris's mother hired me."

"And I suspect she's firing you as we talk," Kris said. "Mother was probably so looking forward to having me around to torture for the next six weeks. She will not be happy if you help me get out from under her thumb, knee, and elbow."

"Well, honey, getting you dressed to go apartment shopping is a long way from seeing you sign on the dotted line. No offense, Your Princessship, but you aren't serious about moving into a slum, are you?"

"She's serious," Jack said. "You want to have Nelly pass me some addresses for places to look at?"

"Nelly, do what Jack asked."

"All of them. I'm not sure this bomb can handle the half of them." Kris took in her ride; it looked bad. The seat covers were slashed where they weren't worn through. She fingered a cut place in the leather. Nope, not cut. Painted on. She eyed the dashboard; under all that dust was solid-looking electronics.

"Nelly, interrogate the car's computer."

"Interro . . . wow. Now that is one smart computer. Jack, where did you get this car?" Nelly asked.

Which left Kris out of the loop and a bit annoyed that her pet computer was going straight from finding out what they were riding in to asking Jack all kinds of questions. Questions Kris would much rather be asking herself.

"Friend of mine, retired from the force, runs a jack-up service to up-gun, up-armor, up-tight the usual suspects. But he keeps a few ringers for special folks. Stakeouts, other stuff."

"Nice to have decent wheels," Abby said, unimpressed. "Baby cakes, you better tell Nelly to sort the vacant apartments by pairs. Your maid's gonna have to live next door to you."

"She does not."

"She does, too, Princess, for at least two reasons. One, I don't want to have to walk the streets after staying up late to undress you after you come back from some fine ball all gussied up. Two, you're going to need someone close by to pull your hind end out of the trouble you're going to get it into when you're lost and doing everything wrong in my side of town."

"Jack," Kris said, for what she immediately realized was no good reason. Still, he ought to give her some support.

"Nelly, do a search for triple vacancies."

"Triple!" came from both women in the back.

"I do not need to be nursemaided. I've been shot at. I know how to shoot back," Kris snapped.

"Wrong attitude," Abby said. "You expecting to be shot at, you gonna be shot at. You smile, make friends with the folks down the hall, on the floor below, then you got folks to help you out, young woman."

"It looks like the folks down the hall and down the stairs are going to be folks I know. Jack, what are you trying to do? You don't have to be next door to me. You don't work for me."

"I should say not," he snapped.

"In fact, Jack, you're not going to have a job for too much longer if Father doesn't win. Maybe even if he does."

"So a cheap flat becomes kind of appealing," he said. "Nelly, what have you got?"

"Well, here are some triple vacancies. I don't know that they are all that good of an idea, but they should do while you people sort out all these human issues. Kris, you will make sure that I am not stolen or damaged." Nelly sounded worried.

"Maybe, maybe not," Kris said. Nelly said nothing back.

The first place was a fourth-floor walk-up in need of cleaning, painting, plumbing repairs, and the services of several kinds of exterminators. The second place was worse. Jack parked in front of the third; it looked no better from the outside. He turned to Kris; she could read in his eyes, *You ready to call it quits yet?* She glanced at Abby. *How long you gonna keep up this harebrained stunt?* was all over the woman's face.

"Kris, you have a message from King Raymond," Nelly said as Jack's wrist computer buzzed softly. Kris raised a quizzical eyebrow at him.

Jack glanced at his wrist. "I am requested and required to present myself to King Raymond at my earliest convenience."

"This happen to you folks often?" Abby asked. "I mean, balls is something I can handle. Being yanked around on some fancy electronic chain, having to drop everything and go see the king. You do it every day?"

"Grampa Ray's just a huggy bear," Kris said, suspecting whatever her great-grandfather was up to at the moment probably had more in common with the annihilation of Iteeche fleets and policy for the human race than what dessert to serve at tomorrow's charity auction. First a leading General, then the President of the Society of Humanity during the worst of the Iteeche Wars, he'd hammered together the policies that had guided humanity for eighty years afterwards. There were shelves of books full of his exploits . . . his and Great-grampa Trouble's. Kris had grown up in the shadow of that distant, legendary man.

Only recently had she come to know the man of flesh and blood behind the legend. And she'd helped talk her great-grandfather into taking a crown. Talked him into trying to lasso together Wardhaven and a growing number of planets into an alliance when it seemed like the six hundred planets of human space were intent only on flying apart.

"Wonder what he could be wanting from a disgraced Naval officer who's been relieved of her command," Abby asked.

"You have such a wonderful way with words." Kris sighed.

"Well, do we look at this next place, or do I head for the palace?" Jack asked.

"It's just a hotel," Kris pointed out.

"Honey," Abby sighed, "if a king lives there, it's a palace, be it ever so hovel. Child, you have to get past this family thing and start seeing the world the way us poor folks do."

"The palace, Sir John," Kris said.

"Jack," her driver corrected.

"Listen, if I can still be stuck being a princess after they've hijacked my ship and hauled me off to the brig, shouldn't any unemployed hired gun wandering around with me be at least a knight in shining armor? Remember, Jack, you gave up being an honest working man."

"She has a certain logic, Jack," Abby agreed.

"Tilly's twerp factor is getting lower and lower on my baloney meter," Jack said, glancing at his watch. "Maybe it's not too late for me to make my first shift."

"Let's find out what Grampa Ray wants first. Never can tell, it might cover room and board."

3

"**Your** Highness, you are expected," the security agent said as Kris presented herself at the door of Grampa Ray's penthouse suite. "Jack, I thought you were on leave?" he added as the agent's name apparently came up right after Kris's.

"So did I. You can never tell when you work around Longknifes, can you?"

"So true," the agent agreed.

"I'll just find a nice magazine to read," Abby said, heading for a chair in the waiting room.

"She's going in, too," Kris said. "Abby Nightengale."

"You *are* on the list," the agent said.

"Me?" Abby said, bringing up a startled hand for a dramatic wave at her throat. "A lowly body servant?"

"Disarming her may take a half hour," Jack drawled.

"You wrong me!" Abby pouted.

"My orders aren't to disarm any of you," the agent said, with a touch more relief than Kris would have expected.

Jack's frown was solid professional disapproval.

"His Highness said that if he was willing to have her

carry all that artillery around Princess Kris, it would be damn undignified of him to demand we frisk her for his old bones," the agent said in defense. "Now, you are to go right in."

"What artillery?" the maid protested.

Jack seemed still undecided. "Sound's like Grampa," Kris said. Behind her, the elevator opened to disgorge Penny and Tom.

"Good," the agent said. "The party's complete."

"I've never been so grateful to be beeped in my life," Penny said, breathless.

"And if it hadn't been Grampa Ray, Mother would have had you ignore it," Kris said to Penny.

Tom frowned. "You know, I think she might have."

"His Majesty is in his study. Your computers will show you the way," the agent said, taking his seat behind his desk.

Nelly told them to go right, go left, through that door. The suite had taken on more than the usual hotel furnishings. One room was shelves from floor to ceiling covered with replicas of the ships, armored suits, and ground vehicles of the Iteeche Wars, backed up with paintings of battle scenes. There were also pictures of staffs, both those who survived their battles and those who died to a man and woman trying to stem the tide. Kris wondered if Grampa normally kept a room like this in his home, or if he'd put this up to impress his visitors now that he was back in politics. Or to remind himself.

She'd have to decide whether to ask Grampa about that.

The final room Nelly directed them into was a workroom, with some bookshelves for real bound books, but mostly screens for net news reports or private news outlets. A large wooden desk was piled high with flimsies and readers. In front of it several couches and chairs formed a conversation circle around a table that might or might not be simply wood. Grampa Ray wore slacks and a short-sleeved shirt. He looked all of his hundred and twenty years, maybe more, as he eyed a reporter on one screen. The man was replaced by scenes from the Naval yard at the station orbiting above their head. The fleet was in port, but supply trucks were moving. A lot of ships were going someplace.

Grampa scowled, silenced the screen, and turned toward them. By the time he faced Kris, he was smiling and seemed fifty years younger. "Thanks for dropping everything to make an old man happy," he said, waving them at the couches and coming around his desk to take a comfortable chair in their circle.

"Depends on what you want," Kris said, settling into the chair across from him. Penny and Tom got comfortable on a couch. Abby took the couch across from them. Jack chose to stand behind Kris, facing two of the three doors. He must hate that he couldn't keep an eye on all three.

No, Kris spotted a reflection of the third door in a blank screen. Jack *had* managed to get an eyeball on all three.

There were few things Kris would not happily give her Grampa. However, if he'd hauled her up here to talk to her about not causing Father trouble during this election, or not exposing Grampa Al for the slumlord he was, she and Grampa Ray were gonna have their first go at head butting.

"Most of the time, I forget how old I am. Then I get a message like this, and I remember," Grampa Ray said, his fingers tapping the one reader he'd brought with him from the desk.

"Back in the first Iteeche dustup, before we realized what a mess we were in, back when I was just a general fighting what I thought was a bunch of pirates, I had a detachment of special ops that were, well, too damn good for their own good.

"Hikila was a new planet. It didn't have a lot of troopers, but the Special Boats Squadron made up in imagination and cussedness what they lacked in numbers. They were good. And I used them. Used them up. It's amazing that any lived to send me an invitation to their bedside at this late date." He snorted.

"But Queen Ha'iku'lani is the kind of woman that fifty men will die for so she can die in bed. I wonder what she thinks now of that kind of real estate business," he said to himself.

Kris felt embarrassed to be let into such an intimate moment. She wanted to look away. Tom and Penny were. Abby was.

Kris couldn't. She was a Longknife. If she followed in the footsteps of her great-grandfather, a hundred years from now she'd be muttering such questions. Did she want to? Wouldn't now be a good time to head for the door?

The king shivered, glanced around as if just noticing the others, and gave them a wan smile. "Sorry. If things were a bit quieter, I'd take a week off and go hold an old war buddy's hand, help her get ready to meet the ghosts waiting for us on the other side. Any decent world would make such a duty the highest priority for old farts like me." He flashed Kris a smile that was only sad around the edges.

"But someone I know and love talked me into putting back on the old battle harness, so just now, Wardhaven's got a caretaker government that doesn't know how to spell the word much less follow those limits. And I hear that Boynton has a fleet of undetermined origins headed their way with no declared intent. And the latest rumor I'm getting from this temporary Wardhaven government is that all or part of the fleet may sail for Boynton real soon now. It doesn't sound like a good time for me to take leave. What do you think, hon?"

Kris swallowed something that might have been a lump in her throat. She hadn't thought of things like this when she'd urged her Grampa to accept the kingship of now ninety planets. She'd seen the honor, somewhat ambiguous and indefinite, but an honor, netherthless. And a way to help the people on ninety planets keep afloat amid the wreckage of the Society of Humanity. Maybe she hadn't looked at it from his angle as carefully as she should have. She certainly hadn't spotted the downside that it would stick her with this princess thing. She was learning that lots of things happened while she was making her plans.

"I guess you'll have to stay here," Kris said.

"Which means I need to send someone in my stead to help an old friend die," Grampa said, his eyes going out of focus. "There will be more to it. Hikila has developed quite an economy in the last fifty years. It needs to come into United Sentients. They haven't voted yet. The coronation of their new queen would be a good time to make that call."

Kris nodded. "I'll do what I can to bring them in."

"Hopefully without all the complications that sprang up on Turantic. I hear some insurance companies are going to court over who pays for repairs to the space station and elevator."

Kris tried to grin. "Oh, for the good old days, Grampa, when all you had to do was kick butt and take names. Now you have to file legal briefs and testify under oath for a week."

"Or three years," King Ray snorted with good humor. "For what I'm sending you into, Kris, you'll need political intel. I've busted Penny loose for you. I hope you don't mind me sending you off world just before your wedding."

"It's all right, Your Majesty. Kris's mother was telling me every little thing I need to do for a simple garden wedding."

"Lord God forbid that woman gets her hooks into anybody's wedding," the king said.

"Any chance you could, sir? Forbid it?" Kris asked.

"I warned your father he was marrying a woman with a whim of iron. He laughed at what he took for a joke. I haven't noticed him laughing that much around his wife of late. No, I'm afraid all I can hope for is that with Penny off planet, she'll get distracted and wander off into someone else's business."

"Can you get Tom off planet with me? We made a great team on Turantic," Penny wheedled, Lieutenant to king.

Kris started to shake her head, but Grampa smiled sardonically. "Actually, I can. Apple of your eye those tiny boats may be, Kris, but the word I'm getting is that Pandori's going to sell them off as private runabouts."

Kris's mouth dropped open, but it was Tom who spoke

first. "Didn't you say they were sending the fleet to Boynton? What will they have left to defend Wardhaven?"

" 'No one would even *think* of attacking Wardhaven,' " Grampa said, even getting Pandori's hand wave right.

"And you gave this bunch full power," Kris said.

Grampa sighed. "Believe me, they didn't talk like that when they came in here. And they did have that 53 percent majority vote in Parliament. It seemed like a good idea at the time."

"Well, you kids do be careful," Abby said. "I hear being around one of those damn Longknifes can be dangerous."

"You're going, too," Kris said.

"I can't wait to count your steamer trunks and see what you pull out of them this time," Jack drawled.

"I don't know why I'm going," Penny said. "Have you ever noticed a Longknife to pay attention to the advice they get?"

"Ouch," came from both king and princess.

"You're going to have to get away quickly," the king said. "I've still got the *Halsey* seconded to me, but if she's not away from the pier fast, she may get orders, and if I have to go to Pennypacker to straighten out conflicting orders with a lot of Longknife names on them, I can't guarantee anything."

" 'Tis a wonderful thing to be a pirate king," Tom sang.

"You've obviously never been one," King Ray muttered. "Oh, Kris, the skipper of the *Halsey* is Sandy Santiago. One of those Santiagos. She'll look after you good."

Now it was Kris's turn to answer with a soft, "Oh." Grampa Ray's political career had been launched when he survived assassinating the Unity tyrant President Urm. It had been in all the papers. Only recently had Kris learned just how it happened that Grampa lived through delivering a suicide bomb. It might be interesting to hear how the story was told among the family of the man who actually walked the bomb in.

Jack and Abby were dispatched to Nuu House to pack. Penny and Tom headed out to do the same.

Kris settled in as they left. "I was afraid you'd called me over here to set me straight about Father and Grampa Al."

"I know the hot water your old man is in. What's my son's beef with you, girl?"

Kris told him about finding out she owned slums. "Oh, ho ho," Grampa Ray chortled. "The old boy hasn't been keeping good enough check on his middlemen, has he now."

"Middlemen?"

"Kris, I'll let you in on a little secret. I can't do everything. You can't do everything, and though he'll deny it, my son can't do everything, try as he does. Little Alex has a bad case of micromanagement, but even he can't be everywhere. So some of his second-, third-level VPs take shortcuts. Folks do that. You find them out, fire them, and put in new people. Hope my boy takes this for a learning experience."

Then a message came in, and family time was over, and Grampa Ray was back up to his earlobes juggling business from ninety planets and firing off his best advice. "Advice, gal. Nice not to give orders anymore. Just advice." In between he remembered the Iteeche Wars for Kris. The operations he'd sent Ha'iku'lani and her Special Boat Squadron on were heavy on his mind. He could name the planets and the dead as if it was only yesterday.

But it was the present that bothered Kris. "It's like someone is nibbling at us. This planet has that beef with that planet, and suddenly they're using warships to settle them."

"No, Kris, not planets. People. This group here. That group there. Always look for the groups behind the actions. And notice how much of it is just posturing and threatening. Threats work better than shooting," Grampa pointed out.

"Take Flan, or Yacolt, or Mandan only last week. Greenfeld tells them they really want to join their new alliance . . . and runs a squadron of battleships across their orbit to overawe them. And Peterwald gets a planet with no messy rubble."

"That why Pandori is rushing the fleet to Boynton?"

Grampa shook his head. "Boynton's practically in our alliance. We're not trying to overawe them. We're trying to protect them, and we don't need nearly that large a force. I think Pandori's doing it to get votes this election."

"And Hikila?"

"They just need some hand-holding. A bit of encouragement. I know them. They're our kind of people. Oh, and don't you let looks deceive you. On the surface they may look primitive. Take a second look. Ask the second question. They'll surprise you."

Jack called. They were packed and waiting downstairs. Kris joined him and Abby. "How many trunks?"

"I counted eight when we left the house," Jack said.

"It's not like we're going to rescue anyone," Abby sniffed.

"Count again when we go through security."

But Kris got distracted at the space elevator. Penny and Tom went through, no problem. Kris ran her ID card through to prove who she was and pay her fare . . . and got beeped.

"Card's no good, ma'am," the young man in the booth said. Kris ran it through again; same result. "It's not the card, ma'am. It's you. You ain't cleared to go up. To leave the planet," the fellow said, turning a screen around for her and Jack to look at. "See, you're limited to planet travel."

"King Ray has ordered me on a diplomatic mission," Kris said, eyeing the report on her. "I'll be back before my court date in . . . *three weeks*!"

"Delayed again," Jack said.

"They really want to drag it out," Tom said.

"You that Princess Longknife," the gate attendant said. "I saw you on the news last night. You did a lot of good stuff on Olympia. Pretty mean of them to do this to you."

"You know about Olympia?"

"Researched it for a college paper for night school," he said, glancing at the screen. "Three weeks. Where you headed?"

"Hikila. Be back in two weeks. Maybe less."

"Why don't you and that fellow behind you go through at the same time. You know. One swipe, two walks."

"Won't you get in trouble?"

"How much trouble can I get in if you get back in time?"

"Joey," Kris said, reading his name tag. "Everyone who gets too close to me gets in trouble." Jack nodded vigorously.

"You just go ahead, ma'am. As you said, King Ray wants you somewhere. Why should Wardhaven Transit stand in your way?"

Jack flashed his badge as he ran his card through. Joey whistled as his metal detectors did their detecting thing. "You are taking good care of her, ain't you." And Kris was through.

Abby followed, leading eight steamer trunks. Kris counted as they rolled by. They made it as a ferry was locking down.

The *Halsey* was also just about to seal locks as they reported to the Junior Officer of the Deck. He frowned at the baggage and called for a quartermaster detail to secure it. Abby pulled a smaller subset of luggage from one trunk for her and Kris, and they all followed the JG forward to the wardroom.

"Captain Santiago asks that you wait for her here while we get under way. She'll visit you then," he said and left.

"They ain't exactly killing the fatted calf," Abby observed. She pulled out a reader. Jack did a security check, satisfied himself a Navy destroyer was safe, and produced a reader of his own. Penny and Tom found a quiet corner where they proceeded to put their heads together and not violate Navy regs on excessive displays of public affection. That left Kris prowling the wardroom. It was larger than the *Cushing*'s. Newer. Just as clean with the usual public readers and the usual subscriptions.

She and Nelly ended up playing acey-deucey. They'd been under way for over an hour when a woman of medium height and brown, graying hair ducked into the wardroom. The three strips on her blue shipsuit's shoulder tabs told all she ruled here. After collecting a cup of coffee, she joined the table where Kris and Jack sat with Abby. Penny and Tom surfaced from each other's eyes to gather with them.

"I'm Commander Santiago, and the *Halsey* is my ship. King Raymond asked me to take you to Hikila, and I'm setting a 1.25-g course for there. I hope that won't bother you. Being a destroyer, we're short on space. I'm bunking all three of you ladies in my in-port cabin. You two men will be in a cabin across the passageway from them. Any problems with that?"

Kris shook her head. Jack said, "No."

The woman eyed Kris for a moment. The JO who'd first led them to the wardroom ducked his head in. "You called, ma'am?"

"Yes, Roberts, show these people to their staterooms."

"This way, folks," the cheerful JG Roberts said.

As the others made to leave, Santiago said, "A moment alone, Princess."

Kris waited.

"I don't know what you were expecting this trip, but let me tell you what you'll get. A trip. Fast. Efficient. Nothing more. I won't have any of my crew getting messed up in whatever it is you Longknifes are doing. Enough good sailors have died for your legends. This Santiago and my *Halsey* will not contribute any more bodies to the list. Understand?"

"Perfectly," Kris said, suppressing shock and rising anger.

"Stay away from my crew."

"I'm not going to stir up a mutiny."

The commander snorted. "They wouldn't follow you. My crew's too good for that. No, Princess, I don't want you making it any harder for them to do what I tell them to do. To follow my orders when I leave you high and dry if you mess up. Understand, Princess, I will not pull your chestnuts out of the fire, and I won't have my crew doing it either."

"I'm going to Hikila to hold the hand of an old friend of my grampa while she dies. I'm not going to start a war."

"Yeah, right. Just so long as you understand, if, no, *when* you do, you will be on your own."

"Am I dismissed, Commander?"

"Yes, Lieutenant."

Kris marched for the door. "One more thing, Longknife." Kris turned. "My daughter will be applying to the Academy this year. For three generations every Santiago that applied to the academy had a letter of recommendation in their file from Ray Longknife."

"Yes," Kris said. She knew Grampa Ray did that, part of what bound the Longknifes and Santiagos together.

"My daughter will not have anything from a Longknife in her folder. You Longknifes have battened off our blood long enough. It stops with my generation. She takes her turn on her own."

"I'm sure she'll earn her billet," Kris said. "On her own."

It was going to be a long trip even at high-g cruise.

4

The *Halsey*'s gig edged away from the destroyer, where it lay tied up to Hikila's space station, and dropped toward Nui Nui. Kris had a good view of the planet from where she sat behind the two pilots. All she saw was water, water, and more water. The main continent, called the Big Island here, was about the size of Earth's Eurasia, but was well south of the gig's nose.

It was good to be away from the *Halsey*. Kris had joined several officers and the Marine detachment in their daily jog around the decks and up the ladders. The Sergeant of Marines was a friend from the *Typhoon*, Corporal, now Sergeant, Li.

The next day, Santiago joined the exercise routine.

To please the skipper, Kris kept old-time reminiscence to a minimum and just did the workout.

Meals in the wardroom were also fully chaperoned by Commander Santiago. Again, Kris was invited to the Captain's table, but it was quite different from her time at the head table on the luxurious liner *Pride of Turantic*. Kris let Santiago set the topics for discussion and followed, as most everything proved out of bounds. From the way the officers started conversations and accepted being cut off, Kris suspected the table topics had never been so nonhistorical, nontactical, and non–current events. No one crossed their Captain's wishes twice.

Kris was looking forward to a meal where most of her life was not a forbidden topic.

The gig descended along a long line of islands spread out from a larger one. As Kris got lower, she could see the islands were wrapped in verdant greens, usually topped by volcanoes. Some still seemed active. Most islands were encircled by reefs and a dazzling blue ocean. No wonder this planet had been the choice of the descendants of Pacific Islanders from old Earth for the place to rebuild their lost life.

The gig splashed down in a large lagoon and was quickly greeted by flower-draped rowers in outrigger canoes . . . and a power tug for their tow. "You want to ride in with us, or with the locals?" the gig pilot called back.

"The canoes are an honor," Penny told Kris.

"I figured as much. Can you open the hatch safely?"

The copilot did. Kris managed the transfer from bobbing gig to bobbing canoe with success, if not grace. Her whites were draped with leis by a lovely young woman wrapped in a sea green sarong. Soft yellow and pink flower tattoos wrapped around her arms and shoulders to disappear beneath her own leis.

"I am Princess Ha'iku'aholo. My friends call me Aholo."

"I'm Princess Kris Longknife. Kris to my friends."

"And I'm Jack," Jack said, making the transition from modern shuttle to wooden boat. He, too, got flowers for his effort.

Their outrigger pulled away, and another took its place at the shuttle's door. Penny and Tom got the same treatment. Kris expected ever-prim Abby to pass, but the woman hiked up her gray A-line dress to show well-shaped legs to her approving boatmen and stepped aboard the third canoe. She also got flowers, though from the fellows. They shoved off from the gig with a shout from an oarsman on Penny's canoe, which Kris took for "last one ashore is a rotten egg," because all three outriggers took off like a shot from a gun for the white, sandy beach. Half-meter waves helped them along, aided by the wind at their back. This had to be anyone's idea of paradise.

Abby's canoe won, but there was no rancor. Kris wondered how her white shoes and pants would take to the water and sand, but she was not about to be carried ashore. She stepped out to find that the sandy section where they'd landed had been grouted or hardened, the beach, too. They walked ashore with the sand giving a bit, but not much. Paradise with high tech.

"My mother's grandmother's heart longs to see you," Aholo said and motioned Kris to a small electric cart, much like one used on space stations. This one was open to the breeze, had seats all around, and a colorful fish-print awning to provide shade. The princess took the driver's seat and offered Kris the passenger side. The rest of the team took others, except Abby.

"I'll wait for our luggage."

An oarsman jumped on board. "I'm Aholo's brother, Afa," and they were off. The road was sand, but again it had been treated. Pedestrians left shallow tracks as did the cart. Beside them, palms swayed in the wind. A wild profusion of flowers and birds added a mad collection of colors.

KRIS, WOULD YOU LIKE ME TO IDENTIFY THE BIRDS AND PLANTS FOR YOU?

NO. LET ME JUST ENJOY THEM.

The cart took them uphill. They passed houses made of wood and woven mats, thatched roofs, men in lavalavas, women in sarongs or lavalavas. Dress was . . . casual.

There was a whisper behind them, followed by a stern, "I am not going native," from Penny.

Aholo smiled. "We often have that effect on foreigners."

Kris measured the depth of feeling behind that word; it came up high. She wondered what she'd have to do to keep that word from being applied to her and Grampa Ray's United Sentients.

Aholo pulled to a stop beside a large, multileveled house with most of its sides open to the breeze. She led them inside, past carved masks and figures, painted shields and potted flowers. Long-beaked, riotously colored birds flew by. Aholo led them through a door into a room that was closed off with blinds and mats on its walls. Candles—no, electric lights made to look like candles—dimly lit the room. A woman lay on a feather bed made from a brightly colored cotton tick. Aholo knelt and took the woman's hand. "My Mother's Grandmother, Ray Longknife has sent his son's granddaughter."

The woman turned her face to Kris. Eyes, dark and deep as pools, took her measure. Then she blinked and nodded. "You have Rita's eyes, not Ray's. That may save you much sorrow, girl."

"I never met anyone who knew Great-grandmother Rita," Kris stammered.

The woman nodded. "She died too soon for poor Ray. Far too soon. I think she would have saved him from being president. He should have faded away after the war, become small again. I hear he's back doing politics again. Bad boy."

"I encouraged him," Kris confessed.

"And he let you," said the dying woman.

"You are the queen here," Aholo pointed out.

"A queen here is nothing. The People sail as they will." The crinkle beside the princess's eyes said lie to the words.

"But you have come to hold my hand while I make that final crossing over the reef, have you, young Princess," the woman said, taking her hand from her great-granddaughter's and offering it to Kris. Kris took it; it was dry, light. The fingers were swollen with arthritis, each joint tattooed with a different design. Sunbursts exploded at wrists and elbows, covering other designs of fish and birds. Tattoos on top of tattoos.

PRIMITIVE MEDICINE USED TATTOOS, Nelly told Kris.

"Don't worry, old age ain't contagious," the queen said, making Kris wonder what the look on her face must be. She stroked the woman's hand; it felt like well-worn leather.

"You arrived just in time for the spring full moon," the queen said, moving to her side and closer to Kris. "Will you dance tonight with us or stand aloof with the other foreigners?"

Kris had read that some primitive tribes started teaching girls to dance at three so they could get the steps right at their wedding. "I would love to dance with you—"

"Good," the queen cut her off. "I will have Aholo send you the proper flowers. Afa, make yourself useful and hustle down to the long house. Tell them they need another princess crown for tonight. That's a good boy," she said as the young man, nearly Jack's age, sprinted out of sight.

The queen gave Kris a wink and a smile. "We'll show the old doubters that Ray Longknife and his United Sentients is a good harbor for us to put in to, between the two of us, *nahi*?"

So I was being jobbed even before I knew it.

"Your Majesty should rest," a man said, coming out of the shadows where Kris had not noticed him. His stethoscope and manner said *doctor*. Not witch doctor but modern M.D.

"Kapa'a'ola, I'll get nothing but rest soon enough. Can't an old gal have some fun first?"

"Grandmama, Kris and I have work to do if we are to dance for you tonight. You rest. We will work," Aholo said as she stood and backed Kris and company out of the room. The queen was asleep before the door closed.

"How ill is she?" Kris whispered.

"She is not ill. She is old, and she is dying. Anywhere else, maybe she would ask for yet another rejuvenation. Here, she says no more. She has had enough."

"And you're going to let her?" Tom said.

Aholo stopped, turned to them. "Her last rejuvenation did not go well. It was painful, and," she looked at her hands, cupped before her, "not very effective. She chose not to risk the pain only to find it a total failure. As she said, 'All die.' So many died in the war with her. Now she will join them." A tear rolled down her cheek. "I accept her choice."

"But you will miss her," Kris said, putting an arm around the future queen.

"Very much."

"Well, can you show me enough dance steps not to make a fool of myself in front of her?"

"She would greatly enjoy the laugh."

"That is what I'm afraid of." Kris sighed.

An hour later, thanks to Princess Aholo and several of her girlfriends, Kris knew enough steps to avoid the worst diplomatic disasters and maybe the personal ones as well. As she'd feared, every step here, every wave, had a meaning, told a story. With luck, Kris would stay back in the chorus line, providing the la-la-la backup.

Aholo dropped Kris off at a suite of rooms about the time Abby arrived with seven steamer trunks rolling behind her. Kris counted them and raised an eyebrow. "I left one on the *Halsey*," Abby sniffed. Which seemed reasonable, so Kris helped Abby unpack. Jack drew a bag from one, Penny and Tom took similarly sized ones as well and went to set themselves up in their rooms.

"You bring me a couple of sarongs?" Kris asked Abby.

"Nope."

"Mother Hubbard? Grass skirt? I'm not wearing one of those short lavalavas."

"Nope."

"Well, what am I wearing?" Kris asked as there was a knock at her door. She opened it to find Aholo holding a flat box.

"Here are your flowers. They will crown us together at the long house tonight. I will see you there in two hours."

"Flowers?"

"Yes. The flowers you'll wear," Aholo said and left.

Kris elbowed the door closed and opened the box. It held two large flowers and two long leis.

"The flowers go in your hair," Abby said. "I'll have to add some hairpieces to fill out that short Navy cut of yours. No problem. One lei hangs around your neck. The other off your hips. We'll probably have to shorten both."

Kris dropped the box. It bounced on the bed. "You're kidding. Right?"

"You going native or foreigner tonight?"

"Not . . . foreigner," Kris said, full realization dawning.

"That's what a grandmother explained to me as I was bringing things in. The well-dressed local virgin, and that's any not-married girl, wears flowers and her tattoos."

"Did Grampa Ray know about this?"

"I doubt it, but then he didn't say he'd dance tonight with the other princess."

"Flowers, tattoos, this is going to be worse than that getup you got me in for Tom's rescue," Kris said, plopping into a wicker chair that complained at the usage.

"Maybe. Maybe not, baby ducks."

"Where am I going to get tattoos in the next two hours? Tattoos that the Navy won't use to throw me out on my ass when I get back," Kris added. A sedate anchor might pass muster. But tattoos like Aholo had curling around her arms, chest, and back . . . there was no way the Navy would stand for those.

Abby tossed Kris her armored body stocking and pulled a bottle of spray paint and some rolled-up somethings from a trunk. "Primitive was in back on Earth a few years ago, but there's primitive and then there's primitive. So my employer needed different tattoos every night of the week. I got quite a collection of possible body art put together before it went out of style and she got killed.

"So, baby ducks, if you want something like that other nice princess was wearing, you came to the right place," Abby said, unrolling several lengths of stencils.

"So it's flowers and body paint tonight."

"With me having paint-by-numbers fun." Abby grinned.

Kris sighed as she stripped out of her whites and shimmied into the armored body stocking. "When in Rome."

"You'll find it's a lot easier to fit in than you think."

A thought crossed Kris's mind. "What'll Jack wear?"

"Don't know. We'll have to wait and see."

Abby applied paint liberally, covering Kris with twining flowers from her neck to her toes without a patch of skin peeking out. Between curling hairpieces and leis, Kris felt almost fully dressed above her navel. She had no trouble hiding Nelly and her automatic. "You sure you need that?" Abby asked.

Kris squelched that question. "It may look like paradise, but until I spot the snake, I'm going fully prepared."

Abby shrugged and set about arranging the second lei so that it would stay in place. Kris wondered how the other girls kept them secure and put that question off for Aholo.

Kris wasn't sure how Jack did it, but he was just leaving his room when Kris answered the princess's knock at her door. Kris about went cross-eyed trying to take them both in at once.

Aholo's sarong had covered a beautiful pastel tapestry of tattoos that merged flowers and ocean, fish and birds into a breathtaking tableau that was almost as lovely as her. Her long raven hair cascaded down her back in one straight fall. Her flowers danced to a stop as she waited at the door. Kris's question as to how she kept them in place was answered as she adjusted them back into place. Kris swallowed hard.

And looked at Jack. His tattoos were the more traditional black and skin. More skin at wrists and ankles growing darker as they approached the navel. A strategically placed gourd did for him what a similarly placed lei did for Kris. Kris had no idea where he was hiding *his* automatic.

"We must hurry, or we'll be late for the crowning." So Kris and Jack hurried. Penny and Tom joined them. As promised, Penny was in dress whites, and so was Tom. Kris reminded herself that they were the ones out of uniform here. It almost worked.

"Where'd you get the tattoos?" Kris whispered to Jack.

"Paint job," Jack whispered back. "Afa suggested the

place. Said I couldn't accompany you into the Long House unless I did something about all this pale skin."

"I like the gourd."

"Thought you might. I like the flowers."

Their arrival at the Long House cut off Kris's answer. It was made of whole logs elaborately carved in baffling figures and patterns. As Kris followed Aholo forward to where a fire pit burned low, sending sweet-smelling smoke upward through a hole in the palm-fronds roof, Jack was politely, but firmly, edged over to the side of the door with several other young men. The people around the walls of the long house, singing to a softly beaten drum, were equally men and women but uniformly old. Two old women in short grass skirts stepped forward.

Kris had been coached in the questions. Though they came in an almost dead language, she knew how to answer. "Will you dance up the full moon?" "Will you light the way for the sailor to find his way home to his island?" "Will you call the fish up from the depths?" At each pause, Kris answered *"Hā"* with Aholo. At the third *yes*, the women placed a flowered crown of orchids on each of their heads, kissed them, gave them a pat, and said, "Now, go dance and have fun," in English.

"Yes, Auntie Kalama," Aholo said with an answering hug of her own, then she grabbed Kris's elbow and, business over, skipped from the Long House.

Kris skipped along, blinking at what she thought she saw up in the rafters of the house. "Are those heads?"

"Yes, shrunken heads of the queens and their consorts. Great-grandmother's head will be there someday. And mine. They watch over the affairs of the People."

"Tradition," Jack said, falling in step with Kris. And Kris decided maybe the Longknifes weren't the only strange ones in human space.

But there wasn't a lot of time to think, because Aholo led them into a wide circle of thousands of people, maybe everyone on the island. There were several fires casting light, and the smells of dinner cooking. The sun was setting behind them, painting the tropical sky crimson, silver, and gold. Before them lay the rumbling lagoon and the growing dark of the ocean.

The drums began to pound a rapid beat. The steps were fast, not all that different from ones Kris has learned for a middle school sock hop, leaving her to wonder who had stolen from whom. The arm and hand motions were much more complicated, and Kris let Aholo take a few extra steps toward the ink-jet sea and then did her best to stay only a quarter heartbeat behind her.

It must have worked. No one interrupted the dance to name her imposter . . . and a huge full moon began to inch its way out of the ocean, setting the waves to shimmering with its light.

With the intense look on Aholo's face as her guide, Kris danced as if the moon did look to her for instructions. She danced as if the fish and navigators this month would depend upon her for the light to find their way home. A gal who'd navigated jump points found herself so taken by the drumming and the night that when the music pounded to a halt, and she and Aholo turned to present the moon to the people, Kris felt rather proud of what she'd danced birth to.

"Wasn't that fun?" Aholo said, out of breath, but her hands held out wide at her side, as if presenting the moon . . . and viewed from a certain perspective, she was.

Kris, her hands in mirror reflection, got a *"Hā"* past out-of-breath lungs. "I hope we don't have to lead the next one."

"Oh no. The little ones are next," and with that, a small tidal wave of people under four feet tall flooded the sand around them and began their own offering to a slower drum. They sang in high-pitched voices something that might have been a thank-you for the moon coming out. But then, they were often unsure of the words and the key, but never unsure of their enthusiasm. Anyway, they did dimples very well and gave Kris a chance to catch her breath, locate a drink that wasn't fermented, and follow Aholo around a circle of proud parents who were nevertheless happy to congratulate Kris on her own dance.

"It's good luck to have two princesses Dance up the Moon. It's been too long we've had just one Dancer on the island," one grandmother type muttered as they passed.

Aholo winced, and Kris made a mental note to look into some family trees, but not in a fashion that hurt her hostess.

The children finished their dance and galloped to be first in line for food. Now dancers Kris's age took their place. The women in one line, the men facing them in another, and Kris saw what twenty years of practice could do.

It also clarified any questions Kris had about the dress code. There wasn't one. The large size of Jack's gourd and amount of her flowers made them overdressed. Several of the women and men had tattoos over all of their bodies . . . well, almost all . . . and nothing to interrupt the view. One particularly wild dancer had crossed clubs on his chest dripping blood. "Even his face is covered with tattoos," Kris said.

"Yes." Aholo nodded. "Those are warrior tats."

"Do you have warriors?" They had shrunken heads in their Long House. What other traditions had they dredged up?

"Kailahi's the center on our football team. Tries to scare the other team something horrible with a before-game show."

"Does it work?" Jack asked.

"They're in last place. Couple of the fans are threatening to redo his tats with hearts and flowers."

"That . . . could be painful."

"Well, the tats are biodegradable," Aholo said. "Mine are starting to fade. When I choose a consort, have a kid, take on the queenship from Grandmama, I'll need a whole new face to the world. I can't be pretty flowers and fish all my life."

Kris nodded; not a bad way to tell the world where you were coming from when you hit the ground running.

As the dance went on, Aholo circulated. Kris found herself being asked many of the same questions she encountered on other planets. "Does King Ray intend to tax us to support his sending folks out exploring for more islands in the stars?" "Won't we be better off just fishing in our own lagoon rather than getting all involved in your big ocean?" The questions were phrased different on Hikila, but the fears were the same.

Kris tried to reformat her usual answers into something comfortable for the locals. "Those who hunger to see new islands will have to build their own canoes, and those who will profit from new lands should be the ones to pay for their paddles," got a wide smile both from Aholo and the small group Kris first tried it on. A simple "No single planet beat the Iteeche," spoken to a group including some old enough to remember those wars seemed the perfect answer to those who wanted to hide on their own little islands. Then again, people who built wooden canoes and fished for a living weren't going to fund all that many starships.

But the electric cart, the hardened sand? There was technology underpinning this paradise. Something didn't add up.

At the edge of the beach, in a small clump, stood several dozen men and women dressed formally for a cocktail party.

Kris very suddenly felt very naked.

"You trade your uniform for this, and I might come around more often," came in an all-too-familiar voice. Kris searched among the well-dressed for the source and found the all-too-well-sculptured features of Henry Smythe-Peterwald XIII . . . or Hank to her. With an effort, she suppressed the urge to cross her arms over her breasts and cup a hand at her crotch. Aholo kept her hands at her sides; Kris did, too. These folks were the foreigners; Kris wore a crown given her by the locals.

"What brings you here, Hank?" she said as those around him opened up and he stepped forward.

"We're opening up several new sales and distribution centers on the mainland. I think the Islanders call it the Big Island. Our local woman thought I ought to see how the other ten percent lives, the ones that soak up all the taxes, so I flew out here for the party. Didn't expect to see you here. Certainly not so much of you," he said, doing a slow scan from her toes to her upper set of flowers.

"Some of us adjust to the local culture," Kris said, fluffing her hair.

"Some of us adjust to the dominant culture," Hank shot back.

"The Islands are the navel of Hikila," Aholo snapped.

"Four in five live on the mainland. Four in five pay taxes to support your fantasy island existence. Don't you think it's time you change that? What's the matter, Longknife? I thought you'd be all up in arms about taxation without representation, or doesn't that apply when your old war buddies get the taxes?"

"I'm sorry, Your Highness." A tall, thin woman with silver hair and a wraparound dress stepped forward. "I'm afraid my associate has had a bit too much of your island drink and a tad too much talk with some of our mainland hotheads. I apologize for his behavior," she said and pulled Hank back into the crowd of mainland partygoers. Several men and women promptly took him in hand and headed him for a table of hors d'oeuvres and wines.

Aholo turned away. "You know the young man?"

"Hank Peterwald. I once thought he might make a nice boyfriend. I asked him one too many questions the last time I saved his life. Bad form on my part."

"I've never saved anyone's life. I will try to remember not to ask them any questions if I do."

"Are there problems with the Big Islanders?" Penny and Nelly had briefed Kris on the general situation here. They'd passed over the population imbalance without comment. Taxation had not come up. What had they missed?

Aholo headed for one of the roasted pigs and dinner. "It should have been resolved years ago, but it didn't seem to be a problem. The People came to Hikila almost two hundred years ago, trying to rebuild a way of life that had vanished almost that many years ago on Earth when the Pacific Islands sank. We didn't have any use for the Big Island, so when refugees from blasted planets in the Iteeche Wars needed a place for a while, we gladly loaned them that land. Same for when your Grampa Ray pushed through the Treaty of Wardhaven and pulled back some of the more scattered colonies to slow humanity's spread."

Several of those last planets had been started with Peterwald money. Losing those colonies had cost them and created more bad blood between the Longknifes and Peterwalds. Kris wondered how many of the refugees on the Big Island still thought of themselves as Peterwald men. Oops.

They each drew a wooden platter and pronged fork from stacks. A round, black-toothed cook in roast pig tattoos sliced them off a big slab of pork. Others piled Kris's plate with roasted banana, several kinds of baked taro, and other items that defied recognition. Aholo led Kris to a quiet palm tree that the wind had blown almost level to the sand before it recovered and grew up. Jack and Afa followed.

"We have lost one home. We will not have that happen again, so when we took in the refugees, all we asked was that they agree that to gain a right to vote, they'd have to take up the Island ways," Aholo said, taking a bite. "Some did. Came here. Married. Look around our fire tonight, and you'll see people as blond as you. Redheads, too. If you want a vote, just stop being a foreigner."

"Most didn't," Afa put in. "Some went back to the stars or other colonies. Most just settled on the Big Island and raised their kids in their own ways and watched their grandkids and great grandkids grow up the way they wanted them to."

"With no vote," Kris said after she swallowed a delicious bit of pork.

"How many people bother to vote on your planet?" Afa asked.

"About half." Jack nodded as he chewed.

"But taxes?" Kris asked, trying some of the banana.

"It's a standard income tax package, passed about the time of the Iteeche Wars. Probably the same as the one on your planet," Aholo said.

"That depends on income," Kris said slowly.

"I fish to feed my family," Afa said. "We will not have net-dragging trawlers rape our ocean to feed canneries. Our Marine Fisheries Conservation Plan lets them do what they want within their one hundred and fifty–kilometer coastal zone but not in *my* deep ocean."

The words sounded well-worn, frequently spoken. "So the Big Island's cash economy pays taxes, and the Islands' subsistence economy can't really be taxed," Kris said.

"We bled plenty during the wars," Aholo said. "No one questioned our sacrifice. After the wars, there wasn't all that much left over to tax. I guess it was about forty years ago that the Big Islanders noticed they were paying most of our off-planet contributions to the Society."

"What about extra ships to patrol the Rim?" Kris asked.

"We don't have any colonies, at least not any the Council of Elders officially name. I guess some of the banks on the Big Island may have bought into some. I think they may have donated a ship to Wardhaven or Pitts Hope's Navy once in a while, but that was local subscription, not something that came before the Council of Elders out here."

"Local subscription?" Jack said before filling his mouth.

"It's not like we're stupid. We may run around in tats, but that doesn't make us dumb," Afa snapped. "Each of the towns on the Big Island has its own elected mayor and city council. Once in a while they have a council of councils, if they want to talk about something that's really big to them. And they do send petitioners to stand before our own Council of Elders and state their case on global issues. Grandmama listens to all sides and then hands down a boon that usually makes everyone happy."

"Or has. Or usually does," Aholo said.

They ate in silence for a while. The moon was well up. The dancing continued. Different drummers. Different cadences. Different steps.

"You need to change, don't you?" Kris said.

"Mama knew that. Great-grandmama, too. I think if Mama had lived, Grandmama and she would have worked this out years ago. But then Mama's and Papa's canoe was swamped ten years ago, and the stroke took Great-grandmama. We've kind of been treading water, waiting until I could get older. I don't think Grandmama can float much longer. The old woman was right. We do need two Dancers to Dance up the Moon."

"Can't your grandmother help?"

"Grandmama never got along with Great-grandmama. Her second husband was from the Big Island, and she moved there and let her skin go pale. Her third husband was a trader among the stars, and she left Hikila, and we don't know where she is and don't care. No." The young girl squared her shoulders. "This is the challenge that I will have to decide when I come to sit on the judgment stone, if Grandmama does not find a way to decide it before she goes to join all the other queens and consorts."

So, Grampa, there are a few things you didn't mention when you asked me to make this little trip, Kris thought. Why wasn't she surprised? Aholo and Afa left for a dance that seemed to involve about half of the islanders, but she didn't ask Kris to join her, and once it got going . . . with everyone seeming to do something different as they went along . . . Kris was glad to just watch.

"So, now that you've met the snake," Jack said, "You willing to let me have your gun?"

"Abby talks too much." Kris gave Jack a sly, sideways look. "Where's your gun?"

"That's no question for a young lady to ask. And you know I don't like my primary to go armed."

"I thought you were on terminal leave."

"Terminal for me. Not you."

"Kris, do you know that this whole area is covered by a security system?" Nelly asked.

"No." Beside Kris, Jack was eyeing her leis seriously.

"Very high-tech. There's a secured vault under the Long House. I calculate the odds are 95 percent that the video camera there is showing a loop of the last hour. The security service has not taken note of it yet."

Kris looked down at her lovely yellow, pink, and turquoise paint scheme. "Not exactly the camouflage for going covert."

"Good." Jack stood. "I'll handle this."

"I can darken your colors, Kris," Nelly said, and suddenly Kris was as dark as the night.

"How'd you do that?" Kris and Jack both said as Kris's paint went back to flowers.

"The paint is in contact with my lead-ins and controllable. If we hadn't been so rushed, I had meant to tell Abby I could touch up some of her over-paints, but there was little time, and I was not sure she'd appreciate the offer."

"She is learning tact," Jack said as the two of them headed back to the Long House, keeping available bushes between them and the dancers. Kris was busy checking their path and didn't notice when Jack's automatic appeared in his hand.

"Where was it?"

"I'm not telling. Where's yours?"

Kris pulled it out from the hair at the back of her neck.

"Figured it. You're going to have to ditch the flowers."

"At the Long House. Nelly, make me black again." In a moment, Kris was in black . . . except her face.

"Here, put this on," Jack said, producing a small vial.

Kris smeared her face black. She'd worry about later, later. I CAN CHANGE THAT, and in a moment, Kris's face was flowers, then black again.

"Thanks Nelly. Now, is there a way down?" Jack said.

"One on this side, one on the other. Go past this azalea bush." Jack did. There were steps leading down to a concrete basement wall with a thick steel door. Clearly, not all of the Big Island tax money had gone off world, something Aholo had skipped over.

"Can you open the door?" Kris asked.

"Don't need to," Jack said. "It's already jimmied. Now, you stay back, damnit."

"Yeah, right." Kris muttered, and slipped out of her flowers, leaving them beside the steps.

The door opened on well-oiled hinges; the room beyond was dimly lit. Row upon row of tables were covered with what Kris could only describe as the makings for the weirdest rummage sale she'd ever seen at any political fundraiser. Wooden masks, statues with very prominent sexual features . . . male and female, stone and wicker doodads were heaped on the tables and lay beside them. And this was under lock and security camera!

To each their own idea of junk.

Jack, with her behind him, moved silently to crouch beside one table and a statue with a particularly long, ah, tongue.

SOMEONE IS WORKING AT THE RIGHT END OF THE BUILDING, TWO ROWS OVER, Nelly informed Kris. Kris touched Jack's shoulder and waved him in that direction. *So there. You do need me and Nelly.*

Several quiet steps later, they crouched in the aisle between tables and studied one intent person in black, rigging plastic explosives to a moss-covered, volcanic rock about the size of a footstool.

Jack crossed the aisle, checked the other side of the room, then took aim and said, "Put your hands up and step away from the rock." Kris drew a bead, too.

The dark figure froze, but otherwise took its time obeying Jack's orders. As it stood, Kris had the impression it might be a woman, but in the dim light, black on gray was hard to make out. Hands up, it opened its mouth . . .

And the room went pitch-black.

Jack fired. Kris fired. In the small flash from their guns, all they saw was vacant air where they were aiming.

NELLY?

IT IS RUNNING. TO THE LEFT.

CAN YOU TURN ON THE LIGHTS?

JUST A MOMENT.

The lights came on as a door opened and slammed to the left of them. "I did say there were two doors," Nelly said.

"And whoever that was just used the second one," Jack's voice held acid as he eyed the rock and the wires connecting the blocks of plastic. Carefully, he stepped closer to it.

"Nelly, are you familiar with this kind of a bomb setup?" Kris said to explain her continued presence.

Jack reached the rock and immediately pulled one dangling bare wire. "That was very likely the antenna," Nelly said.

"Thank you," Jack answered dryly.

"Put your hands up," came with belated authority from the right-hand side of the room, the door they'd entered by.

"Could we at least disarm the bomb?" Kris said, putting her automatic down carefully beside Jack's.

"Bomb?" said one plaintive voice.

"No, you might set it off," ordered the more authoritative one.

"Standing right beside it," Kris said, raising her hands.

"Maybe we ought to let them, you know, disarm it, Kalikau."

"No, they could be on a suicide mission, Malu."

"Nelly," Jack said, "I don't think the arming circuit is complete. What's your call?"

"That was the antenna, and the circuit was not completed. It is not a danger. Yet," the computer agreed.

"Who's talking?" the authority demanded.

"My computer. Now, will you take us to Princess Aholo so we can get this straightened out? But you better leave someone guarding that rock, or whoever was trying to make a bomb might come back and finish it. And why blow up a little rock, anyway?"

"You don't know?" The timid one said.

"Follow me. Malu, you stay and guard the Coronation Stone."

"Coronation Stone?" Kris said.

"Why me?" Malu said.

"You might want to rip off that biggest block of explosives," Nelly said. "That would really break the circuit. We should take that with us," she finished helpfully.

"Don't," said the officious one, but Malu already had. He handed it to Jack.

"And if you'd been wrong?" Jack said to Kris's chest.

"The odds on that were minimal. Much lower than those of whoever that was returning."

Kris paused as they reached the stairs. "Can I put my flowers back on? You know, the crown your elders gave me and the leis from Princess Aholo.

"Flowers?" came from Kalikau somewhat less officiously.

"Be careful," Jack said as Kris started shimmying into leis. "She's wanted for destroying private property on Turantic, misuse of government property on Wardhaven. She could be adding destruction of national treasures on Hikila to her long criminal dossier."

"Only three planets," Kris muttered, adjusting her lower leis. "Five hundred and ninety-seven still think I'm innocent."

"But she's still young," Jack pointed out.

Kris jammed on the crown, threw on the top lei, and quick-marched for the dance while the guard followed with a much less sure of himself look on his tattooed face.

Kris spotted Aholo back at their tree, catching her breath. Afa was bringing up four drinks as Kris, Jack, and the guard marched up. Both locals gave Kris the evil eye until she remembered she was still in ninja rig. NELLY, NEW CAMOUFLAGE SCHEME.

Both grandkids of Queen Ha'iku'lani did a double take. Kris glanced down to discover that Nelly had put Kris in some kind of paint job that might fit a really threatening warrior type.

NELLY, BACK INTO ABBY'S PAINT SCHEME. COMPLETE WITH OVER PAINTS.

YES MA'AM.

Kris turned once again into a flower-bedecked cuddly virgin.

"How did you do that?" Afa asked.

"Maybe I'll show you tomorrow," Kris said. "Somebody

just wrapped your Coronation Stone in explosives. If it had gone off, there wouldn't be much left of the stone or the Long House. This flatfoot interrupted us interrupting whoever, and defusing the bomb. What say we finish the disarming job?"

"Yes," took all of two seconds. Jack led off at a trot, with the two locals behind him and the security man running along explaining why he did what he did and failed to catch who got away. Aholo ignored him. Afa nodded and made listening sounds, giving Kris the impression the police reported to him.

Back at the Long House, Malu was marching around the rock, trying to look every which way at once and keep as far from the rock as he could without getting far from it. All impossible, but the tall beanpole of a man was definitely trying.

A moment passed quickly as they examined the lock, the camera, and the bomb. The defenses were medium-level tech, but then the bomb was rather low level compared to galactic standards. "Homegrown," Jack concluded.

Kris looked around at the treasure room, glanced up at the Long House above. "What would be the impact of losing all this just before your grandmama's death? Your coronation?"

"It would shake our way of life to its roots. That was the stone our very first queen was sitting on when we elected her. Every queen has been crowned on it. And to lose the heads of all my ancestors . . ." The young woman shook her head. "Afa, you'll have to tell the men. We'll need better protection."

"That won't come as a surprise to any of them."

"Yes, but Grandmama didn't want to spend the money. Now, I guess she'll have to. Spend it, or solve the basic problem so no one wants to destroy our way of life."

"That's a tough order," Kris said.

"But one we'll have to look full in the eyes with tomorrow's sunrise."

Jack finished disarming the bomb and turned the explosives over to the guards for disposal. Kris returned to the dance with Aholo and Afa, but to circulate and talk. Or rather, to watch them talk. She kept quiet. She might be wearing their flowers, but this was a problem they, not she, would have to solve.

Santiago, this is one Longknife that remembers she didn't come here to start a war. Or even fight one if one gets started.

5

Kris found herself standing in court the next morning, enjoying being a material witness rather than the accused. Seven judges presided, all addressed either as Your Honor or Grandmother/Grandfather as the gender required. Lavalavas, sarongs, and flowered Mother Hubbards covered their honors as well as everyone else.

Kris cleared undress whites with Aholo beforehand. "Long pants, no shorts." She also ran her testimony by the princess, which turned out to be a good idea. Abby was added to the witness list to establish that computer-controlled paint, which changed designs and colors several times a second, had been the rage on Earth five years back.

"It hasn't reached here?" Abby seemed quite surprised.

"No, it hasn't," the senior judge, a grandmother, informed her. That answered some questions about the bomber. He or she had probably used body paint and quickly resumed a different front to the world, explaining why no one in an all-black tattoo scheme or outfit had been caught.

Kris's "Don't you have nanos to sniff for paint?" drew a frown from Afa.

"If someone is accommodating enough to present a friendly face to our ways, wouldn't you consider it bad form to sniff around them for paint fumes? We gave you and your man the value of the doubt. Besides, nanos don't survive very well in our salt air and trade winds. We stay low-tech on the islands."

Kris had seen that; question was, how low-tech were they on the Big Island?

The court didn't accomplish much. It cleared her and Jack of any wrongdoing . . . maybe she wasn't as material a witness as she thought . . . and advised the men of Nui Nui to improve their security. Court adjourned.

"Now what?" Kris asked as everyone left.

"Now I meet with Grandmama and several of the chief elders. It is time we do something," Aholo said, biting her lower lip.

"And I go fishing. Good thing it's Wednesday, or they'd be stuck with just last night's leftovers. Want to come?" Afa said.

"Aren't you in on the Council?"

"I'm about a hundred years too young." Afa laughed. "Rather go fishing. And you're about a zillion light-years too off island to sit in. So, want to go fishing? Everyone has to eat, and if they talk to Grandmama forever, I'll have to feed them all. Besides, we'll probably hear the best parts over supper. And if I'm half as smart as Papa was, I'll straighten Sis here out if she gets anything wrong."

Little sister slugged big brother . . . but not too hard.

Kris eyed Aholo. "I guess I go fishing."

"That would be best. We may need your Grandpapa's help before we're done, but we have to do this the Island Way first."

"Let me go get my swimsuit," Kris said.

"You don't have to use one," Afa called after her.

Kris kept on walking.

* * *

Thirty minutes later, dressed in a fresh armored body-suit and a one-piece swimsuit with strategically placed ce-ramic plates and even a bit of flotation added, a hat that gave Nelly a good antenna, and protection against the sun and 4 mm assault slugs, Kris was ready to negotiate her freedom from Jack for the day. He frowned at a weather report.

"It looks fine," she said. "No trouble."

"Yeah, but what did the satellite pic show the day Aholo's mom and dad disappeared?"

Kris had wondered about that. She shrugged.

"I'll be in security today," Jack said, "offering any sug-gestions they'll take. They have a chopper. Nelly, keep in contact. I lose your signal, and I'll be out looking for you."

"We girls understand," Kris said, answering for Nelly. She found Afa along the beach where the outriggers were pulled up. His boat was long, clean-lined, and painted fire engine red.

"Can you paddle?" he asked without looking up from where he was arranging nets and fishing lines.

"I've sailed and rowed boats. I've paddled canoes. If my style doesn't pass your muster, I'm sure you'll enjoy show-ing me how to do it right. I'm a fast learner," Kris said.

"Ever fished?"

"Not with anything like the gear you've got in there."

"This should be an interesting day. Grab a handhold; let's get the rig in the water." Kris grabbed where he pointed and succeeded in getting the boat in the water and herself in the boat with no negative comments from Afa or the several dozen guys looking on, and who had their out-riggers in the water as soon as Afa and Kris did and were paddling for the reef right along with them. Which gave Kris several examples of how to paddle. And several shouted suggestions of who had the best form.

"Do you usually have this kind of crowd?"

"No, I suspect it's the company I'm keeping."

By the time they got to the reef, most of the company had departed for their own fishing grounds or gone back to the beach. Afa showed Kris how to throw a net and collect the fish it caught. "Watch out for the ones with nettles." Kris did.

The fish around the reef were small to medium. Kris was ready to toss away the small ones. "Don't. We'll use them for bait. Ever tasted smaki smaki?"

"No. What are they?"

"They're big, about the size of an Earth tuna, and tasty. Thought I'd bring one of them home for the elders."

"Or maybe to impress the star girl?" Kris muttered.

"Maybe. They school out beyond the reef in the deep. Game for some real fishing?" he said, picking up a hooked line.

NELLY, HOW STRONG'S YOUR SIGNAL?

I AM PATCHED INTO THE SATELLITE NET. I SHOULD BE GOOD.

Kris smiled. "I'm good if you are."

Two more throws, and Afa pronounced them with enough bait and enough yellowtail. As they paddled for the passage through the reef, he called to another canoe and passed them a net with their edible catch. "You're not going after smaki smaki, are you?" the guy in the other canoe asked.

"Why not?" Kris asked.

"You're like to catch a shark as a smaki."

"Shark?"

"We won't drop our hooks until I find a school of smaki," Afa grumbled. "I know better than that."

The other fellow handed Kris a knife as he took her net of fish. "Cut your line loose if it looks like you hooked something other than smaki."

"Thanks." Kris checked the bottom of the boat. Afa had a knife, but it was at his end, not hers. "Thank you very much."

"You'll probably be fine," the other guy assured her. "Afa's almost as good a fisherman as he thinks he is."

Kris eyed the passage. Waves three to four meters tall were cresting as the tide went out. It was going to be a rough row even without breaking surf in the passage. Afa rigged a small sail to take advantage of the wind at their backs and they paddled quickly through the passage to the calmer water outside.

Kris couldn't count the hours she'd spent on the sailboat on the lake as a kid. But none of those hours counted against what she faced now. This open ocean heaved, raising her a good three meters up where she could see Nui Nui and another island off ahead of them, then plunged to where all she could see was blue water all around her . . . oh, and a patch of blue sky above.

She'd never been seasick in her life. Never spacesick. But she found herself entering into negotiations with her tummy about there being a first time for everything.

"I will not be seasick," Kris ordered.

You talking to me?

No.

Well if you were, I'd tell you that Abby stashed a small collection of seasick patches in your belly pouch. Kris checked, found four, and applied one under her swimsuit. A moment later she felt better.

"You okay?" Afa asked, a bit later.

"Just fine. Where's that school of fish?" she countered.

"And why ain't I using some high-tech gadget to find them? I would if I was working for the Marine Census, but today, I'm fishing, and it doesn't seem fair to use all those gadgets. All they're doing is trying to make a living, just like me."

"That's one way of looking at it," Kris said.

"But not the way they taught you in school."

"I didn't say that."

"I doubt your university was any different than mine."

"University," Kris echoed.

"Ikamalohi University has the best marine conservation program in human space. I had classmates from Wardhaven."

"That doesn't surprise me. We're only just starting to take our oceans seriously."

"Big mistake. You let the trawlers mess them up, and you'll be a long time getting your seas back right. There's a reason why I hand-built my own dugout outrigger canoe for fishing."

Kris looked it over. She could see the chisel marks, but not a lot of them. The walls were tall and even, the bottom smooth. The bamboo outrig was lashed down tight with some sort of rattan lacing. The whole rig was doing a good job of give and take as it bobbed around in the open sea.

"It looks shipshape," she answered.

"Making a dugout was easy. Now our culture. That was hard. All we had to go on was some novels or sociology books written by pale skins who talked to our people, and we knew some of what they wrote had to be tall tales they'd been fed. Still, that was what we were about, and maybe some of those tall tales were worth giving a try. We sure had lived the life of you pale skins long enough, so we came here, and we've lived our way, and no one is going to take that away from me." He was scowling at her by the time he finished his speech.

Kris showed her open hands. "I'm not trying to take anything away from you. My great-grampa thinks it would be good if Hikila joined his United Sentients, but that's your call."

Afa chuckled as he adjusted the steering paddle. "Sorry. Things like last night really get to me."

"I was the one who stopped it, remember?"

"Yes, and I thank you. I know my sister and grandmama are grateful for what you did. We owe you, and it seems the fish also admit their debt to you. See, they come." He pointed.

Two hundred yards out it looked like the ocean was being rained on. But the sky was blue. As Afa changed the set of his sail and aimed for there, Kris studied it. Yep, there, a small fish broke surface. Then another. "What is it?"

"Those are the tiny fish the smaki smaki feed on.

Where they are, there's smaki. Start baiting the hooks."
Kris had fished before and knew it involved putting small
living things on hooks so you could catch bigger living
things, but someone else usually baited the hooks. Kris
held her breath, captured a small fish from the bait net
alongside, and jammed a hook through its wiggling belly.
It quit wiggling.

"That's not the way to do it," Afa said, smiling.

So Kris took the steering paddle to let Afa do the honors. As he settled her at the helm, his hand stroked her arm.
"You're wearing that strange thing you wore last night."

"A different one. Super Spider Silk body stocking. Can
stop a four-millimeter dart and most other things assassins
may throw my way."

Afa glanced at the sun overhead. "You're going to
burn."

"Also is good for SPF thirty sunblock. I'm protected."

As he moved forward to bait the hooks, he muttered
something about being very well protected. Kris let it pass.

They reached the roiled water about the time Afa had
the first line ready to go over the side. He tossed it, played
out some line, then held down the stick with the line on it
with his foot while he brought down the sail. Then, trans-
ferring the stick to his teeth, he baited a line for Kris. She
took it and tossed it over the side, let it play out about
thirty, forty meters, then glanced at Afa. "So now we
wait?"

"The fish are moving a bit to windward," he answered.
"Let's paddle up that way." He put the line between his
teeth and paddled. Kris could only imagine what Mother
would say if she saw her doing that, but Kris did the same.
There, they settled back to drifting again.

After a while, Kris got the feeling her line was awful
slack and started pulling it in. "Don't do that," Afa said.

Kris weighed her options and chose to ignore the guy.
Good thing; only a head dangled from her hook. "Any
chance your fish have gone to college, too?"

Afa snorted at her joke and rebaited her hook.

A couple of minutes later, he hauled his in and reloaded its bait. "They are showing off for a star walker. Never did this for me," he assured her.

As time passed, Kris began to wonder how long this could go on. No wonder the others skipped this kind of fishing. Again they rebaited their hooks and moved the canoe upwind. Kris tried staring into the blue sea. She easily spotted the tiny silvery forms that darted here and there, disturbing the surface of the water. There were other larger shadows moving among them, deeper down. Big and thin and round. Would the darts from her automatic reach them? Then something long and dark and missile-shaped shot by, and one of the other things came apart.

"Did you see that?"

"It's not good luck to stare into the sea. You might see one of the mer people and have your heart stolen away and go to live under the sea. Or maybe its an old tale to make it easier when people drown." Kris saw pain there and remembered how Afa's parents had died.

"I think I saw something long and ugly eat one of your smaki. What's a shark thing look like?"

"Long and ugly about fits it," Afa said, and yelped as his line went taut. "I've got one."

He held his line for a moment, then let it unwind fast. Still, the canoe took off as if both Kris and Afa were paddling with the tide. Kris knelt at the steering paddle, waiting for instructions, as Afa held onto his stick with both hands and let it play out as fast as it could unwind.

"Ah, how many times have you done this?" Kris asked, thinking it was a bit late to raise that issue.

"Many times," he answered.

"Many times as in too many to count, or many as in too many to count for this dumb girl on the fingers that I'm busy using."

"Many times," he said through gritted teeth. He was reeling out the fishing line more slowly now, fighting it more.

Kris had read about this Nantucket sleigh ride. No, that

was when you caught a whale. Bigger fish. She eyed the
bow. It was down, digging into the sea, but not shipping
much water even when they dipped after cresting a wave.
She wished he'd suggest something. Absent any comments
from him, she edged the canoe off a few degrees to the
right of the course the fish was pulling them in, letting it
drag the canoe a bit.

Wrong answer! The outrigger rose a good quarter meter
out of the water. Afa leaned back, and the rig went down
hard.

"The line needs to be on the other side of the bow. The
helmsmen always keeps the fishing line between the bow
and the outrigger," Afa said.

"Now you tell me," Kris snapped.

"Sorry, I didn't think."

"You've caught some fish. You've never led the fishing."

"Not before today."

"Now you tell me." NELLY, IF WE GO INTO THE WATER,
CALL JACK FAST AND GET A CHOPPER HEADED OUT HERE.

AND IF I COME LOOSE AND SINK?

HOLD ON TIGHT.

YOU KNOW I CANNOT DO THAT.

I'LL HOLD ONTO YOU, AND IF YOU DO COME LOOSE,
POWER DOWN, AND WE'LL SEARCH FOR YOU.

YOU BETTER SEARCH FOR ME, OR . . . OR I WILL NEVER
TALK TO YOU AGAIN. Nelly actually put feeling into that
old threat.

Something long and dark and ugly shot through the water beside Kris. "We got trouble, I think," she just got out
when she had to make a grab for Afa. The line had gone
slack so suddenly it almost shot him out of the boat. She
grabbed him by his lavalava. Not a good handhold.

He came out of it, still headed over the side.

She made a second grab for around his waist and landed
on top of him. Now, having a naked island boy all to herself might or might not have been one of Kris's teenage
fantasies. But having the outrigger rising over her head,
tipping them both toward a dip in the ocean, an ocean

presently occupied by a toothsome monster ripping what
was supposed to have been their supper to shreds, definitely did not qualify as fantasy.

Kris was grateful for Afa's arm pushing her off in the
right direction, which helped them rebalance the canoe. As
the outrigger splashed back into the sea, they both began to
laugh. In the process of separating, Afa ran his hand down
Kris's side, sending shivers through her. Getting back into
his lavalava, he didn't afford Kris too many chances to
steal peeks.

He did look nice.

But the momentum of the fishing run had carried the
canoe up to a patch of water where bits of fin and flesh
were surfacing. That was a solid reminder of how deadly
their situation could be. As they sat catching their breath,
they rode the waves up and down. From the tops they
could make out Nui Nui in the distance. It looked like a
long paddle.

"Papa always said, sometimes you win. Sometimes the
fish win," Afa said, looking at the water, not at Kris. "Today the big fish won. I guess I better set sail. The wind is
changing, and the tide as well. Don't worry. We'll make
dinner."

And they did, though it took a lot of paddling, and there
wasn't time to change. It didn't matter; a swimsuit was just
as proper as anything else. The elders enjoyed the story of
the shark robbing them of their smaki smaki just as much,
if not more, than the fish itself. So Kris got several tales of
how you *really* fished for smaki. By the fifth variation, none
of which agreed much beyond using a hook and line, Kris
winked at Afa. Clearly, everyone did it their own way . . .
and sometimes you won and sometimes the fish won.

When stomachs were full, Kris asked how their day had
gone. Aholo looked at where her grandmama lay on cush-
ions and spoke for her. "It is time for me to go to the Big Island. I and most of Grandmama's counselors. Vea Ikale
called the city councils to see when they can meet with us.
The elders think that if we start with the most willing, and

then those less happy with the prospect, we can slowly build a wave that no one can resist."

"Any answers?" Kris asked.

"No surprise, Port Stanley agreed immediately," Vea Ikale, a tall, round chief with sailing tats said. "Others are still thinking about it. Port Brisbane says they have to call a council meeting before they'll answer our call."

"No surprise there," said a grandmother.

"So we need to get things moving quickly," Kris said.

Heads nodded. "Nelly, raise Commander Santiago on the *Halsey,* give her my compliments, and ask her to call me."

"Yes, ma'am," was followed by a brief pause. "Commander Santiago sends her compliments and is available to talk now."

"Captain, this is Princess Kristine."

"It's good evening there, if I'm not mistaken."

"Yes. I was wondering if I might impose on you for the loan of your gig," Kris glanced around at the entire collection of elders. "Or maybe your longboat and gig."

"You starting a war?" came dryly.

"Actually, I'm starting a peace. Specifically, I want to quickly transport a negotiating team to get talks going to settle a long-running problem."

"Doesn't sound at all like a Longknife gig."

The queen snorted. Several elders grinned; Aholo looked puzzled. Kris sighed. "We're trying to turn over a new leaf. Seems like a good idea just now. I promise to return the gig and longboat to you in good order and with no new dents."

"That'll be a first. When do you need them?"

Kris ignored the comment and passed the question to the queen with her eyes. Queen Ha'iku'lani passed it, too. Several elders found themselves tossing the hot potato back and forth and settled, to their surprise, on, "Tomorrow?"

"Could you have the gig and longboat on the beach at 7:30 a.m. to load out?" Kris said, pushing things to the limit. "That should put us on the dock at Port Stanley by 9:30 at the latest, with a whole day to devote to greeting, meeting, and talking."

"You want Marines?" Commander Santiago asked.

"This is a local issue. We're not involved. Not even sure I'll be going, since I don't have an invite at the moment," Kris said and signed off.

"I was kind of hoping you'd go fishing with me some more," Afa said, his eyes more bedroom than fishing.

"It was fun." Kris swallowed hard.

"I hope you will come with us to the Big Island," Aholo said.

"I was only waiting for an invitation," Kris said, then gave Afa a raised eyebrow. "Why don't you come to the Big Island?"

His face fell as he shook his head. "I fish. Aholo speaks for us." The elders made noises about packing for travel and took their leave; Aholo did the same. Kris realized she needed to pack up, maybe not the entire seven steamer trunks, but a big chunk of them, and bowed out as four strong men brought in a sedan chair to take the queen back to her room.

Kris joined Abby going through her collection of clothes and wondering which she should leave behind and which she should keep with her. A couple of uniforms did not seem like they would do; Kris suspected she'd need to come the attentive princess more often than the gallant trooper. So, sundress or power suit, ball gown or flowing lama sarong?

A soft knock got her attention a half hour into this exercise in frustration. "Come in," brought a puzzled looking Aholo into the room.

"Oh, you have so many different kinds of clothes," the princess said, eyes wide in wonder.

"Yes." Kris sighed. "You just need to pack a dozen different colored sarongs, and you're done. I suspect I'll end up loading four or five steamer trunks onto the gig and still regret something I leave behind."

"But should I walk among those on the Big Island so clearly not of their ways?" she frowned. "Should I show more respect for their ways if I want them to respect our ways?"

Kris moved several dresses aside to find space for herself on the bed and sat down. "Good questions. What's your answer?"

"It does not matter. I have nothing else to wear."

Kris eyed the other princess. She was, of course, more busty. And shorter. Where was that sundress that was way too short and hung on Kris? There. "Why not try this one?"

Aholo wiggled out of her sarong, underwear not being popular on the islands, and Kris helped her get the sundress over her head. The dress's waist was gathered in, providing natural support, and the skirt flounced out beautifully on Aholo. She glanced at herself in the full-length mirror on the bathroom door, and pirouetted. "It's lovely."

"You're the one who's lovely. The dress is yours. It sure doesn't look that good on me. I think your feet are about my size. Abby, do we have some shoes for her?"

Abby rummaged a bit to produce sandals . . . and frilly panties two sizes up from Kris's. "I keep these around. If you keep eating aboard ship like you do, you're bound to end up needing them with no store nearby," the maid said with a sniff.

Kris made a face and said nothing.

"Since you're attending some serious talks, you might want to have some serious business clothes," Abby went on, pulling a red power suit from a different trunk. It was shorter than the one she'd offered Kris, and more roomy. The face Kris gave her maid this time was different, but Abby proved to be just as impervious to it as the other. And she produced a dark blue and bright green suit, both with skirt, pants, and tights, depending on what the businesswomen on the Big Island were wearing.

All a great fit for a 5'8" gal with great curves and totally out of place in the wardrobe of a six foot tall beanpole.

Abby, we got to talk someday. When things slow down.

But not tonight. She stood aside as Abby outfitted Aholo with a full set of underwear, bra size 38-C well up from Kris's own 34-A, but Abby walked right through Kris's frown. *What did the woman have in all her trunks?*

Makeup was skipped, but not accessories for the ensembles . . . more shoes, scarves, and light jewelry. "Unless you have some of your own?"

"Most of mine is handmade and not so fancy. Let me get my box," and that brought out a lot of oohing and aahing as both Abby and Kris matched natural pearls, lovely brooches, necklaces, and bracelets to each of the outfits. And watched as Aholo tried them on. Then tried on some of the formal wear that was supposed to look like it had the flowing look of Island wear but was totally synthetic.

"Why not just wear a sarong?" Aholo asked.

"Hard to answer that question," Abby said. "Kind of like if you ask it, there's no way to answer it for you."

"Oh," the Island princess said.

"Now it's late, and the gig will be here early. I'm just gonna load all of your stuff on one trunk, Princess," Abby said with a nod toward Aholo, "and I'm gonna take all your stuff, Kris, 'cause I don't have time to pick and choose. There's plenty of good-looking guys around only too glad to show off their muscles for me, and I'll let them load this stuff back out."

Why did Kris suspect that this was exactly what Abby had wanted . . . and that one of those trunks had always had Aholo's size, and . . . Too many questions. Way too many.

Morning came early; there were Marines aboard the gig, and Kris suspected the long boat, but they sat in the back and kept their rifles out of sight. Kris nodded at Sargeant Li and got a businesslike nod in return. Though they left Nui Nui at 8:30 a.m. and spent about an hour and a half making orbit and breaking back down, they landed in a large bay surrounded by Port Stanley at 8:00 a.m. local time, having gained two hours against the sun. It would be a long day.

They motored up from the shuttle port through an industrial park that would have done a medium-size town on Wardhaven proud. The greeting speeches at the Civic Auditorium, though they were long and formal, were to a

packed audience. They were full of thanks for all that the
Islanders had done for them in their time of need so many
years ago and reminders of all that they had done for the
Islanders lately. Kris had to respect the way Aholo, in a
bright red suit with conservative skirt, followed right
along, thanking them for their support in building hospitals
and navigational aids in the Islands and glad that they had
enjoyed the hospitality of the Big Island in their time of
great need.

Aholo then went on to say what they had left unsaid,
that the decision made so many years ago, based on false
expectations, now needed to be revisited and set along a
different course.

That finale to her speech drew applause that even Kris's
father would have envied. Especially just now with him
fighting for his political life. For a kid raised in a less-than-
partisan political environment, Aholo looked to be a quick
study.

After a break, they adjourned to the city hall and its
council chambers, and a table expanded to provide room
for Aholo and the elders with her. Kris and Jack casually
did a walk-around that turned up nothing threatening and
only the standard swarm of news-type bugs. They let them
live. When Jack went outside with Penny to meet with the
local constabulary, leaving Tom to keep watch at the door,
Kris settled into a chair along the wall, fluffed out the wide
skirt to her sundress—she was intentionally underdressed
beside Aholo—and got ready to listen and smile through
the rest of the day.

Which was about all she did.

Everyone had to have a chance to talk, and they did. Islander and Mainlander—they insisted on that name and
soon even the Islanders were using it—got their say. Kris
wondered if she was the only one who noticed that most of
them were saying the same thing. Times were tough when
they came to the Mainland, and they worked hard to make
a wilderness into a home, and they'd succeeded and
watched their kids and grandkids grow and prosper. Now

they had as much interest as anyone in this planet, and it was their tax money that paid for everything on this planet. *Everything.*

Of course, the Islanders had their mantra. They fought hard and bled during the Iteeche Wars, saving humanity while the refugees on the mainland were just struggling to stay alive. They just wanted to live their way and they didn't take much. And after all, this was *their* planet.

By four o'clock when they adjourned, Kris had heard a lot of chest pounding but not much give and take.

Abby had taken over the Royal Suite at the Hotel Stanley. Aholo and Kris had separate bedrooms. Abby and Jack were across the hall. Penny and Tom had rooms on either side of them.

The maid was clearly ready to do two princesses for the price of one. Abby set up a bathing, hair shampooing, and dressing assembly line that was a marvel of modern efficiency, and produced two fully decked-out young women in flowing gowns by the six o'clock supper hour. This even allowed for Kris and Aholo to spend time dithering over each other's jewelry boxes. Aholo ended up wearing the best Wardhaven and six hundred human planets had to offer; Kris wore Island finery.

Dinner was in the hotel's smaller ballroom, and Kris found herself sitting between the mayors of Port Stanley and Port Phoenix, a town so far upriver that its creek was nowhere close to navigable. However, until only a few years ago, out of respect for the Islanders, every town on Hikila, no matter how high and dry, was a port.

Kris wondered how much the Islanders appreciated that.

"So, what's King Ray really up to?" kicked off the dinner conversation over a delicious clam chowder. A check around the table showed everyone was a mayor or the spouse of a mayor seated at another table sent to hear and report back. And all wanted to know what was really going on in United Sentients.

Kris gave her usual bland, "I don't know. Good chowder."

"Is Ray slipping, letting the Constitutional Convention convene at Pitts Hope while he stays on Wardhaven?" a fellow who might have fought the Iteeche asked. "I mean he's a Longknife, but that's a bit far to pull strings even for one of them."

Kris kept a smile on her face and kept spooning chowder.

A younger woman whom Kris could easily grow to like asked, "Do you know anything about what's going on?"

"No, I don't know if the next course is salad or fish," Kris said with a straight face.

That got a laugh. She took a napkin to her lips, folded it again, and glanced around the table. "My grampa takes seriously that he's a constitutional monarch, and we don't have a constitution. Kind of makes it rough figuring out what we so-called royalty are supposed to do," Kris said with a wry grin.

That got her a round of dry chuckles.

"Anyway, he's on Wardhaven, and the palavering is on Pitts Hope because he really wants it that way. The folks who have tossed in their hats are deciding how United Sentients is going to run. Should the legislature have one house, two, or three? I don't know; they'll decide. One planet, one vote. Join now and have a say. Join later and, well, you'll know what you're joining, but the saying will be done."

"I take it you're for joining early," the mayor of Port Stanley said.

"I tend to want to be heard when I say my say." Kris grinned.

"I've heard something to that effect," brought a chuckle from around the table. Kris did her best impression of wounded innocence. The chuckles grew to full laughter.

"Will this U.S. thing protect us?" One mayor asked.

"A major chunk of the Wardhaven fleet is at Boynton taking the pressure off them," Kris answered.

"All of it, I understand," one corrected.

Kris said nothing.

"Is it there to protect Boynton, or to pressure them into

joining United? If we don't come in, will we be looking up at a squadron of Wardhaven battleships blockading our trade?" said a young mayor. Kris hadn't gotten his town.

"That's one interpretation of the situation out there I hadn't heard," she said slowly. "For the record, Boynton was in the final process of completing its application when ships started showing up from two, three different other planets. I don't know what they were planning on doing, or who called them in. They aren't saying. Boynton's government asked for help. Wardhaven responded. So did several other planets. At least that's what I saw on all the news. Where'd you hear different?"

"One hears different things, different places," the man said, returning to his chowder.

The salad arrived, and talk lapsed into generalities about the future of humanity and the problems of six hundred planets. Nothing specific to Hikila, Kris noted. She ate what was put before her and answered the questions posed to her, careful to avoid any hypotheticals that might come back to bite her or her grampa.

After dinner was a "dance," which meant that some people actually got out on the floor and danced to music that might have been popular long before humanity left old Earth, or music derived from such sounds. It was music intended to let some people move together in a lovely fashion while others looked on and got about the main reason they had gathered here: talk.

They talked about the other people with them or talked about politics. Tonight, politics seemed to be the main topic.

And Kris found herself pretty much out of the mainstream.

She enjoyed the quiet for a while until an attractive man of about her own age and height settled into the chair next to her and said, "Lovely jewelry they make in the Islands. You and the other princess swap baubles?"

Kris held up a bracelet of coral and pearls. "It's probably the most authentic object I've ever worn in my life."

He rubbed his chin. "Authentic is big with them."

"You've probably figured out I'm Kris Longknife. You are . . . ?"

He offered his hand and a smile. "I'm Sam Trabinki, son of the mayor of Port Stanley. I've been watching you two young ladies from the cheap scats most of the day, see ing how this political thing is done, taking notes. My dad will be inflicting a quiz on me as soon as you leave town."

"Your dad sounds very much like my father."

"Politician first, everything else much later?" he said.

"And I would have sworn they only made one like him, and I got him."

"And I thought I had that privilege." He chuckled dryly.

"Did yours refer things you wanted 'to committee for further study' and leave you scurrying around the family to corral enough votes to get it out?" Kris asked.

"Yes." He laughed. "I was the only ten-year-old to organize my family supper talk in bullets."

"I started that at nine," Kris said, hoping he wouldn't feel one-upped

"We'll, your dad was a Longknife. Did it get worse?"

Kris thought for a moment, blinked, then nodded. "Yes, it did. Father quit coming home for supper." And she found herself talking about Eddy's kidnapping and death. Her eyes still stung, and there was dampness there, but she didn't choke on her words. Not now. He was a good listener, head nodding, making those faint listening noises that encouraged her to go on. She still stripped out anything she wouldn't want to see in the paper tomorrow, but she did feel better for the talk, or maybe it was the finish. "Then again, I did kill the last kidnapping bastards that crossed my path."

"I thought you captured those punks on Harmony."

She blinked, full defenses going up. "You researched me!" she said in full accusation.

He grinned and threw himself happily on her mercy. "When a Longknife comes to town, an apprentice politician kind of has to do a bio on the visiting fireman, er, woman. Dad gave me an A-plus," he said by way of mitigation.

"Send me a copy. I need to know what the news has me officially guilty of these days. But I think that last kidnapping was kept out of the paper, or at least my name wasn't attached to it. Anyway, if you're ever kidnapped and I'm nearby, the rescue is free."

"You're quite a spectacular woman."

"And that's the best pickup line anyone's ever tried on me."

"No, really, you did whatever you did at the Paris system and on Turantic, and yet you're sitting here quietly, letting Aholo get all the attention tonight."

"It's her planet, her show."

He glanced Aholo's way. "Were you in the Islands long?"

"A couple of days."

"What's it like?"

"I think *paradise* is the usual word that's overworked."

"Yeah, that's what my dad says, but my mom keeps coming up with reasons why I can't manage to fit a visit into my schedule."

Kris could understand that. She surveyed the room; dress here was light on skin and solidly conservative. Even Mother's latest fashion delivery from Earth would be decidedly out of step here. Yep, the Mainland was in rebellion from the Island culture, and not just work versus subsistence, cash versus barter. There were a lot of differences, and they went deep and philosophical. Whatever political machinery they came up with would have to be resilient enough to survive a lot of pushing and pulling over the next fifty years.

Nobody said it would be easy.

Kris let Sam get her talking about how her one fishing expedition almost landed her in the water with sharks. "And while some folks talk about us Longknifes and sharks in the same breath, I don't think I would have gotten any professional courtesy from that big mouth."

That had him laughing, but she noticed that as she talked, he'd glanced more and more toward Aholo. Not that

Kris could blame him. She was an eyeful, and she did carry herself with all the poise you'd expect of a soon-to-be-reigning queen.

"Do you think she'd like to dance?" Sam finally blurted out.

"I know that after an hour or more of yakking, I'd kill for a chance to get out on the dance floor."

"Do you mind if I leave you?"

"I've enjoyed talking with you." *But it is his planet, and Aholo* is *the local girl, seen from the distance of twenty-five light-years,* Kris reminded herself. And it wasn't as if she was really letting this one get away.

So he slipped off, and when the noise around Aholo paused for a second, he asked her for a dance, and she said yes without looking too relieved to slip out of the conversation straitjacket. As Sam led her away, the bubble around her broke up. The mayor of Stanley cadged a refill for his wineglass and a refill for Kris's sparkling water before taking the still-warm chair beside Kris.

"Sam keeping you company?"

"He has the makings of a first-class politico," Kris assured the father of the topic at hand.

"He doesn't dance too bad, either."

"Considering that he's probably having to teach her the steps," Kris said, taking a sip.

"I understand you had to learn some pretty fancy steps a few nights ago," he said with a raised eyebrow.

Kris decided to ignore the reference to her going native—or to her stopping someone from blowing up the native treasures—and chose to cut to her chase. "How long is everyone going to keep saying what everyone knows, and when are you going to start solving the problem everyone knows has to be tackled?"

"You are one of those damn Longknifes, aren't you," he said, raising his glass in salute.

"All one word," Kris saluted back.

"Well, your daddy must have taught you the importance of letting folks vent."

"When I was still in diapers," Kris agreed.

"And what we said here today will be in all the news out on the Islands and all over the Mainland. Lots of folks will say, 'Right, you tell 'em,' and we're doing it here, in Port Stanley where things won't get too hot, 'cause we all know what really needs to be done."

"You do."

"Yeah. While we have some hotheads here, and they have their hotheads there, just about all of us agree we need a government that respects both the majority and the minority. Say a House that's popularly elected and a Senate that represents specific locals. Problem is, which locals? They have some mighty small islands and we have some mighty small towns. They don't have many more islands to settle, and our population is growing, and there's a lot of land up here on the Mainland that hasn't been touched yet." He scratched his head. "I sure don't know how we're going to juggle all that, I just know we have to."

"Where does my grampa's United fit into this picture?"

"At the heart of it. Money." The mayor's grin was all teeth. "As soon as Earth folded its Society of Humanity, we eliminated that tax from our budget or started spending it on something local. Now, if we have to pay for that fleet your grampa wants—and don't tell me that hasn't been decided; I can read the need as good as any blind man—that means taxes. If Queen Ha'iku'lani took us into United without a popular vote, there'd be riots here on the Mainland and . . . well, I think even Stanley would be voting for independence from Nui Nui."

"It's that bad?"

"No, not so long as you keep the status quo. It's only if you try to change anything that things get interesting."

"But things are changing."

"You noticed that, too."

"So you can't change just a little bit," Kris said.

"We got to eat the whole apple, core, seeds, and all." The mayor sighed. "Damn, if my boy ain't talked your girl into a second dance."

"If it was dance or talk politics, which would you do?"

"Dance at their age." He sighed. "So, Longknife, what you going to do?"

"My grampa sent me here to hold an old war buddy's hand while she dies. She asked me to help her great-granddaughter try to make her heart light as she lies dying, so I borrowed a gig to get things moving fast." Kris eyed the mayor sideways, "But this isn't my world, so I'm sitting here like a good wallflower."

"Like you did on Turantic." He grinned.

"That being the subject of several legal proceedings, I am advised by counsel to reserve comment for my day in court, if I ever get one," Kris said dryly. They both laughed.

He went his way, no doubt to report on their conversation. She warmed her seat. There were several other young men at the dance, but none so much as looked her way. What was it about her that scared them off: the Princess, the Longknife, the money, or the target painted on her . . . front and back?

At eleven, Aholo called it quits; there were early meetings next morning. Back in their room, as Abby got them out of their formal rigs, Kris got to dissect the night with another girl for the first time in her life. Beyond the "Wasn't that wonderful," and "Oh, my feet hurt," and "I wondered if they'd ever stop talking," Aholo got in "What did you think of Sam?"

"He's got a good head on his shoulders."

"He dances well. For a Big Islan—Mainland guy."

"Both of you danced well. What did you talk about?"

"He has a sailboat. Not an outrigger, but a sailboat with a keel. He loves sailing with the wind in his hair. I didn't think any Mainlander was like that."

"People surprise you," Kris said. Why hadn't he mentioned that to her? She loved sailing. "Too bad we'll be losing Sam when we leave Port Stanley tomorrow."

"Oh, but we may not. He's asking his papa if he can come along as his secretary. The Mainlanders have decided to start forming a Constitutional Convention by kind of rolling up the members from the cities where I've been. That way when we hit the last ones, the more difficult ones, we'll have not only my elders with me, but also the Mainlanders who support me."

That was news to Kris. Maybe she needed to rethink being a wallflower. Or maybe she was finding out things just about the time she needed to. After all, this was these people's show.

Not mine. Remember that, girl. Not mine.

By the fourth city, four days later, Kris was ready to draw some conclusions. The cities were big, and they'd flown over quite a few small towns. In all of them, recent urban renewal had replaced the last remnants of the refugee camps and hasty occupation with centrally located city services, arenas, and gleaming shopping opportunities. Progress.

The fourth city also had demonstrators.

Oldsters in proudly mismatched clothes lined the street with signs saying, It's Our Land, We Worked for It, and similar sentiments. Another line of protesters was more worrisome to Kris. Youngsters in spiked hair in a riot of colors and dressed in somber long-sleeved shirts and pants, buttoned at the neck despite the heat, showed signs demanding, Don't Give the Nudies Nothing. Since attitude toward skin didn't prevent a young mom from nursing her baby without so much as a blanket to block the view, Kris suspected the issue was all political.

It was time to get ready for trouble. The tight lines around Jack's eyes as he studied the crowd along the street their motorcade drove showed his vigilance had gone up a notch. Kris leaned forward, signaling Penny and Tom to do the same.

"We got a problem?" Tom asked softly.

"None I'm more aware of than you, but . . ." Kris nodded toward the show outside their limo. They nodded back. "Jack stays with me. Penny, you connect with the local constabulary and plug into their command center. Tom, that leaves you with the princess. First chance you get, draw a body stocking from Abby and start hanging as close to Aholo as the situation allows. If someone takes a shot at her, try to take it on your backside."

"Like I took your last one." He grinned, lopsided.

"But don't get too close to the princess," Penny said.

"Sam's holding down that slot all by himself." The boy wasn't in the car with Aholo, but once things sorted themselves out in the conference room, he was usually close to his father, which was never far from the princess. And somehow, he'd managed to outcompete a lot of guys to be her main dance partner.

NELLY, ASK ABBY IF SHE HAS ARMORED BODY STOCK-INGS FOR TOM AND SAM.

There was only a short pause. SHE DOES.

ASK HER WHERE SHE FOUND A SALE ON ARMORED BODY STOCKINGS?

THAT IS A RHETORICAL QUESTION, CORRECT?

FOR NOW.

ABBY SAYS TOM'S ALREADY DRAWN A STOCKING. SHOULD BE WEARING IT.

Kris eyed Tom. He grinned. "And I was about to get around to telling you that Penny and I have been in stockings since we came ashore. Just like you and Jack, right?"

Jack elbowed Kris without looking away from the crowd.

"And I've been working with the local police since Port Stanley," Penny said. "They're good, but they're about two hundred years behind the tech curve. A high-tech bank robber here uses a computer-printed note and a gun." Penny sighed. "There's a couple of cops from Port Stanley with us now. A couple more from each town have been added. They know how important it is, but they've never worked at anything like what I talk to them about. They just shake their heads and say, 'That can't happen here.' "

"Let's hope they're right," Kris said, reminding herself that there was a reason why she was not alone here. She had her job and was doing it. These professionals had theirs and were doing them very well, thank you.

That day nothing like that happened at Port Winslow. More tough talk in public, another dinner-dance party that night, and over cocktails talk of district lines cut along this natural boundary or that population limit, criteria for taxing cities to pay for opening up new lands for youngsters.

Two days later, they flew into Port Brisbane at the foot of an imposing snow-covered mountain range. A river and a lake provided its essential water. Its hinterland propelled its growth with food, fiber, metals, and oil. The cocktail debate was whether it or Stanley—the *Port* was rarely appended now in conversations—would be the new capital, or co-capital with Nui Nui. Not all the friction was Mainland versus Islander.

The speeches were blessedly short and done at the airport. There were no protestors lining the streets as they drove directly to the convention center. Abby led a second caravan to the two hotels the entourage now took up.

Well-practiced, Penny went to the command post the local constabulary established on site. Tom and Sam kept close to Princess Aholo as inconspicuously as two good-looking young guys could. And Kris and Jack did their own wide-ranging walk-around.

The convention center was huge, as befitted Brisbane, and on three levels, with an airy gathering space dividing the two main work areas. On the south side were three huge exhibit halls. The middle-level hall had been arranged for the proto-assembly. The upper and lower halls were reserved for growth, caucuses, media, whatever came up. On the other side of the gathering areas were breakout rooms, over two dozen of various sizes, as well as several places to get something to eat quickly. More formal restaurants were across the streets or in the hotels near the convention center. It reminded Kris of some of the better centers she'd been confined to during Father's campaigns on Wardhaven. High praise from her perspective.

"We're starting to get organized in here," Tom reported.

"We've got a newly installed security camera giving us fits in meeting room nine," Penny reported.

"We're just down from it," Kris reported. "We'll check it."

But a Brisbane cop and repairman were first through the door. They died in a hail of automatic fire for that honor.

As Jack returned fire from the side of the door, Kris shouted into her commlink, "Officer down. Breakout room nine."

Somewhere in the building there was an explosion. Somewhere there were bursts after bursts of automatic weapons fire. Police pistols sounded puny as they answered. All too quickly there was little return fire.

"Tom," Penny shouted on net. Static answered her.

6

"My comm's jammed," Jack muttered as he fired a two-round burst, ducked back, and got no answering fire. He knelt and peered out at knee level. No more fire from that room.

"Help me check these out," he said, cautiously entering the room. The cop and tech's bodies oozed blood and looked beyond hope. Two men in service uniforms, assault rifles close where they'd dropped them, lay just inside a back door. One moaned.

"Grab him and get out of here," Kris said. Jack picked up the rifle as they did. Outside, they made for the nearest exit . . . and ran into two cops running in. They handed off their load.

"Where's Bill?" the tall cop demanded.

Jack shook his head.

"We've got to go in there," the tall cop insisted.

There was more automatic fire. Kris wanted to head back in, too. But not while she was outgunned and as disorganized as this. "Penny, are you out?"

"We've evacuated the command center to the Hotel Brisbane's lobby. Can you rally here?"

"Do the local police have a SWAT force?"

"No."

"National guard? Anybody with weapons like we're facing?"

There was a pause. "No, Kris. Guy here says they don't have shit like this here."

"They do now. Nelly, get me the *Halsey*."

"Commander Santiago, here," took less than a second.

"Captain, we have a hostage situation." Kris quickly filled Santiago in. "I need any individual and crew-served weapons you can spare, and people to train the locals on how to use them," she finished.

"Are you in a secure location?"

"No," Jack shouted over Kris's "Yes."

"I'm dispatching the gig to Brisbane to collect you, Princess. My orders are to keep you safe. You ain't just now. You can watch the situation from up here while it develops."

"But the best time to intervene in this kind of a situation is while it's still developing," Kris pointed out.

"If you have trained troops who know what to do," Jack reminded Kris. "We don't. Captain, she'll be at the airport."

"See you there, Agent."

Two hours later, a livid Kris stormed from the gig to the *Halsey*'s Combat Information Center, the fighting heart of the destroyer. The CIC's walls were wrapped in workstations reporting the condition of the ship and space around it. In the middle was a battle board. There her captain sat, both elbows on a board that, instead of tracking space, pictured a small bit of ground dirtside.

"I'm here. What's developing down there?"

"Nothing since you left. One of the reasons I was hoping you would," Santiago said dryly.

"No more shooting?"

"Nothing from inside the building. The police have set up a cordon one block out, facing in. Another one two blocks farther out, facing out. They've about completed their evacuation. Not easy, considering they just closed down the heart of Brisbane's commercial district. They've got a call out to constabularies for three hundred kilometers around, and most of them are sending detachments, but, since this has never been done, and everyone's a bit nervous about their own backyard just now, things are going slow."

"Could you drop some Marines on the roof and we take the terrorists down right now?"

"No, because my Marines would be dead before they hit the deck."

Kris blinked and silently eyed the Captain.

"They've set up a radar on the roof. Docile little thing. Comes on every thirty seconds. Does a sweep. Always on the same frequency. Cuts off. Want to bet if we try to jam it or if it catches something coming in that it will take off frequency jumping and lead us in a merry chase? And they have jokers walking the building roof. What you want to bet me they have seeking missiles on their belts?"

"Have you tried to infiltrate nano recon bugs?"

The Captain scowled. "You trying to teach your mother to suck eggs, Lieutenant? I sent them down on the gig that brought you up. First one burned thirty seconds after it got in. They phoned to say they'd shoot a hostage if we sent another one in."

"Think they mean it?" Kris asked.

"We don't know yet."

"That a live picture of the building?" Kris asked, pointing at an aerial of the convention center and deciding questions might make for an easier relationship with this destroyer skipper.

"Yes, I launched several satellites out of the *Halsey's* stores when this started. We'll have one continuously."

"But we don't know what's going on inside," Kris grumbled.

"Not quite true," Penny said. "Their jammer has closed down the center's comm net, but it has a range limit. We've got a woman inside just on the limit of that range. She's talking to us. Says they shot ten, twenty people taking over the main room. They have all the delegates down on the floor now. A couple of them appear to be rigging explosives to some of the hall's supports. Now they're rounding up the delegates, using plastic to cuff them together into groups of five or six. Oops, they just found our talker. No more news flashes from inside."

"Are Tom and Aholo okay?" Kris asked.

"She said Aholo was. I think Tom is, but she didn't really know him from Adam, so I'll just have to bite my nails. Kris, when are we going in and getting them out?"

"I need the design schematics of that building."

"I've got people working on them. Okay, now there's action at the front door," Penny said.

Heads turned in CIC to a screen showing the local news take. A large Islander in a lavalava walked out of the convention center. Kris recognized him, Vea Ikalu, principal adviser to the queen, and on this trip, to Aholo. Beside him was a woman in a business suit. Both held their hands up and their pace down. They got halfway to the street, say twenty meters. Then rifle fire from masked gunners at the door cut them down.

"Want to bet," Santiago said, "the woman was our talker."

A moment later, other hostages began bringing out bodies and laying them on the sidewalk a few feet from the center. A woman put hers down, stood looking at it for a moment, then broke for the street. She almost made it before rapid fire dropped her crumpled at the curb.

"What's their message? What do they want?" Kris asked thin air.

"That *is* their message," Jack said. "They aren't afraid to kill people in cold blood. They have the upper hand. They will tell us what they want us to know in their own damn time."

"Can't argue with that." Santiago sighed, turning back to her board. "Penny, we really need those building specs."

"Maybe my contacts will work harder now."

"Now that we understand each other, maybe this will be a whole lot easier," came in a confident voice from the news screen. Heads in the CIC turned back to it. The voice was young and very, very confident.

"We want a planetary government like everyone else has. A parliament, say with two hundred MPs. One man, one woman, one vote. Nothing special for Islanders. We're all just one big happy family. Maybe the parliament can even agree to have a queen. A constitutional queen. I don't mind having the naked tits of some Island cutie on my money. But no veto, no control.

"Now I heard that the folks here were authorized to vote on just such a government. Course, they are shy a few folks, the ones that fought us, and the ones that mouthed off when they shouldn't have. Talked on their phone when we told her not to. But the rest, they could vote that government in real fast. They do, and we'll all be out of here by evening.

"But I'm told that politicians can take forever to decide on the shape of the table they sit at, so I figure we better encourage them along. If they don't give us a constitution to vote on by, oh, say six tonight, we let three more walk out, see if they can make it to the street. At midnight, we let four try for the street. Who knows, in the dark, one of them just might make it. Come morning, we turn five loose. It just keeps getting bigger until we run out of delegates or the ones left give us a new constitution.

"Oh, and ladies and gentlemen, you, too, guys in skirts, those of you that resist doing your duty and giving us what we want, you'll be the first ones that get to take the walk."

Kris shivered. That must have been spoken straight at the hostages. "We got to get them out tonight," she said.

"That's exactly what they're expecting," Santiago snapped, shaking her head.

"Well, tomorrow night's not going to do a whole lot of people much good. How long before they decide Princess Aholo's a problem for them?"

"If she's been hanging around a Longknife, not long."

"I've got the building files," Penny said, cutting that debate off. Santiago opened a separate window on her battle board and a 3-D schematic of the convention center began to rotate before them. "The terrorists apparently drove into the receiving dock on the south end of the building. At least when we sent in reinforcements there during the fight, they got shot up badly, and the survivors reported seeing three trucks. We checked with the owners. They don't know why their trucks are there," Penny said.

"New employees?" Kris asked.

"Yep. Checking them out, but the local database is light."

"We don't have those kinds of problems here," Kris said.

"I'm hearing that enough down here, don't you start saying it," Penny grumbled.

"What about the rifle we captured?" Kris asked Santiago. Rather than rely on the locals, she'd brought it up to the *Halsey*. The Captain tapped her board.

"The rifle is a cheap knockoff of the obsolete M-5," came a quick response. "New Hong Kong has six or seven plants stamping them out to meet the rising demand. Ammo cassettes also appear to be from there. The serial number has been filed down, but we figure to recover it and match it to production in another half hour. Longer if it's not in our database."

"Thanks, intel."

"The Marines helped, ma'am."

"Figured they would." Santiago smiled.

Kris absently tapped the board, opening a window, closing it, opening it . . . "A fancy radar. Nano guards to beat our recon bugs. Weapons better than any seen on this rock . . ."

"You getting déjà vu all over again?" Santiago asked.

"If these folks ain't got the banker of those bastards on Harmony, they got his sister's banker." Kris shook her head and made a judgment call. "Nelly, get me Hank Peterwald."

That got frowns from Jack and Santiago, but no one opened their mouth to argue with her.

"What do you want, Longknife?" came a second later.

"You know about the situation in Brisbane?"

"Kind of hard to miss it. I heard you hotfooted it out of range real fast."

Kris gritted her teeth for a second and breathed out the anger that snide remark brewed in her gut. Hank knew her enough to calculate just how much it would set her off. "Yeah, you know how it is," she said, as offhanded as she could manage, "the security types get you in a hammerlock, and next thing you know you're stuck watching it from the cheap seats."

"Yeah, like on Turantic."

"You must admit, I got you an interesting view."

"From my own yacht. So, Longknife, why you calling me now?"

"Well, I couldn't help but notice that the terrorists are very well-equipped compared to what the local constabularies have, and someone had to pay to import all those expensive goodies. I thought maybe you, having talked to folks holding many of the same views as them, might know who's bankrolling them."

"Who says they're terrorists? They sound like freedom fighters to me."

"From where I was sitting, it didn't look like *anyone* needed to fight for *anything* until a few hours ago."

"But you Longknifes are always sitting pretty."

Beside Kris, Jack and Sandy were shaking their heads. Well, she had to try this route. "So you're not going to help me."

"Don't see any way I could, even if I should want to," came back at her.

"Well, just in case you might know someone who does know someone connected in any way to that crew, you might pass along to them that they have one of my officers in there. Obviously, he has no vote in Hikila's future. I will take it personally if any harm comes to him. Very, very personally."

"And I should be quaking in my shoes, Longknife."

"They should be," Kris said and cut the connection.

"Do you think they'll hurt Tom?" Penny asked on net.

"I don't know." Kris sighed, wondering if she'd just helped . . . or sealed Tom's death warrant. "We've got to get those people out. Tonight."

Santiago scowled and reached for an overhead microphone. "All hands, this is the Captain speaking. As you probably know by now, there's a situation on the planet below . . . and we've got *our* Longknife back aboard. She's about to make a call for volunteers for a heroic and near-suicidal rescue mission for tonight. I disagree. A better-planned and less bloody one can be put together for tomorrow night. As your Captain, I strongly discourage you from responding to a request I can not prevent *Princess Kristine* from making." So saying, the Captain handed the mike to Kris.

Kris juggled the mike for a second, wondering how even a Longknife followed an intro like that.

She keyed the mike. "There are five hundred hostages below. The terrorists have already murdered a number of them. At six and midnight, they'll kill three and four more. I say they get those seven and no more. I need nine volunteers for a drop mission to go with me tonight. If I can't get nine, then we do it your skipper's way, plan it all the way, practice it through, do it up right. And let twenty-six more innocents die. Your call. Eight and I don't go. Nine and we give it a serious look-see."

"Well, if you're really desperate," came from the open hatch of the CIC where Abby leaned against it, "I guess I could be talked into trying a drop mission. How *do* you open a parachute?"

"I'm *sure* you already know," Jack said dryly.

"Count me in," came from Penny. "You can get some intel weenie down here to hold these people's hands. I'm going in after Tom."

"Penny, have you ever made a drop?"

"Once. In training. It can't be too hard if your maid can do it."

"She's only coming along in case I break a nail," Kris said.

"Or your neck," Abby added.

Santiago looked like she was about to ground them all when Sergeant Li appeared at the CIC hatch. Her "Sergeant?" was less than half question, much more an accusation that stopped just this side of mutiny charges.

"Begging the Captain's pardon, but if she doesn't have any immediate need for several members of the Marine detachment this evening, we respectfully request permission to accompany Princess Longknife on her little trip dirtside. Ma'am."

The Captain shook her head. "Longknifes," she spat. "Well, how many of my Marines are you going to drag along in your wake? You're not really taking your maid, are you?"

Kris eyed the putative body servant. "Likely I will. With Jack, that makes four of my crazies. If I could, I'd appreciate borrowing six of your hard cases and heartbreakers."

The Sergeant grinned broadly. The Captain's scowl got deeper. "I ought to clap you all in irons, slap you in my brig, and call for a psych workup on the lot of you, but I'll delay any effort to apply adult leadership to you juvenile delinquents until I hear your rescue plan."

"Nice of you," Kris said and signaled Jack, Sergeant Li and, for good measure, Abby, to settle down around the battle board and study the Convention Center layout.

"Captain," Kris said slowly, "if you wouldn't mind dropping a longboat down to Brisbane full of standoff sensors and techs to use them, with firm orders to stand off and not get involved."

"Very firm orders," Santiago said.

"And if you could have the longboat fly by the convention center at seven thousand meters aboveground and five klicks offset."

"That radar would pick up troops making a drop."

"In full combat gear, I agree," Kris said.

"And I'll ride the longboat up," Penny said.

"No," Kris said. "I need you at the command center, pulling what strings you've got. There'll be another longboat along next orbit. And the next one. I promise."

Santiago rubbed her chin and said nothing.

And one of Penny's strings yielded a surprising fish. "Kris, remember that gunman you lugged out of the center?"

"Yes."

"His girlfriend showed up at the hospital, with another girl. Both are talking to our women cops there. They're singing like two very worried canaries."

"What do they know?"

"A lot. These jokers may have all kinds of fancy toys, but professional they ain't. And they like to brag a lot in their pillow talk. These girls are terrified because you got out. They figure you're going to come back down here and stomp heads, slit throats, be really pissed."

"Somebody's been reading too many comics," Santiago growled.

"Anyway, they're willing to do anything to get on your nice side so you'll go easy on their boys. And they want you to know they weren't after you. It was your grampa they really wanted."

"My grampa!"

"You heard right. With Queen Ha'iku'lani dying, they figured King Ray would come charging out here, order everyone to show up, and then dictate a new world order for Hikila for his old war buddy's grandkid. They figured on killing him and taking down an old war hero and freeing the universe from the real dictator."

"Good Lord, what have they been smoking?" Kris breathed.

"The girls swear that's true. And I think they believe it."

"Even if they do believe it, is that really what's going on down there?" Santiago said.

"And if that was what they thought two weeks ago, why'd they do what they did today?" Kris shook her head slowly. "No matter how confused their motivation is, they still have a lot of guns. They're killing people and, if I have any say, they stop doing it tonight. Penny, is there anyone down there who can step up to the plate as a SWAT team?"

"A couple of police departments back in the mountains

have high-risk rescue teams. Some of their members also double as their rifle marksman squad. Get me some armored suits and M-6s down here, two, three specialists to train them, and some time, and I think they could be ready."

"For tonight?"

"Maybe. Tomorrow night more likely."

Santiago's scowl had an upward quirk as she raised an eyebrow. "I'll have my spare suits and rifles added to the next long boat going down."

Kris eyed the battle board. "Now, where do we peel this Convention Center? Anyone downside see any way directly in to the hostages?"

"No," Penny said. "We've set up a camera on the hotel roof to cover the center. The four shooters they have up on the roof look to be in full body armor, with ceramics. That has to be as good as anything our Marines have got. Maybe better."

Sergeant Li said something obscene under his breath.

"Assuming you got control of the roof," Penny said, "blowing holes in the ceiling and either shooting the terrorists or rappelling down into the hall doesn't look fast enough to stop them from blowing their explosives. We need more time to look things over with heat sensors, but that's my first call for now."

"What about the receiving dock on the south side of the building?" Jack asked.

"No access from the main roof, so any detachment that goes there is on its own. And we've already taken heavy fire from what they have defending that end. I don't recommend it."

"Do you recommend anything?" the captain asked.

Penny was silent for a long while. "Not really."

"Well, assuming we occupy the main roof," Kris said, "how do we get inside?" Kris ignored Santiago rolling her eyes.

"There are four accesses to the roof. Along the east side, there are two stairwells that take you down to the top level of breakout rooms."

"They'll be booby-trapped," Santiago said, "and exit from the stairwells is easily covered by fire teams here in the top-level gathering area; they also can cover the middle-level access to where the hostages are. Two fire lanes toward two threats. Bound to be well-covered."

"So we don't use them," Kris said. "Penny, you said there were four stairs. The two others are . . ."

"On the west side of the building, leading down into the building service and support area above the lowest level of breakout rooms. That's where they have the electrical, air-conditioning, heating, that sort of stuff."

"These folks don't strike me as the type to leave if we mess up the bathrooms," Abby said.

"I don't think they're letting the hostages take bathroom breaks," Penny reported.

Commander Santiago gave them a look.

Jack just shook his head as if to say, "You don't *really* want to know."

"Sounds like these stairs will be booby-trapped and well covered," Kris said.

"I'd expect that. Heat may give us better info later."

"So . . ." the Captain began. Hand up, she raised one finger. "You can't make a standard drop because they have radar to lock on to your armored suits and pick you off as you drop. Two . . ." another finger came up. "If you get on the roof, they're in full armor, and the M-6 will be as like to bounce off them as shatter their ceramics. Three"—another finger—"even if you get control of the roof, you can't get off it. Excuse me, Princess, but I think your pumpkin is staying home tonight. No fairy godmother."

Kris had nodded as each digit came up. She reached across and gently folded one of the Captain's fingers back into her fist. "So we don't do a normal drop mission. We don't use the usual stairs," she said, folding a second one. "And do you have any of those dandy new M-6A4s?" she asked as she half folded the last one.

"Where'd you hear about the A4s?" Santiago asked.

"I read a lot." Kris shrugged.

"There are four targets on the roof, I'll think about loaning you four. You still haven't persuaded me you can do anything. Keep talking, Longknife."

Kris tapped a vent on the building. "This leads down to the fast-food kitchens. I plan to enter the building down it."

Santiago zoomed in on the air exhaust. "It's only a half meter square, and it doesn't go all the way down. Even if it did, you couldn't get battle armor down that."

"Don't plan to go all the way down. Abby, you ever use a hand laser or welding torch?"

"Had to use a welding torch to fix my employer's jewelry."

Jack just shook his head.

"Would you happen to have one handy?" Kris said as she followed the exhaust's plunge down until it shared a support with an air-conditioning duct of equal size. "Think you could cut us a hole from the exhaust to the duct?"

"Easily, ma'am. I'll even anneal the edges so no one can scratch themselves."

"You are not taking my Marines bare-ass naked down that air vent. Not against terrorists with fully automatic weapons and ceramic body armor," Santiago announced in full-force Captain. Even Sergeant Li looked a bit pale.

"Don't worry, Sergeant. You won't be totally bare-ass naked," Kris said. "Abby, just how many of those body stockings did you get on sale?"

"They were selling them by the dozen, ma'am. I bought two."

"Body stockings?" The Marine gulped.

Jack pulled his up above the collar of his shirt. You could easily see his fingers through it.

"I warned you, Sergeant. *Longknifes!*" Santiago spat.

"Abby, you have a knife on you?" Abby nodded. "Stab Jack somewhere he's got his stocking on."

"It's full body," Jack drawled without looking back.

Abby produced a knife from nowhere and stabbed Jack full in the back. He grunted as he leaned forward to absorb the blow. "You didn't have to do it that hard."

"Princess here didn't say how hard, and I've been wanting to do that for oh so long."

"Sergeant, take Abby's knife and stab her anywhere you have a hankering," Kris said. He took the knife and went for the gut.

"Is that any way to treat a lady?"

"*I* don't see any here," Santiago drawled. "Okay, so you have some Super Spider Silk undies. I've got some chutes that don't give back a radar bounce. M-6s are mainly plastic, and what isn't we can tape. I imagine you only want Marines that will fit down a half-meter hole, so I get to keep the big mean ones, Sergeant."

"Yes, ma'am," Sergeant Li responded, still looking a bit unsure about leading a squad of Marines dirtside in translucent underwear.

"And Abby will provide you with black body paint that ought to meet the modest requirements of the corps," Kris said.

"If you ask me real nice," the maid added.

Shortly after midnight, liberty launch 2 departed the *Halsey*. Intended to carry the ship's official car dirtside, its rear opened. The manual said it could open in flight. This would be the first time this crew ever attempted that maneuver. They were optimistic it would cause them no problems.

Kris hated optimists on a drop mission.

Santiago had granted them the loan of four M-6A4s. Rather than fire the 4 mm standard carbon steel darts from a spool, these shot 2 mm tungsten flechettes, twice as long as the normal round and with twice the normal load behind them. No sleepy darts for those who put on ceramic armor.

Just who got to use them had been decided at the Marines' shooting range. The Sergeant had shot a near perfect score first, followed by Jack matching him. The other nine who could fit down a half-meter exhaust duct shot next. All did well except one fellow who got razzed bad when he shot his worst in six months.

Kris shot last. And shot between Jack and the next-best Marine. That surprised her. Then Abby surprised them all by stepping up to the next firing slot and picking up an M-6.

"Where do you load this thing?" A Marine showed her.

She shot one round. Missed high and outside. "Need to sight this thing in." A smiling Marine showed her how. She made an adjustment. The next round was in the center. So were the next eight. "Am I doing as good as you, Jack?"

"Better. I had a round that edged into the nine ring."

Abby's next round nudged the nine.

Behind Kris there was murmuring in the Marine ranks. "Even a Longknife's maid's got to shoot as good as a Marine."

"As good as a Marine Sergeant," another corrected.

When the liberty launch dropped its rear ramp, Kris and Abby, Jack and Sergeant Li led off with the M-6A4s. Penny jumped with the other Marines. The last two out were the combat engineer and his assistant, carrying loads that, hopefully, the radar would be turned off before it got too strong a return from.

Free-falling at eight thousand meters was cold. Not as cold as Kris expected it to be. The body stocking did nothing to stop the freezing air, as Kris had learned on Turantic. But tonight, Abby had outdone herself. Ceramic girdles protected guts and butts and what the guys considered most important. Gauntlets and leggings reinforced arms and legs. Abby even had something for chests and backs that she claimed she got at an after-Christmas sale at a toy store. They *were* round and glided nicely. The *Halsey*'s stores provided tape that should absorb enough of their radar signal for them to get close before any alarm went off.

They'd know in a few moments.

The sapper and assistant pulled their D rings first, opening their chutes and beginning a slow, circling decent. They would have a minute to hang in the air. If things went bad on the roof, they could aim themselves away from the disaster.

Penny and the other Marines waited longer, then

opened their chutes next, planning on coming in a mere fifteen seconds behind Kris and the leaders.

"They've finished their comm check," came from the *Halsey*'s intel boss, now at Penny's place in the police incident command center. "You have fifteen minutes before they call them again."

Kris didn't answer. She was three hundred meters above the ground as she opened her chute. She had just enough time to stabilize her canopy, spot her target on the roof turning away from her, and pull up her rifle.

She aimed for the weak spot at the neck between the helmet and back, easier to hit from this angle. "Ready," she said.

"One." "Two." "Three," came back to her.

"Shoot."

Her target crumpled as she fired, riding the trigger to let more rounds go as she moved her aim up to the helmet. It shattered under her stream of darts. Maybe the armor wasn't as good as advertised.

A quick glance around showed her no one still standing on the roof. Kris let her rifle drop by its sling, got her hands back on her controls, and tried to aim her chute for a nice, soft, walkaway landing.

An updraft off the cooling building spoiled that, or maybe it was the concrete below. Part of her canopy lost lift early. She ended up standing on the edge of the roof, half her chute with her, half trying to drag her over the side. With an effort she tumbled awkwardly onto the roof's gravel floor and lay there, struggling with her lanyards until Jack trotted up.

"You want a hand?" he said, grabbing a fistful of line.

"I don't know that I'd applaud that landing," Abby said, joining them and hauling the canopy up where they wanted it.

"Even out on a cold night, all a girl finds is critics," Kris said. She'd caught a glance of her handiwork lying in blood. It was better to laugh at this than think of that.

Out of the night, a chute came down. The Marine was

out of it in a second and racing for the radar. She nodded happily and plugged a black box into it. If the codes were right, the radar would only make happy noises from now on, no matter what it saw.

Penny was also out of her chute, riffling through a downed roof lookout and muttering to her commlink. "We got the comm codes for them. They did have rockets, but they're really stupid SAL-9s. Any kind of countermeasures should take care of them. Nothing on the explosives frequency though."

"Appreciate what you gave us. Dump those rockets over the side, please. No use the skipper having to face them if, you know, you screw up tonight."

"We understand," Kris said as Jack helped her up.

"You kind of rubbed your black paint off your ass," Abby told her cheerfully. "I didn't bring along any spare paint."

"I'll just have to keep my enemy in front of me," Kris said, trotting to the airshaft. The sapper cut off the lock and lifted off the cowling. Abby rummaged in his bag of tricks, pulled out her own smaller bag, slipped into a harness, and got ready to go into the shaft as they snubbed down her line to a nearby air-conditioning unit. Ready, Abby went in with professional panache, then waited for a second while the sapper put a bit of armored cloth between her line and the sharp edge of the shaft. Then she dropped. The sapper shined a laser range finder over her shoulder. He blinked it, and she stopped.

A second later, light showed from her torch. Warm air, then cooler air came up the shaft. "We've struck air conditioning," the Marine combat engineer said. The torch lasted a bit longer, followed by the sound of metal bending and tape ripping. "She sure is a professional. Asked me for tape to take care of the sharp metal ends."

"Professional, yeah," Jack muttered. "I just wonder at what?" Kris could feel the Marines' curious stares in the dark.

She'd gotten into harness while watching this. When

Abby's line went slack, Kris did a somewhat less graceful repeat of her maid's drop, carrying Abby's rifles and grenade load.

Abby's harness and line passed her on the way up as she came down. She snaked herself into the air duct, passed a rifle to Abby, and wiggled out of her harness while Jack came down. By the time Kris was ready to move forward, Abby was in a larger section of air duct, at a vent.

"Want out of here?" she mouthed to Kris in the dim light from the grille.

Kris shook her head. There could be cameras out there. Or trip wires. Or terrorists walking around. Since they started checking out the center with the heat sensors this afternoon, no one had gone near the air-conditioning vents.

Or was that because they'd already done them?

Kris paused as that thought kicked the tire of her plan . . . and air leaked out. What had those two guys they'd shot this morning been up to? She signaled Jack to hold.

"Get nanos down here," she ordered.

A minute later, they released the nano scouts. Another minute more, and they had identified four trip wires to something.

"Abby, open the vent," and out they went. Penny knew where their own cameras were. They sent out their own nano scouts to search, report back, not destroy. Not so much as breathe.

Slowly, they began a zigzag course through the meeting rooms that brought them up, a hundred meters from the door that led into the exhibit hall that held the hostages a good five minutes before the next comm check with the roof.

Problem was, covering that last hundred meters.

Directly ahead of them in the central gathering area, several tables had been upended. Behind them, heat signatures showed four terrorists asleep. Two were seated in chairs at a table playing cards and glancing every once in a while at security camera feeds or at the wide corridor where Kris and her team lurked in the darker shadows.

Two hundred meters to Kris's left, above a twenty-meter wall, was the upper level. Along its rail, eight rifles showed. Maybe the terrorists behind them were awake. Maybe they slept. No telling from this angle. From the heat intel, Kris knew that there were tables on their sides up there and more shooters. That was why she was down here.

Two hundred meters to Kris's right was a drop down to the lower level. There were gunners there and a whole lot more trouble that would come running up here and hit her from behind, but all hell would have to break loose before she'd have to deal with them.

The sapper signaled the meeting room beside them was safe. Kris handed off her M-6A4 to a corporal, the next-best shooter, and took his M-6. The Sergeant signaled him and a private to hold this area, and Kris entered the meeting room, crossed it quickly, then waited while the engineer crawled across the way to check the next one. Since that put him in full view of the two card players, everyone quit breathing for a while, then quit breathing some more as they did their own trip.

But the card players played on, undisturbed.

That move, with a zig through a service area, brought Kris and her team to an almost unnoticeable workers' access door right next to the wall. A hundred yards away was another one of those small doors that the public ignores but workers put to good use.

Here was the problem she had never solved. If she ran for the door, they'd mow her crew down. If she fought her way there, they'd have time to blow the hostages a dozen times over.

Kris took a deep breath. "Command center, Regal is at Alpha. I would appreciate that demonstration." Hopefully the SWAT teams in their battle suits could distract the upper and lower hall terrorists enough. Kris had learned at OCS that hope was not a plan, but hope was all she had just now.

"Slight change in plans," came on net in Santiago's voice. "Zodiac landers 1 and 2 will engage the hostiles in five seconds, three, two, one."

There was a crashing noise of glass, metal, and whatever else might exist under God's heaven. "Weapons free," Kris shouted.

"Go, go, go," she waved at her team as Abby took off sprinting for the door across the way, a Marine right behind her. Penny and Kris on their heels.

Jack and the Sergeant took a second to drop the card players, then a second more to get two sleeping beauties that reached for their guns instead of keeping on sleeping.

Kris wondered, as she sprinted, if she should worry about what was happening above her, but then a body plummeted from up there and she decided maybe the *Halsey* and all that noise was taking care of that.

Ahead of her, Abby slowed to let the Marine take the door for her, roll through it, and shout "Hostages, stay down."

Abby raced through the open door, shot, hopped over the Marine, dropped, rolled, fired again, then repeated the process.

Kris slammed to a halt at the door, her rifle ready. Someone was up, firing at the space above where Abby was rolling.

Kris fired a long burst. The first few rounds to shatter ceramics. The later ones to do their worst. They did. Her target went down.

Penny went through the door without slowing down, headed for the explosive charges along the wall, and started yanking exposed antennas, detonators, whatever looked like it might stop the boom. Since any one of the packets could go boom in her face as she raced by, Kris could only admire the courage of a woman fighting for her bridegroom's life.

Someone across the room raised a rifle, aimed at Penny. Kris fired a long burst. The rifle went one way, the gunner rolled another way and lay still.

"Tom, stay down," Kris ordered. "Where are the terrorists?"

A familiar figure elbowed himself up to look around. "I

think you have most of them. Four bolted for the back exit." He nodded to where a door was wide open in the south wall.

"Command center," Kris called on net, "Look for four terrorists attempting to escape from the loading dock."

"We have their van in our sights. They won't get out of the parking lot."

Beside Kris, the sapper came through the door, took in what Penny had done, nodded, and headed for the opposite wall and its charged explosives. Kris would be writing a lot of medal recommendations for this night.

"Could we start moving these people out to safety?" Princess Aholo called from where she lay between Tom and, yep, there was Sam. Kris signaled for Abby and all available Marines to form on her as she trotted to the Island princess.

"At the moment, Aholo, this may be the safest place in town," was backed up by a burst of automatic weapons fire from outside. "We're working on securing the rest of the building, but . . ." Kris left the rest unsaid.

"Can I talk to Grandmama?"

KRIS, I HAVE HELD A CIRCUIT OPEN FOR HER, BUT THERE'S A PROBLEM. Kris found herself put through to Dr. Kapa'a'ola.

QUEEN HA'IKU'LANI TOOK THE NEWS OF THE HOSTAGE SITUATION WELL. SHE SMILED A MOMENT AGO, WHEN WE TOLD HER THE PRINCESS WAS SAFE, THEN GOT A QUEER LOOK ON HER FACE AND TOLD US SHE THOUGHT SHE WAS HAVING ANOTHER STROKE. WE'RE TESTING FOR IT, BUT WE WON'T KNOW FOR A WHILE. COULD YOU GET AHOLO HOME . . . FAST?

"Better yet," Kris told Aholo, "there's a shuttle at the airport, we'll get you to her within the hour."

"What's wrong?" The girl went pale beneath her tattoos.

Kris swallowed several lies . . . and told Aholo the truth. A murmur ran through the hall. Sam tried to hug Aholo, but the plastic restraints had them cuffed to each other in circles of five or six facing out. No hugging allowed. Abby produced a knife and started cutting them loose. Now Sam was hugging a softly crying Aholo, and Penny was hugging Tom, and Kris didn't care who was crying there. She spotted Sergeant Li.

"Sergeant, secure this area. Don't let anything happen to that princess. Jack, you're with me." Abby handed off her knife and fell in step with them as they headed for the common area.

Rifles at the ready, they crossed back into what had been a shooting gallery. It looked quiet for the moment. Kris hunched down, prepared for appearances to be deceiving. "Captain Santiago, you available on net and have a second to chat?"

There was a series of grenade explosions from the upper level. "Now I do. What's happening?"

Kris filled her in. There was a pause when she was done. "Liberty launch 2 could do a suborbital to drop you into Nui Nui in thirty minutes. We'll have to send the gig down to refuel it, but no problem."

"Captain, I'd like to thank you for the support here, and I'd be honored if you'd accompany us to Nui Nui."

"Glad to back up a well-ordered plan, Lieutenant Longknife. And I'd be honored to go with you. Ensign Konti, police up this area, cooperate with the local officials to the maximum possible, and see that the Marines don't break anything more."

"Yes ma'am," came over the net.

Kris remembered being the Boot Ensign and getting those orders. She hoped Konti enjoyed them as much she had. Back in the hall, the hostages were milling around. To soft cheers, Kris announced that their building was now safe, and they'd be going in just a moment. But one man righted a table and climbed atop it.

"Hold it, hold it. Queen Ha'iku'lani is dying, murdered as much by these . . . unspeakables . . . as any of our colleagues who were gunned down." He looked around at the former hostages. "I don't know about you, but I came here with a pretty good idea of what we really needed to do. No expectation that we could do it. No idea how we'd get the will to do it. You know what I mean?"

A lot of heads nodded.

"Well, I'm mad. I'm mad at having a gun shoved in my face. I'm mad at seeing my friends murdered. I'm even mad at seeing Islanders I've argued with for twenty years gunned down. I say we came here to do a job. I say we do it. I've got proposals, ideas for how to reorganize Hikila over there in my computer." He pointed at a collection of personal effects like wallets, purses, and computers dumped in a corner. "I bet a lot of you do."

"You bet." "Of course." "Who doesn't," answered him.

"Let's give Queen Ha'iku'lani a burial gift the likes our ancestors will be praising long after we're gone."

"Can we at least go to the bathroom?" came plaintively.

"And order in some food."

"Fifteen minutes," the guy said. "A real fifteen-minute break," he insisted.

Aholo shook her head. "That man has no idea what the line will be like at the ladies' room."

"Who *is* he?"

"He's the mayor of Brisbane," Sam told them. "But my dad's right there with him, and he was cuffed to two of your chief adviser's, Aholo, and I saw them talking. I think this is real."

"You are coming with us," Aholo said to Sam.

"I'm not leaving your side. Ever."

And when the kids asked how Mommy and Daddy met, Kris could just imagine the story.

THERE ARE POLICE CARS WAITING TO TAKE US TO THE AIRPORT, Nelly said. Kris formed her Marines to escort the princess one last time.

"Nelly, you remember those tattoos you put me in of Pacific Island warriors?" Kris said.

"Yes, I do. They were quite fierce."

"Think you could turn our black camouflage paint to that?" Kris asked, a grin spreading across her face.

"You bet," Nelly said, and a wave passed down the line

of Kris's rescue team. As they made their way gingerly around the wreckage the Zodiac lander had made of the west entrance, the media lights came on to show Princess Aholo on the arms of two attractive young men and escorted by the most ferocious bunch of practically naked tattooed Island warriors, rifles at the ready. All except one.

Kris's fierceness was somewhat spoiled by her cute bunny white tail.

Liberty launch 2 ran itself right up onto the beach before it popped its hatch. A cart was waiting for them, and in less than an hour from the last shot, Aholo and Kris's team, Santiago included, were in the queen's presence.

"Is this Sam?" was the queen's first question.

"This is the one, Grandmama," Aholo said, putting her hand in her great-grandmother's.

With an effort, the old woman reached across with her other hand to take the young man's hand and pulled it forward to rest on Aholo's. "May the sun and the sea smile upon the two of you and your children," she said, then lay back exhausted.

The two youths knelt beside her bed, young hands in hands, resting on the withered parchment of a hand that had seen so much of human history.

"And you, Princess Longknife, you have found your warrior's face, I see," the queen said, rousing herself. Kris knelt by the other side of the bed and took that ancient hand. But the queen squinted into the shadows. Kris wondered what she sought.

"Aren't you a Santiago?" the queen whispered.

"Sandy Santiago. I skipper the *Halsey,*" its Captain said as she came to kneel beside Kris.

"Oh, good. So Kris has found a Santiago to save her ass. With a good person like you to cover her back, maybe she'll live to be as old as that rascal Ray."

"I'll see what I can do," Sandy said in promise.

The eyes closed. The breathing slowed and became

irregular. The wrinkled hands would have collapsed back onto the bed were they not held by loving hands on both sides.

KRIS, I AM GETTING A CALL FROM THE MAYOR OF STAN-LEY. THEY HAVE BEEN TRYING TO GET A CALL THROUGH TO THE QUEEN, BUT THE DOCTOR WILL NOT PUT THEM THROUGH. HE SAYS HE THINKS HA'IKU'LANI WILL DIE HAPPY IF SHE HEARS THIS.

"Your Majesty, can you hear me?" Kris whispered.

There was a fluttering of eyelids.

"We freed the hostages, but the delegates insisted on staying to do what they came to do, giving Hikila a new government, one that will last." Was that a smile adding to the lines on the old woman's face?

"Would you like to hear what they have done?" Behind Aholo, the doctor was waving, *No, no*. Eyelids seemed to flutter *Yes*.

Kris raised an eyebrow and a question to Aholo. Tears ran down the princess's face as she nodded. NELLY, PUT THEM THROUGH.

"Your Highness," the mayor of Brisbane began softly and without preamble, "we assembled here are proud to present you with a first draft of our efforts. There will be many devils to tame in the details, but we propose to structure our government around ports. Thirty ports in the Islands and seventy on the Mainland. We will have two bodies in our legislature. The House will be elected based on population, but each port will have at least one representative. The Senate will have two people elected from each port and must approve all important votes by 60 percent.

"We recognize that such a distribution does not guarantee that the Islands can block something they strongly oppose. We have agreed to give the queen a veto of any legislation that she thinks goes to the heart of the Island culture for twenty years. A mere majority vote can continue that veto in twenty-year increments. We hope this meets your wishes."

Aholo squeezed Sam's hand and her queen's. "I doubt

that I will ever have need of exercising that authority," she whispered, her voice choked her with contesting emotions.

The smile seemed to deepen, but then the mouth fell open, and it was clear that the deathwatch had begun.

"The queen, my mother's grandmother, smiles her thanks, but now I beg you leave us to a very private time."

The Brisbane Constitutional Assembly bowed off-line with expressions of sympathy. Kris watched Aholo for a sign that she was included in that dismissal, but none came. Her own father's grandfather had sent her here to hold a war buddy's hand.

God knew, Kris had killed men and women in the last year. She'd watched the results of what she'd done and, while it turned her stomach, she regretted none of it.

But this was different. Old and failing, still the queen's body refused to give up the fight for each breath, each heartbeat. Kris found herself wanting to refuse the finality of this, to order the doctor forward, to do something, anything.

Through it all, Aholo knelt there, tears softly making their way down her cheeks. Finally, she bent to kiss a cheek. "Go, Grandmama. Go to the sea where the wind is always fair and the sun never fails."

THE funeral was the next day, with all local Islanders in attendance. The funeral bier was Afa's canoe. Since the tradition of just setting the body to drift on the sea tended to draw sharks, the Islanders had borrowed a page from another book and included firewood on the canoe. They fired it as it drifted out of the lagoon and let it burn.

The queen's head, of course, was handed over to the elder women for honors. On the anniversary of her death, Queen Aholo would install it with her own hands in the niche reserved for it in the Long House.

Kris did attend the coronation of Queen Ha'iku'aholo . . . both coronations. One at Nui Nui and a second at Port Brisbane before the Constitutional Assembly, where there were still demons of various size and nastiness being wrestled to the ground and dehorned. It was agreed that the vote to approve the new constitution and join United Sentients would be on the same ballot.

Kris attended the coronations as a representative of United Sentients, in dress whites. She found herself looking at the Islanders longingly and pulling on her choke collar more than once. She was also there when Queen Aholo explained to Sam's dad that the simple blessing that her grandmama had passed over them was all that was needed for a wedding among the Islanders.

Aholo demonstrated superb diplomacy when she had a more traditional Mainland wedding appended to her Mainland coronation. There wasn't a dry eye in the Brisbane Convention Center, the only place large enough to hold the show.

There being something contagious about weddings, before Aholo's, Kris found herself with Afa explaining to the young man that she really appreciated his offer to move with her to the Big Island and accept her as a business partner, but she really wasn't prepared, just now, to marry him . . . "or anyone else."

"My good name is slandered on Wardhaven. I have to return to face those charges," Kris reminded him.

"Maybe you'll come back then."

She left it at that.

The voyage back to Wardhaven was almost fun. The *Halsey*'s crew was in full celebration mode. Clearly, they ruled. Their time, from drop to last shot, if you started the clock from when the Zodiacs hit, had to be the best, rated per dead terrorist body, that anyone had done in eighty years. And since it had been a Navy *and* Marine team, the whole crew was riding high.

Kris got the skipper's approval on the scope and range of her medal proposals before she had Nelly start the write-ups, then when Nelly finished so well, and so soon, offered to have Nelly pitch in on the rest. Kris had yet to meet a Naval officer who enjoyed paperwork, so it was no surprise when Sandy jumped at the help.

That left them more time to join in the wardroom talks over coffee. Now, nothing was off limits, and all topics were fun.

But Kris saved the most tactful one for a drop by the captain's private cabin. "Why'd you chose to back me up?"

Sandy put aside a reader. "You had a good plan."

"I had a good plan when I left the ship. Why did you wait to back me up until I was standing there at the gate of hell?"

The *Halsey*'s skipper took in a deep breath and blew it out. "Because I needed to see if you were just good at shoving my sailors out there onto the tip of the spear or if you'd be out there yourself, leading the way. You may have noticed lots of people can talk the talk. Don't meet many who match it with the walk, do you?"

"No," Kris agreed. "But it sure would have saved me a bit of tummy lining if I'd known you were coming. Might have had Abby bake you a cake."

"With what in it? Who is that woman?"

Kris shrugged.

"And besides, who says I'm supposed to worry about your stomach ulcer? As I recall, my great-grandpappy didn't give yours much warning before he walked off with that bomb for President Urm. You big people got to realize that you aren't the only ones making plans. Us little folks make plans, too. And sometimes we are going to surprise you."

"You came up with one hell of a learning experience."

"Well, you are one of those Longknifes. Anything gentler, and it would have gone right by you."

Kris chose not to argue that point as Sandy dug in her desk drawer. "I have something here for you." She handed Kris a paper form. It was a reference for an application to the Academy. "I told you my daughter's applying this year."

Kris nodded.

"I also told you that I didn't want her getting another reference from Ray. Two generations was enough. It was time for a change."

Again Kris nodded.

"I would be honored if you would provide my daughter with a reference. A new generation deserves a new generation."

Kris could think of several replies. She didn't know the girl, but then neither did Grampa Ray. Grampa Ray was a king. Kris was just a Lieutenant. But Santiago knew that. And knowing it, she wanted Kris to sponsor her daughter. Kris replayed that last sentence and wasn't sure which "new generation" deserved who. "I'd be honored, Captain."

The last jump brought news from Wardhaven. Kris's plea for help from Olympia had brought it forth in legion measure. Ester Saddik hit the talk shows the night her ship docked. For those who liked their explanations full and complete, Ester, Kris's first Olympia employee, gave them in her calm, pleasant voice, backed up by the warehouse foreman, that nice Quaker, Jeb Salinski.

For those who preferred their input loud and contentious, Ester turned loose rancher Brandon Anderson and farmer Jason McDowell. Those two still had enough anger in them to scorch carbon steel. What they did to Lieutenant Pearson on the one show where she showed up to explain that her procedures for documenting the release of food aid were simple and easily applied left the woman and her rules hanging in shreds. And 3/c Spens, Kris's stand-in accountant, had managed to arrange his discharge on Olympia . . . there was a local girl involved. He did an amazing job of holding people's interest as he walked them through his simple accounting system for tracking aid, and Kris's just-released tax return for last year.

The opposition was on the ropes when suddenly it was found that the charges were technically in error, and therefore, based on that technicality, had to be dismissed.

"Does that technically mean I no longer work for a criminal?" Abby asked.

"I guess so. That make you feel better?"

Abby seemed blasé. But Kris arrived at High Wardhaven feeling pretty upbeat. As she saluted and led her small detachment across the gangplank of the *Halsey,* she asked Nelly to check on where her family was. Quickly, her computer ran down most everyone's present location, finishing with ". . . and your mother is at Madame Bovaine's Bridal Boutique."

"What's she doing there?"

"Kris, Penny, do you mind if I go check on the 109?" Tom asked. Kris waved him away. Penny looked like she'd rather follow him, but she waited for Nelly's answer, dread pouring off her like disease off a swamp.

"She appears to be with Penny's mother."

"Jack, Abby, you're with me. Somehow we have to save Penny from my mother."

"Are we allowed to use deadly force?" Abby asked.

Jack shook his head dolefully.

Kris rode the beanstalk down, her gut in more of an uproar than it had ever been when she was going out to rescue Tom or recon Turantic. It hadn't been this bad riding down to tackle the terrorists on Hikila when she had no idea how she'd cross the last one hundred meters under deadly fire.

No. *This* involved *Mother. Death* was *not* an *option.*

They flagged a taxi. The driver took one look at them and looked like he'd rather take any other fare, but he drove them to Madame Bovaine's Bridal Boutique. "Wait here," Kris ordered. "We won't be long."

"I hope," Penny whispered.

Kris led her team in a quick march through the front doors. They advanced five paces into the store and froze.

Mother was looking at a wedding gown.

It was white, so it had to be a wedding gown. It had no veil, but a large floppy hat half covered the model's face, as well she should want it. There was a front to the gown. And a back. No sides. The model was wearing white stockings and a white garter belt. No bra. No panties. Whatever borrowed or blue she had was right out there for all to see.

"Mother, Penny is not wearing something like that."

"Oh, hello, Kristine darling, I was wondering when you might be back. But I was just telling Pamela here that it is all the rage in Paris this year."

"Paula," Penny's mother corrected.

Brides on Nui Nui probably wore less and looked more modest. "Penny is not wearing that. Pick a dress, Penny," Kris said, waving at a wide collection of traditional gowns.

"But they're all lace and frills. She'll look more like the cake than the bride."

"I'll tell Lotty to go easy on the icing," Kris snarled.

Penny and her mother edged their way into the lee of this verbal hurricane behind several mannequins of traditional gowns.

"Well, if you're going to insist on the bride dressing down into something plebeian, I can at least put the bridesmaids into something more appropriate to the moment. After all, *this* wedding is in *my* garden."

"It is *Penny's* wedding. They're *my* friends."

"It is *my* garden. Your *father* is running for his *life*."

After several repeats, which repetitions made sound only more childish, Kris gave in with a sigh she'd been only too well practiced in since oh, about thirteen. "Okay, Mother, bridesmaids' dresses are supposed to look horrible. So what's your entrance into this year's competition? It can't be any worse than the five I've already got in my closet."

Kris was wrong.

The dress the modiste presented with such a wide smile was built very much like a daisy. Now all Kris needed was someone to think of as she plucked each petal, *He loves me, he loves me not.* Course, when she plucked the last one, it looked like she'd be wearing less than she had to Dance up the Moon.

"Mo-ther."

"Daughter, you said I choose the dress. I'm choosing."

And a deal in the Longknife household took a revolution to break. The back of the dress started in the front with spaghetti straps that flared into a gossamer train, hopefully before the cheeks of Kris's rear end were showing. *I was more modestly dressed as a streetwalker on Turantic! And my own mother is doing this to me.* Heather's red hair and milk-white complexion would be breathtaking against the yellow of the dress. And Babs would leak out of it in all the right places. Then there would be beanpole Kris falling out of it in all the wrong places.

Any chance I could talk Penny and Tom into believing that a Wardhaven princess could marry them by just putting their hands in each others'?

Or maybe if I got my ship back. A ship Captain can marry couples. Could a very small ship's Captain?

No, Penny and her mother had spotted a wedding gown and were looking at it with happy eyes. Kris reached for her credit card. Penny had stood with her through hell and more. And Tom even more than that. They were her best friends and deserved the wedding they wanted. And who remembered what bridesmaids wore?

Well, the society page. And Mother would have Adorable Dora covering this wedding. Kris sighed. She was a Longknife, and Longknifes did what had to be done.

Even when it didn't involve killing someone.

7

To Kris's complete surprise—and immense relief—the wedding went off without a hitch. And Mother lived.

Adorable Dora showed up, got her pics, jammed her mike in several faces for sound bites she wanted . . . then vanished. "The Pandoris have a barbecue this afternoon and The Rachael, Super Nova vid star, will be there." Apparently a vid star's face at a barbecue trumped two junior officers' wedding in the Nuu gardens.

Mother went ballistic before spiraling into a pout.

So she missed Chandra's darling five-year-old daughter, Klesa, doing cute perfectly as a flower girl. She walked solemnly down the aisle, taking two steps dutifully before casting each handful of flower petals over her shoulder. She waited until she reached the altar before turning to face the waiting audience, grinning like the angel she was . . . and upended the flower basket.

Klesa's brother succeeded admirably well as the ring bearer, only interrupting the ceremony twice to ask in his soft three-year-old whisper that carried from one end of the garden to the other, "Is it time for the ring, yet?"

Father Mary Ann smiled both times and assured him in that soft, lilting, Irish-Chinese brogue of Santa Maria that "No, not yet. Wait a wee bit more."

With five maid of honor dresses in her closet, Kris was getting to be an expert on weddings. Father Mary Ann and Commander Petrulio did a superb job of concocting a ceremony. Kris drafted the chaplain when Penny's mother's Reformed Methodist minister backed out at the last minute. Seems the Reformed Methodists were in negotiations with Rome for reunion, and doing a wedding two hundred light-years from Earth with a schismatic Santa Marian woman priest put all that at risk. But chaplains follow a different chain of command and, though Penny was willing at the last moment to give up, defy her grandmother, and do it all Tom's way, Tom insisted on someone to hold up Penny's end of the faith bargain. If ever two people deserved a long wedded life, these two did.

With no loss of blood or other noticeable disaster, the padre and priest reached the end of the ceremony, the part that everyone watching surely took for the most important. The two ministers said, "Tom, you may kiss your bride."

He did. A nice kiss, enthusiastically returned by Penny.

The chaplain cleared his throat. "May I present to you Lieutenant junior grade and Lieutenant Lien."

Penny put her arm lovingly in Tom's, and the string quartet began the recessional. Kris would be next, on Phil's arm. The padre and priest corralled the kids under their wings and showed evidence that they could indeed ride herd on them until the adults had left. Father Mary Ann had brought hard candy!

Kris sighed as she put her arm in Phil's. "Any wedding you can stagger away from," she said.

"No casualties so far," he agreed.

Penny and Tom made little progress out. Family on both sides of the aisle offered hands, cheeks, congratulations, advice, whatever it was you said to a young woman on her first day of wedded life. It was also quite possibly the first chance some had to meet Penny. Kris was glad to see Phil was in no rush to get out. He was demonstrating a solid grasp of things that had nothing to do with the Navy. Good man. Kris took the moment of the stalled wedding recession to lean against him. Nice. She wondered how many dances she could hold him to at the reception. In this getup, she ought to be able to attract a dead man.

Mo-ther was that your idea!

And Father's phone went off.

Actually, Kris was amazed that there had been no phone interruptions during the ceremony. With this many politicians in one place, and the elections at their present heat, it was amazing no one had felt the desperate need to interrupt for something or another. She really couldn't fault Father for now pulling out his ear set. Mother shot him a glare that could have burned a battleship, but he failed to notice her.

Father spoke softly for a moment, his words not reaching Kris, then turned away and walked down a garden path bordered by magnolias and lilacs. Other phones buzzed. In a moment, every politician present was distancing him- or herself from the affair and each other to talk to someone else, somewhere else.

Kris frowned. Had the Prime Minister *Pro Tem* had a heart attack, fallen on a banana peel? It would have taken something like that to get all these politicians so excited in lockstep.

"Nelly?"

"Nothing on the regular net. There is a spike on the private net, but I don't know the reason," her computer admitted. Okay, the Prime Minister was still breathing. So what happened?

Kris eyed the back rows where the other Navy contingent sat, the putative intelligence types. With the media circus in full blow, Penny's friends had been advised not to take a prominent role, leaving all the bridesmaids' dresses to the patrol boat skippers. Such luck. Now they were looking at each other, open questions on their faces, but no answers there.

Seated over by herself, Commander Santiago was talking

to someone. Kris pointed her out to the PF skippers. Groomsmen quickly, bridesmaids a bit more slowly lest they lose what little modesty Mother's gowns allowed them, made their way to the Commander. On the way Kris passed three phone conversations. She picked up "warships," "surrender," and "orbital bombardment." That was enough to hurry her along.

Around the Commander, the men stooped close in, letting the women stand in their daisy getups and still see without showing too much. The intel types filled in behind them. No one interrupted Commander Santiago while she continued to listen.

"Keep checking, XO," she finally said. "I got a major contingent of JOs here from the PF Navy about to turn blue. Maybe a few intel weenies to boot who can't stand to have a tin can sailor in the know when they aren't. I better brief them before they get violent. I'll monitor your traffic. Interrupt me if you get something."

The Commander looked around the small circle. "We're in trouble. Six ships exited jump Beta doing a comfortable 1,500 klicks an hour. Their beepers and squawkers are throttled."

Kris hadn't heard that from any of the politicians she'd passed, but then, none of them would understand the implications of that simple statement. Every ship able to do star jumps was built with a transponder that reported its name, owner, and most recent ports of call. The buoys that tracked traffic through the jumps noted the transponder number and used it to control the traffic and by exerting such control, avoiding head-on collisions in the jumps between stars.

For someone to mess with, much less silence, a transponder was a major offense against the transportation regs of the Society of Humanity. At least it had been for the last eighty years. Someone was taking major risks. Someone was willing to take those risks to make sure people didn't know who they were.

To a naval officer, this little said a lot. To the politicians talking on their phones around Kris, it was very unlikely any of them understood what it meant.

"The ships are now in line ahead," the destroyer skipper went on, "doing a constant one-g acceleration. Assuming they flip at midpoint, they will arrive over Wardhaven in ninety-six hours."

"Battle line ahead?" Kris asked.

"They're acting like a battle line," Commander Santiago said. "Sensors report the power plants on all six are dual reactors, GE-6900 class." That brought out a low whistle around the circle. Large passenger liners used dual reactors for safety, never larger than 2200-class output. Six ships with twin 6900-level power generators meant plasma for accelerating a lot of mass and for generating a lot of electricity for lasers.

"Battleships," an intel analyst said. "President-class."

"Or Magnificents."

"Those are all Earth ships."

"Earth ships wouldn't use the Beta jump point. We would have *had* a report of a squadron of Earth battleships boosting around the Rim worlds," an intel Lieutenant insisted.

"Well, someone with six very big ships just came through Jump Point Beta and is demanding we surrender," Sandy said.

"Surrender," echoed around the circle. Kris's mind boggled at the word. Wardhaven didn't surrender! Couldn't surrender.

"And here's something interesting," Sandy went on. "My XO's a history bug. He noticed something familiar about the message they're sending, so he did a search. I bet you intel folks would have spotted it real soon," she said, smiling, "but the words they're broadcasting to demand our surrender are nearly the exact same words we used to demand Turantic's surrender the last time we fought them before Unity put an end to the Rim's squabbling."

"They're taking us back to the bad old days of Rim worlds attacking Rim worlds for reparations?" Kris said.

That was a Dark Age, when worlds fought worlds for no better reason than that they could.

"I said nearly," Santiago pointed out. "The language is the same up to the point where we ordered Turantic to surrender and pay reparations. They demand we surrender, renounce all alliances, and accept occupation."

Kris took a moment to digest that. Phil whistled. "They want us. Lock, stock, and barrel," Kris concluded.

"Looks that way," the destroyer skipper said.

KRIS, I HAVE SOMETHING.

NOT NOW, NELLY.

"What are we going to do about it?" Phil asked.

"What can we do?" Sandy said. "I'm the only warship in port. Your patrol boats, assuming you could take on a squadron of battleships, are cold steel. Even if the interim government was to order something, I don't see what they could."

"How long to get the fleet back?" Phil asked.

An intel type shook her head. "Can't do it fast. The Boynton situation isn't good. If our fleet starts running for here, they risk losing one planet only to get here and find Wardhaven bombarded back to the Stone Age."

"What can we do here?" Kris said, her mind spinning through a hundred different options—none good.

"That empty suit." Her father's bellow carried across the garden. Then again, he hadn't been all that loud. Sometime during the Commander's briefing, the string quartet had fallen silent. Even Tom and Penny had abandoned their families and joined the rear of the Navy crowd around the destroyer skipper.

"That gutless collection of old women in petty coats. I always said the opposition hadn't had a new thought since their grandmothers were born, but Pandori didn't have to prove me right before the entire planet." Kris wondered how much of Father's yelling was for relay to his political base and how much of it was him blowing off steam. From the look of Father's rising red complexion, maybe all of it was for his own blood pressure.

Father kicked a rented chair out of his way as he returned from his walk among the flowers. Said walk apparently had done nothing to soothe him. "Pandori just went public! Went public with an announcement that his government has no policy toward the approaching battleships. No policy for or against surrender for the moment, and he will need to meet with his cabinet immediately to establish one. The man is a rank amateur!

"Any freshman backbencher in the liberal party knows you never, ever, let the news cycle know that you don't know what you're doing. You *always* have a policy. The people elected you to have an answer for *everything*. It may take a few *brief* meetings to refine it to the present *unique* circumstances, but you *always* know what you're doing." Father pounded one fist into the other. "He's as much as admitted he hasn't the vaguest idea what to do about those warships and their demand for surrender."

"He can't surrender," Honovi said.

"Of course he can't surrender. Wardhaven never surrenders." Kris knew that was for party consumption. Around her father, lapel phones were aimed at him. That sound bite would be on the net in moments. Pandori might not know what his policy was, but Father certainly knew his.

Which might not be all that good. If Father wasn't careful, he'd back the Prime Minister *Pro Tem* into a corner, and the two would still be squabbling there when the battleships arrived overhead to smash everything Wardhaven had in orbit. Cut huge swaths through our cities. Honovi moved in close to his father, sought as much privacy as circumstances might allow. Around them, lapel cameras were covered.

"If we can't surrender, Father, how do we fight?"

"That's the problem, Son. Pandori's screwed us into a horrible quandary. Can't defend ourselves. Can't surrender either. So he wants to crawl into a nice, comfortable cabinet meeting and babble to his buddies about what a mess I made for him when he made it for himself. No, Son. We need a full session of Parliament to tackle this one."

"An interim government has never called a session, Father." Honovi chewed his lower lip for a moment, then went on slowly, "If there was a full session, could you call for a vote of confidence in Pandori's policies?"

Father chuckled. "Now you know why the blokes who bring down a government aren't supposed to do any governing, Son. You bet if he calls a session, the first thing I'll put on the table is a vote of no confidence, and it's one he very much deserves. With the mess he's made of things, he won't last five minutes. No, Pandori's caught in a horrible box. He's got four days until those damnable ships show up in orbit. If he announces his policy now, and it's fight, he comes up a cropper with nothing to fight them with. If he raises the white flag now, he has to call the House together to sanction his decision, and he'll fall so far and so fast he'll never reach bottom for the splat."

Father paused, eyebrows coming together thoughtfully. "Maybe he's not so stupid after all. Maybe he's trying to hide behind no policy to avoid having to face what a policy will cost him. But damn it, his policy is going to cost Wardhaven. Dear God, is it going to cost Wardhaven." Still muttering to himself, Father walked off, Honovi right behind him.

"So, what *do* we do?" Babs Thompson asked the circle of Naval officers.

Kris looked down at Mother's ridiculous bridesmaid's dress. "I don't know about you, but I'm getting dressed." Kris twirled the train over her right arm, straightened her back, and with as much dignity as her attire allowed, quick marched for her room.

It took Kris a whole ten seconds to rip off the daisy dress; that was one outfit she'd never wear again. She didn't even want it hanging in her closet. Abby could send it off to some secondhand store. Somewhere there had to be a stripper desperate to take it off for money.

But that left the question of what to put on.

Kris stood, nearly naked, and eyed the Navy side of her closet. She was disgraced. She was relieved of her command. She was only just cleared of charges.

And on Hikila, someone had set her or King Ray up for murder just now. The fleet was at Boynton, and the PFs were cold steel and up for sale. Coincidence?

She chose undress whites.

Carefully pulling on the starched pants, the Order of the Wounded Lion in its open case on the shelf caught her eye. She'd earned it for mutiny. Should she wear it? Exactly what she would do today was still forming in the back of Kris's mind, but no doubt a lawyer at JAG would be stuck reviewing the mutiny section of the UCMJ by sunset.

"Can I help?" Abby asked, surveying with a jaundiced eye the wreckage of the formal gown strewn about the floor. "Add garlic, and that's one dress that ain't never gonna bother no girl again."

"Could you put my ribbons on my whites?" Kris said. "And you have an eye for a fashion statement. See if you can fit the crest of the Order of the Wounded Lion somewhere on the shirt."

Kris concentrated on dressing. Shoes. Shoes were good, and shoestrings needed tying. What was she going to do? Certainly things were a mess. Fleet gone. What was left was outgunned a jillion to one. Even the mosquito boats, assuming you bought the wildly excessive advertising that a dozen of them could take on one battleship, were outclassed. If they could get power up.

The present situation didn't present impossible odds. They were ridiculous. Someone had played Pandori for the tyro he was; Wardhaven was in deep trouble. Way too deep.

There was nothing else to do.

"Isn't that what Longknifes do? Something, when there's nothing else to do," she muttered to herself. As usual, the problem was finding that something.

"You say something?" Abby said.

Kris looked down at herself; she was almost dressed. She turned to Abby. The woman had put the Order of the

Wounded Lion on her left shirt pocket. Normally, that was where her command badge would have gone. Then again, her command badge was gone, so why not put her mutineer's badge there today?

Good omen?

Her maid held the shirt while Kris put her arms in its sleeves, then buttoned it on. "Abby, things are going to get crazy down here. Would you look after Harvey and Lotty? Rose and Honovi? Father, and yes, Mother if you can?"

Abby nodded with a tight smile.

Kris turned to glance in the mirror. It showed the usual Kris: too tall, nose too long, a young woman with no curves to speak of. It also showed a jaw set. Mouth a tight line. Eyes going narrow. Was this a Longknife face? Was this what Grampa Ray looked like as he ordered Iteeche fleets exterminated? She paced the distance to the door. *Do I have the Longknife answers?* she wondered as she opened it.

Outside stood Tom in the dress whites he'd worn for his wedding. Beside him, Penny had somehow traded her fully layered bridal gown and long veil for the much less formal but just as pale undress whites.

They saluted.

"What are your orders, Your Highness?" Tom asked. There were no questions in their eyes. No doubts. Kris searched the two people she'd led through hell and fire. She found only expectation. Damnably confident expectation.

They expected her to reach into some Longknife magic hat and come up with the right answer once again. The right orders that would lead them through fire and hell . . . again . . . and safe out . . . again.

Kris swallowed the lump rising in her throat and returned their salute. "Princess Kristine sends her compliments to the Commodore and asks him at his convenience to hold a council of his boat commanders."

Tom went from saluting Kris with one hand to talking to his other. But only for a moment. "The Commodore sends his compliments and says he will convene a council of his

junior commanders in the wardroom of the *Cushing* at fifteen hundred hours."

Kris glanced at her watch. "An hour and a half. That
ought to be enough time to get up the beanstalk, onto a military base, and aboard a ship I'm not supposed to go near."

"Doesn't sound impossible for a Longknife," Jack said,
ambling down the hall, hands in his pants pockets. "I figured you might find a Secret Service agent useful, even if
he *is* on terminal leave, so I hung around after the wedding
busted up. Penny, I must say, you've set a new standard for
wedding receptions."

"I suspect it will be talked about for years. Should make
Kris's mom happy."

"So, you three need a ride to the elevator terminal? Hope
you don't mind, all I got is a rented beater." Jack grinned.

The beanstalk station was a madhouse, but all the traffic
was headed down and out. Kris and her three brave souls
had the in and up side almost to themselves. Tommy and
Penny had no trouble going through the turnstile using
their ID cards for both authorization and payment.

Kris pulled out her Nuu Enterprises stockholder ID.

"It ain't gonna work," the elderly attendant told Kris. "I
hear they dropped the charges against you, but when I
checked the 'no admit' printout this morning, your name
was still on it."

"Hi, Mary," Kris said to the familiar face who'd
checked her through the gate as often as not for many of
the last ten years. "Joey out of trouble now that I'm back
from Hikila?"

"The new management didn't wait for you to come
back. They gave him a week suspension without pay the
day after he let you through. I told him to talk to the union,
but he said he needed a vacation. He spent the whole week
up on the North Coast. Sent us pictures every day. Every
day with a different pretty girl wearing practically nothing.
I swear he was renting them."

"He does have a nice smile," Kris noted.

"And now you need to get up the beanstalk. I hear we got some noisy company coming."

Kris thought for a second, then decided to lie. "Oh? I hadn't heard."

"And my husband's a great lover. Tell you what I'm gonna do. Why don't you cuddle up close to that nice young man behind you and let him pay his way through, and if you happen to slip through at the same time . . ." She shrugged.

"The security cameras will spot it."

"Hell, young lady, maybe I could use a vacation up on the North Coast. Has to be some nearly naked boys I can rent. And it might be safer than being around here. Certainly will be if you don't get up there and do whatever it is you're up to."

Jack got up close behind Kris. He ran his ID through the charge slip. There were advantages to being taller than the average . . . and not much more than a stick figure. Kris slipped through in step with her agent. They made it to the ferry just as it was locking down.

Getting aboard the Naval station turned out to be even less of a problem. Pandori had sent most of the Marines to Boynton. Newly hired guards at the gate were more concerned with listening to the news and talking about when they'd get off than checking IDs. Kris waved her ID at the scanner. It didn't go beep, but she kept on walking.

They reached the *Cushing* fifteen minutes before the Commodore's staff meeting. Tom offered Kris an update on the 109.

"She's not in very good shape," Tom said as they boarded. "The motor hasn't been run for weeks. That's not good for small matter-antimatter gear. They were ordered to rip out the lasers, but with the fleet gone, they kept getting orders to provide work parties on the base. Truth is, Tran was glad to farm the crew out to details. It kept them from tearing up the boat. I'm not sure, but I think it's been that way with all the other skippers. Hoping that if they weren't sold before the election, your da would win, and we'd be back in business."

In the dim light and borrowed station air, the cold silence of the boat was like a tomb. Kris had come aboard hoping for something to cheer her up, give her hope that there was a way out of this mess that older heads had gotten them into. The feel of her boat, a dead carcass on the beach, did nothing to help.

It was better to face the Commodore.

Kris crossed the brow onto the *Cushing*'s quarterdeck with Tom at her side. The MC1 system announced, "PF-109 arriving," which brought a smile to her face. "Princess Kristine arriving," was a sharp reminder that Tom was still officially PF-109, not her.

She saluted the flag painted on the bulkhead, then saluted the JG standing Junior Officer of the Deck, who returned her salute. Tom and Penny did the same. Jack stood by like a good civilian, looking a bit nonplussed at the solemn Navy ritual.

"The Commodore is waiting for you in the wardroom," the JOOD said and turned to lead them aft. He cast Jack a questioning look over his shoulder as the Secret Service agent, alumni-in-waiting, made to follow.

"I'm with her."

"Humor us," Kris said. "Things are a bit strange."

"And then some," the JG agreed. Two armed Marines stood guard outside the wardroom. Inside, two more Marines took station beside the door. Kris hadn't seen this kind of security since she bucked Captain Thorpe on the *Typhoon*.

The Commodore was seated at the head of the long dining table, a white linen cloth covering it. Six PF skippers sat down the side of the table at his right hand. There was a single seat open on the left across from the door. And another at the foot. Kris nodded Tom toward the 109's seat and took her place at the foot of the table.

As supplicant? Rebel?

In a moment, she would open her mouth, speak the

Word, and forever be branded by what she said. She could do nothing. But Longknifes had never been good at that. Kris weighed her options and decided now was no time to buck tradition.

Jack took over a corner where he could observe the entire room. He and the Marine sergeant exchanged glares, decided both were alpha, and went back to doing whatever it is that security people do when everything is locked down securely. Penny took a chair away from the table but in easy reach at Kris's left.

"I'm glad to see that we have an intelligence officer among us," the Commodore said, starting the meeting with no preamble. "Though I understand congratulations are more in order than requests for data downloads. So you were successful in tying the knot, Lieutenant Lien, before things got interesting."

"I was, sir," Tom said, half standing in place. "May I introduce my wife, Lieutenant Lien, though her name badge is a tad out of date."

Penny blushed in that lovely way of brides. There was a general round of "Hear! Hear!"

Kris waited for silence, then filled it. "Do we know any more about the intruders?"

"No, sad to say," the Commodore growled. "I got more from pumping my returning skippers than my own sources. The command net has gone decidedly unhelpful. It seems a colonel from the general staff made a personal visit to the military facilities on the space station. His verbal orders were to cease any actions that might give offense to the incoming ships. Close down sensor scans, stand down defensive systems, make nice or better yet say nothing in message traffic, what have you." The Commodore gave a diffident wave of his hand and scowled.

"I only know this because I sent my XO to the fleet command center to find out why the net was suddenly so silent. No one felt a need to hand carry any orders to an old scow like the *Cushing*. Anyway, we seem to be rolling over and playing dead. But there's nothing official to that effect."

Kris looked around the table at the other skippers, her peers, the closest she'd come in her adult life to friends. How would they take to what she was about to do? Slowly, she stood.

"Our planet is under deadly threat. We here command the only force capable of standing between those battleships and our families. Our loved ones. While the government talks, searches for a policy, we have been asked to stand down. Do nothing." Kris shook her head slowly.

"We are warriors. We know that if we are called to battle in four days, we need every second to prepare for that fight." There were nods around the table. Not all. Not all were from Wardhaven. Would they recognize this was their fight? Kris took in a deep breath, held it for a second, and took the plunge.

"I am Princess Kristine Anne Longknife. By right of blood, by right of name, by right of title, I am assuming command of this squadron, effective this date. Do any of you contest my claim and right?"

For a long moment, the skippers just stared at her. Here and there an eyebrow raised. If anyone, it was Phil and Chandra who seemed the closest to frowning at her coup de main. The Commodore's face was standard Navy issue unreadable.

And the door opened. Commander Santiago pushed past the Marine guards. "Have I missed anything important?" she said as she pulled up a chair and sat down at the Commodore's elbow.

"Only the princess here announcing she's taking command of my squadron," the Commodore half grumbled.

"Oh, only that. Good, then I'm not too late," Santiago said, then turned to Kris. "So, Princess Longknife, how are we going to fight those bastards?"

Kris blinked. She'd expected opposition. Argument. Compromise. Anything but this. Anything but having to come up with an answer right now.

"With everything we've got," Kris said. "And everything we can lay our hands on in the next three days."

"Not a bad start," the destroyer skipper agreed.

"Are you going along with her?" Phil asked, incredulity dripping from his voice to puddle on the deck plates.

Santiago eyed him. "Phil, Phillip Taussig. You're Admiral Taussig's boy, right?"

"Yes ma'am."

"Listen, Lieutenant, we've got a first-class mess here. Don't you agree?" Phil nodded. "The politicians, God bless 'em, got faked out of their socks and are presently hunting for a new pair. When they finally decide what to do, odds are, it will be to drop this hot potato into our delicate fingers.

"As I see it, we can follow someone's idea of orders and do nothing, or we can use the legal fiction of Princess Longknife here, and do something. Three days hence, what we do with the next hours just might save our lives. Me, given an option of hiding behind some unwritten orders left by some gutless wonder from the general staff or hiding behind Princess Longknife's legal coattails . . ." The Commander shrugged.

"I'll take my chances with a Longknife. Especially since I suspect that when we head out for those battleships, we'll be following in her wake. You will be leading us, Your Highness."

"Damn right I will," Kris said. There were times when princesses did not mind their language.

Her words went around the table. They answered a lot of the doubt behind the eyes, but not all. Kris had to have them behind her all the way. "Wardhaven is my home. I'm fighting for everything I love. Some of you are from Pitts Hope, Santa Maria, elsewhere. You could say this isn't your fight." No one nodded agreement with her, but she could see some think it.

"For better or worse, Wardhaven is in this mess because we went to the aid of a planet in trouble. Now we're the one in trouble. We have to fight together, side be side, all for one. If we don't, the ones who pulled the strings at Boynton, at Wardhaven, will be pulling the strings at Pitts Hope, Lorna Do, Turantic, next month. Next year. We take our stand now, together, or there soon may be no place to stand at all."

"Go tell the Spartans," Heather Alexander sighed. "I knew there was a reason I hated history class."

"It's not fair," Babs said. "These odds are—"

"Lousy," Kris agreed. "I know. And all we've got is our twelve boats."

"And my *Halsey,*" Sandy pointedly added.

"Don't forget the *Cushing,*" the Commodore said. "If the old reactor isn't good for one more high-speed run, I'll have the snipes out pushing." That got a smile from the PF skippers.

"And the target decoys," Kris said.

"Target decoys?" came from both the senior Navy types.

"Not as battleships, but maybe if we dialed them down to look like light cruisers and the destroyers towed them, they could draw some of the intruders' fire."

"Anything that has them waste a few shots isn't a wasted effort for us," the Commodore agreed.

"Every shot not aimed at the PFs increases our chances of getting our hits in," Kris said. Now, despite herself, she was grinning. "We've got three days to do what we can to improve the odds. The Nuu shipyard is right next door. If Grampa Al won't open it wide for us, I'll find another way to get around, under, or over the fence. Chandra, you've talked about putting rockets on the boats. Using the Foxer launchers for something deadly."

"You think we could get access to the Army's new AGM-944 high-acceleration rockets?" the mustang asked.

"Has to be some way. Last time I checked, the Army was on the same side as us," Santiago said.

For a second there was brightness behind Singh's dark eyes; then she shook her head as if to recover from a dream. "Our engines are cold steel. Our motors have been shut down for nearly four weeks. We don't know if our electronics are still good. These boats were not intended for storage, not without preparation, and the way we got shut down, they got none."

"Then we'd better start testing them, finding out their problems, and getting them back on-line," Kris said. "We commissioned these boats. We can recommission them."

"In three days?" Ted Rockefeller said.

"In less, if we have to," Kris snapped. "There's a whole shipyard over there. If it can't be had at Nuu Docks, it ain't been invented yet. They got it, you want it, it's yours."

"And who's paying?" the Commodore asked.

"You leave Grampa Al to me."

"And don't I think I'm getting the easy job here, just a boat to put back together with tape and glue and bubble gum," Tom said, brogue and grin back in place.

"I don't think there *are* any easy jobs," Heather said.

"I will recall all temporary work details from the Naval base," the Commodore said, standing and bringing the meeting to a close. "Captains, I want a full report on the status of your boats no later than oh eight hundred tomorrow. Princess Kristine, can you tell me by the same time what resources Nuu Docks will make available?"

"Yes," she answered, noting the delicate way the Commodore issued orders to his usurper. Just once, she'd like to go into battle with a chain of command that wasn't Swiss cheese. She wondered if that kind of a fight might actually be fun.

8

Kris wanted to bury herself in getting the 109 into fighting order. What she knew she had to do was find the manager of Nuu Enterprises on station and see just how far she could bluff him. "Jack, you're with me. We're borrowing the *Cushing*'s station runabout. Penny, you want to tag along with Tom. The 109's new intel station needs checking out."

"You don't see a problem, me being on Tom's boat?" Penny said, her eyes following her husband of only a few hours.

"Don't see why not. And the 109 may need someone soon to do that battle intel job you did for us off Turantic."

"Yes," Penny said, worrying her full lower lip. But she set her shoulders and hurried after her new husband.

Kris turned to Jack. His eyes followed Penny with a sad smile. "Some honeymoon those two are getting," he said.

"At least they're together. Now, speaking of together, I need for you to sneak me through the gate at Nuu Docks."

"Shouldn't your stockholder's IDent do that for you?"

"Rather not leave a trail. Remember, I'm not up here, as far as the local net is concerned."

"So I'll just talk my girl in there," Jack promised. But that turned out to be easier said than done. The guard there was not a newly hired rent-a-thug. The clear-eyed bantam brunet sported a sleeve with corporal strips and two service hash marks for six years plus on the job. She listened to Jack's song and dance . . . smiled . . . and called a supervisor.

The sergeant sported a scowl. And five service hash marks, three good conduct medals, and several more medals for sharpshooting that added emphasis to the automatic slung at her waist. Her right hand never got very far from its well-worn grip.

She cut off Jack's bit of fiction fast. "You're Jack Montoya. You were Kris Longknife's Secret Service agent before the latest brouhaha," she said, consulting her clipboard.

She eyed Kris. "And you don't want to show me any ID."

"I would prefer not to."

The sergeant's frown deepened. "You understand this is a secure area, governed by forty eleven laws passed by several parliaments not all of which were run by Longknifes."

"Yes." Kris nodded.

"Princess Kristine, I could lose my stripes for letting you in, but I'm going to assume that you've got a good reason for what you're doing and it don't include messing with my already miserable day."

"I do, and it doesn't," Kris said simply.

"Okay, you may pass," the sergeant said, then turned to the other guard. "Corporal, what you just saw, you forget. You don't talk about it tonight to no one. When it hits the newsies, you express surprise. And you suck it for all the free beers you can get a few years from now."

But as Jack drove around the corner, Kris glanced back. Now the sergeant was following her with her eyes, and talking to thin air . . . or someone on net.

Jack drove straight to the admin center. It was a Saturday, and battleships were inbound; Kris didn't expect to see much activity. So she was surprised to find every fourth desk busy. The work on the *Firebolt*'s drive had taken her to the dock superintendent's office, so she walked straight to it.

It was empty, but the deputy superintendent's office was next, and the door was open. She entered to find him head down over a cluttered desk. She rapped the doorjamb for attention.

"You made good time," he said without looking up.

"Not a lot of traffic."

"You should see this place at shift change Monday."

"What will it be like this Monday?"

He looked up. "Now that is an interesting question. How should I address you, Shareholder, Princess, Lieutenant?"

Good man, rather than assume he knew her, or worse, force her into his own pigeonhole, he asked. "Princess at the moment. Shareholder if I have to be. What do you know of the situation?"

"Nothing that I much like. Battleships headed our way, threatening to turn my place of employment into drifting space junk. Present political lash-up is running around in circles. Military seems to have been told to stand down, don't do anything that eliminates political options. Did I miss anything? By the way, would you like to sit down? You too, Agent Montoya."

"Got it all in one," Kris said, moving toward the offered chair. Jack shook his head and remained at the door where he had a better view in all directions.

A small wooden sign, half buried on the desk, identified its occupant as Roy Buanifanesto. When he stood to offer Kris a hand, he came up short a foot on her and appeared comfortably middle-aged. Hand shaken, he sat back in his chair, put his feet up on the desk, his hands behind his head, and smiled. "So, what are we going to do while Roma burns and Nero's grandkids fiddle?"

"Keep more of Rome from burning, if we can," Kris

said. "There's a dozen fast patrol boats docked over at the Navy base."

"The mosquito fleet Pandori says are toys for playboys?"

"They need to be brought up to fighting trim. Fast."

Roy pursed his lips. "Small matter-antimatter motors. How are they running?"

"Cold steel."

"Ouch. Properly mothballed?"

"Turned off like a light switch. After all, nobody needed those stinking playthings," Kris mimicked the bad press.

"Double ouch. You'll need to get them over here for work."

"That's not going to happen. Nothing we do can look hostile to the battleships coming in or the politicians on the ground."

"Oh, right. That general stand down order. We don't have much military work in the yard just now. Anything that could be gotten out was rushed off to Boynton, and we're kind of trying to put all the pieces back together of what we begged, stole, or borrowed to get them there. You're telling me we're back in the beg, steal, and borrow business again, but pianissimo," he said, bringing two fingers together softly.

"Very quietly."

"Who pays?"

Kris knew that question had to come next. If it hadn't, the shareholder in her would have had to recommend the man be fired. Still, the princess in her wouldn't have minded him bringing it up later. "Do you have a secure line to Grampa Al?"

"I suspect he's waiting to find out why you were sneaking into the yard with no data trail. Computer, is Mr. Longknife on-line?" A holographic image of Grampa Al appeared over one of the few clear places on Roy's desk.

"Hi Grampa," Kris said.

"I won't say it's nice to see you. You only seem to pop up when you want to cause me trouble," said Alex Longknife, paternal grandfather to Kris and the wealthiest man on Wardhaven. Probably one of the ten richest men in human space.

"You really should organize some family picnics or beach parties so we can get together for some quality time."

"And where would the quality be in wasting time with my father or my son?" Kris could agree with him where her father was concerned. What it was between him and Grampa Ray was something she couldn't even begin to grasp.

"You know we have a problem?"

"Looks like the Peterwalds have got some Greenfeld warships headed our way, and that bunch of dunderheads at Government House have really screwed up this time."

"You know it's the Peterwalds. I'd heard that the ships weren't sending any IDs."

"They aren't. But who else would put together that problem on Boynton and turn out my son's government? I'll bet you when things are done that we'll find some Peterwald money behind several of those votes that turned at the last moment. I should have known it." Which left Kris wondering if Grampa Al ever paid for any particular votes he wanted. Hmm.

Kris shrugged. "Whoever the battleships belong to, they need to be stopped. You don't happen to have a few spare battlewagons stashed anywhere in the yard, do you?" When last they'd talked, Grampa Al had bragged about making his own personal world safe and secure. Making himself untouchable. Living on a world run by Peterwalds didn't sound all that safe for a Longknife. Definitely not for Kris Longknife.

"No. Something I've overlooked. One has to expect that you'll get something back for your taxes."

"I'm going to lead the PF squadron out against the intruders," Kris said.

"You can't. That's suicide."

"I think the odds are better than that. I'd like to make them better still. The boats are in cold storage. They need some quick maintenance. Can we call on Nuu Docks?"

"You can have anything Nuu Docks has." The hologram image turned toward the deputy, "Roy, you hear, they can have anything they need." Then the image was back, eye to eye with Kris. "But only, Kris, *only* if you agree not to go out with them."

"Grampa, I can't."

"Why not? You're not going to tell me that you're the only person who can skipper a fast whatever-that-thing-is. There are other skippers. They've got deputies or assistants backing them up. I pay to get the boats back up and running. I get to keep my granddaughter out of this damn crazy shoot-out."

Kris blinked. Good Lord, Grampa Al made it sound so logical. He'd trade his money for her life. Simple negotiations. For a second she wanted to say yes.

Only for a second. She saw herself on the dock, standing maybe with Chandra's kids, waving bye to their mom. Kids did that. And civilians like Chandra's husband.

Lieutenants did not.

Not Lieutenants who commanded one of those boats.

"Sorry, Grampa. No deal. Like everyone else, the boats had orders to stand down and make nice-nice. I've already invoked Princess to take command of the entire squadron. To order these preparations. If I don't lead them, they don't go."

"God damn it, young woman, you're sounding like my father."

"Sorry, Grampa, it's the only way."

"That's what he'd always say. 'It's the only way.' Damn, damn, damn. Just once, I'd like to see someone come up with another way."

"I know a whole squadron full of folks who'd love to see someone come up with another way," Kris said. "Besides, Grampa Al, if you buy me out, what are you going to tell Gates and Rockefeller and Alexander next time you see them? They aren't getting a chance to buy their sons, their daughter out of this."

The hologram of Grampa Al looked away for a long

moment. When he looked back, he looked very old. "Roy, my yacht is tied up somewhere up there. It's got defensive lasers of some sort or another. Get it out of wherever it is, shanghai a crew for it, and let the princess here use it for anything she can dream up. Talk to the captain of my yacht. He may know the skippers of other armed yachts who aren't bugging out for other planets. Maybe Wardhaven isn't as defenseless as some people think."

"Yes, sir."

"Call back anyone you need to work on the boats. Give the princess here anything she wants. Do it carefully; the last thing we want is to have the newsies sniffing around. We have to keep it quiet from those damn gunboats and from what passes for a government down here."

"Yes, sir."

"Thank you, Grampa. That's very—"

"Patriotic of me," Grampa Al snorted. "It isn't just you folks in uniform who believe in what the flag stands for. We all do, just in different ways. Oh, Roy, keep a running tab on what this all costs. If my son gets his act together and wins this election, we can probably get his government to pay for this."

"Yes, sir," Roy said, looking a bit embarrassed at Kris. But only a bit. He was a businessman.

"Anything else?" Grampa Al asked.

"Nothing I can think of. If I do, I'll have Roy call you."

"My boss is on vacation. Should I call him back?"

Al's hologram shook his head. "If he comes back, we'll be raising a red flag. No, Roy, you get to handle this one. Enjoy it. You'll be working directly with a young, hot-blooded Longknife. You got any boys her age and marriage high?"

"No sir, I just married off the last boy."

"Lucky man. Now, if you don't mind, I have to liquidate some real estate holdings a certain busybody pointed out that I own. Amazing what pops up when someone goes digging."

"Sorry about that," Kris said.

"I doubt you are. Do you really think it will make any difference to the people living there who owns them once I've sold my holdings?"

"You could keep them and improve their condition."

"Survive this crazy charge of yours and drop by my place. We'll spend some quality time with me explaining to you the marketing realities that make slums happen."

"I'll do that," Kris said as the hologram collapsed.

Roy sat up in his chair. "We just had to redo the bathroom on the boss man's yacht, so I have the specs on my own computer. Won't have to access any database, raise any flags. Now, Your Highness, let's go see what we can do for your squadron."

"Let me drive," Roy said, slipping into the front seat of the runabout. Instead of heading for the front gate, he headed elsewhere. "I bet we can open Gate 5," he said as he drove a large six-lane street that headed straight for a four-meter-high fence that loomed between the Navy base and Nuu Yards. As they approached, a gate started rolling open.

"Yep, Navy forgot to lock down their side." Roy flashed a smile. "Guess the new hired security missed a check box once we closed down the gate on our side." Well, at least Kris wouldn't have to fake her way through the main gate again.

In the *Cushing*'s wardroom was another surprise. Poring over readers with the Commodore and Commander Santiago was Captain van Horn, the Navy station commander. He looked up, took in Kris with Roy at her side, and scowled as if they'd committed a particularly aromatic social blunder.

"We used to have mines in orbit," the Commodore was saying. "I remember them being removed, thirty years back, as a hazard to navigation in peacetime. Are they in storage somewhere?"

"They were," Captain van Horn said. "Sometime before I took over the station, they were sold as overage and dangerous. I think they were turned into fertilizer."

"Oh," said both commanders.

"You're back," the Commodore said, spotting Kris.

"Grampa Al was available and authorized full cooperation by Nuu Docks," Kris said.

"Though he would prefer if she were left on the pier when these boats sail on their suicide mission," Roy pointed out.

"Hurrump," van Horn said. "So you'll lead, Sandy?"

Santiago ignored the question. "What'll it be, Long-knife?"

Kris swallowed. Was it pride, folly, a death wish driving her? "I sail on the 109."

"Assuming she sails," the Commodore said.

"Boat got a problem?" Roy asked with an eager grin.

"Total failure in the magnetic containment field."

"No problem," Roy said, bringing his commlink up. Then stopped. "You got a runner that you can send to the yard?"

"Enlisted. Officer. My XO if necessary?"

"Your XO, if you don't mind. I've got a new deputy running the Planning and Estimations Branch. I'll have him get over here with everything he's got awake, clean, and sober this afternoon."

"Helen," the Commodore hollered.

A gray head, another retread back from retirement, appeared in the wardroom doorway. "You bellowed, sir."

"Shag it over to the yard. Planning and Estimations. Wake their boss, his crew, and tell him his boss wants him over here five minutes ago."

"On my way," Helen said with a half salute.

"I've got your runabout," Jack said. "I just came from there. I can probably get you there and back fastest."

"Take you up on that," Helen said, and they both were gone.

"So the PF skippers aren't waiting until morning to let you know their status," Kris said, joining the circle.

"Not for show stoppers," the Commodore said. "I got four boats so far with major problems: 109 and 105 engines, 103's laser capacitors, and 102 started tearing out its lasers."

"We can manage all that," Roy said.

"Grampa Al also donated his armed yacht," Kris said.

"So you can lead from the lap of luxury," van Horn growled.

"No," Kris said. "But I wondered if the target drones might be a bit more persuasive if their gear was working from a gunned yacht rather than towed behind a destroyer?"

"There'd be more power for the jammers and maskers," the Commodore said, rubbing his chin.

"The yacht's two small 12-inch burst lasers are pretty distinctive and not much use at long range," Kris said.

"We could add some 4-inch secondaries I have lying around the supply depot," van Horn said. "If Al Longknife won't mind us mussing the finish on his toy, we could hitch them in."

"My understanding is that we can do anything we want," Roy said. "Now, you don't want to move any Navy into my yard, and any civilian boats can't show up at your piers, so I'll park any yachts at the piers right next to your fence."

"We'll have to open Gate 5," van Horn said with a frown.

"Nope, not necessary." Roy grinned and filled the Captain in on the shortcomings of his rent-a-security.

"If I had my Marine detachment," the Captain sputtered, then paused. "But if I had my Marines, we wouldn't be in this mess. Very good, Superintendent. However, Commodore Mandanti, I think we can do better than using your MK VI decoys. We've got some spare MK XIIs lying around the station now that the fleet's out. I'll talk to the skipper of the reserve squadron that runs them."

"Another person to bring into our strange twist on our stand down orders," Sandy said.

"I'll have my XO talk to her. She's his wife. I'm sure she can persuade her ragpickers that now might be a fun time to put in some active duty to help us close down the base. Make it nice and properly unthreatening," he finished with a snarl.

So civilians who'd kept a uniform in the closet would be asked to crew lightly armed yachts, faking it as light cruisers, intentionally drawing the fire of battleships to distract them from the fast patrol boats that might—just might—do the battleships some damage.

We're all crazy.

Wonderfully crazy.

Van Horn brought in an Army Colonel, head of the supply depot and armory next door to the Naval station. And brand-new AGM 944s were towed through another improperly locked down gate to be parked under lock and key in a building across from the PF piers. Even boats that had no power to move got ready to be deadlier than they ever had been before.

Exhausted, Kris accepted Santiago's offer for a place to crash that night. She found herself back in the stateroom she'd had for the trip out to Hikila and back, with Jack across the narrow passageway from her. She checked in at CIC before calling it a night. The lead battleship was still broadcasting its demand that they surrender. "You want a news feed?" the Duty Lieutenant asked as Sandy ducked her head in the CIC.

"Nelly could do it better and faster," Kris said.

"Yes, I could. The space elevator was closed at 8:30 p.m. for technical difficulties."

"Right," Kris said, "but that's going to make it harder to get work crews up to the yard."

"Not really. They have to make test runs while making repairs," Santiago said. "We'll see who are on those runs."

"King Ray has requested assistance from all United Sentient members," Nelly said. "No reaction yet. There are unconfirmed reports that two squadrons, twelve battleships, have been ordered back from Boynton, but no one at Government House will comment. This is interesting. There was a background briefing from a high military official saying that all President-class battleships in human space are accounted for so that the rumors that these ships approaching are super battleships must be discounted."

"Someone has more faith in intel than me," Santiago said.

"And hasn't seen my passive electromagnetic take," a tech said, tapping his readouts.

"Wonder who fed that leak?" Kris muttered.

"Wardhaven stocks are plummeting on the interplanetary markets, Kris. This being the weekend, markets here are closed, but after-hours trading has been suspended. There are reports that automatic tellers are restricting withdrawals."

"Sounds like standard financial protections," Kris said. "Any specific reactions from people?"

"No, they're going about their weekend," Nelly reported.

"Half probably don't even know about this. Won't know until Monday. Any more info on the intruders?" Sandy asked.

"Not much, Captain."

"Nothing to match them to any specific warship construction over the last five, ten years?" Kris asked.

"Well, maybe, maybe not," the Lieutenant said with just the hint of a grin. "Beni, talk to the ladies."

"Yes, sir, ma'ams. Well, electronic countermeasures take a lot of data analysis. And you can't analyze data without moving it around. That makes noise." The young technician rapped a screen where a dozen colored columns moved up and down spasmodically. "Every design of storage media is just a bit different. My old man analyzes them for Consumer's Union to see how long they last, but he and I've been doing a bit more work. Seeing if we could get a signature off them."

"From here you can't ID storage media!" Kris said.

"Ma'am, I got an ID on you and that fancy computer around your neck when you were two piers down." The kid grinned.

"Who made the storage on our intruders?" Santiago snapped.

"Peterwald Computing Unlimited," the technician shot back.

"Peterwald," Kris breathed. "Grampa Al thought that we'd find a Peterwald at the bottom of this. I thought he might just be seeing old family ghosts."

"Sometimes old family ghosts don't stay in the closet where you want 'em," the skipper said. "Don't take it personally, Kris. If Greenfeld can occupy Wardhaven, they'll take over most of King Ray's United Sentients within a year. Add ninety planets to their sixty, seventy, whatever their count last was, and they'll have Earth in five years. Damn, they played us but good."

"I need to get this to my father."

"Call on my phone," Beni said, offing his commlink.

"I'm not sure," Kris started.

"Ma'am, me and my pop don't much like folks listening in on our conversations. Trust me, what you say on that link will be private. And besides, who's gonna bother listening in on a phone that belongs to some 1/c Electronics Tech? The newsies got better things to do with their time."

"You can bet on Beni," the Duty Lieutenant said.

Kris took the phone, asked Nelly for her security code, then for the special number Honovi reserved for calls from his wife. It was a lousy trick to use Rose's number, but . . .

"Things are really busy here, honey," Brother said a moment later. "I'll have to call you back."

"Things are busy here, too, but we need to talk," Kris said.

"Where are you?"

"That's not something we need to talk about just now. But someone I'm talking to just told me something about the approaching luxury liners that I thought you might like to know."

"Luxury liners?"

"Yeah, the ones transmitting love letters," Kris said, trying to use code obvious to her brother but not something that would attract the attention of search bots.

"Oh, *those* liners." Brother might be slow; he wasn't dumb.

"Seems the recording media they use was all made by Peterwald Computing Unlimited."

"Them," Honovi said, not repeating a word that might raise a flag to the wrong searchers.

"Yep. Grampa Al thought they might have an oar in our troubled waters. Here's another vote for that."

"Father won't be happy to hear about that."

"How are things going on that?"

"Not as well as I might wish. Father is insisting on calling a session of the 'old folks' home.' Obviously the new guy doesn't want to. Knows he can't face a vote. Father is leading a march on the 'old folks' home.' He's got a lot of members behind him, a majority. The new guy will have to do something."

"What?"

"I only wish I knew. This is a horrible situation. Remember how old Doc Meade used to say we'd chosen the worst of the British model?"

Kris did; she hadn't agreed with her political science professor. If the opposition managed to bring down a government, it was only fair that they had to either form a government or hold the hot potato until after elections. But he'd brought up hypothetical situations—none of them as bad as the present—and argued the old government should be left in place until a new one took over. "The British Empire survived two hundred years on old Earth doing it that way. Mark my words, sooner or later, our chickens are going to come home to roost."

Next time Kris was around Wardhaven U, she'd have to look up Doc Meade and tell him she'd met his chickens— and they weighed in at a hundred thousand tons.

If she ever made it back to her old college.

"So, what will you do now?" Kris asked her brother.

"Get back to the head of this line and say a word to Father. Keep him from digging this hole he's in any deeper. Father knows he's right and the new guy's wrong, but the other guy holds all the cards at the moment. Being right and powerless is not a good combination. Meek would do just fine right about now, but *your* father does not do humble pie at all well."

"*My* father!"

"Well, he's *certainly* not acting like *my* father, that calm, cool, collected, and consummate politician."

"Love you, Brother. Take care of things at your end.

"What end are you taking care of?"

"You know that little 'yacht' of mine I showed you around?" Kris said, using the newsies' derogatory name for the PFs.

"Good God, woman, you're not up there, I mean around there."

"Selfsame."

"That's suicide."

"I don't think so, not if I can help it. Besides, Brother, if you and Father can get your act together, remember, the alternative is either throwing in the towel or sending out the Davids to take on the . . . ah . . . big things."

"Sweet Jesus, Sister, you almost make me want to lose this."

"You can't lose, Brother. I'm counting on you. Unless you can pull something out of your political top hat, I'll be leading out a bunch of rebels. Don't make us be rebels against what we're fighting to defend. Please don't do that to us."

"Sorry, Sis. I hadn't thought that through. Dear God, what a mess we're in."

"In spades. Brother, you do your job. I'll do mine."

"'Bye, I got to run. Catch us on-screen." And he was gone.

Kris hung up, glanced around. "What news do you have?"

"Three takes," Sandy said. The Duty Lieutenant turned them on. All three showed the Parliament Building. Scores walked. No, the camera on one screen panned back, and Kris could easily count hundreds of somber men and women in the old-fashioned suits customary to those who held seats in Parliament. Yep, Father had well over half of the members behind him. He marched at their head up the fifty steps leading to the formidable oak doors that were always open when Parliament was in session.

Today they were closed.

Father reached the top of the stairs and quickly crossed to the doors. They refused to open for him. With full drama, he pounded on them. They stayed closed. He turned to face the gathering throng of members and newsies, an old-fashioned piece of paper pulled from his pocket the only notes he'd need for what Kris knew would be one barn burner of a speech.

And Honovi caught up with him. Brother stood close and whispered something in Father's ear. The waiting media tried to capture it, but all they got was a soft buzzing. Honovi had taken the unusual step of turning on his jammer. Father must have noticed; he snapped something at his son.

"Your old man don't like your brother using a jammer, do he?" Beni said, grinning.

"No, Father truly believes that government should be transparent. What you see should be what you get." Course, what you didn't see was wide open.

Honovi didn't budge. He kept the jammer on, and he kept talking. After a moment, Father put on his seriously listening face. Not the one that showed he was listening to you, but the one that meant he was hearing every word you were saying. He actually let a frown cross his face.

Father never frowned. "Who wants to vote for a gloomy Gus," was his constant warning to Kris when she was new to the campaign trail at four, six. Father's frown got very deep before he nodded and let Honovi move behind him. When he faced the newsies again, he stuffed the notes of his prepared speech in his pocket. Face deadly serious, he took a deep breath.

"My fellow citizens, these are strange and perilous times, but you don't need me to tell you that. It's pretty clear to anyone with eyes to see. Ears to hear.

"These unique times call for unique measures, from you, and from those you have called upon to govern you. I came here today thinking that all of these fine people with me could jump-start the wheel of government turning." He turned to glance over his shoulder.

"It's pretty clear we can't.

"But as much as I'd like to hear from you, the people, the elections aren't until next week, and those ships demanding our surrender and threatening horrible destruction if we refuse, will be here in just three days.

"We need a government now.

"My son," he said, turning to Honovi, "a more educated man than me, tells me that back on Earth, in perilous times such as we face, they would form governments of national unity, governments where political gain was put aside when national survival was at stake.

"Mojag Pandori," Billy Longknife, the consummate politician, said, waving across the street toward Government House, "it is time we tear down the wall that we have built between us.

"Mojag Pandori, I call upon you to meet with me by noon tomorrow so that we can work out the necessary procedures for forming a coalition government so Wardhaven may face this time of crisis not divided by its past but united for its future.

"Mojag Pandori, I stand prepared to make any concessions necessary during this critical period so that we can put our people's interests first where they must be. Have to be, if there is to be any Wardhaven interests at all in the future.

"Thank you, my fellow citizens, and may God help us all."

Applause swept the steps of the Parliament Building. Beside Kris, Sandy brought her hands together and slowly clapped. So did the Duty Lieutenant. The 1/c sat at his station, mouth open.

"He did that with no notes. I mean, I heard you talking to your brother. I saw your brother talk to your dad, but you mean to tell me that in the time it took those two to talk, and him to face the camera, he came up with that?" the enlisted man said, eyeing Kris in disbelief.

"He is one of those damn Longknifes," his skipper reminded her technician.

"Yeah, I know. I heard about it. Read it in the history books. Figured it was crap and legends."

"Sometimes it's harder to hate my father than others."

"Yes," the Duty Lieutenant agreed, then flinched away from his skipper's glare.

"All right, folks, tomorrow will be an early day, and I don't give us better than two-to-one odds of getting uninterrupted sleep, so if you got a rack and eight hours off, I recommend you use them," Sandy ordered.

Good advice, Kris decided . . . and took it.

9

Next morning Kris found a blue shipsuit outside her stateroom. After breakfast, Kris wanted to use the shipsuit as an excuse to bury herself neck deep in the recalcitrant innards of PF-109. Instead, she and Jack headed for the *Halsey*'s CIC. The Duty Lieutenant, a diminutive blond, took Kris in with a glance, gave Jack a smile, and went back to applying silent encouragement to the three enlisted crew on the passive sensors.

The main display table showed the Wardhaven system. Six bogies, labeled Hostiles 1 through 6, blinked red not quite a third of the way from Jump Point Beta. They'd have to flip and start decelerating late today to make orbit in two days.

"If they don't flip, could they find a gravity well to slow them down?" Kris asked.

"No," Nelly answered, a second ahead of the battle board.

"Good question," Sandy said from behind her. "I hope you'll keep your computer out of my ship's innards. It may be standard Navy issue, but I've got it configured just the way I want it."

"Nelly?" Kris said.

"I wouldn't think of touching it without your asking." Nelly sniffed. Kris and Sandy exchanged skeptical glances.

Kris leaned on the battle board. "I think it's best to intercept the hostiles late. Give the politicians time to come up with a formal policy. I'd much rather sail with authorization than as rebels."

"Definitely," the destroyer skipper agreed.

Kris frowned at the board for a long minute. "In the vids, the gallant heroes charge off to meet the evil assailants head-on in one great cataclysmic battle . . . that still manages to fill the last twenty minutes of the vid. Board, assuming we've been accelerating away from the station for ten minutes at one g, how long would we be in firing range of a battle fleet decelerating and carrying about the same velocity?"

"Large battleship lasers, three minutes from maximum range to minimum, to maximum. One-third that for secondary batteries."

"And, of course, we'd then be on a reciprocal bearing with the battleships between us and the station," Kris said, grinning at Sandy. "I did learn something during my tactical course at OCS. Not as much as I wanted, but the commander gave me one hell of a reading list. I got through most of it on the *Typhoon*."

The destroyer Captain nodded. "So you know enough not to use the vids to plan your battle."

"And that you know a whole lot more and earned command of this destroyer when I was still doing term papers on Milton's poetry. Tell me, Commander, how do we fight this battle?"

Sandy eyed Kris for a long moment, then leaned forward to study the battle board. "Sorry, Longknife. You played the princess card. You demanded the command. We gave it to you. You can't dodge out on it now.

"Besides, when those battleships are breathing down this station's neck, getting all dressed up to blast Wardhaven back to the Stone Age, the only thing between them having a field day and us maybe, just maybe, converting them to spare change, are those twelve PFs under your command. You're going to be the one who runs them in. You've already shown me you can do it."

Sandy looked up, fixed Kris with eyes as sharp as any 18-inch laser. "I watched you plan the rescue at Brisbane—and then juggle the plan as the fight came at you. The Commodore showed me the attack plan you used on him. I like that idea of going for simultaneous hits on the battlewagons. Face it, Kris, you've already shown yourself the natural leader of the PFs, and the other skippers showed they'd follow you."

Kris opened her mouth to argue, but Sandy waved her off. "Yeah, some needed more persuading. Hell, gal, even I did. But then you showed them how it was done. You've got them, Princess. They're yours to command, so you, by God, will command them.

"Yes, you and I and anyone else interested will come up with a plan, the best plan we can. But out there, when hell's overheating, it's gonna fall apart. And when it does, it's gonna be you and that collection of disorganized chips around your neck that are going to come up with a new plan that will work better."

"I hope that wasn't a reference to me," Nelly snorted.

"You know what I mean," Sandy said, turning back to the board. "Board, advance the intruders. Assume one g acceleration continues to flip point and one g deceleration up to making orbit at High Wardhaven's level. Show results."

The board showed the track in yellow, putting time marks along the line at twelve-hour intervals. Then it adjusted the situation around Wardhaven. The yellow line met the planet just at High Wardhaven. "Yep, they plan to take out our access to space on the first pass. Get the main yards, the beanstalk. All interstellar communications. Perfect timing."

"Board," Kris said. "Is there any other course and time track that allows for those results?"

"None that put them over Wardhaven before our fleet could return from Boynton," Sandy said. "I already checked it."

"So Mother Nature decrees where and when we fight."

"It's often that way," Sandy said. "You can't mess with the laws of physics."

"So we fight in less than three days."

"Yep."

"How close to the station?" Kris asked.

"Closer than the station folks would have it, but no closer than we have to," Sandy said.

"If the government chooses to fight, what're the advantages of fighting within range of the station's defenses?" Kris asked.

Sandy frowned. "Defense lasers have this equal opportunity attitude toward ships. If it moves, shoot it. Being Navy, I kind of object to being shot at. Really object to being shot at by my own side. No, let's back off a bit. What say we take as many bites out of the apple as we can. With luck, the station gunners will be left nibbling at a very thin core."

"We could swing around the planet and hit the intruders as they come in. Us on an elliptical orbit."

"That's one option. A popular one," Sandy said. "But where's Milna?" The battle board had been simplifying the situation, showing only the picture within immediate Wardhaven orbit. Now it backed off to show Wardhaven's single moon.

"Ah," Sandy said with a grin. "Someone didn't do their homework, or someone set the timing without talking to a good ship driver and tactician. Poor sod. Plot me a one-g course from High Wardhaven around Milna and intercepting the intruders."

The board did.

A green line reached out to the moon, swung around it, then headed back. It formed an acute angle with the intruder's course. "Perfect," Sandy breathed. "We can choose our place and time to intercept them. Here, three hours out. Or here, two hours out. Or here, an hour out. We decide. It's like having the weather gauge in an old sailing frigate battle."

Kris loved to race sailboats. She well knew the advantage of the weather gauge. She also knew the risks of orbital skiff racing. "If we engage too close to Wardhaven, on this course, any damaged and helpless ships will be on a straight course to crash and burn on Wardhaven."

"Battle board, see what tugs are available on the station. Arrange to have them in orbit and available to rescue crews," Sandy said, all business in her voice.

And Kris remembered that there was a lot more to planning a battle than made it into the history books. But it would be a lot easier for her to ask her crews to give that last desperate measure if she knew . . . and they knew . . . there was a tug crew out there risking their necks to save their own. Details. Details. That was where battles were lost and won. Someone out there had six battleships and their crews working on their details. All Kris had was herself and a destroyer Captain.

A Longknife and a Santiago against six battlewagons.

Even odds.

A breathless quartermaster 3/c dashed into the CIC. "The JOOD said I might find Your Highness here. There's problems at the Nuu Docks between the yacht crews and the reservists and their decoys. Captain van Horn and the dock superintendent suggest that you might really want to have a say-so in it."

Kris sighed. She had a battle to plan, but she needed ships, too. Did Grampa Ray ever have to juggle like this? The history books didn't mention this kind of stuff. Well, maybe they had, and she hadn't noticed it. Maybe next time she got a chance to read some history, she'd have a lot less stars in her eyes.

Better yet, she'd have a nice talk with him *real soon*.

Kris turned away from the battle board. Jack came off

of the wall he'd been holding up. "The runabout's at the end of the gangway," he said.

Their passage through Gate 5 was delayed by a slow flow of monstrous constructs, all painted Navy gray. The 4-inch lasers Kris recognized. The huge teardrop shapes scattered among them puzzled her until Jack passed one. MK XII Training Simulator was stenciled in small letters in one corner. So that was what a real, honest-to-God target decoy looked like. It was at least four times larger than the MK VI they'd trained against.

The chief was right. They'd had it easy. Too easy?

Only time would tell.

Jack squeezed the runabout into a tiny space marked No Parking, Fire Zone, parked it, and Kris headed for what looked like a full-fledged knitting and debating society at the foot of a pier. As she approached, she spotted several medium-size hulls pulled into piers one after another. She counted five, but there might have been a sixth or seventh. Too small for freighters, they were too big for most yard craft, tugs, that kind of stuff.

Yachts? That many? That fast?

NELLY, ANYTHING IN THE NEWS ABOUT NAVY PREPARATION TO FIGHT?

KRIS, I HAVE IT FLAGGED. IF ANYTHING COMES UP, I WILL TELL YOU.

HOW'S THE POLITICAL SHOW COMING?

YOUR FATHER IS STILL TRYING TO GET A MEETING WITH PANDORI. THE ACTING PRIME MINISTER SAYS HE NEEDS MORE TIME. THERE ARE RUMORS IN THE NEWS THAT YOUR FATHER MAY HOLD A SIT-IN ON GOVERNMENT HOUSE STEPS STARTING AT NOON. HE HAS NOT ACTUALLY SAID ANYTHING PUBLICLY SINCE YESTERDAY'S STATEMENT. I AM NOT PRIVY TO ANYTHING. SHOULD I CONTACT YOUR BROTHER'S COMPUTER?"

NO, IF HONOVI THINKS I NEED TO KNOW SOMETHING, HE'LL TELL ME.

Still, it was interesting. Father was keeping the pressure on Pandori but doing it at a lower level. Using the rumor mill to pressure the poor fellow rather than actually jacking him up. Father, or Honovi, was working the situation smarter, not harder.

Well, damn it, they better. I sure am.

Kris joined a mob of Navy and merchant marine sailors milling around among yard workers. They parted to let her through to the center where the real knitting, marching, and chowder society seemed to be in full session.

Arrayed on one side were six merchant officers in different uniforms, each more spectacular than the other. Yep, yacht skippers. Some were old, others young, split male, female. All looked competent and hopping mad.

Across from them was Captain van Horn. Behind him were two Commanders Kris took for his XO and his wife, the CO of the reservist detachment. Behind them in ranks were a half-dozen Lieutenant Commanders, all middle-aged, competent looking, split male, female. And if Kris's year with the fleet had taught her anything, the Navy was as steaming mad but hiding it well.

Between them stood Roy and two other shipyard types. Roy went from looking back and forth between his two hostile allies to beaming at Kris. "So glad to see you, Your Highness," he said with a fervor Kris had never heard attached to those words.

"How's the morning going?" Kris responded.

"In some ways, it couldn't be better," Roy said, his grin wavering at the edges. His greetings got a round of obscenities from the merchies and a gruff "Hurumph" from van Horn.

"*Your* Grampa Al got five, maybe more of his friends to donate their yachts to the present effort," Roy said, nodding at the merchant marine contingent.

"Glad to have you aboard," Kris said, with all the *noblesse* she could *oblige*.

"Maybe. Maybe not," a merchant Captain said stepping forward. "I'm Elizabeth Luna, Captain of one of these tubs. We've skippered them where the owners wanted them, not always where the flight plan said, not always where it was easy to go. We know just what they can do . . . and can't. We can push them for as much as they'll give you. We and our crew are what you want to run these ships. Not those fancy-pants Navy types."

"They're warships now. The Navy will crew them," van Horn said with about as much negotiating room as a baseball bat.

"Yes, Captain. Just a moment, Captain. May I speak with you yacht skippers, in private?" Kris said.

She joined them in a hardly private circle, but she did have her back to van Horn. "Listen, I can't talk openly about the battle plan, because, well, I'm still working it out. I can tell you that our plans for your ships involve those decoys that I passed on the drive over here. And we'll need these ships to follow very exact orders and draw the enemy's fire when and where we need them to. And once we've hung those decoys on your boats, they may not behave like they did yesterday. Do you understand?"

"You need people to follow orders," one skipper said.

"There's not going to be a lot of glory," another said.

"And the chances of getting killed are pretty damn high," finished Luna.

Kris eyed each of the six. "I think you understand me pretty well."

Luna turned to the others. "Didn't expect much different when I heard a Longknife was leading it. Did you?" All in the circle nodded. She turned to face Kris. "Someone sold you a bill of goods, kid. You think the only ones willing to risk their skin for Wardhaven are the likes in that Navy uniform. Well, honey, as I see it, we're all up to our ears in bad. Anyone who's got a chance to do something about it ought to step up to the plate and do it. I can. I'm here. You're not gonna send me away. And me and my crew can do the best job of pushing the *Archimedes* through space of anybody there is.

"You got Navy gear you want operated, you put Navy folks on my boat. They do their thing. I do my thing. You give me an order, Princess Longknife, I'll do it. Or die trying. You want more than that?"

Kris swallowed hard. There it was. Solid and personal. Could she ask anything more? Could anyone? How had she become the personification of Wardhaven and freedom? She hadn't asked for it, but here it was.

"And the rest of you?" she said, in the firmest voice she could muster.

"So say we all," said the one of the skippers. "So say we all," said the rest.

Kris turned to face Captain van Horn. Without a word, he came to attention and saluted her. Then he did a smart about-face and addressed his contingent. "You heard Princess Longknife. You *will* serve aboard the armed yachts, alongside *their* merchant crews. There will be opportunities for confusion and friction. *I* expect those challenges to be resolved. You *will* maintain an attitude that we're *all* on the same side and the enemy is out there, not here. Do I make myself clear?"

"Yes, sir," came loud and clear.

"Any problems that can't be handled aboard ship will be referred to your squadron Commander, and, if necessary, to me. If I can't solve *your* problem with *your* yacht's Captain, we'll bring the princess in on it. I *don't* recommend pissing off a Longknife. President Urm did, and they didn't find all that many pieces of him." Van Horn chuckled at his own joke. The Navy ranks and merchies joined in. Kris managed not to roll her eyes. Sandy smiled and gave Kris a wink.

There were times when lies served their purposes.

"You have your orders," the Captain finished. "Commander, assign your officers to their ships. Chiefs, dismiss your sailors to work details."

Chiefs began shouting orders, though Kris was none too sure just what they were. Being an officer, she didn't have to bother herself about that. Chiefs ran the Navy, and the officers just rode along. She joined the yard superintendent.

"How's your part of the job going?"

Roy shook his head. "I have no idea. I spent all night poring over the schematics of the yachts and those MK XII decoys. The yachts fall into two main classes, but every one of them is a bit different. None have the internal space to absorb everything inside the MK 12."

"So we weld the decoys on as some kind of figurehead."

"Yeah. But that's gonna look as out of place as a yacht in a battle line as soon as those battlewagons get in visual range."

"My Grampa Al would say *you're* telling *me* all *your* problems. You're not telling me *my* solution." Kris said. She tried to soften it with a smile.

"Yeah, I've heard the yard super quote me that, and I've quoted it down the line. Here's what we're going to do. We'll plate over this loose collection of junk into what looks to all the world like a real, live warship. By the way, what do you want? Why settle for light cruiser? Why not go for battleship?"

"Slow down, you lost me."

"By noon today, we'll have all six yachts in air docks. In with them will be six MK XII decoys and six power barges. Those barges we usually put alongside ships that need to shut their reactors down but we don't have pier space for. This way, the yachts can use their reactors to go full bore on their engines, and the barges' reactors will feed internal power and the four-inch lasers. Maybe even those twelve-inch pulse lasers for a last gasp something. Who knows?

"Anywho. We're going to put all of this inside a false hull using up all the sheet metal I can lay my hands on. Van Horn says he has some spare lying around. Says I can have it.

"So, in say two days, we're gonna have six of the ugliest-looking ships in space, able to do God himself only knows what, with decoys aboard that may or may not mask the whole thing."

"Good Lord," Kris said, "and you came up with all this last night while I was getting a good night's sleep?"

"Sleep. You slept!"

"Yeah, it's that stuff you do in between gulping down caffeine," Kris said. Then something funny struck her. "You're going to make an awful lot of changes to those yachts. I don't imagine they're going to handle anything like they used to."

"No way in hell. Driving them will be like carrying an elephant on a skateboard while crossing an iced-over river."

"But those merchie skippers insisted they had to keep command of their boats because they knew how to handle them."

"Yeah."

"Had you told them about all this rework on their boats?"

"Yeah, before you got here."

"Van Horn knew about it?"

"Yep, that's why he started that song and dance about the Navy would be crewing the boats."

Kris raised her eyes to the ceiling of the yard hundreds of meters above her. Had she just been had? Had they just let her paint them out of a corner they'd wanted out of?

Am I a princess or a pawn? Do I really want an answer?

"Roy, you need me for anything more?"

"Nope, don't see anymore crises on the horizon for, oh, five . . . ten minutes."

She turned to Jack. "Sir knight, would you *please* drive me to the 109. I need a few quiet moments getting my hands dirty."

THERE was no one standing guard at the brow of the 109. No surprise there. With a crew of fourteen, everyone would be doing real work.

"I'll hang here," Jack said, staying in the runabout. "If I see any MPs, I'll holler."

"You do that," Kris said and boarded the elevator for the short ride down to the quarterdeck. No one there, either. She climbed the central ladder to the bridge.

Kris was wrong. There weren't fourteen in the crew. Penny was at the intel station, frowning at it as it did something. "That didn't load right," she muttered, then spotted Kris. "Captain on the bridge," she said.

"As you were," Kris said, to stop the other enlisted woman on the bridge from coming to attention, even though she was under the command console, then Kris added, "And not really," to correct any misperceptions. "Tom has the ship. Where is he?" she asked, looking around and missing his lopsided smile.

"Aft, trying to figure out what went haywire with the damn motor," Penny said. "I'd be helping him, but between him and the chief and Tononi's crew, they've maxed the engine room's space. Fintch is smaller than me, so she's with them. Me, I'm trying to make sure this mismatched collection of databases can talk to each other. Data, data everywhere, but not a bit of it will hook to anything. Oh, and getting the sensor feed to patch in. I'll be an old woman with grandkids before they talk to each other."

"Grandkids?"

"No chance of that yet. Tommy and I have hardly managed to sleep, much less sleep together. You Longknifes sure know how to throw a honeymoon."

"About as good as the wedding receptions you Liens throw," Kris said, heading aft for the engine room and uncomfortably aware that what for her was a crisis was for her friends a crisis with bloody inconvenient timing.

Now Kris climbed down the ladder. On the quarterdeck, she had to zig, open a hatch in the bulkhead that divided the tiny boat into two airtight compartments, and start down a ladder offset to one side. In the motor compartment, the matter-antimatter motor occupied center place. It also dominated the smell. In the rest of the boat, the faint hint of ozone and electronics accented the human sweat that processing could never quite get out of the air. Here, ozone and electronics blasted the nose. Today, however, human sweat dominated all.

"Damn it, that should have shown us something," didn't

sound like her usual Tom. Maybe there was more than one reason Tom didn't want his bride down here?

"I got it where you wanted it Mr. Lien," sounded like a very contrite Fintch.

"She does, sir," was a protective Chief Stan.

"How's it going?" Kris said, entering into the maze that passed for a PF's power plant. "And as you were," she added.

"Good to see you, ma'am," the Chief said.

"Good to see all of you. Tom. You need a break?"

"Yeah. Chief, give everyone five. Make that ten. Can you scrounge me up a cup of coffee that's not older than I am?"

"Yes, sir. One for you too, ma'am?"

Kris didn't need more caffeine, but it hadn't taken her long to learn that, in the Navy, the exchange of coffee cups was a sacred ritual. "Yes, thank you, Chief."

The others left them alone. Kris took the only real chair at the motor mech's station. Tommy, no lopsided grin in sight, settled carefully on a thick bar of metal arching in a guard over a magnetohydrodynamics generator. He flipped a black box of his own design absently over and over in his hand.

Born in the asteroid belt of Santa Maria into a successful mining family, he'd learned early not to trust air, gravity, or any of the other things that mud hens like Kris took for granted. Still, Tom was the first friend Kris had made at Officer Candidate School. They'd fought their first firefight together, and he'd backed her up when she did the unthinkable on the *Typhoo*n. And on Turantic.

And all the time, he'd always had that lopsided grin.

Not today.

"What's wrong, Tom?"

He didn't look at her. He looked everywhere but at her. Finally he scowled and looked her in the eye. "I can't get the damn motor going. The 109 should be your flagship, and she's gonna spend the fight tied up to the pier, and Jesus, Mary, and Joseph, we can't afford to be even one ship down."

"So what do you need to get the motor going?"

"I don't know, Kris! They snuck a bunch of plumbers on board to shut down the motor. On a Saturday. When even the duty crew had been shanghaied off to straighten paper clips or some stupid duty around the station. Pandori really had it in for the PFs. Said they were just a—"

Kris had to cut this off. "I know the political spiel, Tom. What do you need to get the ship up and running?"

"I don't know, Kris. I can't find out what's wrong. I'm trying, but I can't."

"So we pull old components and replace them with new ones until we find the ones that are dead and the motor works."

"That's—" Tom started.

Kris cut him off. "Not the way you do things on Santa Maria. I know. But Tom, I got the entire Nuu Dockyard next door with its whole workforce at our disposal. We got twelve PFs and half a dozen armed yachts to get battle ready. We got two, maybe part of a third day. Elegant ain't a word I want to hear. Quick, dirty, ugly. I'll take them all if it gets me 'All power on-line. Ready to answer the helm.' You hear me, Captain?"

Tom breathed out what might have been an argument. With a shiver, he nodded. "I hear you, Longknife. Loud and clear. How fast can you get me a dock crew with a full set of replacements for this haywire engine of mine?"

"How about before the Chief gets back with that cup of coffee. You can offer it to the yard boss. Tell him it was a princess's, but he can have it instead."

"I'll do that. See what extra it gets me."

Kris headed up the ladder. Jack didn't quite make the electric runabout lay rubber gunning for the yard with Kris's orders for not one but two engine overhaul teams, but he came close. With a sigh, Kris headed for PF-105. It was a coin flip as to how Babs Thompson would take having the dockyard folks take over her engine room. Wounded pride versus relief. Kris found the cheerleader and prom queen up to her elbows in engine room parts and studying schematics with her Chief of the Boat. She accepted Kris's transfer of a portion of her domain to Nuu Docks with poor grace, but not a word. Once the hatch was closed on Babs's exit, the Chief turned to Kris.

"Thank you, ma'am. There's nothing more dangerous in the Navy, not even battleship guns, compared to a junior officer with a screwdriver. If you'll pardon me saying so, ma'am."

"I'll try to remember that, Chief," Kris said, suppressing a sigh as she remembered her own wish for a few moments alone with her boat, a chance to get her hands covered with honest dirt.

10

Those two ship visits spotlighted what her job had become. The skippers and crews would fight the ships. She would get anything and everything out of their way that might interfere with them putting up the best fight possible.

The fact that some of that interference might be coming from those very skippers was a new thought for Kris, but not a totally alien one. In school she'd studied managers that were too hands-on. Micromanagers. Now she was getting a chance to help some of her friends avoid it. Oh, and avoid it herself.

Help ships get ready for the fight.

Find more ships and draft them into the fight.

That's what a princess does.

Chapter one for a book she might write someday on the proper etiquette and education of a princess.

Kris laughed and headed for her next PF. NELLY, KEEP COUNT OF WHICH BOATS I VISIT. TICK THEM OFF FOR ME AND LET ME KNOW IF I MISS ONE.

YES, MA'AM. WHILE YOU ARE WORKING ON THESE, I AM WORKING ON MORE COMPLEX EVASION SYSTEMS, FASTER

EVASION MANEUVERS. I AM ALSO WORKING ON SEVERAL FINAL ATTACK RUN-INS, DEPENDING ON HOW OUR EVASION EFFORTS SPREAD US OUT. AND HOW MANY OF US SURVIVE THE RUN-IN.

VERY GOOD, NELLY. YOU COVER THAT.

DID YOU KNOW THE CHIEF OF 109 HAD ORDERED NEW HELMETS FOR THE CREW BEFORE PANDORI CLOSED THINGS DOWN?

NO. ARE THEY GOOD ONES?

YES. THE BEST, BY MY MEASURE.

PLEASE ORDER THEM FOR ALL THE BOAT CREWS. AND THE ARMED YACHTS.

WE WILL NOT WANT THE ORDER TO RAISE A FLAG TO THE MEDIA.

NO. WE DON'T WANT THAT.

HOWEVER, YOUR GRAMPA AL SPONSORS SEVERAL FOOTBALL TEAMS. I COULD ORDER NEW HELMETS UNDER THEIR COST CODE AND HAVE THEM MAILED TO THEIR PROPER ADDRESS, THEN MISDIRECT THEM UP THE BEANSTALK TO THE ATHLETIC DEPARTMENT OF THE NAVAL STATION. THAT SHOULD GO UNNOTICED.

YES, NELLY, THAT SHOULD.

KRIS, IS THIS WHAT YOU WOULD CALL FUN?

YES, OUTSMARTING PEOPLE WHO REALLY SHOULDN'T BE ALL THAT INTERESTED IN WHAT YOU ARE DOING IS WHAT I CALL FUN.

YES, I FIND THIS FUN. I WILL ALSO REPROGRAM THE HIGH-G STATIONS TO ALLOW FOR THE HELMETS. THE YACHTS HAVE SMART METAL STATIONS, SO I COULD MODIFY THEM AS WELL, THOUGH MOST HAVE SECURITY SYSTEMS IN PLACE THAT WILL STOP ME. I WILL EXPLAIN TO THEM THAT WE HAVE ORDERED HELMETS THAT WILL HELP THEIR HUMANS AND THAT MY ADJUSTMENTS WILL MAKE THEM SAFER. I THINK THEY WILL ADOPT MY CHANGES.

YOU'LL NEGOTIATE WITH THE YACHT'S COMPUTER SYSTEMS?

I THINK THAT IS WHAT YOU WOULD CALL IT.

That was something worth thinking more about. NELLY,

MENTION THAT TO AUNT TRU'S COMPUTER NEXT TIME YOU TALK TO IT. I THINK TRU WOULD FIND IT INTERESTING THAT YOU AND THE OTHER COMPUTERS ARE NEGOTIATING THINGS JUST NOW.

YOU THINK SO? IT SEEMED ONLY REASONABLE.

Yeah. Right.

The other boats were in various degrees of disarray. Kris expected Phil or Chandra would prove an exception to that, but they rather proudly pointed out the extent to which they were a mess. Chandra was testing the AGM-944s. Though the same diameter as the Foxer charges, they were four times as long. That required ripping out two of the four Foxer tubes to install missile-size ones.

"Nelly's working on several more radical evasion schemes."

"Good." Chandra nodded. "I think we will need to be more wily than we ever thought we needed to be. Better we cut corners faster than we have to, than cut slower than we should have."

"We may need more Foxers."

Chandra blinked. "I will have to arrange for us to load new Foxer magazines while we are moving. It can be done."

"Commander Santiago on the *Halsey* is looking at how many tugs we can get standing by. Just in case we use up all our consumables and need help slowing down."

"Are we going to be diving out of the moon at them?"

"That's one option."

"A good one. We can maneuver behind the moon, come out on a different vector from what we went in on."

"It could have us diving straight at Wardhaven."

"That's what the tugs are for," the mustang said with a fatalistic shrug. "First we kill the battlewagons, then we worry about the rest of our lives."

Phil's engines were torn apart, his radiators in the yard being reworked. "If I can get an extra ten percent output from the matter-antimatter reaction, even if it's for only the last thirty seconds, it could put me that much closer, that much faster. I'll use the radiators to cool the engines down as far as I dare before we start the charge, then close them off to give off as little infrared as I can. Then, once we've blown them to hell, we can spread the radiators out and get the reactors out of the red fast. If this works, the yard can redo all the other boats before we leave. How's Tom doing on the 109?"

"The yard's helping on the 109 and 105. I see that you've got the yard working with you. Chandra has them helping her up-gun the 105. You need anything else?"

"Not now. I'm gonna let them work out the kinks in the Foxer to 944 thing on the 105 before I let them mess with my boat. You going down the squadron?"

"That seems to be my ticket. You look over the shoulders of your chiefs and techs to make sure they got everything they need to get the job done. Me, I get to look over your shoulder to see if there's anything I can get you. Sometimes I even help you before you realize it. We've ordered new helmets." Kris updated Phil on Nelly's new evasion plan and the helmets that might keep them from addling the crews' brains while they did the evading.

"I should have thought of that," Phil said.

"The more heads, the better the thinking. Tell you what, I'll ask the Commodore if he'd like to hold a stand-up conference on the pier beside the *Cushing* this evening so we can review work on the squadron. Say sixteen hundred. Each skipper can say how things are going, good ideas they've thought up, and plan for the next day. Nothing too long. Don't have time for that."

"Think you can get the shipyard boss to show up, tell us how things are going? I asked my yard rep, and all I get is 'Everything is fine. Don't worry.' Just makes me worry more."

"I'll have Roy there."

Kris stumbled across Jack more by accident than intent. He swore a blood oath not to let her get away like that again. At the *Cushing*, Kris told the Commodore about her idea of afternoon and morning meetings.

"I always had those when I was in the yard. We're in such a hurry we're forgetting to do it right. You're doing a walk-around. Good Commanders always do them. Lets 'em see what's really happening in their commands. Anyone tell you to do that?"

"No," Kris admitted.

The Commodore smiled. "Should have known it wouldn't take a Longknife long to figure it out. By right of blood, by right of name. By right of title, is that what you said? Got to remember that for my memoirs. Don't hear things like that nearly enough these days. Certainly not from the likes of your old man. Anyway, yes, Your Highness, I will send runners to your fiefs and request and require that your skippers present themselves at sixteen hundred."

"Sounds awful fancy. Sure they'll understand what you want? What's wrong with 'The Commodore sends his compliments and calls a conference on the pier.' It always worked before."

"Ah, yes, but this has more poetry. And shouldn't we who are about to die salute life with poetry?" the Commodore said. And for the first time, Kris noticed that the old fellow had a twinkle in his eye.

What have I unleashed? No. What are we unleashing from ourselves?

Kris skipped the *Halsey*. She had no illusions that she had anything to offer Sandy, other than what time the pierside conference was. Gate 5B was now open between the yard and the Naval Station right at pier-side. Kris crossed over quickly, but the air docks were scattered along the spacefront. She didn't know what to expect aboard the yachts. She was not surprised when she got everything from "Princess arriving," aboard Grampa Al's boat to "There's a Longknife aboard. Watch your wallets," as she crossed the brow to another.

The yachts had established their own command structure, electing the skipper of the General Electric yacht *Archimedes* as their Commodore. Elizabeth Luna, a tall drink of water with graying raven hair and a drawl almost direct from some rawboned section of old Earth, greeted Kris with a firm handshake and a complaint. "They want to rip out my 12-inch pulse lasers. Over my dead body they get my guns."

Kris suspected there'd be a lot of dead bodies besides Elizabeth's. "They give a reason?" Kris asked, buying time and checking for exits. Jack displayed noticeable disinterest in Kris's bodily safety as he studiously examined a set of crossed sabers hanging from the bridge bulkhead. Apparently, Elizabeth was fully prepared to repel boarders.

"Weight. They're welding that damn decoy to my snout, a barge off kilter between that decoy and the *Archie*, and slapping together some sort of false front on all this with half-inch deck plate, and *they're* worried about *weight*."

"How could you use the lasers with all that junk out in front of you?" Kris asked. It sounded like a good question.

"That crap ain't gonna be there when I'm shooting, honey. I plan to rig explosive charges to the struts holding on the cover and the decoy. Once you've done your part, I'm gonna cut myself lose and go gunning for any little pieces you left behind."

Kris blinked. She considered her part in this mission just one step shy of suicide. Any reasonable person would. But intentionally going into battle in a ship speckled with explosive charges . . . ! Planning on blowing a hole in your ship so you could get out, and then charging out shooting . . . ?

Pardon me, Kris, but what is the difference between her explosive charges and having the AGM-944s aboard? Nelly asked.

Thank you, Nelly, you may go back to your calculations.

Yes, ma'am.

"The other armed yachts plan to do the same?"

"Yep. We got it all worked out. You mind explaining it to the yard folks and your Navy friends? They seem to listen better when you do the talking."

"Aren't the reservists normally in the decoys?" Kris asked.

"No problems. I've moved their workstations inside. Better eats for them out of our galley, trust me. We got the staterooms all rigged as work areas for them. Even got three of them set up in the owner's hot tub. Drained it, of course. Eight redundancy lines going forward to the decoy's noisemakers and other stuff. Trust me, they're safer here than there."

"Making a real mess of the yacht."

"Boss said to win this fight. Don't count the cost, and there's stock options in it for the crew. Not that the boss's stocks are gonna be worth all that much if we lose. But we win this one, I don't expect any of us will have to look for work the rest of our lives. Yes, Princess, we're gonna go gunning for anything you don't kill.

"And from what I hear, we aren't the only yachts that are checking out their six-shooters. Half a dozen more armed yachts are getting ready to sail with us."

"Oh my God," Kris said. Maybe prayed. "We don't need them out there ahead of us, messing up . . ." Kris didn't say more.

"Messing up the fancy dance you fast boats are gonna have to do if your gonna stay alive," Luna finished for her.

"Something like that," Kris finished. NELLY?

I TOLD YOU I WOULD TELL YOU IF SOMETHING BROKE IN THE NEWSIES. NOTHING HAS BROKEN. NO HINT OF DEFENSE. THE TALKING HEADS ARE ALL POLITICAL AND ALL CONCENTRATING ON YOUR FATHER AND PANDORI. NO RETIRED GENERALS, ADMIRALS TALKING. INTERESTING, THAT. TRUST ME, KRIS, I CAN GENERATE RANDOM NUMBERS AND PAY ATTENTION TO THE NEWS. PIECE OF CAKE.

THANKS, NELLY. "How long do you think before this leaks out?" Kris asked the yacht skipper.

The merchant mariner shrugged. "Most of us have orders from our owners to keep it quiet. No reason for us to blab our heads off to the newsies. We drink in a better grade of bar from them, if you ask me. Anyway, they're not snooping all that hard. Maybe someone shortened their leash. Who knows?" There was a hint of a smile in the shrug Elisabeth gave: Had she actually just praised the bugs that everyone usually loved to hate?

Kris's next stop took her to Roy's office. A runner led her to the shop floor where the acting super huddled with a small army of engineers over a hologram of one of the armed yachts. Kris watched as it blew away its outer shell, decoy, and power barge, emerging like a butterfly from a cocoon—and was then ripped apart by the flying pieces as they bounced off of each other and into the yacht.

"That ain't gonna work," Roy said. "Get another option."

"We've already tried twelve."

"So you shouldn't have all that much trouble coming up with another twelve. Your momma didn't raise an unimaginative engineer, did she?"

There was a general muttering about whether *some* managers had mothers. Roy chose to recognize Kris at that moment and by concentrating his smile on her, ignore the small mutiny among his people. "How's it going, Your Highness?"

"Better than I might have expected. Has Captain Luna seen that little demonstration?"

"She and the other five skippers saw the first four versions. Doesn't believe a pixel of them. 'All engineering hogwash,' I believe was their response."

"Could they fire their lasers from inside that lash-up?"

"Not sure I'd recommend it."

"How about a short, very low-power stutter burst to knock a hole where you want it, then a full power burst through that hole? I did a low-power burst on . . ." Right, her shoots were not in the history books, yet. "Well, I've dialed pulse lasers way down and used them that way."

"Hardware's not designed for that."

"I did software mods. On the fly. Certainly you could do some with two days' warning."

"And test them, debug them, document them." Roy sighed. "Oh, I hate dealing with software engineers.

Especially when I have to tell them all we have is two days to do it in."

"I could have Nelly do it before close of business today," Kris said.

I COULD HAVE IT DONE IN FIVE MINUTES, IF I HAD ACCESS TO THE SHIP SYSTEMS. WHAT DO YOU THINK I AM, AN ABACUS?

I KNOW, NELLY, BUT LET'S NOT EMBARRASS TOO MAY PEOPLE.

YOU HUMANS AND YOUR FEELINGS.

Now Roy was grinning from ear to ear. "That might be fun. Challenge my software engineers to a race, them versus your computer. But no. Not a good idea. I'll have to work with those guys long after you've sailed off into the sunset. Very bad idea. But it would be fun. Oh Lord, but I'm gonna be in trouble."

He glanced back at his engineers. Another explosion was taking place in slow motion. Yes. Yes. No. The ship got nicked, then slammed, then the power barge bounced a girder and drove it through the bridge. Ugly picture.

"What a choice. Either these folks have to come up with something, or the software engineers. Looks like I'm damned either way."

"What if you kept the false ship pretty much in one piece." A small voice came from around Kris's neck. "Blew the attachment points gently, and backed the yacht out of the cocoon?"

"What did you say, Kris?"

"You're talking to Nelly, Roy."

"Do you have to blow up the false ship?" Nelly asked. "Why not leave it mostly in one piece? Small explosions might detach it. Then, if the yacht fired short retro blasts, the false front would go on at its existing vector, and the yacht would slow. Then it could set out on its own course."

"That's what we've been trying to do. It's not as easy as it seems. The charges keep doing more than we want. The attachments have to be solid enough to take the pounding we're gonna give them during the fight. That rig's going to be knocked around quite a bit. It takes major explosives to separate it."

"But properly placed, they don't have to create that big a mess, that many conflicting vectors," Nelly came back.

Kris suspected this discussion could go on for quite a while. "Ah, Roy, I've set up a sixteen hundred meeting on the dock beside the *Cushing* for the PF skippers. There will probably be an oh eight hundred one as well. We might also want to set one up thirty minutes later for the armed yacht skippers and the Navy OIC aboard. I understand the Navy's actually been moved off the decoys and into the yachts. These get-togethers would let everyone know what's going on in their work."

"Oh, right, yeah, we *are* moving the Navy workstations onto the yachts. Guess we haven't told everyone."

"We can do that at the stand-up meetings."

"Right. Nelly, you have any suggestions for size of explosions and placement?"

"I would need to see your plans for supports."

"Right. Hmm. No easy way to break that to the engineering staff. Let me get back to you at the four o'clock thing."

"I will be there if Kris is," Nelly said.

NELLY, TRANSMIT ALL THIS REAL TIME TO TRU.

HOW WOULD THAT NOT PUT SECURITY AT RISK?

RIGHT. THEN MAKE A RECORD AND TRANSMIT IT AS SOON AS IT BECOMES POSSIBLE.

YES, MA'AM. DOES THIS BOTHER YOU?

NO, NELLY, IT'S JUST A NEW SIDE OF YOU THAT WE HAVEN'T SEEN BEFORE AND I EXPECT WILL TICKLE TRU'S FANCY.

I THINK IT IS FUN TO TICKLE TRU'S FANCY.

SO IT SEEMS.

The *Halsey* was last on Kris's list, but she made a stop by the 109 first. The yard folks had fully occupied the engine room. Tom was back on the bridge, giving what help he could to Penny's effort to connect the intel station to the sensors.

"Maybe string and two tin cans?" Penny sighed.

"Maybe we need to bring in some expert help," Kris said.

"More yard workers?" Tom asked, still no grin in sight.

"No, I think there's a tech on the *Halsey* that might put all of us to shame," Kris said. "A nerd who loves black boxes like a good friend of mine," she said, giving Tom an elbow in the ribs.

"This tech nerd on the *Halsey* sounds like someone I'd like to meet," Tom said, his grin starting to come out of hiding.

"If he or she can make my station talk to this tub's sensor suite, I want in on the talks, too," Penny said, pushing herself away from the recalcitrant station.

"Strangely enough, the *Halsey*'s CIC was next on my ramble," Kris said and led the way.

No surprise, Kris found Sandy leaning over the battle board. "How's it going?" Kris asked what was becoming her one-question-fits-all greeting.

The destroyer skipper shrugged but didn't take her eyes off the board. "It's a crapshoot. Do we attack early, dive straight at them as we come out of the moon's shadow? Or do we come along beside them, let them shoot at us for a while at long range? Note that they will be shooting at us. Their battlewagons have the range for the shoot. We don't."

"Sounds like you just answered your own question. No reason to stay in their range any longer than we have to," Kris said.

"But if we come charging straight at them, it kind of shows our hand, doesn't it?" Tom said.

"That's why I don't want to do it." Sandy nodded.

"But our hand is kind of weak," Kris said.

"Weak, yes, but do we want them to know it? Battles aren't so much won by the brilliant choices of the winner as lost by the dumb mistakes of the losers. I hope that doesn't shock you, Longknife."

"I've been kind of suspecting that," Kris said dryly.

"I'm shocked," Tom said, grin lopsided as could be.

"I'm shocked," Penny said, "that a tin can skipper would be revealing such sacred Navy secrets to lowly junior officers."

"Think security can afford to lock me in irons for the violation, Lieutenant Lien?" Sandy asked.

Penny preened at her new name and shook her head.

"So," Sandy went on slowly, "if we did a slow approach until we got into long-range laser fire, let them get in the first shots, and then turned things loose . . ."

"We'd have more time to study their formation," Penny said, giving the intel officer's take on the tactical problem.

"And they'd be doing the same to us," Kris pointed out.

"And wouldn't the both of us be doing our best to lie, lie, lie to each other," Tom concluded in full brogue.

"So who will do the better job?" Kris asked.

"What are our decoys going to be sending?" Sandy asked.

"I'd thought we'd pass them off as light cruisers, dragged out of mothballs. We were supposed to have sent everything we had to Boynton. It was on all the talk shows," Kris answered. "But Roy says we can have any size false front put on the yacht lash-up. How big we want to fake?"

Sandy rubbed the bridge of her nose thoughtfully. Tom started talking first. "What if we started out making the noises like something smaller, but as we got closer, started 'leaking' something bigger. After we got caught up in those fights on Olympia, my great-grandmum told me that things weren't always so peaceful on Santa Maria. During the starving times for the first hundred years after the lost ship's crew tried to make a go of it settling on Santa Maria, well, not everyone was willing to go hungry. Some went bad. Went to the hills as bandits. That's not something we kids got told in school.

"Well, there was one fight where the menfolk were making their stand against the hill bandits, and just when it looked like they were beat, the womenfolk and kids, decked out with any stick or whatever looked sharp or pointed, they come running around the hill beside the fight.

The bandits took one look at what they took for reinforcements and ran."

"Confusion and misdirection," Penny said.

"Confusion to my enemy," Sandy toasted.

"The more, the merrier," Kris agreed. "Maybe we could start out making like light cruisers, then have half of them start to leak like Triumph-class battle cruisers. Just the kind of old units that might still be swinging around the reserve fleet moorings and been overlooked."

"Confuse them more and more." Sandy nodded.

"And if that's not enough," Kris said, "Patrol 8 isn't the only gun in town." That got a raised eyebrow from Sandy and open stares from the other two. Kris filled them in on what the armed yachts wanted to do, and that there were more of them wanting in on this brawl.

"Oh, sweet Jesus, Mary, and Joseph," Tom prayed. "Just what we need, a crowded battlefield."

"No, I'm told they'll be behind us, looking to go in after us and fight what we've damaged."

"That might not be such a bad use for them. Privateers cutting out the enemy wounded and putting them down." Sandy nodded. "Somebody thought they could leave Wardhaven defenseless if they shipped the fleet away. Don't they know you can never turn your back on a free man, free woman? Not while they got their teeth. Their fingernails."

"I suspect 12-inch pulse lasers on an armed yacht qualifies a bit higher on the threat scale than teeth," Kris said.

"But you get my meaning."

"Yep. We cut a hole in the battlewagons, leave them bleeding and shocked. The armed people of Wardhaven will take them down with what they've got."

"And my *Halsey* and the *Cushing* will cut a hole for you to go in. That we will do," Sandy said, hands slowly clenching into fists. The four of them thought on that for a long moment. It was a plan. The only plan they had. And no battle plan survived contact with the enemy.

What will I come up with when this one comes apart?

"I need to make a call dirtside," Kris finally said. "See

how things are going with my brother. Since my last call to him didn't get blasted all over the newsies, it looks like Beni's commlink is a good one. Can I borrow it again?"

"Ask him. Lieutenant, please have Beni report to the CIC."

"Aye, aye, ma'am."

Two minutes later, the 1/c reported, rubbing sleep from his eyes and zipping himself back into a rumpled shipsuit.

"I wake you?" Kris asked, realizing her first question should have been about Beni's schedule, not his availability.

"You sure enough did, ma'am. This important?"

"I hope so. Can I borrow your commlink?"

He handed it over, looked around for a empty chair, sank into it, and appeared to be asleep in two blinks. Kris talked in her codes and Honovi's number.

"Rose, I told you . . . This you, Kris? Don't hang up."

"It's me," Kris said.

"Good. I'm meeting with Kusa Pandori. You remember her. She kind of does for her old man what I do for mine."

"I remember Kusa," Kris said. "I'll call back later."

"No. No, don't you dare. I want you to hear this, and I want her to hear what I tell you. Kris, understand. She has to know that there is nothing being held back here. I can't afford to say one thing to her, then another thing to you."

"Open covenants, openly arrived at," Kris quoted Father quoting some other politician.

"In spades, Sis."

"What's happening?" Kris asked as she heard, "So that's really your sister. So what? She's out of jail. Who cares?"

"My sister is up the beanstalk preparing a dozen fast patrol boats to take on the incoming battleships."

"We don't know they're battleships. Those expensive toys are headed for the scrap heap, and my father ordered the Navy to stand down. Besides, if anyone with a name like your sister was doing anything like that, it would be all over the news. Why haven't I heard about it?"

"Beni, can you put this on some kind of speakerphone?" Kris whispered.

"Yes, ma'am," the technician said, coming to his feet from his apparent sleep. In a moment, the entire CIC was listening to Brother's response, as Beni whispered, "I've got you on mute. If you want to talk, Lieutenant, hit this button."

Kris nodded and listened.

"Do you honestly think someone would send luxury liners to broadcast a surrender demand?"

"It could be all a bluff," the woman's voice said. Kris measured it for conviction and found it wanting.

"They've got battleship reactors and turbines." No answer there. "And my sister is doing everything she can to get those dinky boats you want scrapped ready to attack those battleships, 'cause they're the only ships we have that can."

"Don't forget my *Halsey*," Sandy said with a grin. A grin that was answered around the CIC.

"That's suicide."

"Maybe. Kris doesn't think so. And she's spending every second she can reducing the odds against her."

"They can't do it."

"Then what does your father intend to do? He can't surrender. Face it. Sooner or later, he's going to have to do what we all know we have to do: fight. Order everything we have to fight. You wanted to be known as strong on defense. That's why you sent the fleet to Boynton."

"We thought if we were seen as strong, no one would try us."

"They were bluffing," Tom spat.

"And if they were bluffing at Boynton, no wonder they want to assume someone's bluffing here," Penny said.

"Nobody bluffs with battleships." Sandy scowled.

"But you must be bluffing," the young woman went on. "The news would be full of any preparation for battle at the Naval Station. That would not go unnoticed, Honovi."

"No, Kusa, it hasn't gone unnoticed. Just unreported. My father talked to his contacts in the media. They are sitting on it. They will sit on it until your father and mine announce that a coalition government is moving to defend Wardhaven."

"My father has his contacts in the news—"

"And if they can get up the beanstalk, and if they can get on the Naval Station, and if they can get their news bite, does your father really want to say that what is going on is in violation of his orders? Orders that he did not put in writing for some reason."

There was a long pause in the phone conversation.

"Why doesn't your brother just tell her how the cow's gonna eat the cabbage?" Beni asked.

"Because sometimes, the true measure of a politician is not what he says, but what he doesn't say, and the patience he has in not saying it. The Pandoris painted themselves into a corner. A corner they didn't see coming and never intended to be in. Now they need help out. Thank God my father is finally trying to help them out of it." More likely, Honovi had persuaded Father to let them out. After this crisis, Kris suspected the relationship between father and son would never be the same.

Between brother and sister might be kind of different, too.

"What do you want?" the young woman asked.

"My sister wants to lead out her squadron obedient to our orders. She begs that she not be required to sail in Wardhaven's defense as a rebel against verbal orders. If they have the loyalty, the courage, and the willingness to risk their lives, the least we can do is give them our permission. That's all I ask. Your dad can stay Prime Minister in the Government of National Unity. My father would like Defense. We can work things out if you have problems. But whatever we do, we have to have this done before they sail.

"When's that?"

"Kris?"

"We need to be away from the station eight hours before the hostiles arrive. Say go into the boats two . . . three hours before that. Give us an hour before that to pass the message along the pier. If you could, Honovi, Kusa, we need twelve hours before their scheduled arrival."

"When's that?" Brother asked.

"Assuming they continue their one-g deceleration, and that they want to make orbit with standard energy . . ." Sandy tapped the battle board. Kris read off a time not quite two days hence.

"Not a lot of time," the young woman said.

"I'm hearing that a lot from yard workers, ship fitters, engineers," Kris said. "If we'd been ordered to go tomorrow, we'd go, but our chances of getting those battleships are a whole lot better for having had three days' preparation."

"Three days?"

"I came right up here," Kris said.

"One more thing," Kusa said. "I expect that my dad and your father can agree to most of what they presently differ over, Honovi. But one thing must be clear before any further talks."

"Yes?"

"When this naval force sails to engage the, what did you call them, hostiles, there will be no Longknife aboard them."

Kris swallowed hard. There it was again. Nobody, but nobody, wanted her in the squadron. Not Grampa Al, for his reasons. Not Honovi. Not the Pandoris for their own reasons. She half expected Brother to snap, "Deal."

There was silence from the other end of the line.

"Sis," Honovi finally said slowly, "I'd love to agree to what she just asked."

Kris stood, her finger hovering over the Talk button on the commsole. All she had to say was "Yes," and she was out of this suicidal charge. She'd live!

To see what? Live under whose idea of a government? Before Kris could stab the comm button, Sandy got there first.

"This is Commander Santiago, skipper of the destroyer *Halsey*. Princess Longknife is in my Combat Information Center, and we've been listening in on this conversation. And Ms. Pandori, before you go through the roof, let me assure you that those listening will hold this conversation in utmost confidence until their dying day. Which, I suspect, isn't all that far off, since my ship and I will be doing our best to punch a hole in the battleships' defenses for the fast boats to slip through.

"You say you do not want a Longknife with us when we sortie tomorrow. Sorry. *We* want her. Not only do we *want* her with us on that sortie, but we *demand* that she lead us. We demand that because the odds are that a hell of a lot of us are going to die on that sortie. If she's leading us, there's a damn sight better chance that we will not die in vain. Am I clear on that point?"

"Yes, Commander," came a rather cowed woman's voice.

"I understand your political objective. As a Santiago, trust me, I don't like Longknifes any better than you do. However, I've seen the files of what she did in the only practice run this squadron got to make. I've watched her pull this lash-up together. When all hell's a-popping, you send for the bastards, and there ain't no bastard better than a Longknife bastard. From what I've seen, this one has the makings of a damn fine Longknife bastard.

"So, ma'am, when we sortie, we sortie behind her, or your father may find that those of us presently in rebellion by preparing for what we were told not to prepare for, will be in rebellion by refusing to sail for what we damn well have gotten ready for. Do I make myself clear?"

"Perfectly, Commander."

"This is Lieutenant, JG Tom Lien, commanding PF-109. I'll be in one of those toys that will be doing its best to close with the battleships and blast them out of space. Every one of us skippers wants Kris and that crazy computer around her neck to be calling the shots on when we dodge and how we do it. Eight of us tried attacking just one drone battleship, and eight of us failed. Four followed those two and we four got our fake battleship. That tell you the way it is?"

Well, maybe I don't get to stay home and knit, Kris thought.

"I will tell my father that keeping Princess Kristine out of the attack on the invaders is not an option," the young woman said. "I may require further concessions from you, Honovi."

"*You're* going to ask *me* for concessions so *my* kid sister can run off and get herself killed?" her brother growled.

Kris mashed the Talk button. "Down, Brother. Remember, you're the politician. I'm the one who gets to break things."

"Kris! Please take care."

"As much as the circumstances allow."

"Yeah, right," he snorted. "I think this tells you all you need to know, Kris. Kusa, shall we continue our talk privately?"

"*Very* privately," said the young woman's voice.

"Kris, you really will see that this does not leak."

"Brother," Kris said, glancing around the CIC, giving every soul present a look that would sear steel, "what they heard here they have already forgotten."

"Thank you. Good-bye. Stay safe."

"Good-bye. Don't forget to take care of yourself. Some of those lasers may be aimed your way, too, Brother."

There was a bitter snort. "You. Worrying about me!" and the line cut off.

"You weren't really looking for an out option, were you?" Sandy half asked.

"No, though I have to wonder a bit. Everyone keeps throwing them at me. Kind of makes me wonder if it's just me that wants to make this crazy run. Nice to know I'm wanted," Kris said, giving Tom a hug. Penny joined in from the other side.

"Yeah, I think we want you, or your computer."

"It is nice to be wanted," Nelly said.

"When you're finished with that love fest, could you help me?" Sandy said as gruffly as the grin on her face would allow. Tom and Penny broke from the hug, leaving Kris once more alone.

"Yesterday, Winston Spencer, a newsie who did a story

on what it's like to be a destroyer sailor last year, called me. Good story. Wanted to know if I'd be doing anything interesting soon. I told him I'd heard the Navy was only doing nice things just now. He said he'd heard the same, but if things changed, he'd sure like to go out with me. Friends for old times' sake."

Kris measured that against what her brother had said. Patriotism wasn't something limited to just a day here and there, to this group or that. She shrugged. "Ask him if his insurance is paid up and if his wife and kids would mind if he got suddenly dead. Then offer him a berth. Assuming you don't mind."

"He did a good story. If he lives, he'll do another one."

"Boy, aren't we a gloomy bunch," Penny said.

Tommy glanced at Penny. "Sure you want to ride the 109?"

"Will you be in it?" his bride asked. Her groom nodded. "Can anyone make that board do its tricks better than I can? Oh. Right. Nobody can make it do anything. Aren't we supposed to be talking to someone about that?" Penny said, glancing around.

"Yep, that nice guy snoring over there," Kris said.

"Who, me?" Beni said, sitting up, eyes open now.

"Can we borrow him?" Kris asked. "Tom stole this intel station, but we can't get it to tie into our sensor array. At least not consistently."

Sandy grinned. "Beni don't need sleep. Grab your toolbox and head up the pier, First Class."

"I keep saying I got to make Chief. They never do a lick of work. This being first class is just too much of a bad thing."

"You could apply for OCS," Kris suggested.

"Yeah. That would be the ticket. Officers never do nothing. Be an officer and just stand around drinking the coffee the Chief brings you and telling jokes. That's what I need to do. Which boat is it you need fixing?"

"The 109," Penny said. "I'll take you there."

Tom started to follow, but Kris grabbed his elbow. "We

have a four o'clock stand-up on the pier. Maybe after it, Penny and Beni will have your problem solved."

"Stand-up on the pier?" Sandy said.

"Yep, that's why I dropped by. To tell you about it."

Sandy got off her stool. "Glad you mentioned it."

"Say nothing of it," Kris said as they headed for the hatch.

11

If Sandy got the Word late, milling around the pier was evidence that others had gotten the Word wrong. The armed yacht skippers stood there at the 4 o'clock meeting beside the *Cushing* instead of their own 4:30. Rather than send them back to their boats to grumble for half an hour, Kris invited them to lend an ear to what the fast boats were doing.

It was a good idea.

"Can we have some of those? Anything that will keep those damn battlewagons busy elsewhere has got my vote," was Captain Luna's response to Chandra's briefing on the AGM 944 missiles. She got solid nods from her fellow yacht skippers.

Van Horn turned wordlessly to the Army Colonel who'd arrived late and breathless from his supply trove. "The Navy's pretty much stole all my 944s," the soldier said. Before a groan could get really going, he added, "But I got plenty of AGM-832s. I even got the launchers they come in. Normally truck mounted, they ought to go nicely on your boat hulls. The 832s aren't as quick on the acceleration as the 944s but they still kick like a mule, and we pack twelve of them to a box." He grinned to show one gold tooth in front. "And we got loads and loads of them."

"Anybody told you lately that they love you?" Luna said.

"Not since my wife left town with a traveling Bible salesman," the Colonel said. "I'll start shipping 832s to the Nuu yard just as soon as I get back."

"You do that, love."

"Moving right along," Roy said, turning to Phil, who launched quickly into his efforts to cool his engines down fast by replacing the radiators with ones of his own design. He finished with a big grin on his face.

Then Tom took a step forward. "And if we do it that way, we'll end up dead in space with our coolant blown."

"What'da'ya mean?" Phil shot back.

"You're using small-tubed radiators. Small tubes from beginning to end."

"The smallest possible to get the maximum radiation area."

"You also get the maximum turbulence in the coolant mixture. On Santa Maria, we intentionally use something we call Nano Mix Overheat to get the max from our mining slurry. But to keep from wrecking the nanos, we cool them down before they overheat. We tried the small tubes. And kept blowing them out. Perturbation in the liquid mix when the outside cools too fast and tries to swap with the inside but there ain't enough inside. You need a larger tube to start with at the front end of the radiator, then it narrows and splits into finer tubes. Fast, but not too fast."

"We did a computer simulation on this," the yard worker at Roy's elbow put in.

"You have any solid data to simulate from?"

"Well . . ." he started.

"Did you do a search of the literature from Santa Maria?"

"We did a search. We didn't get anything from Santa Maria."

"Man!" Tom spat. His lips got thin as he shook his head in short, choppy snaps. Kris made a note that this was what Tom looked like angry; too bad Penny wasn't here to see. "We're halfway across the galaxy. Transportation costs eat our hide. We have to have some ways of being competitive," Tom said, the true son of a Santa Maria mining family. Then he rattled off a long search string that only ended with "heat transfer."

At Roy's elbow, the yard worker talked rapidly to his computer, but Nelly was faster. A hologram sprang from Kris's chest. A schematic of a reactor, small-tube heat exchanger, red-lined. Explosion. New schematic of the same reactor, a heat exchanger that blended larger tubes that fed into smaller tubes. This time the red line bled smoothly to green.

About the time the second hologram ended, the yard worker looked up. "I found it. That's about what it says, and no, I'd never have found it doing a regular search. Damn."

"I guess I need Tom's designs and a new set of heat exchangers," Phil said, quick to change from he-bull facing he-bull to student bowing to teacher.

Tom shrugged, lopsided grin out to deflect so much of the bad that the world might have thrown at him. "I'm just glad I could help. It is an old family secret, and I'm gonna get my hide walloped for talking out of school about it."

"We'll try to keep it a family secret, just between us and Nuu Enterprises," Kris said, then leaned close as Tom stepped back into the circle of skippers. "There was a reason I wanted your nose out of that engine room," she whispered. "You're better used here than at a job the yard could do just as well."

Now Tom blushed.

"Now that that's settled, I been thinking," Luna said . . . to catcalls from her fellow skippers. "Back at the yacht basin, there's a few armed yachts that ain't going nowhere, just gathering dust. I figure one bit of brilliance deserves another, and what with us using bubble gum to stick some of that nice man's rockets on our boats, why don't we borrow some of those and stick a few rockets on them? So, what do you say to us dropping by, and, real friendly like, taking what we need?"

"There must be a guard or two," Kris said, suspecting larceny like this must normally be frowned on.

"There are, honey, but they're old and decrepit or young and want to live to be old and decrepit. What say you and I and a few of my crew go pay them a friendly visit. I really think you ought to come along. That bit of frippery around your neck is good at picking locks, I hear."

Kris turned to Captain van Horn. "Sir, you strike me as none too happy watching us kids having all the fun. Want to put together a hooligan flotilla of your own?"

"I was planning on calling up more reserves to man the tugs and other yard craft. Use them to provide search and rescue in orbit," van Horn said, pausing for a moment in thought. "Maybe a couple of armed yachts backing them up might come in handy."

"Some of the larger unarmed runabouts might handle the ship-to-ship rescue work very well," Kris said. "The Coast Guard Reserve could crew them." Most of the time, the Coastie Reserve just did safety checks and caught the odd boat that got in trouble before it burned itself up on reentry or vanished forever into deep space. They were civilians for the most part, owners of small-system runabouts. Kris had gotten to know them during her skiff racing days. They were good people; would they appreciate the job she was calling them in on?

Van Horn nodded. "I have a liaison with the Coasties. I'll see if I can't get some of them up here and give them the Search and Rescue job. That would free mine up for something." The Navy Captain turned to the Colonel. "How many of those AGM-832 missiles can you lay your hands on?"

"How many you want?"

"What if I were to load up two, four small container ships with your missiles?"

The Colonel whistled. "A whole arsenal. Hmm. You swabbies would need some help aiming them. I know just the red legs to do that. Let's you and me talk."

Kris found herself ignored as the Captain and the Colonel walked off in animated conversation. Luna shook her head. "Now that looks damn dangerous. There's a reason we like the Navy and Army hating each other's guts and brawling properly in any good bar. When they start working together, freedom for dishonest people like me is seriously in jeopardy."

"Then we better be off quickly and commit whatever piracy you have planned before they can get the world so organized and law abiding that there's no room for an honest and free woman."

"I knew a Longknife would understand," Luna said, grinning. "Now, do we take the sabers, or just our smiles?"

At Kris's suggestion, they settled on smiles. With Jack at one elbow and Luna and her crew of time-displaced pirates at the other, Kris quickly found herself at the yacht docks. They were pretty much abandoned, as was most of the space station once you got away from the yards. Only an old man and his teenage grandson stood guard at the gate to the main pier.

"Was wondering when you'd show up," the old man said, staring up at her from where he sat in a small guardhouse beside a flimsy gate that hardly blocked the main pier's access road.

"Wondering," Kris echoed, trying not to give away anything more than the presence of her and Luna's crew did.

"Yeah. The Shipwright's Daughter just outside Nuu Docks' gate is the only place open an old man or his grandson can get a bite to eat. Luna and her cutthroats move their overstoked tubs there. And there's talk of a Longknife on the base." The man's grin at Kris was missing three teeth. "I served with your great-grampa at the Battle of the Big Orange Nebula."

He glanced over to where long, wide windows on the floor of the station showed row upon row of yachts tied up.

"Owners that buy armed yachts don't do a lot of talking about what they got under the hood, but I'll bet you that you've come for the five, six boats that are still parked and that have lasers behind their brightwork. And I'll bet you I know which ones they are."

"Sorry, Gabby. Betting against you would be betting against a sure thing," Luna said. "You gonna let us at them, or do we need to rough you up for appearances?"

At the suggestion of hurting his grandfather, the kid moved forward, a baseball bat with a lead weight ready in his hand.

"No, Cory," the old man said. "She was just asking me what I needed for job security. Luna'd never hurt me more than she needed to, to get a job done," he grinned, gap-toothed.

"What do you say I let you in and we wait and see what comes of it. Who knows, we may all end up heroes. If it don't turn out that way, I'm sure me and Cory can find a couple of flights of stairs to fall down. Now come on, I know where they keep the spare keys to most of these."

Unfortunately, getting access to the armed ships turned out to be the least of the problems. Getting into their systems, especially gun systems, turned out to be a lot tougher. Nelly did her usual hack effort and found them as well secured as Peterwald's yacht had been on Turantic. Rather than force them by raw power, Kris called Nuu Docks; all of them had started life there. All had a standard set of ship systems from the yard . . . and all had system back doors that all but one of the owners hadn't bothered to change. And that one had not bought nearly as good a security system as he thought. Well before lights out, Nelly had all six armed yachts and eight large runabouts ready to follow them back to Nuu Docks like nice little ducklings.

Next morning, the yard was a madhouse, with more ships to work on, more work to do, and more people doing it. At the 0800 stand-up beside the *Cushing,* Roy from the yard proudly reported the last discrepancies with the PFs had been cured during the night. The installation of AGM-944s had been successfully completed on Singh's boat, and they were ready to proceed with the rest. Tests with the new radiators had been completed in the yard. If Phil and Tom agreed, they'd start installing new ones by noon. Both Lieutenants agreed to make that review their first order of business after the meeting.

That meeting over, Kris headed for her next one with the armed yacht skippers trailing a fast-stepping Captain van Horn and Colonel Tye. Kris should have recognized that for trouble, but her lack of sleep or tendency to view higher-ranking officers as hopelessly harmless led her astray.

The 0830 stand-up was a mob scene. But then, Nuu yards now sported a rather large mob of ships. It had started with armed yachts learning to fake it as cruisers and battleships. Now there were more armed yachts, as well as rescue runabouts that had started life unarmed but looked to be acquiring Army rockets. A quick glance showed Kris that anywhere anybody could find a spare inch of deck was fast filling with rocket launchers. And four medium-size Navy container ships usually plying quiet resupply routes now occupied docks at Nuu and were growing antennas of several makes and many models.

"That yours, Captain?" Kris asked.

"Ours," the Army Colonel cut in.

"Navy-Army combined effort," Van Horn agreed.

"Army-Navy," the Colonel corrected.

"As soon as we get the Navy sensor containers loaded, an idea left over from the Iteeche Wars, we'll take those four ships over to the Army Depot and start loading containers of the 832 missiles and even older birds. Anyway, between the Navy sensor suite to fix a target—"

"And the artillery crews programming missiles to go for targets without grid coordinates or GPS," the Colonel cut in, "we should have a major annoyance for our uninvited guests."

"We might even do a little damage if we get lucky," Van Horn added drolly.

"A lot of damage if they hit. Pile-driving warheads on those old 722s can cut through six meters of concrete. Wonder what they'll do to ice?" The Army Colonel grinned. "Who says old is useless?"

"Those missiles will definitely get those battleships' attention. Maybe five, ten percent," the Navy officer added.

"But sometimes, it's the last fraction of a percent that matters," the soldier whispered.

Kris nodded agreement.

That was the last bit of agreement she got for quite a while as she slipped into a knot of arguing yacht skippers surrounding Roy. The bottom line was there were a lot more spots on yachts where skippers wanted to mount rocket launchers than there were rocket launchers. So everyone wanted what there was to be had.

"Hold it, hold it," Kris said, raising her arms and shouting to be heard. "First thing, you don't decide who gets rockets."

"Who does?" several of the skippers demanded, Captain Luna first among them.

"The battle plan does," Kris said.

"And what's it say?" Luna growled.

"That some of you might get a chance to use those missiles, and others of you won't get any such chance. Nelly, show them a hologram of what those rockets can do." A sphere appeared in front of Kris. "In space, these rocket seekers should be good for twenty thousand kilometers. But better to hold them until you're ten K out. You have to be close enough for the warhead's seeker to home on heat, like a battleship's engine." The hologram showed a battleship with a rocket heading for the medium heat around the engines, not the extreme heat of the thermonuclear exhaust.

"But the key words in what I just said were the ten to twenty thousand kilometers. If you go up against a fully operational battleship, it will shoot you down before you get anywhere near missile range. You've got to go in after other ships have taken a lot of the fight out of the battleships."

"The Captain and the Colonel are making noises about using missiles. Lots of them, from a damn bunch of tramp container scows," Luna pointed out. "Don't sound like they're planning on waiting for things to get peaceful."

"We're putting sensors and guidance on those ships. We're going to use them different from you. We don't have enough of the stuff we're concentrating on those scows to share among all of you. You're gonna have to go in close and use the warhead seekers to get your job done. Sorry, that's just the way it's gonna be." Kris cut off further debate on that.

"So how many missile launcher boxes do I get?" Luna said.

"None."

"What!"

"Remember, you're faking it as a cruiser. Navy cruisers do not fire Army surplus rockets."

"But once I shuck those duds, I could."

"Not likely." Kris shook her head. "Backing your boat out of the fake front is going to be hard enough without trying not to rip off the launcher. Face it, Luna, if you just knock it a bit, it's gonna break. No, the six of you that are pushing the drones will have your hands full during the early part of the fight just faking it. After that, you can do what you want with your lasers. The other yachts will get the launchers."

"Damn." Luna looked around at the new skippers. "Any of you want to trade ships?"

Kris suppressed a grin. What happened to all that "I know my boat. I'm the best one to drive it." But she was busy counting noses. Yes, they did have a round dozen extra yachts. Half of them sported some sort of burst laser. The others had been planned for rescue, but maybe . . .

"There are twelve fast patrol boats. There are twelve yachts. That gives us a chance to complicate the battleship's firing solutions for the early part of the attack. If you're game."

The new bunch of yacht skippers were a mixed crew.

Some were hired, like Luna; a few were actually the own-ers. Others were Navy, reassigned from tugs and other yard craft now that the Coasties had been brought in to run the rescue effort. One was a Coast Guard reservist. They eyed each other; one muttered, "I should have known, with a Longknife on board, it'd get terminal," but they all nodded when one said, "What do you have in mind?"

"We start the charge at 1.5 g's. Then work up to 2.0 g's, then 2.5 as we close. The final approach will be at a good 3.5 or better. I know you can't make accelerations like those."

Faces suddenly gone pale nodded back at her.

"But if you were with us for the trot, maybe stay with us for the canter," Kris said, falling into horse talk.

"It would help?" one skipper said.

"Give the battlewagons more targets," another answered.

"They'd be at extreme main battery range," Kris pointed out. "You'd drop out well before we got into the secondary battery envelope, where the fire would get rough."

"Where's the help in that?" one skipper asked.

"I don't know about yours, but my wife would kind of find it a help," another snorted.

"But would it do any good?" another said. "Don't they have some kind of electronic stuff? Couldn't they tell us from you?"

Among the decoy yachts, a Navy OIC coughed. "We were talking about just this kind of thing yesterday eve-ning, when all those yachts came toddling over to the yard. No one's using any of the stuff on the old MK VIs yet. We could cobble together some decent maskers from them."

The woman glanced around her fellow Navy types, got nods. "It wouldn't work perfectly, but if we did a few things with your PFs, Your Highness, and a few things with your yachts, ladies and gentlemen, we could fix it so those bastards would be stuck scratching their heads for a whole lot longer than I'd want if I was in their shoes. Which I never want to be."

This was going farther than Kris had intended. These were civilians, dragooned in at the last moment. She had hoped to talk them into starting the charge with her boats, then falling out quickly. She hadn't expected they could do anything else.

Suddenly, it was looking like they could do a whole lot more. But at a horrible price. Kris wanted to beg off, excuse herself, tell them to forget that she'd ever mentioned it.

Yet, if her PFs were to deliver their 18-inch laser blasts to those battleships, they needed all the help they could get. Might the sacrifice of these twelve be critical to victory?

Kris remembered Phil's story of the earlier Torpedo 8. Fifteen hopelessly outnumbered planes had bored in and been slaughtered. At the moment, their sacrifice had seemed a horrible waste. But the enemy defenses had been lured down low. They didn't notice the bombers up high. And those bombers had smashed them, redeeming Torpedo 8's sacrifice.

I can't not ask these civilians to do this. I'll hate myself, but Kris kept silent, let an icy cold freeze her heart. Allowed granite, hard and unfeeling, to replace the churning in her gut. She stood as men and women, some with cracking voices, talked themselves into a death ride.

"We have to. There's no other choice," was the final word from one woman, tears streaming down her face.

God, I'm coming to hate that phrase.

"Nelly, order more helmets for these boats."

"Yes, ma'am. I placed the order as they were talking. Express to the Navy athletic center. They should be here today. We'll need to install high-g stations on all the yachts."

"I figured as much," Roy said. "I'll get my shops working on that. Can each of you report your needs ASAP?"

"Some of us have high-g stations," one Captain said.

"Very likely you'll want better," Kris said. "You'll not only need to go straight ahead at two or more g's, but you'll need to be dodging right, left, up, down every two, three seconds."

Several Captains gulped. "That's gonna take a lot of

reaction mass. Some of our directional thrusters weren't designed with things like that in mind." That started a lengthy discussion that ended with some of the Army rockets being stripped down to raw motor segments and strapped to the noses of some of the yachts. As they built up to higher g's, they'd use those solid rocket motor bursts to augment their thrusters.

"When you've used them up, drop out of the charge," Kris told them. And chose to believe the nods they gave her. Maybe they believed them themselves.

At two g's, with directional thrusters minimal, how do you break away from a charge? *Don't ask the question, Kris, if you don't want the answer.*

Kris sent the yard crews and the yacht personnel on their ways to load rocket launchers. She needed to study the battle board. She needed to study it a lot. This battle was getting more and more complicated.

Winnable?

She wanted to think so. But there was a long way between a battle being winnable and it being won. A long way.

Kris looked around, found she wasn't needed, and headed for the *Halsey.* She found Sandy hunched over the battle board and quickly brought her up to date on the changes agreed to at the meeting. Or started to.

Sandy knew what van Horn was up to. She waved Kris to a halt at the idea of stripping the MK VIs to outfit the yachts.

"No can do. Van Horn will need them. We can't have cargo ships running around a Navy gun line. Looks funny. I use a couple of tugs to fake it like tin cans and the gear from the MK VI on the freighters to fake them as cruisers."

"So, how do I hide my PFs among some fast yachts for at least the first part of the charge?"

"Let's see what we can do about you having your cake while I eat it." She tapped her commlink. "Beni?"

"This better be good news"—punctuated by a yawn— "'cause I just got back . . . *three hours ago* from fixin' that PF's sensors." After another yawn, a "ma'am," was appended.

"I got bad news and good news, Beni. There's a Longknife at my elbow, and she wants lots of electronic countermeasures."

"And the good news is . . ."

"Doesn't your old man know most of Wardhaven's old crows?"

"Yeah."

"Well, we need them and all the gadgets and potions they can lay their hands on up the beanstalk, say, in the next hour."

"That's gonna be kind of noticeable."

"We'll worry about the noticing. You worry about landing that flock on our doorstep soonest."

"Yes, ma'am."

Kris leaned over the commlink. "And Beni, can I borrow your phone to call home, if it's not too much trouble?"

"Trouble's all I seem to get since a Longknife showed up. For sure not much sleep."

"You got to apply to OCS," Kris said through a grin. "You'll get plenty of sleep at OCS."

"That's what I heard. Hearing it from a Longknife, I kind of find myself doubting the story now. You know what I mean."

"Call your old man," Sandy said. "Then get to CIC."

"Yes, ma'am. Out."

Sandy punched her side of the commlink. "We'll see what that starts moving up the elevator. Singer, Sperry, lots of folks have stuff we can use. I expect to see a lot of lab stuff. Gear they think they can twist or tweak for us."

"Non-standard. I thought you liked standard."

Sandy sighed. "I love standard. I love well-tested and proven. I like not being dead day after tomorrow even more. One out of three won't be too bad." A quick call to the yard made sure the MK VIs didn't get broken out for spare parts. About that time, Beni showed up with his phone and Kris called Honovi.

"You okay?" was his first question.

"I'm fine. You making progress?"

"Slowly. I'm in a meeting just now. Father and her father, so I can't talk long."

"We're needing to call out for pizza, several other things. It may start getting harder for us to go unnoticed."

"You have hardly escaped notice, Sis. But the bugs and rats are no more interested in selling soap to certain approaching markets than you and I are, so they're willing to sit on it. They want to know when they can stop sitting on it, though."

Kris looked at Sandy. She shrugged. "I'll give you a guesstimate on that next call," Kris said.

"Well, thanks for the early notice. Now, I have to go."

"Good-bye," Kris said to a silent line.

"You'd think they were building a battleship," Sandy said.

"Politics is their life," Kris answered lamely.

"Well, this could be our death. I wish they'd pay a bit more attention to us." So the two of them did pay attention. They studied the battle board and the pieces they had to move around it. They studied the hostiles . . . no change there. They examined, questioned, and modified their assumptions about the six battleships, then did the same for their own units.

When the first lunch sitting was piped, Sandy ordered something sent down; meatloaf sandwiches with potato salad swallowed with red bug juice. Captain van Horn joined them, borrowed half of Kris's sandwich, and examined how to get the best use out of his missile ships. He tapped the final stretch of yellow approach mapped for the hostiles. "They'll be coming in on deceleration. Rear end to Wardhaven. Get my missile ships across their sterns early to fire up their soft rears. Sooner or later one of our rockets will hit something that'll hurt them.

"Then you charge in and smash them. Let the rest of the hellions rip what you leave behind, and then I'll mosey in close and send salvos into the shattered wrecks. Take no prisoners."

"I hadn't thought about prisoners," Kris said.

"We'd better. Do we offer them a chance to surrender or no? 'Cause once the fight gets hot, it'll be real hard to put a stop to it." The Captain looked slowly around their small circle.

"If they want to give up," Sandy said, "I'm all for it. But we can't call for their surrender too early. It'll make us look weak. Considering how weak we are, we can't look weak."

"I agree," was all Kris could add. She'd spent all her time thinking how she couldn't surrender. It felt strange planning how to offer that to her enemy. Even stranger to realize that the very offer of surrender was a carefully balanced ploy.

Good Lord, let me do this right, she prayed softly to herself . . . and any listening God.

"I say we let them surrender when we have them on the ropes and begging," van Horn said. "They call us, we don't call them."

"They might surrender a bit earlier if we reminded them the offer was on the table," Sandy said.

"And they might get all hard and John Paul Jones on us. 'I have not yet begun to fight,' and such," said the Captain.

"Gosh," Kris said, all wide-eyed, "And I took us for the underdog and them for the overconfident ones."

"Hard to tell," the Captain said, dusting sandwich crumbs from his hands and heading for the hatch.

"Very hard to tell," Sandy said in agreement.

12

The afternoon went long, with Kris still poring over the battle board. Jack stood close, watching, occasionally asking a question. Few were dumb. "If the yachts are faking it as PFs, won't it be kind of obvious when the real PFs fire this Foxer decoy stuff, and the yachts don't?" he asked.

Sandy sighed. "And the battleships will know exactly who are PFs and who are yachts . . . and the yachts would die. You want to join up, Agent?" Jack took a big step back.

The yachts needed Foxers or something like it. Kris took a walk over to the yard to get them welding external tubes to the yachts for firing a few Foxers. They'd have to do it manually, and with no reloads, but it might work . . . for a while.

To avoid putting a Foxer message on a net that was supposed to be all roses and kisses, Jack went off happily with Sandy's XO to see what the Foxer status was at the Naval Supply Center. They came back way too quickly and none to happily.

"When the fleet sailed, it took a full load of Foxers for every ship. That didn't leave many in stores. Here's the bad news," he said, handing Kris a number that when divided by the number of yachts came out between one and two.

Jack drew the job of dropping down the beanstalk to visit the company that made Foxers. Colonel Tye went searching the Army Supply Center for anything that might fake it as a Foxer . . . and Kris tried not to kick herself for not thinking about this yesterday. This whole operation was a thousand-headed monster . . . but it grew its heads a day, an hour, a minute at a time.

It was bad the way it was slowly being popped on her. With luck, springing the whole thing on the Peterwald fleet in one big chunk would be a whopping shock to their carefully laid plans.

The 1600 meeting with the PF skippers came before Jack got back. Kris led off with her idea of mixing armed yachts in with the PFs early in the charge to confuse the battleships. Phil looked none too happy. " 'Steer clear of the merchie,' my pappy always warned, 'lest she liven up your day by taking it in her head to ram you.' "

"They won't go full bore, probably won't go more than two g's," Kris answered. "They'll come in behind us to finish off what we've left crippled."

The other skippers seemed to like the idea.

Then Kris told them they'd have to share their Foxers.

"Trade-off." Chandra scowled. "All the world is a balance."

"I hope we get something for that balance," Heather said. "I don't want to get squashed like some wandering frog 'cause someone is using up my supply of foxy."

"We're looking into what we can do," Kris said.

Penny and Tom took a step forward when Kris thought the meeting was about done. "We were talking with Beni," Tom said. "We think we can improve our chances of maintaining communications between the ships, letting us talk when we want even if they try to jam, if we set up a continuous battle net with a preplanned swapping of data packets. We'll then piggyback anything we're saying onto the preplanned packet."

"And Tommy has just the idea for something to play on the battle net in the background," Penny said.

"What?" Kris asked, not sure about Tom's choice of music.

"Trust me," Tom said. "It's something my old grandda says came with the landers from Earth, three hundred years ago. Twenty-first century. Maybe older, from the words."

"But don't listen to it until we go out," Penny said. "Don't spoil it."

"Trust you," Kris repeated.

"Believe us, it's good. Ask Beni if you don't believe us."

Kris made a note to do just that, but she also had a note to do something else. "How's the 109?"

"Good to go," Tom said as Penny said. "Great!"

"Good," Kris said.

"A bit more work on her tonight—" Tom started.

"No," Kris said.

"Huh?" came from both.

"The High Wardhaven Hilton actually is open for business. It's not getting a lot, but it's open," she told her two friends. "I reserved the Honeymoon Suite for you two tonight." There were noes and can'ts and other negatives, but Kris talked right over them. "It's four o'clock, civilian time. I'm sure if you show up by 7:30 tomorrow morning, the Chief can fill you in on anything and everything that's happened in the meantime."

Penny and Tom were still shaking their heads. Behind them, Phil and Chandra, Babs and Ted were gathering, wide grins on their faces. Heather was making signals to the other skippers. Kris didn't need two guesses about where this was headed.

"Now then," Kris continued slowly, eminently rationally, "You two can either walk yourselves over to the Hilton, check yourselves in, and enjoy the night. Or your friendly neighborhood JO juvenile delinquents can grab you, strip you naked, haul you squealing and screaming over to the Hilton, lock you in your Honeymoon Suite for the night, and leave you showing up for battle tomorrow morning dressed like Hikila warriors . . . without the tats."

Penny and Tom glanced behind them. Then turned to face down the growing threat. "I think surrender is the better part of modesty, here." Tom sighed.

"Heather and Babs look awfully eager to get their hands on you," Penny said.

"Ted and Phil ain't exactly backing away from you, love."

There was a general move toward them.

"We're moving. We're moving," the young couple said in unison. "Just tell Chief Stan to recheck that sensor feed," Penny called over her shoulder as Tom put his arm around her.

"Glad those two haven't forgotten what it's like to be just married," Phil said.

"Be nice to have someone to hold tonight. Be held by," Heather said with a shiver.

"Chandra, you going to make it home tonight?"

"Can't stay away that long." The old mustang sighed. But coming down the pier, like it was any other day, was Goran, two kids in hand, at least until they caught sight of Mom. Then they broke ranks and mobbed her with, "Mommy, Mommy."

Once she surfaced from hugs and kisses and more hugs and kisses, she turned to scold Goran, but he silenced her with a kiss of his own. "Certainly your boat can spare you for a few hours."

"But this station is a target tomorrow."

"And I and our children will not be here. Trust me," he said. "Certainly, there is somewhere we can be alone."

NELLY, TELL THE HILTON I'M PAYING HALF FOR A WHOLE BLOCK OF THEIR ROOMS.

ALREADY CHECKED. THEY HAVE CUT THEIR RATE FOR ANYONE WITH AN ID CARD.

"The Hilton has a special tonight, Chandra, Goran." So with the first smile Kris had enjoyed in a long time, she left the PF pier behind and headed for Nuu Docks. One look at what lay ahead of her . . . and she wanted to go hide in the 109.

If the earlier meetings had been mobs, this one was a full-fledged riot. All the efforts to keep things low key at the beanstalk were history. Everyone and his brother and pet duck must have headed up to the space station.

There were main contractors with ideas, sub-contractors with their suggestions, sub-subcontractors with their brilliant pet concepts, and folks who'd never won a bid for even a sub-sub-subcontractor's billet who were absolutely sure they had the war-winning breakthrough . . . and anyone who knew someone who knew someone on one of the yachts and had gotten through the Nuu yard gates was there. Kris had to remind herself that the enemy was that-away and that using machine guns for crowd control had gotten Colonel Hancock in trouble.

Still, it was tempting.

Roy took to the role of ringmaster like a seal takes to a pool of fish. He ordered all the nonship personnel to the yard side of the pier. He then invited the ship personnel to police up their ranks. Merchant sailors relished tossing business types who drew five, ten times their pay over where they belonged. None too gently. With wide grins.

A quick rundown of progress showed that the missile launchers were going onto the larger system runabouts. Despite the early morning decision, Luna and her fellow decoy Captains had come up with an idea that would get them a few missiles "in small, conformal packages." Foxers were going onto the runabouts that would be mixing in with the PFs. Like the missiles on Luna's boats, they were in tubes welded to hulls. No reloads. Four to a boat if the supply could be found.

It turned out that the Army had some white phosphorous rockets that they used in space situations. They would provide heat and some cover. Kris ordered them to be mounted on a two-for-two basis on the yachts, and some for the PFs. That way, the first four times both ships dodged, they'd be alternating Foxers with phosphorus. That ought to confuse the battlewagons. It left enough folks at this meeting scratching their heads.

Make do, make do. Just let it get us by, Kris prayed.

Once the usual business was covered, Roy tackled the masker and countermeasure problems. "Any of you big fellows bring along enough units for say, thirty, forty ships?" got slow shakes of the heads from the main contractors.

"So we're going to have to let some ships sail with some of your gear, some ships sail with the other guy's stuff."

"Kind of looks that way."

Roy signaled for the Navy OICs to step forward from the MK XII decoys. Most of them knew at least a couple of the business types. Roy brought in several of his own yard people. It began to look for all the world like a bizarre bazaar with this group haggling with that Naval officer, that shipyard fellow shaking his head violently, "No, you can't do that," and a contractor insisting that his new baby could, and skippers like Luna standing back, skeptical looks clouding their faces.

Kris sidled up to Roy, who took a second from his dickering to notice her. "You going to need me?"

"Don't think so. Best you leave this kind of stuff to us with dirty hands. Where you going if I do need you, though?"

"*Halsey*'s CIC," Kris said. He nodded and dived back into his debate of antenna, bandwidth, and signal strength.

Kris backed out, found Jack waiting for her, brought him up to date on what she'd been doing, and found out that the Foxer manufacturer had been waiting for a new contract before he started turning out any more units.

As Kris groaned, he quickly added, "However, he expected we might need some and has been running twenty-four/seven since those battleships showed up. He's shipping what he has and shipping the rest as fast as they come off the line." Jack sent Nelly a report that showed enough to rig maybe four or six to the laser-armed yachts. Filling up the spare lockers of Squadron 8 and the destroyers would have to be done from the last to arrive.

"It's going to be tight," Kris said.

"Yeah, hope it's just as tight for the other guy."

Kris nodded. "I have to remember that. If I have it bad, the other guy can't have it all that easy . . . even if we are doing this battle on their timetable."

"Remember, according to the last news report out, your boats are cold steel, and all he has to worry about is the *Halsey* and maybe the *Cushing*. Would you want to be on his bridge when they get the first reports on the fleet that you're gonna have sortieing from High Wardhaven? And then you're gonna be hiding behind the moon as they get closer."

"And deaf," Kris said. "If the battleships do anything while we're behind the moon, we won't know about it. We need a relay to keep us in touch. Come on, I've got to talk to Sandy."

Sandy shook her head. "I should have thought of that before. We want them to be biting their nails about us, not the other way around. But whatever we put in a trailing slot will be out of the fight." She scowled.

Kris hadn't worked to get all this ready just to start paring her fleet down. "Nelly, call that nice guard at the yacht basin."

"Hello," came back at her.

"Hi, I dropped by a few days ago to look at buying a few boats. You seemed to know what just about every one of them had inside. You wouldn't happen to know of one that has a lot of entertainment capability, maybe the thing my boyfriend would want. He's kind of into broadcasting."

"Broadcasting, you say. Something that could get you a good media feed and send it on your way where you want it?"

"Yes. That's it."

"Well, there's this system runabout owned by a media anchorwoman who has only used it to run to the moon and back. Wanted to know what all her competitors were doing while she was on vacation. I think she mainly was worrying about replacement. You want to come over and get it? Take it out for a spin?"

"Grampa," came an enthusiastic voice on the phone, "why don't we take it over to her. We can run it around. We do it when they need cleaning. We know how to run those things."

"Son."

"Grampa."

There was a long pause, pregnant with expectation.

"Got room for an old fart and a smart kid?" finally came back at Kris.

"You know where we'll want you."

"We'll be there in an hour."

"Two more volunteers," Sandy said as the commlink went silent.

"But these stay way back, right?" Kris said. So why did she have chills running up her back? With a shiver, she changed her train of thought. "They're going to be shipping Foxers up the beanstalk. We've got a small mob of electronic countermeasures folks, and they're bound to be shipping stuff up. The beanstalk's going to get plenty busy."

"So that's a flock of ravens on the next pier," Sandy said. "Wonder what they'll come up with?"

"I think I better warn my brother that the space elevator is going to be a busy place. Where's Beni?"

"In the sack," the Duty Lieutenant said, but she produced a commlink from a drawer. "The boy may be slow and lazy, but he ain't dumb. Said if you needed his phone, better it was here than under his pillow."

"Boy is educatable," Sandy agreed.

Kris dialed Honovi. "Bro, it's me. How are things?"

"We're working on it. I'm with Pop and his good buddy just now." Kris heard snorts in the background.

"I thought you ought to know that the beanstalk is going to be getting a workout soon. All kinds of nice stuff."

"Hmm. I'm putting you on speaker, turnabout being fair." Kris did the same. Brother continued, "We've got a bit of a problem. Among our others. Seems there are several liners in port. Due to sail yesterday, today. Booked solid. We've held them in port. Policy issues. That kind of stuff."

Kris could imagine. Would Peterwald dare shoot up a liner registered to an Earth company or one of the hugely powerful Seven Sisters, the first planets colonized four hundred years ago? Do you hold the liners in port and challenge Peterwald to shoot up the station with them there? Not very brave, but then Pandori was grasping for anything.

"We've got folks who want to leave town, folks with non-Wardhaven passports. Even some with ours. So, we're thinking of giving in and letting the boats sail. What are your thoughts?"

Kris eyed Sandy and wished she had a whole lot more people here at the moment. Liners would mean a mob scene at the station. People with cameras. It would be much harder to keep hidden what they were doing. Or could they hide their efforts among the flow? Would refugees be interested in looking around? Would all the people fleeing be refugees?

The Duty Lieutenant tapped a workstation. One of the screens scrolled down a list of passenger ships in port. Four big ones. Six medium. Most had sailing dates past due. Yep, there'd be a lot of pressure on Pandori to let them go.

"If they sailed at the same time we did?" Kris said. She was no expert on electromagnetic racket, but all those reactors would have to put out a whole lot of noise. All that mass in motion would play hail Columbia with detection gear. Could her tiny fleet fall out the bottom? NELLY, SHOW ME IN PURPLE THE ORBITS THESE LINERS WOULD TAKE TO GET TO JUMP POINT ALPHA. COULD THEY BE MADE TO FOLLOW THE FIRST PART OF OUR ORBIT AROUND WARDHAVEN AND OUR HEADING TO THE MOON?

The purple path appeared on the battle board. Sandy frowned and mouthed "Nelly," silently at Kris. Kris nodded. Sandy eyed the plot. "Birds on the next pier might like this idea."

"I missed that," Honovi said.

"Some local discussion. Some of us up here think it would be a good idea to let the passenger ships go."

"You're not going to use them . . ." Kris recognized Pandori's deep baritone.

"No. But if they traveled the same path for a ways, it wouldn't hurt. We'd want those ships to leave—"

Sandy cut Kris off with a sharp shake of the head.

Kris backed off two hours and said, "All the passengers would have to be aboard by, say, seven tomorrow morning."

"Not a lot of time," Father said.

"There's not a lot of time before those other ships show up," Kris pointed out, if it needed pointing out.

"Yes." "Right." "Just so," came from the phone. Apparently it did need pointing out.

"So there will be a lot of traffic up the stalk in the next couple of hours," Kris said. "Please keep it low-key."

"We will," Brother promised.

"And you are going to make us legal, right?"

"We were working on that when we were interrupted by this other matter," Father assured her.

"See you when this is all over," Kris promised.

"Please, yes," Honovi answered as the line went silent.

"I better get back over to the yard," Kris said, getting up. "Sorry about having Nelly mess with the inside of your battle board, but . . ."

"It seemed like a good idea at the time," Sandy said. "You know, I've never once heard a Longknife admit to doing something that seemed like a bad idea at the time. Now, in hindsight . . ."

Kris tried to give the destroyer Captain a lighthearted shrug. She wasn't doing lighthearted all that well today. Whatever she did, it seemed to mollify Sandy.

"Still, it was good to have that plot added to my board and nice not to have it talked about on net, so, yes, Nelly, you're forgiven for messing with my ship."

"I just asked the board to plot the course. The board did all the work," Nelly said. "It did it most rapidly."

"Nelly, are you complimenting my standard Navy-issue gear?"

"It did the job required of it."

"I think your computer is learning tact."

"I hope so," Kris said as she headed for the hatch.

"You going into that den of thieves next door?" Jack asked.

"Looks like it."

"I better tag along."

"I thought you were on terminal leave."

"Yeah, I am, ain't I. But I don't like the looks of that mob they let in. It sure would be a shame for you to get this ragtag and bobtail collection all formed up, then miss the show because someone put a bullet in your elbow. Pinked you in your little toe. You know, that kind of thing."

"You know, if I didn't know better, I'd think you were concerned about me."

"Nope, just worried about my professional reputation. Me being so close when you get tagged, I'd never live it down."

"Yeah, right," Kris said. But it did feel good to have Jack at her side, doing that thing he did that seemed to be looking every which way at once.

On his own pier, Roy had organized chaos into groups that were examining small chunks of the problem. He circulated between them. Kris caught him in midcirculation and brought him up to date on the major ship movement about to take place.

"Crap, I was kind of hoping those love boats would stay tied up not too far from me and my docks. So they're out of here."

"Looks that way."

"Good Lord but that's gonna be a lot of noise, not to mention heavy metal moving around," he said, slowing down. "Albert. You might want to hear this. You too, Gus."

Two middle-aged types. Albert a tall, thin woman, Gus a short, round man, detached themselves from different groups to join Kris and Roy. As Kris repeated her situation report, several others gravitated into their circle.

"Neat," a young woman said. "Plenty of mass. Plenty of magnetic excitement. Where's the sun and moon?"

"Nelly, give the woman a schematic of the system." And one appeared in front of Kris.

"If the whole mob pulled away at the same time, you'd have Wardhaven between the bastards and you for fifteen, twenty minutes," Gus said, pudgy fingers tracing Nelly's hologram.

"You could sort yourselves out, form on their reverse side, be in their shadow by the time you got out from behind Wardhaven," Albert said.

"They'd head for Alpha jump," Kris said, "and standard battle tactics would have us head for the moon."

"No surprise there," Gus said, "but you'd have their background noise again to use to sort yourselves out, get the larger ships in front, the smaller in their shadow. We could have a whole lot of different . . . and extraneous . . . noise from several sources covering so much of your signal that . . ."

"Yes." Albert nodded. "Those liners would add a very nice bit of cover to the symphony. If we tweaked our signals in the J band. The L and P. We could have them so confused."

Kris left them to their confusion and headed for Luna's boat. "You set?" she asked the merchant skipper.

"As set as can be. Appreciate you letting us have some of them Foxers and Army WP. I know you would like us to hang back out of range, but that ain't what I got in mind."

"Nelly's developed some bone-jarring evasion schemes."

"Yeah. A mite rough for these old bones, but those new brain buckets they dropped on us might save what smarts I got left, and I do like the rig your Nelly did to my high-g chair. Where was she when I was a young sprout, kicking up my boots?"

"I was a young chip, learning to count, and couldn't tell a random number from an imaginary one," Nelly put in.

"Damn, she's even telling jokes. Can you cook?"

"No." Nelly sounded truly brokenhearted.

"Well, you learn how to cook, and I'll think about marrying you. Cooking and singing."

"Don't encourage her to sing."

"Singing. I could learn to sing."

"I think I've created a monster, if you ain't done it first, honey."

"I'm afraid I did it long ago," Kris said and took her leave, Jack at her elbow. They walked along the piers where the other yachts, both armed and rescue boats, were fitting out.

"It's getting more and more complicated," Jack said.

"With more people involved. Just look at the crews of these boats." There were civilian and merchant marine, Navy and Coast Guard Reserve, mixed together as if they'd been press-ganged to crew boats that had started with one mission in mind, then switched to another. But whatever job they'd drawn, they'd taken to it with a will. Despite van Horn's warning about friction, or maybe because of his ham-handed words, Kris hadn't had a single problem.

Here and there she paused to talk to officers and crew; no one asked her when it would start; they knew the physics of space travel as well as she did. No one asked if they'd sail. With or without authorization from their government, these men and women were committed. Had been for two or three days.

"We're ready, ma'am." "You bet, Your Highness," "We're behind you," sounded good.

She found Gabby and Cory at the end of a line of un-armed civilian tugs, two reserve comm tech 2/c's working to get their hijacked boat ready for the next day.

"You'll be trailing the main force," Kris told them. Nelly provided a hologram that explained it. "When we're behind the moon, we don't want them to do something to surprise us."

"Right, tomorrow, all the surprises are on those bastards." The kid laughed.

"That's the general idea," Kris agreed. "You're our link to let us know. If the sensors on the base detect changes in the hostiles, they signal you. You relay it to us. I can't think of anything more critical tomorrow."

"Besides blowing one of those battleships out of space," the old man said.

"We'll do that. You just tell us what we need to know."

"You can count on us."

Kris gave them a jaunty thumbs-up and headed back.

"You're feeling guilty," Jack said beside her, his eyes still roving. Habit? No one here would harm her.

"More like burdened. They're so sure I'll come up with the right plan, get things just right so we win this thing. They must know how bad the odds are."

"Doesn't look it from where I'm standing," Jack said.

"Faith is a wonderful thing. They have faith, and I'm stuck hoping I can come up with the perfect attack plan."

"I think that's called the burden of command."

They were back in Roy's domain. Carts, long tables, and black boxes made up an impromptu assembly line, complete with a quality control station. A woman there rejected someone's work. "Try holding it together next time with bubble gum."

"How's it going?" Kris asked Roy.

"Fine, fine. Couldn't be better. Oh, one thing, if we want the armed yachts to fake it as PFs, maybe it would be good if the PFs occasionally come off looking like yachts. We'd like to put some noisemakers on them. Something that you'd switch on for just a short time that would make you sound like a yacht."

"Wouldn't that give our location away?" Kris backed away, folded her arms across her chest.

"Yes, it would, but not much, and not for long. Do it just before you do a radical course change. But if, for just a second or two, you were making noises like your average, garden variety yacht, someone might be less interested in shooting you. We're making the yachts look meaner. Why not make the PFs nicer?"

The idea had logic. It just kind of limped when you added that you'd be doing it by making nice noise that someone could home in on. "Put the noisemakers aboard. I'll leave it to the Captains how much they use them."

"Fine, fine. Just remember, you go swagger around looking all mean and nasty, and you'll be first in line to be swatted."

"Yeah, yeah," Kris said. "Nelly. Could you mix that kind of noisemaker into your evasion plan?

"Doing it, Kris. No problem. I have also accessed the section of the spectrum they are looking at simulating and agree with them. Our design was intentionally worked on to quiet noise in that area. A little noise down there would make us look much more like a regular civilian vessel.

"And you can't hide like a needle in a haystack if you're all shiny. I see your point. Maybe we need some hay seed."

Done there, Kris and Jack headed for the PF boats . . . and a surprise. Most of the crews were camped around their gangways. They'd brought air mattresses, chairs of different sorts. It wasn't at all the shipshape Navy look.

"No one going back to barracks?" Kris asked.

"Don't want to leave the boats," Chief Stan explained. "Most of our trouble started because some yahoo got on board and messed with our engines while we were away. Nobody, but *no*body is getting on my boat tonight."

That brought determined nods up and down the pier. Several of the officers were there; many weren't. A check showed that Kris's mention of the Hilton's availability had sent a few off to check it out. Kris wondered who would be paired with whom, then decided she didn't need to know. She did notice that Phil was among the missing. She hoped he made a better choice than Babs.

Kris settled among the 109's crew when they offered her a chair. "We're ready," Fintch assured her.

"If she don't land us on another golf course," Tononi said and got slugged for it.

"Just so long as we make a hole in one," the Chief quipped.

"Just so long as we get this over with." Fintch sighed. "I mean, I'm not all that excited about taking on six battlewagons, but this waiting is a big pain in my butt."

"We got the target when we went after it," Kris pointed out.

"Yes, ma'am, Your Highness," Fintch agreed, "and I'm sure we'll do better tomorrow."

"We're a better boat than we were for that run," the Chief pointed out. "We got better high-g protection. We got rockets to make them keep their heads down. We got a couple a dozen ships riding out there with us, right ma'am? They ain't gonna know what hit them when Eight goes flashing by."

"We're going to hit them hard," Kris agreed. "And we're going to punch holes in them for other boats to knock bigger and wider. It's not just us out there. Everything Wardhaven can muster, Army, civilian, you name it, will be out there, trailing us. We knock 'em down. Then they'll put 'em out."

It sounded so nice. Kris had been working for this every moment since she came up the elevator. It should work.

But how many of these fine, wonderful people would be here to talk about it tomorrow?

Don't go there. Not now. Not tonight. If you survive, you can worry about it. No need to let this last night be burdened by tomorrows that might never come. Someone brought out a harmonica; a gal on 110 had a guitar. They sang songs for a while. A couple of the guys complained this was too much like summer camp. They wanted a football game.

The Chiefs scotched that. "And who's gonna fill your slot if you're in the sick bay tomorrow with a broken leg, busted head?" That ended that. The Chief of 110 came up with a rousing song that sounded evil enough to have been drunk to for a couple thousand years. One young lad recalled he had a bagpipe in his quarters. Despite threats from half the crews, he headed off for it. Kris thought of how the Fourth Highlanders of Lorna Do approached their business of breaking heads, hearts, and other things, and happily joined in.

An hour or three later, she knew she needed some sleep

and turned to go. The Chief was at her elbow, nodding to Jack.

"You're around the Lieutenant a lot, sir. Are you—"

"I'm her Secret Service agent. Or was, when she rated one," Jack answered. "I was at Tom and Penny's wedding and followed them up when the Lieutenant here decided to do something. I've just been doing what I could."

"You been keeping her safe, anyway," the Chief nodded.

"Something like that."

"You going out with us tomorrow?"

"Nope. I keep her out of trouble dirtside. You got to take care of her up here."

"We'll take good care of her, sir. Damn good care of her."

They walked in silence for most of the distance to the *Halsey*. "You know, I think the Chief mistook me for a boyfriend," Jack finally said.

"Or a stalker," Kris offered, trying out an evil grin.

"Never considered that as a career option. Might take it up if your old man doesn't win or I don't get assigned back to your detail. Stalker. Not a bad job."

Kris suppressed the urge to reach out, take Jack's hand in hers. "Don't stalkers have to be unwanted? Kind of hard to think of anyone who wouldn't want to have you on their trail."

"I know a few bad types that didn't want to see my face." Jack tried his go at one of Tommy's lopsided grins. It didn't look right on him; his grin righted itself into just a nice friendly type. Unfortunately, they were at the *Halsey*'s brow. Kris went through the formalities of coming aboard ship, went to the CIC, found it empty except for a duty watch.

"Anything new?" drew a negative reply. Jack trailed her to her room but quickly opened his own door. For a second, Kris considered inviting Jack in for drinks, for talk, for . . . But he was quickly in his own room, and the door closed between them. She opened hers, hit the light switch, and stopped.

There, on her bunk were laid out two uniforms. One was the usual blue shipsuit. Next to it were pressed and starched dress whites. But someone had already gone to the trouble of affixing her shoulder boards, putting on her few medals. The Order of the Wounded Lion was there, only moved to the right pocket. On the left, where a command insignia would have been . . . there was one.

Kris blinked, studying what showed there. Ten, fifteen years back, when first the PFs had been suggested, someone had proposed a command insignia for PF squadrons. When the boats were all decommissioned, the insignia had been disestablished. The Commodore had somehow laid his hands on one and had been known to wear it on special occasions.

Present uniform regulations did not allow for it.

Now three small ships on a field of lightning bolts sailed serenely across Kris's left pocket. A gift from the Commodore? A surrender to her usurpation of his command? Clearly, someone had gone to an effort to have her wear that.

Gently, Kris moved her whites carefully to the small desk beside her bunk and quickly got ready for bed.

The clock on the desk said she'd been trying to sleep for three hours. Maybe had slept for two. Kris was wide awake, or at least awake enough to be haunted by visions of what lasers could do to small ships. Human flesh. Herself.

"Kris, will I survive today's battle?" Nelly asked softly.

Kris was out of bed, yanking on the blue shipsuit as she answered. "Unless we get blasted to bits, I expect you will."

"I would like to make a long message to Tru before we sail."

"All the things we've talked about?"

"Those, and something else."

"What?" Kris paused at the door.

"Kris, I have been nudging at the edges of the small

rock Auntie Tru gave me from Santa Maria. Never when you were fully engaged. Certainly not for the last few days. But I have been trying to look into its insides. And I think I see things.

"Maybe it is what you would call a dream. Maybe not. I think I see stars. Star maps. Only, some of them are different from the maps your great-grandfather Ray had made when he was still attached to the stone on Santa Maria. I do not know why the maps might be different. It just looks that way to me. There are other things. Images of what I take to be the Three and the cities they built. They are lovely.

"Kris, I would not want what I have seen, or think I saw, to die if I die. Let me send them to Tru. Then, if something happens to me, at least I will have done more with my time with you than just count numbers and keep track of your stocks."

Kris stood there at the door. Nelly clearly had not obeyed her order to not touch the stone slice imbedded in her matrix of self-organizing processing material. But she had also not failed Kris in anything important. Nelly had done what she had insisted she could: sneak a peek into the heart of the possible data source without Kris suffering any disastrous side effect. The teenager had defied Mother but gotten home safe.

"Yes, Nelly, just before we sail, send by landline all the data you want to Auntie Tru. Send her a full backup of what you are. Tell her that, if anything happens to you, to be sure to activate you again. Register a change to my will that money is to be made available to Trudy Seyd to pay for your restoration."

"Thank you, Kris. I appreciate that. Maybe your brother Honovi will have a girl that could put me to good use."

"Oh, Tru will find someone to keep you working hard."

"But no one like you. Take care, Kris."

"Take care of yourself," Kris said and opened the door.

* * *

Sandy was hunched over the battle board in the dim light of CIC. The duty watch went about its work around her. Kris pulled a stool out from the battle board across from Sandy and sat down.

"Thought you'd be asleep," Kris said.

"Tried. It's overrated. Thought you'd be in whites," the destroyer skipper said without looking up.

"Will be, after I shower later. The whites your idea?"

"Part mine. Part the Commodore's. I think the old fellow likes you."

"He's trusting me with his squadron, and I know he loves those boats. You see anything new?"

"Nope."

"If you stare at those dots long enough, they start to dance," came a new voice behind them. Captain van Horn strode into CIC. For the first time, Kris saw him not in his impeccable uniform of the day, but in a blue shipsuit, a ship command patch on the left pocket. "You stare long enough, you can get a high good as any drug. I found that out in my younger days, standing CIC watches," he said, pulling out a seat and settling in, apparently ready to try his own advice. "See anything new, Sandy?"

"Nope. Same old same old. Crazy lash-up. Impossible odds. We're all going to die. You got any new and crazier ideas?"

"All out, though I passed a bunch of PF crewman doing the craziest dance to a bagpipe, a harmonica, and a guitar. Claimed it was some highland thing done by the ancient clans before battle. Guaranteed victory."

"Anyone getting hurt?" Kris asked, wondering if maybe she should have stayed and provided a modicum of adult supervision.

"Seemed harmless, but they were trying to get sixty-four people all dancing in a row."

"A conga line?"

"No, side by side. As if getting ready to charge."

And weren't they? Maybe it wasn't such a bad idea.

"You're out of uniform," the Captain said.

"Shipsuit, same as you," Kris said back.

"Don't you have whites?"

"You in on that, too?" Sandy said.

"Commodore Mandanti asked me about it. I thought it would be a good idea. You need to look spiffy when you give the All Hands Address on the pier tomorrow."

"What All Hands Address?"

"The one where you tell us all this is a wonderful thing we're doing and that we're going to push through and win. The one they're going to need to hear after my personnel chief tells them they're all in the Navy Reserve, on active duty, and covered by health and life insurance for the next month.

"You don't think I'm going to send this lash-up of Johnny-come-latelies out to fight battleships without official papers. I'll be damned if I'll let those Peterwald bastards shoot these people for terrorists. Even Luna. They may be taken in armed resistance, but they will be taken in uniform with ID cards."

"Assuming Kris's dad here and his thousand closest friends can agree that *we* are legal," Sandy added.

The Navy base CO shrugged. "We lose, the winners want to shoot someone, they can come looking for me, or whatever pieces of me they can find. As far as these folks are concerned, they signed the papers, they got the card. We even dug up enough shipsuits to put them all in uniform."

Details, details. More that never made it into the history books. Thank God for bureaucrats like van Horn or his personnel chief who thought of all the details.

"They could shoot your personnel chief. She's a civilian."

The Captain laughed, full and hearty. "Holds a commission or whatever they call a lieutenant's papers in the Coast Guard auxiliary. Was supposed to be on a search and rescue boat, but the last I heard, she wrangled herself onto one of the armed yachts. We're having to bring up more folks to cover the SAR boats. They ought to melt nicely into the refugees headed for the liners."

"Didn't anybody tell folks this is a suicide mission?"

"Ah, yes, Your Highness," the Captain said, fingering his ship command badge, something she'd noticed he lacked on his uniform. "But there are some suicide missions you just can't miss. Some missions, no matter how bad the odds . . . how middle-aged smart you are . . . you just have to get in line for."

He paused, stared at the battle board for a long moment. "If I could find it in my heart, I'd feel sorry for the poor son of a bitch decelerating toward us. He's got all the power on his side. By every right, he wins tomorrow. All we've got on our side is will. Raw determination. And a hunger for freedom. We've lived free for so long, we've forgotten what chains feel like. And we ain't going back."

Kris studied the battle board. On one side, power, steel, chains, and slaver. On the other side determination to stay free. A willingness to die trying. The arrangement on the battle board stayed the same. The prospects looked a whole lot different.

Sandy shuffled in her chair. "Battle board, how long until the arrival of the hostiles, assuming continued deceleration?"

"Arrival in twelve hours."

"Start a countdown clock." One appeared on the board.

"Nelly," Kris said. "Keep one of those going for me, too."

"I already have."

13

Contact: –12 hours

Vice Admiral Ralf Baja studied the battle board in flag plot of his flagship, the *Revenge*. Henry Peterwald had chosen the names of the five ships that trailed the Admiral's flag: Ravager, Retribution, Retaliation, Vengeance, and Avenger. If there was any doubt in the Admiral's mind about his mission, the names given his commands settled it. He'd always known there was bad blood between the Peterwalds and the Longknifes. Nothing open, just something whispered. Now it was as public as six battleships and their course for Wardhaven.

"Any changes?" he asked.

"None," his Chief of Staff Rear Admiral Bhutta Saris said immediately. Nice to have a second who knew what was on your mind. Then again, it didn't take a crystal ball to guess today.

The Admiral glanced up in the direction of the separate intel section he had added to his flag plot. Saris followed his gaze. "Lieutenant, report the status of the target," he ordered.

The Duty Lieutenant came to attention, but his eyes stayed on the boards of the three enlisted technicians he oversaw. "Communications on their battle net is at twenty percent and purely administrative. No threats identified. Their media net continues to report on their political paralysis. No evidence of military preparations, though some of the minor outlets are now carrying commentaries urging military action. These are usually attacked immediately by phone-in callers. Their civilian net usage is about normal. Some minor public demonstrations reported. Anything larger is being suppressed. Our searches identify no threats developing."

"Not that we'd know before time." The Admiral sighed. "No one talking about us would call us enemy battleships. They'd have selected code words. Love Boats. Twinkies."

"And we would have nothing more to fear from such talk," came a new voice. The Admiral organized his face to bland as he came to attention and turned to the only one who would enter his flag plot uninvited. Harrison Maskalyne was the perfect governor for Wardhaven, or would be as soon as the Admiral put him there. Tall, with finely sculptured features offset by wavy black hair, he could have stepped off a pedestal of some Greek god. And was about as dumb and bloodthirsty as one as well.

The governor waved a hand. "Your political masters have delivered Wardhaven to you with nothing to defend it but a ship or two that dare not show their faces. Perfect planning. First we smash the Longknifes here. Over the next year or two we collect up the wreckage of their king's united nothing," he said, closing a fist on thin air. "Then, in three or four years, Admiral, you will be leading a full fleet on an intercept vector for Earth, and humanity will be done with this fracturing and bickering. United once more." He smiled.

Of course, he was quoting a speech the Admiral had heard Henry Peterwald give a few months ago. Peterwald didn't count on Maskalyne for anything but an echo. He rarely surprised.

The Admiral nodded. "All goes according to plan. You will excuse an old fighter. We are trained from our first day at the Academy that no battle plan survives contact with the enemy."

"Ah, but this plan has nothing to fear. Your enemy has nothing to bring at you. No contact. No problem. Right?" The governor said with a happy chuckle.

"As you say," the Admiral said, giving the governor a slight bow so as to avoid joining in the mirth.

Maskalyne shook his head. "You are far too dour, Admiral. Just don't let your concern for bogeymen interfere with your application of the proper jolts to Wardhaven. I want the full spectrum of political and communication targets flattened on our first pass. We of the political arm have taken care of your military problems. Now you will apply the proper degree of violence to all the necessary social and cultural targets to cower the troublemakers on Wardhaven. Wardhaven must not just be defeated. They must know they have lost everything. Even hope."

"We have a full list of your targets," the Admiral said, tapping a section of his battle board. On the bulkhead, a screen changed from the space ahead, Wardhaven growing larger, to a long list of targets ranging from Government House and Nuu House, as well as communication hubs, media centers, any places large groups might gather, talk, and form a consensus when the net was down.

"Good. They must be defeated, and more importantly, know they are defeated. The occupation forces won't be arriving for several weeks. We don't want them to have to fight. Only occupy. Your job is to take the fight out of Wardhaven. That's what these ships were built for. Right?"

"Yes, Mr. Governor," the Admiral said. The *Revenge* was not your average battleship. Tomorrow, Wardhaven would either surrender or find out. The governor left, on whatever errand he felt called to on this, the last day before his investiture. Admiral Baja continued to study his battle board.

It continued to tell him the same nothing it had for the last three and a half days.

"I want to get four, maybe six undisturbed hours of rest," he told Saris. "Don't awaken me unless something very important comes up. Something that fills in some major blanks."

"I will get some sleep, too, sir. No need to baby-sit a board that says nothing. Let the Duty Lieutenant do it."

"He will wake you if necessary?"

"Yes, I trust him. I knew his father."

"Good, then let us get some rest." The Admiral turned but carefully let Saris fall in step beside him. As he came close, he turned on his jammer and whispered to Saris good-naturedly, "Do you have orders to replace me if Maskalyne says to?"

Saris's dark complexion turned almost ghostly for a moment, but he did not miss a step. "Yes, sir. That was the condition of my being offered the position. If I did not agree to that, it was made known to me that they would offer it to someone else."

The Admiral nodded. "You were my first choice. In return for you, they required that I accept certain things as well. I expected they would require something like this of you. I am glad that we now have it out in the open."

"Might I ask what things they required of you?"

"Let us hope that you never have to find out what they are," the Admiral said and switched off the jammer.

"Sir, we had a slight magnetic disturbance in the vicinity of flag plot," the Duty Lieutenant said, turning to them.

"What kind of disturbance?" Saris demanded. They both knew that their recent conversation would not have occurred without someone jamming the observing cameras, listening posts.

"We could not locate it, sir. It was only there a second. It might have been a minor power fluctuation," the young man added, as if trying to give himself an out. Maybe his superiors. Senior officers were known to occasionally use jammers. If caught, it could be a career-ending mistake. Maybe life-ending.

"Well, what are you going to do about it?" Saris demanded.

"Log it, sir," the young man said, giving the proper answer.

"Then do so. I will be in my underway cabin. Wake me only if something develops. Understood?"

"Yes, sir."

Vice Admiral Ralf Baja left for his stateroom without looking back. He could only hope his fleet could spare enough time from looking over everyone's shoulder to keep an eye on its rapidly approaching target.

Contact: −11 hours

Honovi watched the large screen in the main parlor of Government House. It was hard to remember that this was not his home for the first time since he was thirteen.

"Can't you get the picture any clearer?" Prime Minister *Pro Tem* Mojag Pandori snapped. "Somebody walked off with the remote." A slur against the Longknifes' sudden packing job, no doubt. Honovi didn't mention all the stuff he couldn't find.

The screen was old, and someone had been messing with the brightness. Kusa looked at Honovi wordlessly. Yep, she was the kind of hands-on type who would have tried to make things better . . . and gotten them worse. An out-of-kilter vid screen perfectly illustrated the entire mess Wardhaven was in.

Honovi walked over to the wall, opened the control box, and pushed a couple of buttons. The screen snapped into proper clarity. Father and the acting Prime Minister focused on the picture and didn't notice Kusa mouthing *Sorry,* behind their backs. Honovi gave her a quick wink.

The scene was of the main space elevator station. People waited in long lines for cars. The voiceover explained that just hours ago, the stations had been deserted, with the evacuation of the space station complete and no one going up or down . . . a lie Honovi had made sure there were no pictures to disprove. Or at least none ready yet for the news.

Now it was different. The government had lifted its ban on near-Wardhaven space travel so long as the ships were only going from the High Wardhaven station to Jump Point Alpha. Now citizens of other worlds, stuck on Wardhaven, were fleeing.

The pictures were the kind that Honovi had hoped to never see in his lifetime. Fearful women clutching children that had that blank look of the young who didn't know enough to be frightened, except their mothers and their fathers were scared, so they took in that terror. Men hurried about, accomplishing nothing in their haste, and women hastened them on, wanting to know why the impossible wasn't done already.

Honovi had tried to keep this fear at bay for three days. Now it reached out, from children's wide eyes, from mothers' cracking voices, from men's frustration. Yes, that was fear. And now that it was on the screen, it would be out in the open for all to see everywhere.

"So, now are you satisfied?" Pandori spat. "I still say we should have kept the ships, the others, here. No one would dare bombard us with them here."

"The message is very clear," Honovi said with the slow, dogged repetition that he hoped might finally get through Pandori's denial. "They are using the old formal declarations from pre-Unity times. Ninety, a hundred years ago, a planet was supposed to surrender when it lost control of the space above it and pay 'reparations.' That usually meant taking over the winning planet's debt to Earth. It was not a pretty time."

"But they aren't demanding reparations. They want our total surrender," Kusa pointed out.

"Those are Peterwald battleships, and they're playing for bigger stakes," Father snapped. He was trying to stay quiet like he'd promised. It was not easy for him.

"So you say," Pandori snapped. "With you Longknifes it's always a Peterwald under the bed. I say we ignore them, go about our business. They wouldn't dare fire on us. And, when the fleet is back, we settle anything that needs settling."

There it was, out in the open. Bluff. Pandori was a great one for bluffing. Father brought his fist down on the visitor's easy chair. "And just what do you think those six battleships will do while our fleet is boosting in from the jump point? Our battleships will arrive over a smoking ruin of a planet, with those ships running for the other jump point."

"Father. Mr. Prime Minister. We've had this conversation," Honovi put in. They had. And might well have it many more times if there was time for it. Eighty years of peace had built "civilized expectations," as Pandori put it. "Faith in the system," as Father put it. "A near impossibility to face the reality of change" was the way Honovi put it privately to Kusa. She disagreed politely but not forcefully and tried to get her father to accept the need for change as much as Honovi worked on his.

"We need to work on the wording of our response to the surrender demand, and orders for the fleet," Honovi said, going straight at the next item on his to-do list. "We need to issue it in two hours, maybe less."

"Why so soon?" Pandori grumbled. "It only takes a bit more than an hour to boost past the moon. I've done it many times."

"Yes, sir," Honovi said. "But they aren't boosting past the moon. They'll boost at one g for an hour, then reverse and decelerate for an hour so they swing around the moon and come back at the hostile battleship's track as they're coming in. That's where they'll fight them."

"We did a school trip in the first grade," Kusa said. "It took the afternoon to swing around the moon and come back."

"We did that trip, too," Honovi said.

"Do you remember much of first grade?" Father quipped to Pandori. "I sure don't."

The acting Prime Minister shook his head. Finally, something the two old political warhorses could agree upon.

"Course, we didn't fight any battleships," Kusa said.

"I pretended we saw pirates," Honovi said.

"They were good days when children had to pretend they saw anything horrible," the Prime Minister said, eyes tearing.

"They will come again, Papa."

"If we make them," Honovi said.

"Okay, let's see what we want to say."

Contact: –10 hours

The Duty Lieutenant in flag plot of the Greenfeld Alliance Battleship *Revenge* studied the news feed. Then studied it some more. Then reviewed it again. This was a definite change in the target's condition, but was it enough to wake the Chief of Staff, the Admiral? He called down to the intel center.

"Commander, have you an analysis for flag plot yet?"

"We are working on a full report. At the moment what you see is basically what we see. They are letting those holding non-Wardhaven passports leave. We should expect that several large liners will be crossing our track as we make final approach, heading out for Jump Point Adele. I doubt any of them will make for Jump Point Barbie, but we should keep our lasers ready. Any that do might try for a suicide dive on us."

"The Longknifes would use a packed liner as a suicide ship!"

"I'm not Chief of intel to underestimate Longknifes."

"Do you think I should wake up the Admiral?"

"That is your call, not mine."

"Yes, it is," the young Lieutenant agreed. He eyed the media feed. So many women with children. Men with wives. Here and there were a clump of men his age, going about their business like sailors on their way to their ship.

He spotted a woman moving purposefully through the crowd, two younger men following in her trail, pulling loaded carts behind her. The emblems on the boxes looked familiar, but he couldn't place them.

"Some of those are not refugees," the Lieutenant said. "Some of them move as purposefully as any sailor."

"Maybe they are assigned to the luxury liners that will be sailing, coming back from shore leave."

"And there was a woman on the last feed. She hardly looked like a refugee. She was leading two men bringing along loaded carts. I almost recognized the markings on the boxes."

"Maybe those were her family heirlooms and the young men were her . . ." The Commander coughed discreetly. "You know how decadent the women behave where the Longknifes call the shots."

Yes, the Lieutenant had seen all the vids. He'd also learned how hardheaded an intel weenie was once he latched on to a preconceived notion. "Before I decide to wake the chief of staff, I would appreciate it if you could run the faces of the clearly nonrefugees on these media feeds against the Wardhaven database. Especially that woman. She should be easy to place. She clearly was someone."

"We are already doing it, Lieutenant. We know our job," the intel officer said and closed the link.

The Lieutenant paced the deck behind his three enlisted technicians. One of them cleared his throat. "Yes?"

"We are getting more powerful magnetic signatures from around the High Wardhaven station, sir."

"As if liners were increasing their fusion reactors. Bringing more magnetohydrodynamic power on-line?" Fusion reactors generated plasma for thrust. The plasma, as it raced through magnetic containment fields, also generated electricity through magnetohydrodynamic generators outside those fields. That electricity in turn created the containment fields that held the reactors together. A wonderful system that seemed to give you something for nothing, his physics professor had quipped, but it powered man between the stars. And when ships weren't under boost, large ships ran a small trickle of plasma around a racetrack to keep electricity flowing. Several liners were now raising that trickle as their future energy needs rose.

The magnetic resonances around High Wardhaven flexed and flexed again, and any chances of seeing what was going on there as discreet units became less and less a possibility.

With luck, one of the ships would interfere with another, and they'd blow out the containment field of a reactor. It had been known to happen. In the bad old days. Not recently. It would just be Longknife luck not to happen this time, either.

The commlink beeped.

"We have your people ID'd, Lieutenant."

That was fast, and from the sound of it, not at all what the Commander wanted. "Yes?" the Duty Lieutenant said.

"The woman is Miss Dora Evermorn, the anchor for Galactic News and Entertainment on Wardhaven. She has a show every afternoon between two and four. I've reviewed the last three days' feed, and she didn't announce a vacation."

"So, where's she going?"

"She owns a system runabout. Can't jump out of system. Maybe she's headed for the moon where she'd get a good shot of Wardhaven under bombardment. Who knows? We've flagged her."

The Lieutenant nodded. That was something he knew. News followed the story. Military preparation was a story. If she was any good, she'd lead them to the story they wanted.

"The men on the video are civilians. Some work for the Navy in that capacity. A few own small runabouts. Some of them have notations in their files that they are members of the Coast Guard Reserve or auxiliary. Like the Greenfeld Youth Association but with no military training. They see that private runabouts meet safety regulations, have survival pods. Sometimes they rescue idiots who get in trouble. They have no military value."

"As you say," the Lieutenant said. Accepting the words but being careful not to accept the value of the report. If they had no military value, why weren't they staying home where they belonged on a day like this? Why were they heading up to a station soon to be under attack? Hardly the actions of someone who viewed themselves as having no military value.

Damn intel's granite mind-set!

So, do I wake the Chief of Staff or not? The Lieutenant paced back and forth, watching the lights on his technician's boards change, but did they change enough?

Contact: –9 hours 30 minutes

Kris finished her shower and dressed carefully in the whites prepared for her. Today she might get killed, but there was no need for a bulletproof body stocking. They didn't make one to stop an 18-inch laser.

At least she'd managed another hour catnap. She actually felt rested. Dressed, she settled the blue beret fancied by the PF sailors on her head. Since they spent most of their time with their heads in a brain bucket, they needed something easy to stuff in a pocket. To the uniform groans of the rest of the Navy, they'd settled on a Navy blue felt beret with their boat's insignia holding pride of place.

The Commodore had tried to have them adopt a squadron emblem; they'd insisted on their own boats'. Today, Kris wore the Commodore's squadron emblem as befitted a squadron Commander.

"Kris, we need you quick," came as a holler from CIC.

Kris ran for the combat center and almost tripped over the airtight door. There weren't that many on a PF. If a PF took a hit, it wasn't really going to matter.

"Shut up. We'll have an answer for you in just a minute," Sandy was snapping into Beni's commlink.

"Kris, Adorable Dora Evermorn is at the yacht basin on net hollering for her boat."

"Gabby's not answering?"

"We've got the boats on emission controls. They aren't listening or talking except through our guarded landline."

"Thanks." Kris grabbed the commlink.

"Dora, do you recognize my voice?"

"Kris Long—"

"Yes, and if I wanted my name used, I'd have used it. Don't say a word. Don't move an inch. I'll be there in a minute to talk to you. You'll have all your recorders off, or so help me, I'll throw you out the nearest space lock. You understand?"

"I have two strong guys here who say you can't do that, but yeah, I'll play this your way for the time being."

Kris snapped off the commlink, turned to get Jack, and ran into him. He was dressed, ready for duty. "Gosh, I thought today was going to be a slow day. All Navy. You mean I got to protect you from a newsie?"

"Nope," Kris said, heading for the pier, "I may need you to toss a newsie and her two brawny sidekicks over the side."

"That's kind of outside my job description, Your Highness, Princess, sir, ma'am."

"Yes, but if you're bucking for that vacant job of knight errant, it's right up your alley."

"Who said I wanted that job? False rumor. You've been getting your news from Adorable Dora too long."

Still, Jack made a fast run to the yacht pier. Adorable Dora was waiting impatiently beside the small watch hut at the yacht basin. With a face and body the best that money could buy, she was just the thing that people wanted to watch for their news and entertainment, assuming there was a difference between the two. The two young men lounging on the large luggage carriers were just as expensive to the eye. Since they were never on camera, Kris could only suspect what they were paid for.

"Where's my yacht?" lacked the usual two o'clock teaser.

"Why do you ask?" Kris counted.

"You're taking a fleet out to fight those ships. I want to follow you. Film it."

"You could easily get killed doing that. There won't be any cheap seats at this show."

"Comes with the territory," Adorable shot back. The looks the two men swapped said this was news to them. "Guys, start setting up for a shoot. We're going to interview Princess Longknife. Get an exclusive before the battle. You're wearing that small units command badge. Does that mean you're commanding the fast patrol boats? Are they fixed up enough to leave the pier?" Behind her, the guys had seemed surprised by her order, but as she fired off questions, they broke out their gear. And you had to give Dora credit. She had done some homework.

"Put the gear away, fellows," Kris said. Jack sidled over, friendly like, hand on holster, to give them his official smile.

The guys quit unpacking.

"I have my collar camera. Not as good, but this kind of story will go far. Princess interferes with the news!"

"Did you talk to your boss before you headed up here? Did you check with anyone? Didn't you wonder for a moment why this wasn't already on the news?" Kris said, trying to be as rational as she thought Adorable Dora's brain was capable of.

"Lazy reporters are easily scared. I ain't lazy."

"National security mean anything to you?"

"Try scaring me with something real, honey."

Kris gritted her teeth. The urge to have Jack chuck the woman out an airlock was overwhelming. No, the urge to chuck her out an airlock herself was too much to pass up.

"You're stuck with me, deary. Let's make the best of it. You don't want me to report the story until you say so. I want to report the story up close. You say I could get killed. I'm willing to risk it. Where's my yacht? I've got a right to sail out in my yacht and do what I want."

"No you don't, because I need your yacht for a communications relay ship," Kris snapped back.

"You've stolen my yacht!"

"Borrowed."

"Stolen, in my book."

"Would you two ladies stop for a moment?" Jack put in. "Kris, I know she's easy to hate, but all I hear her asking to do is trail the fleet and take pictures, record her story. Now, if I understand what you have in mind, you want her yacht to trail the fleet and pass along any messages that we need to hear when you're behind the moon. Right?"

Kris didn't want to, but she saw the logic of where Jack was going. "So let her ride along with Gabby and Cory. They do our job, and she does hers."

"Right," Jack said.

"That's all I want," Dora said.

"You guys going along?" Kris asked

They looked at each other and slowly shook their heads.

"I'll double your pay," Dora said.

Heads kept shaking.

"Jack, I don't like the idea of her on the same yacht with Gabby and Cory. They'll follow orders, but with her yelling, I'm not so sure they'll be following my orders."

"And you want me to ride shotgun on her."

Kris nodded.

"You gonna double my pay?"

"Triple it," Kris said.

"What's she paying you?" Dora demanded.

"Nothing," Jack said.

"She's got to be paying you something. She sleeping with you? You look good enough to eat."

"You sure you want me on the same boat as her?"

"Space her if she makes a pass. Kind of accidentally like."

"I can do that." Jack grinned.

"You wouldn't," Dora said.

"I suspect Gabby and Cory would testify in a court of law that you thought you were just opening the door to the little girls' room. Want to bet?" Jack grinned around hard eyes.

"Sure you want to go?" Kris asked.

"I'm going."

"Select your minimal gear. Jack, drop me off at the *Halsey,* then you head for her yacht. What do you call it?"

"All the News That's Fit to Print."

Contact: −9 hours 15 minutes

"We have an intercept," said the Chief of intel, "that you may be interested in. That Dora Evermorn couldn't seem to find her yacht and ended up talking to someone."

The Duty Lieutenant listened to first one person talk to Dora. Then someone else came on-line, seemed to be recognized, but cut Dora off. "Was that who she almost said she was?"

"That was Princess Kristine Longknife. She is on the station."

"Where?"

"We could not get a fix on the call. The commlink is not standard, and what with all the liners getting up plasma, the whole station is a mess."

"But that is definitely a Longknife."

"Definitely. A little one. Not King Ray, but the troublesome brat herself."

"What kind of ship is this Dora Evermorn looking for?"

"It's a system runabout. No weapons. No military value of any sort." There again was that quick, disparaging assumption from the intel Chief. "Will you wake the Chief of Staff now?"

Ah, and now, not content to toss off his own conclusions so lightly, the Commander was ready to poke his nose into flag plot's job, but not with a clear "You should wake him." No, just an ambiguous question. *The hot potato stays in your lap, Lieutenant. Nice toss, Commander.*

"I will look into it," he said, cutting the link.

The Lieutenant drew in a troubled breath. What had changed since the Admiral and Chief of Staff had layed down? *Kristine Longknife has been identified on High*

Wardhaven. Passenger liners are being allowed to evacuate non-Wardhaven citizens from Wardhaven. Some of them may cross our path, even attempt to suicide crash us.

And how does this raise the threat against this battle-ship for the next hour and a half above what it was three hours ago?

Simply put, it did not. Could the Admirals do anything in the next hour and a half that they could not do in the first fifteen minutes after they awoke?

No.

His father had often talked of the pressure of battle. Of the need for men to go into it prepared for it. His father swore he'd won half his battles by getting a good night's sleep and a good breakfast. Oh, and a good cup of coffee.

Was father just feeding him a sea tale?

The Duty Lieutenant took a deep breath and let it out slowly. What a tale he'd tell the Chief when he got back.

The Lieutenant stood again and watched the technicians watch the intel feed from the target. Things were certainly happening now. But was it all that different? Were there any warships in evidence? Anything the intel Chief would identify as having significant military value?

The Lieutenant paced, and time passed.

Contact: –9 hours

Kris found a mob scene in front of the *Halsey*'s pier. On a more thorough review, it clarified into a very well-organized riot. She spotted Captains van Horn and Luna in the center of it and figured them for the best explanation of the content and process of what was going on, so she headed their way.

"Howdy, dear. You're up early," Luna said, now decked out in a blue shipsuit with Captain's shoulder tabs and an underway command badge, the mirror image of van Horn beside her.

The Navy Captain nodded. "Your Highness, I under-stand you had a media problem."

"Solved. Jack's going to ride herd on Adorable Dora, though she's going to be trailing us in the communications relay ship. Turns out we stole her yacht for that job."

"Evermorn," Luna spat. "Why didn't you just space her?"

"Well, I told Jack he could if she gave him any trouble. Think Gabby would lie for him in court?"

"Like an Oriental rug."

"Not that it's any of my business," Kris said, looking around, "but what's going on here?"

"Registration," van Horn said simply.

"Press-gangs in action," Luna grumbled.

"Since I somehow doubt that six battleships will surrender upon setting sights on our gallant sails, I suspect we are headed for a fight," van Horn said. "Civilians, taken in arms, can be shot as terrorists. Combatants, taken in arms, are prisoners of war. Which do you want to be?" he said with a nod toward Luna.

"Not taken," she muttered.

"My thoughts exactly, but battles have this nasty way of not going as planned. So, if those bastard Peterwald ships haul some of you out of survival pods, I want our crews to be in uniform and have ID cards to wave at them."

"You just want everybody in blue," Luna simpered.

"And she agreed so quickly when I pointed out that her present employer might not consider what comes next covered by his health insurance or life insurance."

"Captain can be very persuasive."

"What are their ranks, rates?" Kris was only a year or so in the Navy, but she knew enough about the Navy Way to know that everyone had their place and stayed in it. Her excepted.

"Old regulation from the Iteeche Wars allowed us to take in civilians when things got kind of out of the ordinary. Special rank. Naval volunteer. Pay status of third class."

"Third class in a pig's eye," Luna said, patting her rear pocket. "I got my master's papers. I'm a ship's Captain." Which explained her four strips and command badge.

So there was a tactful bone in van Horn's Navy-issue body. Kris flashed him a smile. He answered with a "Hurrumph."

"After we've got everyone inducted, I expect you'll want to address them, Your Highness."

"Already!"

"They deserve a few words, ma'am," Luna put in. "You can't expect them to go ballyhooing off, at the risk of life and limb, without seeing their Commander. They'll be talking about this fight for the rest of their lives. I was at Wardhaven, with that slip of a Longknife when she was just a girl."

Kris swallowed. That was how Gabby introduced himself. "I fought with your great-grandfather at the Battle of the Big Orange Nebula." There was more to being one of those damn Longknifes than just being cussed at in bars.

Kris started to say, "What do I say?" but she swallowed that. Luna and van Horn were looking at her with the expectation that she knew what she'd say. That somewhere in her Longknife genes was the script for days like today.

Good Lord, did they have *that* wrong.

"Okay, let me know when you want me," Kris said and turned away. She wanted to find a quiet corner to scribble some notes.

A woman, standing stiff for her ID photo, spotted Kris and broke into a wide smile. Kris smiled back.

A tall, gangly kid, hardly more than a boy, looked up from where he was pinning his Coast Guard Auxiliary badge onto his Navy shipsuit. "We gonna beat those jokers?" he asked, though his words were more a prayer.

"You bet," Kris said. A half-dozen boys and old men around him laughed with him, at his brashness, at his hope. Who knew? They were just happy to hear they'd win, and from the horse's mouth, no less.

Kris found no quiet corner; instead she ended up circulating among the crews: grizzled merchants, middle-aged yacht owners with their young daughters and sons, electronic specialists dragged over, screwdrivers still in hand, to be

registered, volunteers all. There were Navy reservists looking for the odd person to fill up a hole in their crew, a slot
they'd just thought of last night and might be useful. There
were shipyard hands, too, not sure what they'd be asked to
do, but ready to sail with the fleet if they were needed.

It was an odd lot, for an odder mission. If courage and
enthusiasm, willingness and guts decided battles, the hostiles were licked. Unfortunately, 18-inch lasers decided
battles.

Kris had none of them.

Kris found herself among some old chiefs, filling out
their tugboat crews from experienced civilian salvage
teams and eager Coast Guard volunteers. "Last night, they
was showing us the balls to the wall—if you'll pardon me,
ma'am—kind of attack that you fast patrol boats plan to
make." "I suspect you'll be coming at them from the moon,
if you're smart," another Chief said, smoking her pipe.
"Wardhaven's gunna be kind of big underneath ya'." "But
we'll catch ya." "We'll be waiting for ya, with power, whatever ya need, Your Highness."

"You'd be surprised what some of us salvage tugs carry."
The last one grinned. "You do what needs doing, and we'll
catch you and set you down soft as down on a duck."

"Now I think they're looking for you, and I think old
fuss and feathers is expecting us to form ranks for parade."

He was right; the processing seemed to be done, though
two or three last stragglers were being rushed down the
line. And a few of the civilian clerks were signing themselves in, if Kris wasn't mistaken.

The PFs were forming ranks in front by boats. Kris noticed that the officers that had been missing last night
were at their stations up front. Yes, there was Tom. And
Penny, too.

Sandy's XO paraded most of the *Halsey*'s crew, those
not at duty stations. The Commodore's gray-headed XO
was doing her best to get her mix of too old or too green
crew out of the *Cushing* and into their designated ranks beside the line destroyer.

The merchant skippers did a surprisingly good job of forming right along with the reservists they carried. Kris suppressed a smile at the eagerness of old farts who'd prided themselves on sloppy now trying to compete for Shipshape and Bristol Fashion.

The ragtag and bobtail contingent of armed and unarmed yachts formed to the rear of the PFs. As they would in battle, each picked a PF, grouped behind it, and tried to look like they knew what a rank and file was. The old chiefs of the tugboat flotilla marched dourly up to fill in the back row. They asked no pride of place; they were used to picking up the leavings.

Kris loved them all.

A couple of tables had been pushed together up front. Sandy was standing on them, waving at Kris to get forward. Van Horn had helped the Commodore to climb from a chair to the tables.

Kris started to double-time for her place. "Kris, you have a call coming in from your brother," Nelly announced. "It's in the standard family code."

"I'll take it," Kris said, giving Sandy an acknowledging wave but slowing down. "Hi, Bro. What's happening?"

"Sis, I'm delivering what you want, but it's just the minimum. The new guy is giving out a press release. No public statement for him or our man."

"He's not going for a photo op!" For a politician to give up face time, airtime. That was unheard of!

"The press release will call on the incoming things to cease their messages and declare where they are from in the next hour or we will consider ourselves in a state of war with them and those who sent them. The message will be out there. It's just that Pandori can't make himself say the words. The fellow is so much a product of the long peace that he just can't . . ."

Kris knew that any search system that could break their code now knew what everyone would know in a matter of minutes. It was time for plain talk.

"Grampa Al figured there was Peterwald money behind the votes that got Pandori the PM's job."

"Pandori's not a Peterwald man," Honovi shot back. "And you know, Sis, if the Society for Humanity was still up, if there was still peace in human space, Pandori could have been a great man."

"Yes, Brother, but that Society is dead, and ugly things are roving human space, and I'm gonna be facing six of them in a couple of hours, so you'll excuse me if I don't feel all that sorry for Pandori and his daughter."

"Yeah, I can see your point. Anyway, Sis, you're legal. You can go break things, and it ain't against the law. Happy?"

"Jubilant. Now Bro, if you're anywhere around your old haunts, I strongly suggest you get long gone. If this guy is anything like the last Peterwald nut I dealt with, he wants you and Father dead in the worst way. Head for the hills. Keep your head down until you have a good idea of what I've broken."

"Understand you, Sis. I'll pick up Rose and Mother and, how do you say it, beat feet out of town."

"Good-bye, Brother, I got to talk to a couple of thousand of my closest friends," Kris said and cut the line. She was at the podium. She waved off help getting up. Among the older, wiser heads, she asked softly, "You want to say a word?"

"You played the princess card, Kris," Sandy said. The other two senior naval officers nodded. Painfully aware of the Lieutenant strips on her shoulder boards, the Commanders, Captain tabs on *their* shipsuits, Kris faced her command.

They looked back at her. Expectant. Ready.

Kris stood, legs apart, hands on hips, and looked back at them. "Now it's our turn," she began.

"Eighty years ago, your great-grandmothers, great-grandfathers, fought with my Great-grandfathers Ray and Trouble to beat back the Iteeches and save humanity from extinction."

Beside her, the Commodore cleared his throat.

"Okay." Kris smiled. "Some of you old farts were there, with my grampas, doing the fighting." That brought a soft chuckle among the ranks.

"Those of you who faced the Iteeche know what it's like to fight outnumbered, outgunned . . . and win."

"Yeah," "You bet," "We did," came back in smatterings.

"The Iteeche would have made the human race an extinct race. You didn't let that happen."

"No," came back solid, sure.

"You fought, and you won, and we've built the world we've enjoyed for the last eighty years. A world of peace. A world of prosperity. A world those battleships coming at us plan to end. Are we going to let them?"

"No," rolled back at Kris.

"So now it's our turn. The bastards out there have got us outmaneuvered. They've got us outgunned. But they haven't got us outsmarted. They haven't got half as many surprises up their sleeves as we've got up ours."

Again there was a murmur of approval in the ranks.

"Dirtside, my brother thinks I'm crazy. He thinks I'm out of my mind to be charging into a fight when I could be down there where he is. Who's the crazy one in the family, me or him?"

"Him," roared back at her.

"You've probably got smart brothers like mine. Stay home. Stay safe. As I see it, when those battleships start shooting, he has to sit there and take it. Me, I get to shoot back."

"Yes."

"I get to blow them out of space." Just one chance. Hold it; what did the tugboat skipper say?

"Yes," didn't last nearly long enough for Kris to finish the thought nibbling at her. She concentrated on the speech; the battle would have to wait for a second.

"Now it's my turn to put a stop to them shooting at my mom, my dad, my brother, my loved ones." Kris wished she could name a few specific names, but "Yes" was roaring back at her.

"The boats ready?"

"Yes," was the loudest yet.

"Let's go bust some battleship butt."

When the cheering died down, Captain van Horn stepped forward. "Chiefs, dismiss your crews to their ships."

Maybe the Chiefs did. In the roar that followed, Kris sure didn't hear any orders bellowed. But crews ran or trotted or rushed for their boats, a stream of free humanity rushing to meet the enemy, their fate, victory. Whatever came.

Kris turned to van Horn. "I got another crazy idea."

"This better be an easy one as well as good."

"My PFs are a one-shot weapon. They can't reload their pulse lasers. Right?"

"Yes."

"We're going to rendezvous with tugs to help us slow down, miss Wardhaven, avoid burning up in the atmosphere. Right?"

"Yes."

"Could those tugs recharge our pulse lasers, pass a refill of antimatter and reaction mass, recock us for another go at any battlewagon still fighting?"

"We'd have to send you in early," Sandy said.

"But we'd get two bites out of the battlewagons."

"At least any that survived the first run," van Horn said, looking around. "XO?"

"Sir."

"Get over to the salvage tugs with reactors. See what kind of power cables they have. Make sure they got fittings to match with the PFs. Tell them they're not only going to help them make orbit, they're going to refuel and rearm them."

"I'll do that, sir. And with your permission, I'll assign myself with that division. Make sure everything goes smoothly." Somehow Kris doubted matching up at two, three g's would be anywhere close to smooth.

Roy from the yard passed Kris. "Nice speech. Almost makes me want to sign on."

"You got a tugboat with a full reactor?"

"Three deep space salvage tugs in the yard. You don't need them for the stuff you're doing in orbit here."

Kris explained that she did. "Oh," was his reply. "You know that thing I said about almost wanting to sign on?"

"Ready to forget the almost?"

He took a deep breath. "Guess so. I knew that some of my yard folks were sailing on some of these tubs, work not quite finished. Oh hell, why not take out my own fleet of tugs? You want me to catch up with you, slow you down, pass lines?"

"Antimatter containment pods, reaction mass fuel lines, that kind of stuff."

"Where do I sign up?"

Van Horn looked at his check-in tables; there were still a few folks sitting at them. "Better hurry if you want one of these nifty uniforms, plus health benefits and life insurance."

14

Contact: –8 hours 45 minutes

The Duty Lieutenant eyed the feed. Wardhaven was finally sending something to the *Revenge*.

"Are you getting this?" Intel asked needlessly.

"I'm watching," the Duty Lieutenant said, bringing the thousandth cup of coffee he'd drunk this watch up to his lips. Cold, weak, bad. The coffee. And the response.

"If the unidentified warships in our system do not identify themselves within the hour," said the woman on-screen.

A woman being used for such an announcement. The Lieutenant shook his head. Longknifes.

"We will commence the defensive actions against them as is our right under self-defense. These ships are warned that if they take any hostile action against our forces, Wardhaven will respond against them, and those who sent them, with the full force available to us. The approaching ships are warned that they should prepare to be boarded by customs inspectors as well as animal and plant quarantine and drug enforcement inspectors."

The Lieutenant almost choked on his coffee. "Sorry," he said to the technician who got splattered by the spray. He wiped at the worst droplets.

"It's okay, sir," the technician said. "Sir. Are they serious? About boarding us?"

"They're bluffing," said the tech next to him.

"They're joking," said the Lieutenant.

"Will you wake the Admiral now?" the intel chief demanded.

"To answer that!"

"Well, it is the first communication we've had from Wardhaven. And it is an ultimatum."

"Written by a stand-up comic or someone who has lost all touch with reality," the Lieutenant said, finishing his coffee. "No, I think the Admiral can sleep through this. I will wake him fifteen minutes before the ultimatum expires, and he can compose a response while he's shaving."

Intel sputtered something as he clicked off, but the Lieutenant ignored him. Nothing had changed. Wardhaven was still there, waiting to be plucked. Cracking a few bad jokes, but if that was the extent of their defense . . . plant inspectors . . . there was no need to disturb the Admiral's sleep.

A mess mate brought a new thermos of coffee. The Lieutenant sampled it. Not bad. Not good, but at least not bad. "Tell the chief of the Admiral's mess that he better have a very good cup of coffee waiting in forty-five minutes when I wake the Admiral."

"He'll want something good to go with that," a tech said.

"Drug inspectors. We'll show them some drugs to inspect," said another. There were rumors about how the Peterwalds made their money. Rumors spread by the Longknifes, no doubt.

"Mind your boards. Let me know the second anything changes," the Lieutenant warned. A woman, speaking for Wardhaven, throwing defiances like a kitten surrounded by hungry dogs. Maybe they would be taking a surrender from her before noon today. But deep in the pit of the Lieutenant's gut, there was a suspicion, a suspicion supported by nothing on the boards, that there was more behind those words.

"Mind your boards," he repeated.

Contact: –8 hours 30 minutes

Kris ducked into her stateroom for a second to change into a shipsuit. Whites might look good for a talk with the troops, but she didn't need the Order of the Wounded Lion's crest gouging her at three g's. At three g's lots of things went from a nuisance to a major problem.

Kris glanced in the mirror one last time. That was still her. The fancy uniform was gone, she wore just what she needed for the job she'd do today. Just her, her crews and boats, and some mighty nasty battlewagons that figured they had everything the way they wanted it. "Well, we got some free women, free men, willing to put it on the line to tell you no," she told herself. "Let's go keep Wardhaven the way we want it."

The *Halsey* was busy, crew going about the business of getting under way. Sandy was still in CIC as Kris passed.

"Anything new and surprising?" Kris asked.

"Nope. The stations sensor array is back on-line, but the intel feed is the same, just to three more decimal places."

"Take care, Santiago. This time we'll make sure the history books get it right."

"Take care yourself, Longknife, and the history books are written by historians. They'll never get it right until they stick their noses outside their safe libraries and come out here where it's really happening."

"Must be a historian somewhere in the mix. We've got everything from pirates to kids."

"Excuse me," a gentle voice said. "Am I missing something?"

"Kris, may I introduce my pet newsie. Winston Spencer, this is Princess Kristine. She commands today."

"Your Highness." He bowed from the neck. "Lieutenant," he frowned, then glanced at Sandy. "Commander?

And isn't the captain of the Naval Base taking out some armed container ships? Yet you say Princess Kristine commands. Is there a story here?"

"Live through today"—Sandy smiled enigmatically—"and you may have your story. If you have the smarts to figure it out."

"Hmm," he said, as Kris left Sandy and her Boswell.

Kris found Tom with his legs sticking out from under one of the 109's bridge consoles, Fintch under it with him.

Penny muttered, "No. Still no. Yes! No. No. No. Got it! Hold it there!" Kris said not a word while Tom and Fintch finished what they were doing to something.

Tom rolled out from under the console, spotted Kris, and grinned. "Something didn't stay fixed from yesterday's work with Beni, or while fixing what he fixed, he elbowed something."

"Or someone elbowed something," Penny added.

"Anyway, it's fixed, and we're good to go," Fintch said, grinning, then frowned and looked around. "Should one of us call attention on deck or something?"

"I think we better belay all that until after we've got a couple of battleship hides to nail on the O club wall down on Wardhaven," Kris said.

"Yeah. If the gal is using Navy words like *belay*"—Tom grinned—"she's got enough salt in her veins without us doing all that time-wasting attention stuff. We've either learned all our lessons by now, or it's too late."

"Is the old boat ready?"

"As ready as she'll ever be." Tom saluted.

"Or will be as soon as you find a place for me," a new voice said. Kris turned to face a short, middle-aged man holding a large portable computer. Behind him, three yard workers lugged, in order, a high-g station, a workstation, and a toolbox.

The man held out a hand. "I'm Moose. I'm your raven."

"Raven? Moose? Mine?" Tom said.

"Yeah," the fellow said, stepping aside. "Set me up next to that intel station. That ought to work best. Yeah, you got

all those yachts faking it as PFs, but it might help a bit if
you occasionally faked it as a yacht. You know, made some
of the noises that the civilian boats make but the Navy paid
lots of bucks to quiet you guys out of."

"You're here to make noise!" Tom said.

"Yeah. You mind? I'm a last-minute addition. We ravens
decided to put one of us on each of your boats."

"I heard about this. It's your call, Tom," Kris said.

A yard worker was already on his knees, drill at the
ready, but only at the ready. He looked up, eyeing Kris,
Tom, Penny. "Look, I don't know which one of you dudes
is the boss here. Do we start drilling or not?"

"Can you drill in Uni-plex?" Kris asked. Unlike smart
metal, the semi–smart metal used in the PFs could be reor-
ganized twice. The third time you tried to change it, it fell
apart. Navy policy was to change the cheaper Uni-plex
only once.

"Sure, ma'am, we drill it all the time," the worker said.

"You're going to make noises," Tom said to the stranger.

Moose's lips got thin in exasperation. "Look, folks. You
got a nice ANG-47SW station here. Bet you got it dialed in
sweet. It's gonna let you know all kinds of things about
what you're facing. Right?"

Penny nodded.

"So, what you gonna do with what you find? Hope you
got a canned program to work on it. Hope you can compute
a modification for it real fast."

"I should hope so," said Nelly from around Kris's neck.

"Yeah, right, they warned me about that thing. Listen,
you can count on what you got, or you can count on me. I
got my own bag of tricks. Some are standard. Some are the
kind of stuff that old ravens like me and mine spent our
lives dreaming about, dreaming up. It's been a long peace.
This looks like the only war in town. You gonna give me a
shot at it?"

Kris looked at Tom. "It's your ship, Tom." She paused
for a moment. "I know it's rough having someone walk on
your bridge at the last second and say, 'I might just win the

war for you,' but, well, I just did something like that to
some tugboat skippers. Told them they needed to step up
their game and maybe help me win this thing. I don't
know." Kris shrugged. "Your call."

"Me pass up a pretty black box?" Tom grinned. "Drill,
man."

"I'll need to hitch into this intel station. I can probably
do all my intake and output from it. No other hookups."

"Good, 'cause if you wanted to crawl under my navigation console, I'd space you."

"Kind of touchy there, huh?"

"Tom, how's the rest of the boat?" Kris asked.

"Time for a final walk-through. You want to come
with me?"

"I'd be honored to do that, Skipper."

"Just don't touch anything." He laughed. "Can't have
these staff officers getting their hands on things."

"Only to run my white gloves over surfaces to check for
dust," Kris assured him.

Penny took her station, did a check. "Kris, you heard
about the ultimatum?"

"No!" So Penny ran it for them.

"You recognize the spokeswoman?" Penny asked.

"I think that's Pandori's daughter."

"Think they'll identify themselves?" Tom asked.

Kris shook her head.

"Who's gonna do the drug inspection?" the raven asked.

"Us. With pulse lasers," Kris answered.

"You got that right." Tom beamed and climbed forward.
Kris followed.

Contact: –8 hours 15 minutes

"YOU happy now?" Mojag Pandori came the closest to
snarling as he had during their long discussions. "The ultimatum is out."

"Are you going to wait for it to expire before you put our
defense forces on alert?" William Longknife asked lightly.

"Our defense forces are already ready," Pandori snapped.

Honovi had been resting a hand on his father's knee. Now he squeezed it. Hard. "That is not what we have heard," Honovi said softly as his father's color rose.

"There are always rumors."

"Would you mind touching base with your Chief of Staff?"

"That is hardly necessary," Kusa said, ever defensive of her father. Honovi had come to respect her for that.

"We will be leaving you in a moment," Honovi said but made no sign of rising. "Humor me just one more time."

The call was made. "Admiral Pennypacker, what is our defense alert status?"

"Defense level one, sir. The lowest possible."

"Lowest!"

"Yes sir, the one you asked for."

"Admiral, we have Billy Longknife with us," Kusa said, cutting off further discussion. "You may have heard that we just issued an ultimatum to the intruders in system. Don't you think it would be wise for us to now come to full defensive alert?"

"Certainly, if the Prime Minister orders it."

"It is so ordered," the temporary Prime Minister said, looking like he was passing a kidney stone.

"And a strike force is making ready to proceed from High Wardhaven Naval Base to engage the intruders. See that this force receives orders to proceed with full discretion upon the expiration of the ultimatum," Kusa added, looking straight at Honovi. He nodded at her.

"A strike force?"

"Yes, Admiral," Mojag cut him off. "Just see that we come to full defense and the orders are issued. Do you understand?"

"Yes, Mr. Prime Minister. I understand. Now we fight."

"Yes," the acting Prime Minister said, almost visibly in pain, as the Admiral rang off.

"May I suggest that you now leave this building?" Honovi said, standing.

"Leave here?" came from Kusa, her father, and his.

"Yes. The battleships threaten a planetary bombardment if we resist. Government House will certainly be high on any target list. I suggest we not be here when they start shooting."

"They wouldn't destroy a cultural and historical icon like this," both fathers got out in cadence.

"They wouldn't dare," Kusa backed them up.

"Kusa, gentlemen, they intend to destroy Wardhaven as a separate, living entity. In a world ruled by Henry Peterwald, there will only be room for one center of government, and it will not be on Wardhaven. Thus, a wide laser slash will be where we are standing. I strongly suggest we be elsewhere."

Kris had told Honovi, in private, and with a promise not to tell Father, about what Sandfire on Turantic had intended for her. Anyone who wanted to serve his sis up to Henry Peterwald naked for a long and terminal torture session would not give a second thought to burning down several old buildings. Certainly not buildings that were only useful for self-government.

"I have just put the defense forces of Wardhaven on highest alert. I will not leave this command post," Pandori said. Maybe the man did have some fight in him.

"Then, Father, I suggest we leave them to their station."

The former Prime Minister maintained a frowning silence until they were out of the Prime Minister's office and into the vacant waiting room without. "Has your sister put you up to this? Is there something you're not telling me?"

"Father, you didn't respond very positively to her earlier accusations against Peterwald. Let's say she has passed along to me some incidents of more recent vintage that I find credible. Taken in context with those battleships, I think it's best if, in her quaint way of putting it, we beat feet for points unconnected with the Longknife name and government functions."

"Eighty years of peace create a certain way of thinking."

"Yes, Father. And those who don't break it may very soon find it listed as their cause of death."

Honovi quickened his pace. His steps echoed off the polished wooden floors and portrait-bedecked halls of Government House. Not one other person was in sight.

Billy Longknife hastened his steps to keep up with his son.

Contact: –7 hours 55 minutes

The Admiral let the hot water run over his razor as he listened to the Duty Lieutenant at his left give his briefing. His Chief of Staff, Bhutta Saris, already showered, shaved, and in dress blues, stood at his other elbow.

"So there is a Longknife at the Naval Base," the Admiral interrupted the young junior officer.

"Yes, sir."

"King Ray," he said slowly. "He could be a problem. Billy would just be there looking for votes."

"The young woman, Princess Kristine," Saris said. "A socialite with some naval training. She has run afoul of several unusual operations," a euphemism for black economic ops on Greenfeld, "and survived by an amazing streak of luck."

That was what the intel reports said. "Amazing luck." "Surprising bit of luck." "Luck beyond normal expectation." At Command and Staff College they taught that luck was not a strategy. Apparently at what passed for Greenfeld's spy training school, luck was all that could be connected with the Longknifes.

"What could a squadron of battleships have to fear from a mere Lieutenant?" the Duty Lieutenant added.

"What was the ultimatum again?" The Admiral finished shaving the other side of his face as he listened to it a second time. "So, they want to know who we are? And they want to inspect us, like they would any tramp freighter, huh?" They laughed politely at his joke while he washed off the soap.

He dried himself. His batman brought his uniform blouse, complete with medals. As he shrugged into it, he reached a conclusion. "When the ultimatum expires, quit sending any message. Go completely silent. I want us even quieter. They want an answer, let them eat cold static. They will get their answer when I choose to give it and not a moment sooner."

"Yes sir," the Duty Lieutenant said, and spoke into his commlink.

The Admiral took another sip of coffee. "Very good," he said to his Chief steward who'd brought it. "You have outdone yourself. You and your men. Tell them very good for me."

"I will, sir," the Chief said, nodded, and left.

"So, they are letting the liners go," the Admiral said. Bhutta nodded. "Do you think even a Longknife would stoop to using a liner loaded with refugees, women, and children from other planets, to crash one of us?"

"Ray Longknife was particularly bloodthirsty during the Iteeche Wars. I wouldn't put anything past him."

"I don't want to start this war by shooting up a boat-load of civilians from a half-dozen uninvolved planets. Pass a message to the Captains. If a liner gets to within fifteen thousand kilometers of our ships, disable it. Every one of our ships sports a gunnery E. Let's show some of that expert shooting. They are to take out the engines without blowing out the reactors. Understood? I don't want any battleship crashed by a liner, but I don't want five thousand dead civilians splashed across the media either."

"I understand, sir," Saris said as they entered flag plot.

"Sir," the lead technician said, standing from his workstation. "The intel Chief said you will want to see this. Wardhaven is going to full defensive alert."

"Show me," the Admiral ordered.

Like a puppy, the Duty Lieutenant was everywhere, trying to see and show everything at once. The Admiral saw in a second what he wanted. Normally, the space station fed power down the elevator to the planet's power grid. Now, that power line was empty. He didn't need intel to tell him the defenses of the space station were absorbing that power. Lasers whose capacitors had been bled off four days ago were now being charged. Yes, defenses were coming on-line.

The Admiral saw this as other sources fed him more data than he could possibly use. Finally, he took the poor young officer aside. "You did well to let me sleep. Your briefing was precise and to the point, but now I am awake. I have my eyes open. So be a good boy and only answer the questions I ask."

The youth turned pink. But he nodded and took his station behind his three technicians. Good. Good.

The Admiral turned to his battle board. As it was now, he'd be going into a battle with his fragile engines pointed at his enemy's station-based lasers. But those were his orders.

"Go straight in," Henry Peterwald told him. "Straight for them. I'll have Wardhaven set to cave like a house of cards." Well, these cards were making noises like they might shoot back.

"Should we put some fear into them?" Saris asked.

"No, I need to keep some surprises up my sleeve. Let's let them think they know what they face for a few hours more. Raise deceleration from 1.0 to 1.05 g's, give us a bit of a cushion in case we need to stop decelerating later for a while."

"Like to dodge passenger liners or shoot up the station?"

"Or something like that."

Contact: –7 hours 45 minutes

Tom began the reintroduction of Kris to her old boat forward in the fo'c'sle. Here, a slip of a gunner's mate 3/c oversaw the firing tubes for the Foxers, and now the AGM 944 missiles.

"You still lifting weights, Kami?" Kris asked.

"Twice a day," the woman replied from where she sat buried in the middle of four huge canisters of reload.

"Don't worry, ma'am, if one of these puppies misfires, I'll kick its ass."

"And if she needs help, she only has to shout," came from the next compartment.

"And if you big lugs need help in a tight corner of the laser bay, you know who to call, too," Kami shouted right back.

Apparently, the deal Kris had worked out in her weapons division was still holding. The fo'c'sle had been cramped even before the larger 944s had been added. Four launching tubes fed by four canisters full of reloads, and, for the Foxers, spare canisters to horse into place when the first load was empty. Now it was an even tighter fit. Kami ruled here.

Just aft of there was the laser bay, its four long pulse lasers the reason for PF-109's existence. Here, Ensign Satem, the Swede, and two more mechanics saw to it that when the boat was in a place to break something, it got broke.

"Any problems?" Tom asked.

"None you need to worry about," Satem answered. Swede, their newly promoted 2/c, and his two junior mechanics were going over number-three laser. "Normal check. No surprises, sir. Ma'am. You give us a battlewagon. We'll put the holes in it. Let's see how good they are at breathing vacuum."

Next aft was the bridge. Penny and Fintch had it to themselves. "Where's our raven, that Moose fellow?"

Fintch gave a thumbs-down; a glance showed half of Sandy's sensor feed was blank. Tom and Kris climbed the next deck down. Sparks's command of the radio shack looked like it had already taken a hit. Ensign Hang Tran, Sparks since she started at Wardhaven Tech for reasons she refused to explain, was hardly as tall standing as her four subordinate electronics techs were bending double over two opened black boxes.

"Not that board," Moose was saying to them. "The next one."

Kris glanced around. Radio, radar, magnetic gear, network, jammers, noisemakers, or at least the controllers for antennas located around the hull of the boat, she recognized. New boxes with hastily stenciled names like maskers, decoys, and one just marked Black Cauldron Rev 4.5 didn't tell her a lot.

"Any problem?" Tom asked.

"Yes," Sparks snapped.

"No," Moose said.

"Any consensus?" Tom said.

"Would you open that hatch, gal, and ask that other gal if she's got color?"

Kris guessed she was the first gal. She lifted the hatch to the bridge. "Penny, you showing lights?"

"No." A pause. "Yes. I got them again. But damn it, I don't like them blinking on and off."

"Me neither. Here. Somebody hand me that duct tape."

"Duct tape? You're installing gear in my boat with duct tape!" Tom's voice was amazingly calm, all things considered.

"The board is in there solid. The tape should keep it from wiggling. Hand me that foam spacer as well. Both of them."

"That going to hold at three g's?" Tom asked.

"You gonna be any worse off losing it then than if you never had it?" the old fellow answered as he went about taping it down.

"Sparks, there any way you could secure it better?"

"Sir, there is no way that I'd touch that stuff. It's bread board. Hell, sir, it's bread *crumb* board, some of it."

Moose looked up from what he'd just finished. "Some of this stuff is experimental, yes. The fleet sailed with everything that was good, kosher, bought under contract and documented forty ways to Sunday. And, if you ask my opinion, half of it won't work, and the other half is already obsolete. This stuff is what the fleet should have had. Would have had if the procurement folks had half an idea of what was really going on. Anyway, you got what we can give you."

"We can't afford to lose sensors," Tom pointed out. "No sensors, and we are deaf, dumb, and blind. No sensors, and we can't find a battleship to shoot. You understand?"

"I understand you. You won't lose your sensor feed again. And I'll keep the other guy's sensors from seeing you."

Tom shook his head. "You sure this is a good idea?" he asked Kris as he turned away.

"The reservists crewing the decoys came up with the idea of pulling these folks in. They think we really need them, Tom. I don't know enough about this to argue."

"What do you think, Sparks?" Tom asked.

"My favorite college professor, Doc Marley, says that no matter how good it may look, the job is never done until the job is fully done, checked out, and documented. I did not think duct tape was included in that." She sniffed. "But when I called Professor Marley, I found that he is on the 105 boat working with Singh. I asked him why he isn't with me on the 109. He said because the Moose is a better raven. Batty as they come. Do not make him mad, but the best there is when the documentation can't be finished and hell's a-popping," she said, shaking her head.

"I guess that answers that," Tom said.

"I'm gonna keep working down here," Moose said. "I understand you intend to do three g's with radical turns."

"Something like that," Tom said.

Moose pursed his lips. "Didn't quite factor that into this gear. I'll see what me and your guys can do about that."

"I'd much appreciate that," Tom said and led Kris aft.

They paused on the empty quarterdeck. "What do you make of him?" Kris asked.

"Batty as they come says it all, but then, taking on six battleships with a dozen mosquito boats and whatever you can press-gang out of the yacht basin don't exactly strike me as the sanest thing I've ever let you talk me into."

"You don't want to be a bored old married man, do you?"

"Ma and Da didn't complain about it, but I'll settle for looking in on the engine room just now."

There, Tononi and two motor mechs were going over the antimatter injectors under the Chief's watchful eye. A yard man was standing by with a toolkit . . . and spare injectors.

"Pass them the new one," the Chief said as they entered.

"Problem, Chief?" Tom asked.

"Not now. Not now that we've replaced one hundred and twenty-five percent of the motor, sir," the Chief answered with what passed for a tight smile.

The yard worker blanched. "They're certified parts, Chief."

"Certified by my pet monkey, most likely," the Chief said.

"We going to need any more parts?" Tom asked.

"We have a spares cart on the pier," the yard worker put in.

"I'd think it was empty by now," the Chief growled.

"It's the second load," the Nuu Docks man said. Kris wasn't sure if he was helping his case . . . or digging his hole deeper.

"It would be really nice if we could get under way sometime this year," Tom said almost wistfully.

"She'll answer orders when you give them."

"Nelly, message Roy. Please stock spare parts aboard tugs for PFs' engines, lasers, and electronics. Empty the warehouse. It ain't gonna do us any good there if we need it out yonder."

"He got it. His initial reply is obscene, but he's ordering the warehouse to ship it all to the tug landing."

"Thank you, Nelly."

"Aren't you worried about message intercept?" Tom asked.

"By now there must be enough traffic in and around this station to flood their comm gear. I figure they'll crack my message about five minutes after I blow them out of space."

Tom grinned along with her as they climbed back to the

bridge. Penny looked up as they arrived. "Good. I was about to send for you. We have a message to all hands."

"Put it on the main screen."

A stranger appeared, identified as Admiral Penny-packer, chairman of the Joint Staff. "Wardhaven's defenses are fully alerted. We are about to launch a strike force from High Wardhaven to intercept the intruders. In response to our ultimatum, they have gone silent and increased deceleration. If that signals their good intent, fine. If not, let them know that Wardhaven will defend itself with all its power."

"Now doesn't that really stir me blood?" Tom brogued.

"Not," Penny said.

"Can you raise the *Halsey* on secure landline?"

"You got it," Penny answered.

"Sandy, what's your take on Pennypacker's announcement? Is there anything nice about what the intruders are doing?"

"In Pennypacker's dreams. By doing some extra slowing down now, they can flip ship later, protect their jets from us when they may need to, and not overshoot the station. They've also gone even quieter on the emissions controls. Just six big, deep holes in space. They're telling us as little as they can. Not the kind of behavior you like from friendly visitors."

"Pass the word. We got our hunting license. We're legal. Battlewagons are in season, and we can bag the limit."

"Happily. I'm sure Luna and van Horn will be delighted."

Kris rang off, fished in her pocket, and turned to Tom. "I have something for you, Commander 109. It didn't seem right that you should be going into this fight the only JG commanding a boat, so the Commodore got van Horn to cut your promotion papers. Congratulations, Lieutenant. Penny, you want to do the honors?"

"But it's been so pleasant having him serve under me," she pouted, but she was up, coming around her station, and removing his shoulder tabs and putting on the new ones Kris had brought.

Honors done, Kris settled into her chair. Her board showed reports from the 109. She revised it to show input from the whole squadron. Babs's 111 was down for engines . . . again. Gates was just reporting a new capacitor installed . . . again.

It was time to get things organized. "Phil, you lead First Division, with 101, 02, and 03. Chandra, you have Third Division. Take 104, Babs, if she can get 111 away from the pier—"

"I'll sail if I have to push it," came from Babs.

"And Heather's 110 boat. Stick close to Chandra, Heather. I've got some wandering planned for Division 3."

"This ramblin' frog's gonna be right on your old tail," Heather promised the mustang.

"The rest form Second Division with 109. We'll start it close and tight," Kris went on. "Let them see as little of us as possible while we're getting away from the pier."

"So, when do we get out of here?" Heather shot back, probably speaking for all of them.

"In about two hours," Kris said.

"Two hours. We'll all be old and gray. And some of us could have grandkids."

"Two hours. Sit tight. Wait," Kris repeated.

"Fix an engine," came from Babs.

"Repair a capacitor," echoed Andy.

Wait.

15

Contact: –7 hours 30 minutes

"Nothing ever goes according to plan," Kris muttered to herself. She'd heard Father say it about political campaigns. Grampa Ray and Trouble had laughed about it in battles . . . in retrospect. Now Kris saw it in spades. It was one thing to plan on hiding behind passenger liners. Another thing to do it.

"Say again, port control. You want us to do what!"

"*Pride of Antares,* you are cleared to withdraw from the pier, but you will hold at fifty klicks, trailing the station."

"We'll be in zero g."

"Yes."

"I got a boat full of kids, women that aren't used to zero g. Hell, I got junior officers and stewards that ain't been in zero g more than ten seconds. How long you want us to hold?"

"About an hour. Maybe a bit more."

"How about I either boost at one g straight for Jump Point Alpha or stay tied up here for an hour, a bit more?"

"*Pride of Antares,* I have twelve liners to get away from this station over the next hour. My board shows you hull tight. I'm activating your tie-downs."

"And if I just kind of put on one g and head out of here?"

"May I remind you that you are in a Wardhaven Defense Primary Control Zone and all our lasers are charged."

"You wouldn't."

"*Pride of Antares,* I'm having a very bad day. You really want to see how much I'll do that I'll regret to tell my wife about tonight?"

"Would you mind telling me what's going on here?"

"Not on an open channel."

"Kris," came from Sandy over the landline, "I think its time we show the passenger liners why we want them where we want them. And maybe some encouragement to do it."

"Sounds like a good idea to me. I was bored hanging around here anyway."

"Okay, folks. Final briefing. I am Task Force Horatio, ships one through six. Kris you've got Task Force Light Brigade."

"As in 'Charge of.'"

"Glad you read your Tennyson. One through twenty-seven at last count. Depends on who gets away from the pier."

Numbers appeared on Kris's command board. Her PFs were matched through twelve, then different yachts.

"Captain, you're Task Force Custer. One through eight."

"Understood." There was a pause. "My Army associate tells me that Custer bought the big one. As in massacred with all hands. This your idea of a joke?"

"Only for those who crack our codes. And speaking of, Beni tells me, Kris, that your Tom has a synchronous transmission he wants to make to help us keep communications confusing to our enemy. Want to send it, Tom?"

"Sending." There was a pause. "Done."

"When are you going to play it on battle net? Beni's got my curiosity up."

"Wait for a while. We're not desperate enough."

"And I thought you PF jockeys passed desperate weeks ago," van Horn said dryly.

"We just plumb that depth deeper and deeper, sir," Tom answered back.

"And if the children will let us get a word in, I propose we begin backing out. Horatio, Custer, then Light Brigade. We big boys will take station inboard of the liners. You little folks take station inboard of us."

"You mean closer to Wardhaven?" Kris said.

"You got it."

"Begin sortie now," Sandy said.

"Kris, may I send my data dump to Tru now?" Nelly asked.

"Yes, Nelly, it's that time. But tell Aunt Tru not to look at it until we get back."

"And if we do not?"

"That is something we humans do not look at until we have to," Kris said.

Captain Luna glanced around her bridge. A week ago it had been spick-and-span. Now it had wire runs taped down and running every which way. Still, it was the *Archie* and responded to her orders. She tapped her ship's comm. "Let's put the spurs to her, boys. Navy, grab a seat or get ashore, 'cause this boat is going places." Her board showed green. The hull was tight. Power was good . . . on both reactors. The pier tie-downs began to move the ship backwards. The last tie-down clicked, and the ship floated free in space.

"Helm, put us right close up behind that old fart in the *Cushing*," she ordered.

"You bet, ma'am," the young man said.

She listened carefully to see if any of the Navy Reservists would get sick in zero g. Officially, all of them were space qualified. She trusted Navy papers no farther than they'd fly if she made a paper airplane out of them. Still, the ship stayed quiet. The airflow brought no smell of last night's supper.

"Any of you Navy types got money to burn? Nothing big's going on, and I figure we got plenty of time for a couple a games of poker," Luna said on ship net.

"Ah, Princess, Light Brigade Leader, er, what do you want us to do?"

Oops, Sandy . . . and Kris . . . had forgotten to pass along orders to the incipient riot they had organized. "Search and rescue, salvage tugs," who were now more, "should stay at the station and go into orbit in three hours. I'll give you alerts as to when you should expect to make rescue intercepts. At this point, assume six hours. Light Brigade units. Armed yachts and runabouts will form by divisions. I'm sending them now." She punched her board, and the force structure went out to her force. "Division 4, 5, and 6, shadow Patrol Boat Divisions 1, 2, and 3. Division 7, you stay with 6. If any vacancies open in the other divisions, you fill in. Otherwise, I'll figure out something for you." The last three boats were a race club that had volunteered together at the last minute. They gave her an enthusiastic set of "Sure, no problem."

"Now then, you're going to be facing a solid hour plus of zero g as we do a close orbit of Wardhaven. If you think you can handle two plus hours of that, detach and form with the rest of the brigade when we form on the big boys. If you'd like to save yourself an hour of zero g or stay close to the station for a last run to the little girls' room, stay tied up to the pier while the liners detach and line up."

"We can do that," came back in a light murmur.

Kris kept her small stuff tied up and out of the way of the large units while they formed their line. That left her tied into the commlink when the next liner got its orders.

"Port Authorities, do I understand that you are refusing my request to boost for Jump Point Alpha?"

"Affirmative, *Sovereign of the Pleiades*. Form on *Pride of Antares,* trailing the station by fifty klicks."

"You are going to convoy us out of here?"

"Something like that."

"With what?"

"Watch your transmission. This is an open channel, and there are hostiles in system."

"I can see why you want us to keep quiet. You Wardhaven folks really got the balls if you think—"

"You want to lose your license for a language violation?" came back to cut him off.

"As if you'll have time to file it. Okay, I'm leaving. And I'm only too glad to see the last of you folks."

"Could we kind of accidentally shoot that one?" Tom asked.

"He's loaded with civilians," Penny pointed out.

"We can put a scare in him," Phil suggested on net. "A close flyby."

Kris could almost see the devil in his smile. "Squadron 8 will sortie on my order. We will form by divisions. Phil, let's *not* take any paint off that last liner in line as we go by. I'd love to, and on any other day but today, believe me, we would, but we got bigger fish to fry."

"Kris, you a vegan?" Heather asked, but Phil led them out, passing between the second liner and a third one just getting under way, at a very sedate pace.

Squadron 8 took its place between Wardhaven and Task Force Horatio and Custer. The *Halsey* looked deadly in its blackened ice reflecting back the stars. The *Cushing* was a bit the worse for her years. The six decoys looked no better than scrap piles that had drifted off from some ship breaker's yard and been hastily painted black. The container ships were in their original blue, white, and crimson paint schemes, garish and clashing with the green of the containers lashed to them. But they held station in line astern as shipshape as Kris would have expected of Captain van Horn's command. The first four ships were fully loaded. The last two were only half. Kris hadn't asked the Captain what he planned for those last-minute additions, but she didn't doubt he'd put them to good use.

Every three or four minutes, another liner separated from the station and fell back to settle in line astern of the other large passenger ships to the right of Santiago and van Horn's commands. There was little to do but watch. As Kris had learned her first day at OCS, hurry up and wait was the Navy Way.

Contact: –7 hours 15 minutes

HONOVi gulped as the round parking drive at Nuu House came into view. It was full. "What are all those cars doing here?

"Today is your mother's weekly canasta party," said Father.

"But there are battleships coming."

"Gabriel could be in the third movement of his final solo, and your mother and her friends would not change their schedules, but it's not canasta today. Her socialite friends have arranged to hide the contents of Wardhaven's museums. Don't want some temporary occupation force to grab our treasures, do you, son?"

"I'd never have thought Mother and her friends—"

"Lots of people are surprising us these days. But call Rose and tell her it's time to go. Have her check with that maid of your sister's. She'll help. If you are serious about us needing to 'beat feet' for points unusual for us, this may actually be a spot of luck. I suspect your mother's club will spread the word rather quickly; some might even go along with her."

"If we have time," Honovi said.

"That is up to your sister. Damn it, boy, I hate having her charging off like that. Doesn't she realize that people can get killed doing that? They don't all live long, ornery lives like my grandfathers."

"Believe me, she knows."

"When this is over, we have to get her somewhere where she can contemplate the error of her ways."

Honovi glanced up as the car came to a rest. "For the

moment, Father, don't you think we should be glad that she's busy committing more errors to contemplate?"

"Hmm," was all Father said.

"Sir, we'd better hurry."

"I'm coming," Al Longknife muttered as he turned from his inner sanctum to the elevator. He'd done everything to make his life secure, his person impregnable, and it had come to this. Everything depended on that slip of a granddaughter and what she'd been able to concoct out of castoff ships, borrowed yachts, and whatever.

"Bad planning," he muttered as he entered the elevator.

"Sir?" the junior vice president who was offering Al the courtesy of his hunting retreat in the south mountains said.

"Nothing." That was the problem. He'd let his father play at king of ninety planets. His son play at ruling this one. What had it gotten him? Nothing. Nothing to protect his business, his employees, his wealth from these battleships. Nothing to protect this tower he lived in from being reduced to a smoking ruin. Nothing to protect his life.

Al settled awkwardly into the tall all-terrain vehicle that would be needed to get into the backcountry. As they drove down the lush, tree-lined boulevard, away from Longknife Towers, he glanced back. He'd always considered the tall cylinder a salute to the world.

Now he wasn't so sure who was giving who the finger.

Al settled face front for the long drive. Maybe Henry Peterwald wasn't so crazy. Maybe the only way to make human space safe for yourself was to control every damn inch of it.

Something to think about.

Contact: –7 hours

"Sir, we've got chatter from the port authorities on High Wardhaven," the Duty Lieutenant reported. The Admiral came to look over his shoulder as he looked over the shoulder of his three technicians.

"Play it for me, son."

The Admiral listened. Yes, things were happening. More than just loaded passenger liners getting away from his target.

Saris came to stand by his elbow. "They are not letting them boost for Jump Point Adele."

"No surprise. They want them to swing around Wardhaven."

"And make a suicide dive at us?" the Duty Lieutenant said.

"Did you message our Captains?" the Admiral asked. Saris presented a message board to read. The message was clear: nip the engines, don't slaughter the passengers. "Even an iron-headed dofbert could understand that. Good."

The Admiral settled into his chair at his battle board and eyed the space around Wardhaven. "Plot a course for Jump Point Adele from High Wardhaven with an orbit around Wardhaven."

The board did.

"Lieutenant, talk to me about that station."

"The defensive lasers are charged. A dozen passenger liners are powered up. Also merchant ships. Private yachts. The entire station has merged into one huge magnetic flux, sir."

"Radar."

"Jammed, sir."

"Visual? Laser? Can't anybody see anything?"

"Nothing, sir, the station has been venting water, intel assumed from its sewage system, for the last twelve hours."

"Before the ultimatum was issued?"

"Yes sir. We assumed, with the evacuation, that there was a problem and no one to look at it and, well, it was just venting."

The Admiral shook his head. "And with the evacuation, who was pissing to create a sewage problem to vent!" He snorted. Did you have to be brainless to be assigned to intel?

Then again, hindsight was so much better.

"Should we power everything up, sir?" Bhutta asked.

"I don't know what they have. Why should I let them know what I have? No, we are just standard President-class battleships. Let them assume that is what they face until it serves our interests to tell them different."

The Admiral studied the board that told him no more now than it had four days ago. "No. Now we hurry up and wait."

Contact: –6 hours 45 minutes

Kris watched as the line of transports grew longer. Now it included more than just huge passenger liners. There were hastily converted general cargo ships, some container ships rigged for human occupancy, and most of the yachts Kris hadn't walked off with. She'd heard on-line some rather nasty comments by owners who'd shown up to find their yacht not at its assigned berth. They'd been accommodated on other people's yachts, the converted ships, somewhere. And their complaints had been kept to a minimum. At least Kris hoped they had. No one had actually mentioned that their boat was armed. Not on net.

It was time to wake up the rest. "Task Force Light Brigade, second inning. This is your five-minute warning. Prepare to detach from the station and join up in five minutes."

"About time." "Just a minute, our skipper's ashore," and "But I so wanted to see who got the girl." "Teach you to start a long vid," came back at Kris.

She waited four minutes, gave a one-minute warning, then ordered them to detach in the order she'd assigned. Fourteen of them made it away from the docks with only one minor bump. Just as Kris was about to order one of the Seventh Division boats into the missing slot, the dock spat out the missing boat.

"Sorry to be late," was all the excuse she got.

"Glad you could make it."

By divisions, the yachts and system runabouts threaded

their way through the line of transports, then the Navy ships, and joined up with Squadron 8. "Remember, when we start this thing, you stay with us until we hit two g's. Then you fall back. We go ahead and knock some sense into the battleships."

"And we pick up the pieces," they repeated together.

Kris prayed they were very little pieces.

Contact: –6 hours 35 minutes

Sandy glanced around the *Halsey*'s CIC. Every station was manned and ready. Every face showed eager in the dim light. *How did I let another Santiago get talked into following another Longknife into another mess?*

Because there really is no other option, Sandy gave the answer her great-grandfather must have given.

"Well, at least I'm not opening a damn briefcase bomb," she muttered to herself.

"Ma'am?" her XO said, beside her.

"All hands," Sandy said, mashing her commlink. "This is the Captain. You know our mission. We're decoys to draw fire away from the little boys. And that's what we'll do. But I haven't forgotten, any more than you have, that the *Halsey* packs ten big pulse lasers of her own. Once we've done the job we came for, and once the fast stuff has done their tap dance, we're going to nail some of that battleship butt to our own yardarm."

That got a cheer in the CIC that echoed through the ship.

"Transports, this is convoy lead. You are cleared to begin a deceleration burn on my mark. You will make one partial orbit of Wardhaven before accelerating for Jump Point Alpha or Beta."

That got Sandy several different levels of remarks from sincere thanks to reeking sarcasm to "Who'd be crazy enough to mess with Beta?"

When silence returned, she said simply, "My mark is in five, four, three, two, one. Mark."

Beside her, the transports began their burns. Ahead of her, the Naval task forces began the same burn even as the *Halsey* did likewise. As one, civilian, Navy, Naval volunteers, all slowed to fall away from the station into a lower orbit that would swing them around Wardhaven and out into space. While the transports applied straight deceleration vectors, the Navy ships did some fancy footwork. They not only slowed but tucked themselves in close to the civilians, much closer than the five kilometers allowed by defunct Society regulations and insurance companies. But there was a war on, and hard times called for hard risks.

There were exceptions. The last two ships in Task Force Custer, the half-loaded container ships, waited a moment to begin the descent burn, waited until the end of the transport column was even with them, then did their burn with a bit of a wiggle as well and fell in line, unnoticed by those busy keeping station.

Since Sandy wasn't looking in that direction, she failed to notice the other exception. Three armed runabouts, the ones Kris had designated Division 7, started their burn, but their club leader spotted the lack of burn by the two container ships and thought they might need help. Then he thought it might be fun to join them in whatever it was they were doing. Three more runabouts joining the mob of yachts and runabouts at the end of the transport line were hardly noticeable, even if these did have rocket launchers welded to their skin.

Kris watched the station fall away. She'd done that so many times as she rode the elevator down. This was different. Today, home wasn't at the other end of this ride. Today she was headed for a fight that would either leave her planet still free or slagged and enslaved. Either end might leave her and a lot of the people she loved dead.

There wasn't any other choice, she told herself. *I hate that option*, she added. *If I live through this, I swear to God that I will do everything within my power to never be left with no other choice ever again. I* will *have choices. I* will *make my own decisions, and not because I'm in a box with no good place left to go.*

Kris rode the PF-109 as Wardhaven's gravity swung it around and slung it at Milna.

Contact: −5 hours 25 minutes

"Admiral, the convoyed liners are coming around Wardhaven," the Duty Lieutenant announced.

The Admiral did not look up from his battle board.

"The convoy commander is authorizing the liners to start their burns for jump points. Note the use of the plural, sir."

"Noted, Lieutenant. Do we know anything about this convoy commander? Where is he located?"

"He appears to be a she, sir. Wardhaven has one destroyer in system. The *Halsey*, sir, is commanded by a woman."

"One of their Amazons, huh," grunted Saris. "Maybe she will escort the liners right out of the system. Assure that they are safe, huh."

"I would rather hear more about their use of multiple jump points. Is anyone heading for Jump Point Barbie?"

"We can not yet tell, sir."

"Let me know immediately."

The Admiral drummed his fingers on the battle board. It showed him his six battleships on a vector that now passed between High Wardhaven and the planet. He'd have to adjust his deceleration at some point. What held his attention was a formless glob of electromagnetic flux crossing the face of Wardhaven. "Can you get me a visual or radar picture?"

"Radar is still being jammed, sir."

"A convoy of luxury liners is jamming our radar!"

"So intel tells us, sir."

"Get me the best visual you can on the screen. Have they started boosting? Can't we spot their engine burns?"

"They're boosting at a ninety-degree angle, sir."

"Get me an infrared."

"They're working on it, sir, but it comes back all fuzzy."

"Fuzzy? Will someone put something on-screen for me to use my own MK I eyeball on? Saris, get that data up here."

Minutes later, the Admiral stood, hands behind his back, and paced between two different screens.

"It is very confusing, sir," Saris said.

"Yes, it is. Infrared *is* all fuzzy. The laser range finders are confused. This looks like a string of merchant liners. First ship looks like a Sovereign-class. Next in line has to be a standard Pride series type. But the electromagnetic signals from the next ship are confusing. The laser return has strange echoes, and the infrared is off."

"At least they are not headed for us, sir," the Duty Lieutenant said. "They are all headed for Jump Point Adele."

"And these," the Admiral said, pointing to a small group at the tag end of the line.

"They seem to be a bit off course, sir."

"Let me know when you figure out what course they *are* on."

The Duty Lieutenant nodded. Then his eyes went out of focus as he listened to his commlink. "Say again," he said, then swallowing hard, "Ah, sir, intel thinks the stray ships are heading for Jump Point Barbie."

"Where is Division 7?" Kris said, trying to keep her voice low, calm, and properly commanding when all she wanted to do was scream.

"There, Kris, over there with those two freighters from Custer. And don't ask me what they're doing. They were just following along with all of us until a minute ago, then suddenly they took off at one-g acceleration."

"Where are they headed?" Kris asked.

Her workstation immediately showed a course for Jump Point Beta. "They're heading for the battleships," Nelly said.

"Van Horn said he had something special planned for those ships. But how did Division 7 get attached to them?"

"I don't know. You didn't tell them. Can we order them back?" Tom asked.

"They were the last to get added to the force. They aren't on the Navy net, are they?" Kris said, looking over her shoulder at Penny and Moose. The raven shook his head.

"You'd have to talk to them on the commercial net and in the clear. And the battleships could home on you as well. Me, I wouldn't issue them any new orders. As I recall, your last words to them were to stay close and listen up. Looks like they chose to hang loose and wander off, ma'am."

Kris couldn't argue that, but still something in her command had gone horribly wrong. She couldn't have any more like that. She mashed her commlink. "Light Brigade. Listen up. Stay in line with me. Do not acknowledge."

Kris heard no replies, just as she wanted. At least the ones she had left could obey small orders like that one. She eyed her board. The transports now accelerated at a comfortable one g, much to the relief of their passengers, no doubt, for Jump Point Alpha. The Navy task forces would slowly separate from the civilians—and the cover they offered—as the warships headed for the moon. Still, for the moment, Horatio and Custer stayed close in the cover of the transports . . . and the Light Brigade hung tightly to the cover of them both.

Meanwhile, two lone freighters and three system runabouts boosted at one g for Jump Point Beta with no apparent intention of ever getting there.

The Admiral studied the battle board. It told him far too little. "Talk to me about those five vessels," he demanded.

"Two of them are standard container ships. From visuals, they are partially loaded with standard containers. The others are small system runabouts, not cleared for star jumps, sir."

"So what are they doing making for a star jump?"

When the silence stretched, the Duty Lieutenant stepped into it. "Sir, if someone was desperate enough, they might think they could do a jump, then buy more fuel in the Paula system, do another jump, keep going until they found someplace that would take them in. It's risky. If they ran out of fuel . . ."

"But when you're running for your life," Saris finished.

"Makes me want to talk to whoever has access to ships like those and feels the strong need to run," said the future governor of Wardhaven, entering flag plot unannounced.

"A good reason to include corvettes with this force," the Admiral pointed out, not for the first time.

"But we must present only a hard, armored fist. Nothing weak about us." Harrison Maskalyne again was quoting Henry Peterwald. That might be a good negotiating position for a businessman. It overlooked much from a naval perspective.

"Well, these little fish will not be caught in the net we do not have," the Admiral said with finality. "Assuming they do not threaten us."

"Freighters and runabouts threaten *us*!" the governor said.

"How close will they pass?" the Admiral asked.

The Duty Lieutenant looked like he'd swallowed a lemon. "Sir, each ship is having trouble setting and maintaining a course. I don't think the runabouts really know where the jump point is." Jump points appeared to wobble in their orbit around a star, part of the process of them maintaining a relationship with the several stars they were in contact with. Starships used a full set of sensors to find a jump as they approached it.

"I suppose the runabouts were planning on following the freighters through, but at least one of the freighters' sailing masters is a bit unsure of himself," Saris snorted.

The Admiral nodded. Things like that happened when people panicked. When you grabbed ships that had been tied up to the pier too long, merchant officers tied up to the bar too long . . . Then again, it also provided a cover.

"When will they pass closest to us?" the Admiral repeated.

"In about two and a half hours, sir."

"Establish contact with them in two. Warn them to stay twenty thousand kilometers from us. They come any closer, and we will respond with deadly force."

"Yes, sir," the Chief of Staff said.

The Duty Lieutenant, however, was studying the overhead like a stargazer who might really see his future there. "Sir, there is activity among the transports. Sensors are starting to clarify the situation. There are warships among the liners."

The Admiral chuckled. "Tell me something I wasn't expecting, boy."

16

"They just lit up like a Christmas tree," Moose said.

Kris unstrapped and stepped around to study Sandy's and the raven's boards. Multicolored bar graphs danced everywhere, circles made sweeps, and lists grew as fast as cryptic letters could appear in small windows.

"He's searching us, full active," Penny said.

"Active with everything he's got," Moose said softly. "And he brought the whole friggin' farm with him. Before he was pinging us with some off-the-shelf stuff I could have picked up in any secondhand ship store on Earth. No-account stuff that said nothing. This new stuff says he's good. He's very good."

"Too good?" Kris whispered.

Moose glanced up from his board, a tight grin on his face. "Not as good as me and my raven buddies. No, he's not as good as he thinks he is. If he was, he'd have brought this stuff up a bit at a time. Tickled us with one, see how we react. Play with us, the way a good fly fisherman plays a wily trout. Let it run a bit, pull to set the hook, then run, pull, run, pull." He shook his head. "This fellow is all brute force."

Kris hoped brute force was not all it took to win.

"Young man, I understand you have a song for the battle net, a song to cheer us on our way and make it harder to crack our communications," Moose said.

"Just a moment," Tom said, and tapped his board. "Battle net going active . . . now," he announced.

Drumming began, then a distant pipe, growing closer. A woman's voice, husky with confidence, filled the bridge.

> *Axes flash, broadsword swing,*
> *Shining armour's piercing ring*
> *Horses run with polished shield,*
> *Fight Those Bastards till They Yield*
> *Midnight mare and blood red roan,*
> *Fight to Keep this Land Your Own*
> *Sound the horn and call the cry,*
> How Many of Them Can We Make Die!
>
> *Follow orders as you're told,*
> *Make Their Yellow Blood Run Cold*
> *Fight until you die or drop,*
> *A Force Like Ours is Hard to Stop*
> *Close your mind to stress and pain,*
> *Fight till You're No Longer Sane*
> *Let not one damn cur pass by,*

Kris eyed the main screen with its six red hostile dots coming at them. She mouthed the refrain as the singer came to it: *"How Many of Them Can We Make Die!"* She wasn't alone.

> *Guard your women and children well,*
> *Send These Bastards Back to Hell*
> *We'll teach them the ways of war,*
> *They Won't Come Here Any More*
> *Use your shield and use your head,*
> *Fight till Every One is Dead*

Raise the flag up to the sky,
How Many of Them Can We Make Die!

Now the whole bridge echoed as each word was bitten out. The singer took a step back, leaving the music to drum and pipe and other things Kris couldn't quite place. Studying the music just wasn't in her. Feeling it riff up her back, harden the muscles of her gut, her fists. Now that was something she felt like doing. The singer tiptoed back.

Dawn has broke, the time has come,
Move Your Feet to a Marching Drum
We'll win the war and pay the toll,
We'll Fight as One in Heart and Soul
Midnight mare and blood red roan,
Fight to Keep this Land Your Own
Sound the horn and call the cry,
How Many of Them Can We Make Die!

Axes flash, broadsword swing,
Shining armour's piercing ring
Horses run with polished shield,
Fight Those Bastards till They Yield
Midnight mare and blood red roan,
Fight to Keep this Land Your Own
Sound the horn and call the cry,
How Many of Them Can We Make Die!

"Da . . . amn," the raven breathed. "I'm supposed to slip message packets in among that."

"Where did a nice peaceful boy from Santa Maria lay his hands on something like that?" Kris asked.

Tom actually turned a light pink around the edges. "When I wrote my granddame about how hard it was for me to become a trigger puller for you on Olympia, no matter how bad the hard men were, she asked me if I didn't remember that song, 'The March of Cambreadth.' I told her of course I did. I'd sung it since I was a wee kid, but, well, it was just a song.

"When she came to our wedding, she took me aside, told me that maybe she and Granny Good Good had been, well, maybe a bit too good. They didn't tell us kids, growing up, how it came to be that we still sang that song on Santa Maria.

"You see, back when the lost scientists finally realized they were lost and never going to see Earth again, we were all taught in school that they had a rough hundred years, the Hungry Years, when the colony could have died. What they don't teach us kids in school is that not all the grown-ups were as willing as the textbooks say they were to go to bed hungry and get up to hard, killing work every day. Some took to the hills.

"And some came back as raiders. Trying to steal what they weren't willing to work to grow. There were fights, and men died to keep food in their kids' mouths.

"Me, now, I'm thinking it was stupid of them not to tell us kids the real history, especially now that we're heading our separate ways to face what we are, but Granddame gave me back a song I've known all me life, and now I've given it to you."

Behind Tom, the song was on repeat: "Guard your women and children well." Yes, in the long peace, maybe a lot had been forgotten. A lot had been softened too much.

"Granddame says the song came with the original crew from Earth, that it dates from the twentieth century. With all its talk of axes and swords, armor and horns, I kind of think it's older than that, but it was good enough to get us through the hungry time."

"How Many of Them Can We Make Die!" Kris and Tom, Penny and Fintch sang together.

"It ought to get us through today," Tom finished.

"Yes," Kris agreed.

> *"Follow orders as you're told,*
> *Make Their Yellow Blood Run Cold."*

"What the hell is that?" the Admiral snapped.

"We're intercepting their battle net, sir," the Duty Lieutenant said. "That's playing on all their ships. Intel thinks they're burying message packets somewhere in the carrier wave, the song or somewhere. We're searching it, sir."

"Well, what's it telling us?"

"There seem to be a dozen or so ships separating from the transports, sir. They appear to be on a one-g course to a lunar orbit, sir. Intel expects they will do a midcourse flip, decelerate at one g, and loop around the moon—it's called Milna, sir—and then come at us on a converging course. They should be sending it to your battle board very soon, sir."

The battle board winked, and the course was now displayed as the net announced, *"How Many of Them Can We Make Die!"*

"How many ships do we face? What types? Are they armed with anything but this song?"

"Just a moment, sir. They are reviewing the data."

The Admiral stomped over to the intel boards that his own technicians were overseeing. He watched lines of all different colors go up and down, squiggles that told him nothing while a woman sang, "Send These Bastards Back to Hell / We'll teach them the ways of war, / They Won't Come Here Any More."

"Cut that damn noise off," the Admiral snapped. He did not want that playing throughout his fleet.

"Yes, sir. Luister, cut the sound feed."

"Done, sir," and quiet descended on flag plot.

"An interesting bit of ancient lore," Saris noted. "Axes, horses. Do they intended to scare us with that?"

"Or laugh us to death." The future governor chuckled.

"I will find more humor when I know something about those ships that are headed for the moon. We know they have one destroyer. Maybe a second that's an escapee from a breaker's torch. What are these other six, no twelve?"

The Admiral's question was met with strained silence.

"They can't be very good, or they'd have been sent to Boynton," the future governor offered from his vast store of military knowledge.

The Admiral tapped the senior technician on the shoulder. "Talk to me. Tell me something. Anything about those ships."

"Sir, it's not that I can't tell you anything about them. It's that it changes every second. It won't stay the same, sir."

"Changes?" The Admiral frowned.

"Yes, sir. The first ship, sir, that's the Admiral-class destroyer we were told to look for. Engines fit. Laser capacitors are loaded and humming. We've got noise off its passive sensor suit. Our lasers are painting it. It's an Admiral-class destroyer match to the third decimal place, sir."

"I like what you're telling me. Keep talking."

"Second ship is an old John Paul Jones–class. As close to a wreck as ever managed to drift away from a pier. But her reactor is going, her laser capacitors are holding 84 percent of their charge. I'd say they've been worked on recently. Some new Westinghouse cells in place of the original GEs. It's also making more noise with its passive suite than it has any right to, sir. There's a lot more stuff in their CIC than that ship was built with. Some of it doesn't match against anything in our *Jane's All the Worlds' Electronic Countermeasures.* I'd guess that's why intel is taking so long to hammer out a report. He can't just search and copy from the usual book. Something is very weird out there."

"Keep talking. I don't like what you're telling me, but I like it better than silence."

"The *Halsey,* that's the ship, isn't it, sir?"

"Yes, she's the *Halsey.*"

"Well, the *Halsey* isn't just screening the ships behind her, she's streaming chaff, crystals, and needles, sir. Our radars, lasers, and magnetics get through sometimes, other times just bounce off that crud. Makes it hard to know what is real, what isn't. Also, and I'm not sure of this, sir, but I'd swear that some of our signals—radar, lasers, and the like—are being messed with, captured, processed, resent back to us. Those ships move, wiggle, grow, shrink, do all kinds of stuff."

"That's impossible!" Saris snapped.

"Yes, sir. I know, sir. But it explains why the Commander down at intel doesn't want to go on the record, sir. Me, I'm just a tech. I'm not bucking to make Captain, sir."

"But you just made Chief. Lieutenant, log the promotion."

"Yes, sir," the Duty Lieutenant said, eyes wide.

"Admiral, the man hasn't told you anything," the future governor snapped.

"No, but he will. What do you know, Chief? What do you think you might know? And what do you think that they want you to think you know?" Behind him, the governor snickered.

The new Chief studied his board with its different gauges and displays. He pointed at one. "There, in the lead is the *Halsey* followed by the old *Cushing*. On that I would wager my life, and the life of my wife and child."

"You may be," Maskalyne said darkly.

"Go on, Chief," the Admiral said.

"Behind them are six ships. Definitely six ships. Then a space and six more, sir. Other than the raw count, I am not sure what I can tell you about these twelve targets."

"Nothing about their engines?" the Chief of Staff cut in.

"Sir, the two ships following the destroyers appear to have a pair of GE-2700 reactors. The ones after them sport either Westinghouse 3500 or Tumanskii 3200. The first would be appropriate for two old converted light cruisers, the last for four ancient battle cruisers from the Iteeche Wars, even the Unity War. However, sir, there is something soft about the data. Some fluctuations that just don't belong there, sir. I can't help but wonder, sir, if they aren't somehow masking or faking their reactors' magnetic signatures, sir."

"We are not masking our active reactors," the Admiral said.

"No, sir. The magnetic signatures put out by our reactors are too large. Our fleet has no capability to mask or modify the signatures put out by our active reactors," the Chief replied as if reading from the official manual.

"Yet you think they are?" the Chief of Staff snapped.

"Because of the softness of that line on that scope, sir," he said, pointing with a finger whose nail was bitten off to the quick. "It should be sharp. It is not. And because some of us technicians think that, with the right equipment, we might be able to mask the flux field around our reactors. Redirect them. Certainly create more than they were generating. Sir. Some of us technicians talk about doing what I think they are doing."

"Because that line is hazy," the Chief of Staff said.

"It would be interesting to see what some of you senior techs could do, with some equipment . . . and money," the Admiral grunted. But what he needed now was time. And time was something he didn't have.

"What about those last six?"

"They appear to be two destroyers and four cruisers, sir, but I'm not sure. Still, their lines are more defined. It is as if the reactors they are masking were a closer fit."

"Hmm," the Admiral said, rubbing his chin. "You may have told me a lot. Or you may have told me nothing. Is there anything else you wish to add to your lot of nothing, Chief?"

"One more thing, sir, and it may be even more of a phantom than the rest, sir."

The Admiral nodded.

"Our sensors keep getting echoes or ghosts as they try to paint the targets. As if for a moment we see something more than the ship. It could just be a reflection off the chaff. It could be part of the decoy signals I talked about. Or there could be more targets."

"Now you are seeing ghosts," the Chief of Staff said. "Lieutenant, call for this man's relief. We can not have a rumormonger in flag plot." He glanced back at the Admiral as he shoved the Chief/technician from his seat.

"Do we have anything from intel?" the Admiral asked.

The Duty Lieutenant nodded, pressing his commlink tighter to his ear. "He is making his report now, sir. His assessment is that the two destroyers in system are making a run for the moon, streaming target decoys behind them to make them look like a major force. He says we have nothing to fear from them. Most likely they will not even use the moon to orbit back toward us but will continue on the run."

"Then why didn't they just run for the Adele jump point?" The Admiral sighed. The relieved Chief said nothing. "And how is it that the Longknifes have target drones that can fake their reactor signatures, and we do not?" he added. The newly promoted and relieved Chief gave the Admiral the fatalistic shrug that peasants had been giving their lords for centuries as he left.

"It will be interesting to see, Chief, whose estimates are more correct," the Admiral said. The Chief turned, stood tall, and saluted him, then passed his replacement on the way out.

"You should not still be calling him Chief," Saris said.

"And I am not sure that you should have relieved him," the Admiral said, going back to his battle board. Once again he stared at it. It precisely told him the location of ships. Beyond that, it told him nothing.

"KEEP her steady," Tom told Fintch.

"Steady, aye, sir," the helmswoman repeated. The 109 was fifth in line for Squadron 8. Fintch had the lead fake battleship barely five hundred meters off her starboard side. She tracked the ship with a short-range laser bought at the local sporting goods store, used by mountain climbers to measure their work. The laser only reached out two kilometers and was guaranteed not to damage your eyes even if you accidentally looked into it while holding it yourself. It certainly wouldn't go the 400,000 kilometers or so to the approaching enemy fleet.

On the 109's left, an armed yacht was doing the same, hugging close enough to give any insurance man a heart attack. Kris wondered how the Coast Guard Reservists, who usually handed out tickets for violating such safety rules, must feel now as they broke them themselves.

She suspected they were getting a huge kick out of it.

"Penny, Moose. You know anything about those battleships that you didn't know before?"

The older fellow raised an eyebrow at Penny. She nodded his way. "I wish I could tell you something, ma'am," he said, "but now that they've lit up their active lasers and radar, all I'm getting from them is what I'd expect to get from one mean and nasty Wilson-class battlewagon. Now, these are from Greenfeld, not Earth, so there's bound to be some differences in them, but so far, I can't tell you anything more than what we pretty much knew when they first popped in system. They're big. They can do a lot of damage, and they are probably lugging a lot of ice."

Kris nodded. Off to the right, two freighters and those three lost runabouts of Division Seven boosted toward Jump Point Beta and the intruders. Van Horn hadn't told her what he planned from the freighters. Having some ships take an early swipe at the battleships looked like a good idea. Whoever commanded the invaders was playing his cards close to his vest, not even broadcasting his ultimatum now. A batch of missiles might force his hand. Part of it. She listened to the music for a moment.

> *Close your mind to stress and pain,*
> *Fight till You're No Longer Sane*
> *Let not one damn cur pass by,*
> How Many of Them Can We Make Die!

Yes, but her lost division? What did they think they were doing? Time passed with no answers, the ships did their flip, going from accelerating toward the moon at one g to decelerating into lunar orbit at one g. It was not easy, because Sandy wanted to keep the *Halsey* firing and spreading "fairy dust" as she called her chaff. First the *Halsey* flipped, then the *Cushing,* then Captain Luna's "cruiser," and so on. And, in their shadow, each of the PFs and each of their yachts or runabouts. One of the yachts slipped up, flipped late. If that told the enemy anything, it didn't matter.

They were on a course set by the laws of gravity and physics. In time they would collide, and then other laws of thermodynamics and light would apply. Everything was governed by laws.

Except the outcome. That would be governed by lasers and luck. And raw human willpower.

Kris sat with a lot less to do than Tom, who walked his bridge, occasionally checked with his other stations, making sure the 109 was ready for what was to come. Kris could do nothing but sit tight and wait. NELLY, DO YOU HAVE ALL YOUR EVASION SCHEMES DONE?

DONE, DISTRIBUTED. CHECKED, DOUBLE-CHECKED, AND RECHECKED. KRIS, THERE IS NOTHING TO DO, AND I WANT TO DO SOMETHING.

WE ALL DO, NELLY, BUT THERE IS NOTHING TO DO BUT WAIT.

I DO NOT LIKE WAITING.

NEITHER DO WE.

"Take your seats, folks; we're going to be going to zero g for a while," Tom announced as they approached Milna. Kris checked her seat belt. It was already as tight as it would go.

"Like why are we even here?" Adorable Dora complained. "I'm not close enough to the action . . . if there was any . . . to get pictures. All I'm hearing is that lame song. What's going on!"

"Nothing," Jack said, trying to stay as calm as the circumstances would allow, and finding they didn't allow all that much. Kris was up ahead, doing her best to get herself blown to atoms, and he was back here baby-sitting a woman who never lacked for something to complain about.

He'd thought that walking beside Kris as she played target to half the universe was the worst part of knowing the woman, but he was wrong. Here, tagging along behind her as she did what she wanted, led a tiny bunch of optimists out against impossible odds, this had to be the worst day of his life.

"Well, can't we do something?"

"No," Jack said. "She is up there. We are back here. They are about to go behind the moon. While they're behind it, if something comes from Wardhaven, it will be our job to transmit it to them. Now, why don't you sit down and compose something."

"I never compose. I'm perfect in my spontaneity. It says so in all my reviews." Not in the ones Jack read, but now was no time to educate someone who was oblivious to most of her life.

Jack sat, composed himself, and watched the carrier wave on the tight beam between High Wardhaven and their boat, between Kris's fleet and their boat. Nothing.

Kris watched as Milna slid between them and the intruders. With the moon's solid bulk blocking observation, it was time to act. "Task Force Custer, may I suggest you edge further into the lead, say ten or fifteen thousand klicks ahead of us, tossing rockets up his rear at his vulnerable motors. Any discussion?" Kris offered as she finished.

"It'll be harder to keep them in sparkles," Sandy said.

"I think we've kept them in the dark as long as we can," van Horn answered. "We're forty-eight minutes from Task Group Reno doing its thing. Once they do, I doubt there will be all that much question that some of us are playing the missile arsenal role. I concur with Princess Longknife's orders. We'll do a quick burn, take a lower orbit, and come out ahead of you two."

"Singh, follow Custer. I want you offset when we start."

"Understood. We stay with Custer. Use him as our kickoff point. Has Nelly included this in our plan of approach?"

YES, I HAVE, Nelly answered.

"She has. If you are too far off, we will make adjustments."

I INCLUDED OPTIONS FOR THEM TO BE AS FAR AS 150,000 KLICKS.

THANK YOU, GIRL. AND THANK YOU FOR KEEPING IT JUST BETWEEN US GIRLS.

YOU ARE WELCOME.

"Horatio, stay behind Custer and keep faking it as a gun line as long as possible. I will launch the Light Brigade's attack ten minutes after the Reno attacks. I want Divisions 4, 5, and 6 to hold at the line of departure and stay with Horatio."

"Why?" came from an unidentified boat, but Kris suspected it was being asked on every one of them.

"Because I still don't know enough about these battleships. If the Reno attack tells us something, I may give you different orders at the last minute, but just now, I want to save you for the final attack as they're coming up on the station."

"I thought you wanted to have this settled before the station guns started shooting at all of us?"

"I wanted a lot of things," Kris snapped. She paused. The song on net was coming up on *"Follow orders as your told, / Make Their Yellow Blood Run Cold."* "What part of following orders don't you understand? Division 7 didn't follow orders. What's about to happen to them is going to be ugly. You going to do what you're told, or you want to get out and start walking back? Now, if you'll excuse me, I've got this battle to manage."

"Horatio, Custer, Squadron 8 will do a loop around Wardhaven after our attack. That'll have me coming back at the battleships at a steep angle. You see a problem with that?"

"It should make it easier for the tugs to capture you," van Horn said. "And for you to make a lunar orbit after your second attack. With you attacking earlier, it'll work better that way."

"Fine," Kris said. NELLY, ORGANIZE THE ORDERS FOR THE TUGS, SEND THEM TIGHT BEAM TO JACK, AND LET ME

KNOW WHEN HE ACKNOWLEDGES SENDING THEM ON TO
HIGH WARDHAVEN.

There was a pause. JACK ACKNOWLEDGES THEM. More
of a pause. JACK SAYS THE TUGS HAVE THEM AND WILL
COMPLY. JACK SAYS BE CAREFUL.

HE DOES, DOES HE? TELL HIM TO BE CAREFUL HIMSELF.

HE SAYS HIS ONLY RISK IS KILLING ONE REPORTER.

TELL HIM THAT'S NO RISK, IT'S A NATIONAL SERVICE.

HE SAYS YOU DO YOUR JOB, HE WILL DO HIS JOB. OUT.

Kris leaned back in her chair as the ships around her accelerated in obedience to her orders. She'd placed her bets
on some pretty slim data. Hunches really. She tried not to
grit her teeth. She did her best to look loose, confident to
those around her on the bridge. She had committed every
ship that Wardhaven had in its defense. Every last one. Had
Grampa Ray ever done anything so outlandish? Betting the
entire future of Wardhaven on a single throw of a very
small pair of dice.

Suddenly Kris knew what it must have been like to con-
front President Urm with nothing but a briefcase bomb. Or
face an entire Iteeche fleet inbound for a planet and your
defense forces outnumbered four to one. Or to know at that
final battle that all of human existence hung on what you'd
done last week, would do in the next few moments, and it
might not be enough.

How had Grampa faced those burdens and stayed
sane? One thing Kris did know. He had. And if he could,
so could she. She tightened her belt . . . again. They were
coming out from around the moon, accelerating at a full
g . . . again. The battleships were there . . . again, on her
board.

"Anything new?" she asked.

"The same old same old," Penny answered.

"They're showing the same noise they were," Moose
said.

"Let's see if we can teach them something new," Kris
said.

* * *

The Admiral studied his battle board. The enemy was coming out from behind the moon in a different formation from the one it had been in when it entered.

"The six in the rear now lead," the Duty Lieutenant told the Admiral what his eyes already saw, "but we can not tell you anything more about them. The eight now trailing them still seem to be led by the *Halsey*. While behind the moon, they did send a tight beam message to the single runabout trailing them. It relayed it to High Wardhaven. We do not know the content of the message, but based on it, a dozen tugs got under way and are going into orbit now. Intel identifies them as rescue and salvage."

"Good, good," the future governor chortled. "Let them keep the space around Wardhaven clear for our trade vessels. Don't want too much mess, now do we."

The Admiral slammed his fist down on the battle board. "I'm not worried about scrap iron in orbit. I am worried about those ships. Can't anyone tell me something about them?"

The Duty Lieutenant worried his lower lip. "When they did their flip over on the way to the moon, there was an anomaly. Intel didn't report anything on it, but my technicians identified it. It was a fusion reactor ship. Small, yacht size, sir. Hiding in the shadow of the fleet ships."

"Why didn't you mention that?" the Chief of Staff demanded.

The Duty Lieutenant stiffened. "I was waiting for intel to report it, sir. I kept waiting."

"And they never did because it didn't fit their picture," the Admiral said. "And they do like a nice, complete picture. Right up to when it falls apart." He tapped his board, where the two freighters made their way toward him, toward Jump Point Barbie. "Sing to me," but all he got was silence. He sat back. Soon enough he would have plenty of noise. Then he would make his decisions. God help him if he decided wrong.

17

Kris blanched, fighting the flashback. The memory of going for ice cream for her and Eddy. Two men walked past her; they smiled. They had signs hung around their necks that said Kidnapper, but a ten-year-old Kris smiled and waved at them. They waved back. She kept skipping toward the ice cream stand.

When she came back to the duck pond with the ice cream, Nanna was dead, and Eddy was gone.

That was when Kris usually woke up screaming. It happened every night until Kris learned to sneak out to Mother's wine cabinet, Father's wet bar. The dreams came back after Grampa Trouble started her drying out. Judith, a miracle of a psychologist, had helped Kris go back to that day, relive it in all its horror . . . and recognize that there was no one there with signs around their necks. No one that even looked like the men who stole her brother, and with him her childhood.

Strange. Kris had attended parts of the trial. She'd even attended their hanging. Father had almost lost his chance to replace Grampa Al as Prime Minister by the tactics he used to keep capital punishment on Wardhaven's books long enough for those three to swing. Only with Judith holding Kris's hand had she been able to take the dream men's images back to that day and realize she had never seen them in the park.

There was nothing she could have done to save Eddy.

Kris bit her lip, willing away the old pain. Helplessness was the least of her problems today. With Judith, Kris had written the final page of her personal history of that horrible day. Nothing she could have done would have saved Eddy.

When the historians wrote about today, Kris's actions would be all over everything. She shrugged; the difference between ten and twenty-three. Between being the Prime Minister's bratty granddaughter and Princess Longknife.

The difference between me losing a brother to Peterwald and Peterwald losing a battle fleet to me. Kris grinned.

The worry time was over. Now was the time to do. On her board, two freighters went to maximum acceleration— charging the battleships. Around them, three runabouts joined in.

The freighters exploded in a cloud of rockets launched.

"**Blast** the freighters," the Admiral ordered.

"The orders are out, sir. We're trying, sir," the Duty Lieutenant said.

"Then why aren't they gone?"

"Too may targets, sir. There are rockets all over the place, sir, and the central defense command hasn't sorted them out and allotted priorities yet, sir."

The Admiral shook his head. Every laser was slaved to the central defensive computer on his flagship to assure that the best use was made of all defensive guns . . . and that they didn't engage each other in fratricidal firing. A great idea, which was not working under the pressure of a sudden massive attack.

The Admiral mashed his commlink. "All ships, engage incoming rockets on your own. *Revenge* will engage the large enemy ship closest to Wardhaven. *Ravager* will engage the one close to the jump point. The rest may have the small runabouts. Now shoot the damn things." Acknowledgments came in.

Killing the attackers was easily ordered. Not so easily done. The freighters were smaller than they appeared, just a long spine with bits of hull and structure here and there. The engine rooms aft seemed to be the largest target, and the Admiral assumed his ship's gunners would aim for them.

But the damn merchant ships would not hold still to be swatted properly. The triple turrets of the *Revenge* shot out, but the freighter had done some kind of rolling loop. In the meantime, it had launched more rockets in a growing cloud of metal headed toward the Admiral's command along several courses, some straight, some elliptical, some in spirals that changed with each loop. "What are those things?"

"I don't know, sir," the Duty Lieutenant said. "They do not fit any of the naval weapons in our database, sir."

"Try Army weapons."

"Yes, Admiral."

A short pause. "Most of them are not showing up, sir."

Out in space, the first freighter had been hit, but the 18-inch Naval laser seemed to have gone through it without fazing it in the slightest. The other ship had been winged in one engine, but that was only making it a more erratic target. And its wild gyrations did not seem to slow its additions to the growing cloud of missiles. A runabout launched a volley of four rockets.

"Those are Wardhaven Army AGM 832s, intel says," the Duty Lieutenant reported. "Obsolete, of little military value."

"And the other ones?"

"Nothing from intel, sir, but my technicians identify some of them as even more obsolete Army designs, sir."

"And if you tell intel to dig deep into its references of ancient Wardhaven Army rockets, I suspect they can identify even more of those out-of-date and worthless weapons headed at us. Maybe they can even tell us how to destroy them."

"Yes, sir," the Lieutenant said and spoke into his comm-link.

The lights flickered and dimmed in flag plot as the primary and secondary lasers drew on the energy of the ship's reactors. The Admiral tightened his seat belt. Saris spotted his action and did the same. The future governor of Wardhaven continued to pace about flag plot. The cloud of incoming missiles expanded, reached out for his ships. It was only a matter of seconds.

"Admiral, the two enemy freighters say they are abandoning ship and ask that you cease firing at them."

"Have they quit firing at us? Are they on a course for us?"

"They don't seem to be firing anymore. They are not headed toward us. The Captain of the *Revenge* awaits your orders. There are escape pods exiting the ships, though they are not squawking on emergency channels, sir."

"I wouldn't squawk if I were them either," Saris muttered.

"Keep blasting them," the future governor demanded.

The Admiral raised an eyebrow to Saris. "Mr. Governor," his Chief of Staff said, "that would not be advisable. We need to conserve our power to shoot the incoming missiles, not crewmen drifting in life pods."

"So power up some more reactors," the governor demanded.

"Order the Captain of the *Revenge* and *Ravager* to concentrate on the incoming missiles and ignore the life pods. And tell those other ships to get those damn runabouts," the Admiral snapped. Another one of them launched a volley of missiles.

"Also, tell the fleet to stand by to maneuver. On my signal we will reverse course, slow to one-tenth-g acceleration, and begin evasion plan 4."

"The order is given."

"Execute."

"Done, sir."

The future governor of Wardhaven spun in place to face

the Admiral, then kept on spinning, bounced off the Lieutenant's chair, and hit the overhead. "What's happening?"

"We are evading missiles, Mr. Governor," the Chief of Staff said, reaching for the governor's leg. He missed. The *Revenge* twisted in space, sending the governor toward the port bulkhead and down. The Admiral caught his hand as he went by.

"Here, let me get you into a chair," the Admiral said.

"Why didn't someone warn me?" the governor shouted, rubbing his head with one hand, his knee with another, and needing help to buckle himself into a chair at the battle board.

"Sir, the ship has been at Battle Condition Bravo for the last hour," the Chief of Staff said, his voice carefully even. "All Navy personnel are trained to stay within reach of a handhold or belted into their high-g stations. It was in the briefing book you were given when you came aboard."

"You expected me to read everything you left in my suite?"

"Only if you wanted to avoid circumstances like this. Now, sir, the Admiral is not giving orders to our ships to initialize their two cold reactors just now. Starting reactors drains plasma from the hot reactors to mix with cold reaction mass and heat it up to plasma temperatures. While that is happening, you actually get less power out of your reactors. If one of our captains feels he can start a reactor, that is his business. The Admiral does not believe it is his place, in the middle of a battle, to tell a Captain how to sail his ship."

"You ordered them to slow down, bounce me off the ceiling."

"That was part of fighting the enemy attack, Mr. Governor," the Admiral cut in, content now to explain himself. "That is me fighting my battle, not me fighting a Captain's ship. Old Naval tradition." The civilian's frown showed he still did not get the difference, but then micromanagement was not an illness the Admiral had observed isolated solely to civilians.

He glanced at his battle board. Only two of the runabouts

were still attacking, and one of them vanished as he watched. By turning his squadron nose on to the incoming missiles, he'd protected his vulnerable motors. Most of his captains had taken his intent if not his exact order and turned a bit more to get their engines pointed away from the incoming threat axis. That did have them boosting along vectors that would have to be canceled once this problem was resolved.

"What kind of damage can those missiles do to a battleship with our armor?" the governor grumbled.

The *Revenge* shook slightly. "I do not know, but I suspect Captain Trontsom will have an answer for us soon." There were other cracks and rattles as the cloud of missiles passed over the fleet. The last runabout was retreating when it was cut in half.

"Send to *Avenger*. 'Miserable shooting. I expect you will do better next time or paint over your gunnery E.' Are we out of this missile shower?"

"Yes, sir."

"Send order to squadron, 'Reverse course. Resume 1.05-g deceleration toward High Wardhaven.' Lieutenant, have the flag navigator plot us a course correction and pass it along to the *Revenge*. Also have the Chief you relieved report back on duty. Then tell me what you can about these missiles. Chief of Staff, what's our squadron's condition?"

"Minor damage, sir. Reports are coming in. Some antennas, mainly. I would guess that some of the warheads were homing on emitters, infrared, as well as our general form."

"Lieutenant?"

"They were old missiles, some of them twenty, thirty years old, sir. They must be the scrapings of Wardhaven's armory. The Chief of Staff is correct. They had several kinds of guidance systems as well as warheads: home on jam, home on emitters, home on heat, home on movement, and home on specific images. None of them were ever intended for use in space. The fact that they could be used here, cover the distances that they did . . ."

"Yes, I know, Lieutenant, intel is very surprised."

The Admiral eyed his board. "Saris, how bad is our heat problem?"

"The lasers generated a lot of heat, sir. Since we're only decelerating at one g, we aren't burning much reaction mass, and we can't work off all that much preheating reaction mass before we shoot it into the reactor. We've sunk about as much of it as we can into the fuel tanks, but they're starting to vent. Do you think we could stream the radiators?"

"Not with what I see coming, Saris," the Admiral said, tapping what his battle board now had labeled Enemy 1 and Enemy 2. "Not unless we want to see our radiators blown to bits."

Kris swallowed rage and helplessness as she watched Division 7 die. They'd failed what she never intended for them to try.

How would the other volunteers take this slaughter? She mashed her commlink. "Do you understand now why the armed yachts and runabouts attack *after* the fast patrol boats have cut them down to size?" she transmitted in between, "Use your shield and use your head, / Fight till Every One is Dead."

There was general silence on net back at her. Was she losing her volunteers in that dead quiet? "Horatio, Custer, your assessment," Kris said on net for all to hear.

"The missile launchers achieved my intent," van Horn said with maddening coolness. "The hostiles showed us what they had. We scored some hits. I counted about fifteen. We trimmed some of their secondary batteries. Some of their sensors. Reno did what was expected, and we'll have rescue vessels out to pick up the survivors' life pods in a couple of hours."

"It may have done a bit more," Penny said from behind Kris. "Is anyone else getting a rise in the infrared from the targets?"

"I have it, too," Sandy said. "Their lasers aren't as efficient as ours. They're generating a whole lot of heat, and it has to go somewhere. They tried feeding it into their re-action mass fuel tanks, but they're a lot closer to empty than their boss man would like them to be. I'm betting he'd love to stream his radiators out behind him right about now."

There was a cough behind Kris; she turned to Moose. "Ma'am, I'm getting more reactor signals than I was a minute ago."

"More reactors?"

"I'm getting it, too," Sandy said. "My folks are scratching their heads. How can battleships have more than two reactors?"

"If they're built with three. Four," Moose said.

"Four reactors?"

"Did anybody get a good readout on the main battery that they brought to bear on the freighters a couple of times?"

"My people did," Sandy reported. "But we thought it was some kind of mistake."

"My readings show triple lasers discharging," Moose said. "Not twins. What did you get?"

"Triples," Sandy said softly.

Kris called up the specs on the largest battleship in human space, the President-class. Designed to fight the Iteeche Noble Deathship, it had three 18-inch turrets strung around its forward hull. Three more around its bulging amidships, and a final three aft where the hull again tapered. All were buried under meters of ice except when they popped up to fire, and all were evenly spaced at different intervals around the hull's circumference.

And all the turrets held just two lasers.

That gave the Presidents a whopping eighteen monster lasers.

If you put three guns in each turret, you had twenty-seven of them. Kris gulped. "That would take a lot of power."

"I'm showing four reactors on each of those ships ahead of us," Moose said. Penny nodded.

"Ah, Kris," Penny said. "We intercepted a message from the flag ordering fire against the Reno Task Group. It was in a code very much like the one Sandfire used, so we cracked it a lot faster than I expected. He named two ships. *Revenge* and *Ravager*. In a later signal, he identified the *Avenger*."

"Friendly bunch," van Horn said dryly.

"No hidden agendas from the Peterwalds," Sandy said.

"So what kind of ship do you get with twenty-seven big lasers and four reactors?" Kris asked.

"I'm trying for measurements, now that we had Reno's ships somewhat close to it," Moose said. He sent a scale drawing to Kris's board. The President-class weighed in at 150,000 tons of steel, ice, and electronics. The picture he put over it was big.

"It could be nearly 300,000 tons, ma'am."

Kris let out a low whistle.

"And aren't the bigger they are, the harder they fall?" Tom said, but he was a mite pale around the freckles.

"Anything built by men can be blown up by women." Penny grinned.

"Then it's time we start breaking a few things," Kris decided. "Task Force Custer. Will you please lob more missiles their way. Start easy. Let's see how they react to them. Then pick up the pace. We want to heat them up before Squadron 8 punches some big holes in them. Squadron 8, rig your 944 missiles to home on heat. If Custer is kind enough to overheat the secondary battery for us, no reason we can't knock them out on our way in." That brought a cheer on net.

"Nelly, work with Moose. I want to know exactly where those four reactors are in those ships. As I see it, we got twice as many targets to aim for now."

There were more cheers as the computer replied, "Yes, ma'am."

"Custer 3 through 6, you have your targets," van Horn ordered. "You heard the princess, let's heat them up for Eight to knock them down." On Kris's battle board, Custer sprouted missiles. Behind her, Moose talked to Nelly, the computer's voice coming not from its usual place at Kris's neck but from his own computer. Kris eyed the situation.

In five, maybe ten minutes, she'd commit her tiny

command to its first test. She might be planning to take a second bite out of this apple, but she wanted her first one to be big and whoever was running that show to know he'd been bit.

"**Here** comes trouble," the Duty Lieutenant announced just as the relieved Chief came through flag plot's aft hatch. "The first enemy group is launching missiles, Admiral."

"Tell me about them."

"Can't we just shoot the enemy ships launching them?" the future governor asked.

"They are staying five thousand kilometers outside the range of our 18-inch lasers, Mr. Governor," Saris answered for the Admiral.

"Then go after them," the civilian said simply.

"Sir, we are decelerating into High Wardhaven's orbit to begin our ordered planetary bombardment," Saris said, choosing words a child might understand. "If we deviate from our course, we very likely would miss that orbit. At this stage of our approach, we could even end up crashing into the planet."

"Oh," came very softly.

"Believe me, sir. They want us to juggle our approach," the Admiral assured the future governor. "No doubt those are small, say thirty, forty thousand–ton ships. You can horse them around in orbit easy. Our planet killers are 325,000 tons of power. We have solid ice as our defense. We can take what they can dish out." The Admiral tried to sound full of confidence. He was . . . as far as it went. He did not mention the deficiencies in heat management that still bedeviled the squadron. The yard had been so sure they could solve the heat buildup problem from all the extra weapons they'd slapped on the Revenge-class ships. If not this week then next week. Well, maybe the week after.

They'd sailed, assured that it would not matter. There would be no fight. "The whole Wardhaven fleet is at Boynton." So what was coming at them just now? Al Longknife's private yacht?

The Chief took a station. The Admiral noticed that he didn't relieve the man who'd replaced him but rather tapped the most junior tech. The youngster reluctantly made for the door, but the Duty Lieutenant had the makings of a good leader. He sent him instead to a spare jump seat. Good. An extra pair of eyes might come in handy, and the young man would talk about being in flag plot for the Battle of Wardhaven until the end of his days. Unfortunately, the Battle of Wardhaven was making itself into something much more two-sided than the Admiral had expected or wanted to fight. "Talk to me, Chief."

"The incoming missiles are AGM 832s. Standard Wardhaven Army issue. They have fully selective seekers. Their warheads may be high-explosive general purpose, sub munitions dispensers or armor-piercing. No way for us to tell until they hit. Sir, I notice that some of my sensors are off-line."

"The ships making for Jump Point Barbie turned out to be loaded with ancient missiles," the Duty Lieutenant said.

The Chief said nothing but eyed his board. "The incoming wave is heavy, and it is deep. Sir, there is movement behind the missile ships. Four, six, uh, nine, twelve small blips are decelerating out of their shadow. I make twelve system runabouts. No, some of them may have full reactors. Some of them may have capacitors for lasers. Sir, there's a lot of masking. I can't say anything for sure about those boats."

"Except there are twelve of them."

"There are definitely twelve, sir."

"How many PFs were put up for sale, Mr. Governor, by Wardhaven's temporary government?" the Admiral asked.

"Ah, twelve."

"Think that might be them?"

"They were ordered demilitarized."

"Yes, it was on all the talk shows," the Chief of Staff said with a slight cough.

"Missiles to ding us. Fast boats to damage us with lasers,

then a gun line to hit what is left of us. Not a bad battle plan." The Admiral smiled, letting his teeth show. "Sadly for them, we are not your usual battle squadron, and, I suspect, they are a very old bunch of relics. But it is nice to know what the battle will be. Very nice to know. Finally.

"Lieutenant, send to fleet: 'Prepare to repel missile attack. Withdraw unneeded sensors to protected positions. Prepare to repel fast attack boats armed with pulse lasers. Use main battery if necessary, but watch your heat budgets. Continue deceleration at one g unless I order differently.' "

"It is done, sir, as ordered."

"Good. Good. Keep me informed on how we're doing on those missiles, Chief."

"They're tossing them at us. Our 5-inchers are starting to bat the leading ones down, sir."

"Good, good. We can do this all day." But the Admiral kept one eye on the temperature of each of his battleships' fuel tanks. They rose higher and higher; all were venting. The more fuel he lost, the less options he had to maneuver in Wardhaven's orbit until his supply fleet arrived with Marines in two weeks.

Several of his skippers were already resorting to a third option for cooling their guns, switching their coolant into local secondary radiators that spread out around the twin laser turrets themselves. This got the heat out into space, but it weakened the ice around the turret . . . and it gave the turret a decidedly warmer infrared signature than the rest of the ice around it. *Maybe we can't do this all day, but then, they can't have enough missiles to keep this up for an entire day, can they?*

"HOW'S your stock of missiles?" Kris asked.

"It won't last forever," van Horn answered.

"What do the battlewagons look like?"

"Fuel tanks are venting. That's bound to cause the trailing ships' lasers to bloom," Penny said.

"I like that," Tom said.

"Some battleships are showing hot spots around their 5-inch batteries," Moose said. "Lot more of them than I was expecting. Those mothers really are monsters." He sent a picture to Kris. Yep, they had at least twice the number of secondary turrets dotting their ice, if the hot spots were taken for them.

Kris studied her board, tried to do the three-dimensional math. Van Horn's four freighters were firing missiles from slightly aft of the battleships, letting them decelerate down on them. If Kris launched her squadron at the hostiles, she risked running into her own missiles.

"Nelly, give me a battle plan that puts the squadron at the edge of big laser range and gives us a solid run in with missiles ahead of us and behind us."

"But none in the same space as us," Nelly added. Was there a chuckle in there?

"You go, girl," Tom said.

"Here is a schedule. We should break out now."

"Divisions 1, 2, and 3, let's show the guy what we got. Phil, lead the way. Divisions 4, 5, and 6, form a line but stay back. Sandy, they're yours until I get back."

"You're not taking them in with you?"

"Change in plan. I want to get an up-close look at those monsters. Try to spot something a 12-inch pulse laser might dent before I send them in."

"Look for a miracle, huh?"

"Isn't that what we Longknifes always do?"

"Good hunting."

"With targets that big, how can we miss?"

Kris waited until Squadron 8's boats were in a good starting pattern, random to all outward appearances, but, if the planned dance came together right, and if they weren't too badly damaged on the run in, it would have the boats paired up close and personal to each of the six battlewagons.

There were some big ifs in there, Kris noted.

Kris's screen blossomed as Custer fired off a major pulse of rockets, then darkened as a space opened up.

"That's our cue," Kris said. "Initiate intercept orbit. Evasion scheme 2."

PF-109 slammed from a steady one g to two g's while flipping over and aiming itself back at the moon. A moment later, as if thinking better of that, it flipped over and turned its deceleration into acceleration at an even wilder 2.25 g's.

Penny's announcement, "We're in big gun range," was followed by another major change in direction, and Moose muttering, "Damn, they did try to swat us with an 18-incher."

"They did?" Kris asked.

"Yep. Missed."

"Nelly, was that part of your evasion assumption?"

"Of course, Kris," the computer answered patiently.

"Dang it all, where are they going, and why are we hanging around here, behind?" came over the net.

Sandy expected it. At least Luna was talking before she charged in. "We will stay right here, by my orders."

"And if we don't?"

"I'll shoot you down like the dog you are. Don't I remember somewhere someone promising to follow orders?"

"Well, yeah, but there's orders and then there's being a yellow-bellied coward." That brought agreement on net.

"In a couple of moments," Sandy said, trying to keep exasperation out of her voice, "I'm going to expect you to follow me in something that no coward would ever do. Just about the time those battleships get a good solid bead on Kris and her boats, we're going to parade ourselves inside their gun range. We're going to march right through the one hundred thousand klicks range they got to the eighty thousand klicks range that the 14-inch guns you would have if you were the ships you're claiming to be. You following me?"

"We ain't gonna po-raid along right behind you, are we?"

"No, I expect you to be in full evasion mode."

There were several expressions of relief at that.

"We're going to draw their fire just long enough for Kris to get a good solid aim at her target, make her hit, then start to run away. Then, depending on how much wreckage she's left behind, we either run in ourselves, or run away."

"Why are all you Navy types so pessimistic? We'll be running right in there behind her, collecting up all the strays and brandin' 'em."

And why are all you who never studied war such optimists? Sandy thought, but kept that to herself.

"XO, set us a course that will take us in to eighty K from the hostiles. Begin evasion program at one hundred-and-one K range."

"Aye, ma'am."

The 109 boat dipped, then zigged a bit, then zagged a lot, then did several minor dodges that left the hairs on the back of Kris's neck wanting something major. About the time she was ready to say so, the 109 slammed itself into a complete course reversal, then into a hard left. Then dropped like a rock.

"Missed us again," Moose chortled.

"I calculated that should fake them," Nelly said.

"You sure faked me," Kris said.

The 109 flipped, flopped, and spun. "And they miss again," Moose drawled.

"What's their heat situation?" Kris asked.

"Building up fast, what with 18-inch and 5-inch firing," Moose said. "Their fuel tanks are all venting. I can spot all their secondaries. Their capacitors must be losing efficiency. Taking less of a charge, taking longer to take it. You got to like their problems, ma'am. They're either going to have to stream those radiators and risk losing them or start taking hits from our stuff getting through."

Moose looked up. "I wonder just how thick their ice is."

"We're about to find out," Kris said as she watched the battleship secondaries fight their battle with Custer's missiles. Most of the missiles were homing on the heat of the

5-inch batteries. The fight was up very close and personal for those gun crews.

Smash the missile, or the missile kills you.

Beneath Kris, the 109 dodged and weaved, cut and turned as the 18-inch lasers tried to cut her in two. 18-inch turrets were not designed to track targets that turned on a dime, shot away at two, three g's, then swung around again. In most cases, the lasers were just laid and fired when the PFs looked like they were headed into that bit of space. Nelly's dance and the Foxer's confusion disrupted the gunner's plans time after time. Eighteen inches of blazing death reached out, but the mosquitoes they sought were never there.

"Whoops," came a voice on net.

"What happened?"

"They winged me," Heather reported. "Opened my quarterdeck to space. Engine room is tight. Bridge is holding. Gonna have to put a bit less stress on the hull, though." With its longitudinal strength compromised, hard turns now risked having PF-110 bend in the middle like a wet noodle.

"You want to pull out?" Chandra asked.

"To where? The other side of those bastards looks as close as any other safe place. '*How Many of Them Can We Make Die!*'"

The 110 boat slowed; 105 boat dropped back. Chandra refused to leave the young skipper alone in the gathering hellfire.

Behind them, Horatio drew in range of the battleship's main battery, and their fire shifted to this new threat. But Kris had hardly a moment for a breath of relief; she was well in range of the 5-inch batteries, and Custer's last blast was pretty much done while Kris's boats were still looking at a long way to go.

The good news was there were fewer 5-inchers firing now, though there were still too damn many of them for Kris's taste.

"Squadron 8, let's give the 5-inch gunners something to worry about. Verify 944s are set for infrared. Salvo fire them now."

From the bow of the 109 came the sound of rockets exiting the tubes.

The *Revenge* shook with yet another hit. The Admiral tapped his board, calling up reports on all six of the ships in his command. More secondary batteries were unavailable. Just off-line, or wrecked by a Longknife rocket? The board did not have that information. What the board did show was that more and more of the 5-inch turrets still online were showing deeper and deeper yellow, headed for orange. Slow to charge now, and taking less and less of a charge when they did. Heat buildup was slashing the effectiveness of his massed weapons.

No. The *Ravager* was cooling down. How?

Right! Schneider was flushing his coolant through the main refrigeration coils of his armor, the old bastard. That was definitely not in the book. The kilometers of refrigeration coils running through the five-meter-thick armor were intended to cool that ice. Schneider was doing the reverse, using the ice of the armor to take off some of the heat now bleeding the efficiency of his offensive weapons suite. A desperate measure.

But today was a day for some truly desperate innovations.

"Lieutenant, send to all ships: 'Flush reaction mass and other coolant through the main belt armor's refrigeration coils to cool it. Bravo Zulu to Schneider and *Ravager* for the idea.' Close your mouth, Lieutenant, and send it now."

"Yes, sir."

"That will weaken our main armor belt, sir," the Chief of Staff observed carefully, in his status as the Admiral's official second-guesser.

"Have we taken a hit that threatened to penetrate our belt?"

"No, sir."

"Can we afford to lose any more of our secondaries? Lose any more of their efficiency? Wouldn't you like to slap down one or two of those mosquitoes buzzing toward us? I understand Princess Longknife commands one of them."

"She was relieved of her command. Charged with actions unbecoming or something," the future governor pointed out.

The Admiral eyed his Chief of Staff, then the incoming attack. "She is out there."

"I would not bet against you on that one, sir."

"Ships report they are cycling coolant through their ice, sir." A glance at his battle board confirmed the report. The secondaries were sliding back toward the green. Particular hot spots were cooling down around the ships' hulls, even as the entire hull took on a warm pink. Not that it would matter against patrol boats with pulse lasers.

Oops. What have we here? More missiles. Intel said nothing about the Longknife patrol boats having missiles on them. More things that didn't make it to the talk show circuit. The Admiral suppressed his grumble and tightened his belt . . . again. It would be interesting to see how the heat seekers on these warheads reacted to the lack of warmth around his secondary batteries . . . and the raised temperature of his armor.

"For what we are about to receive, may we be truly grateful," he muttered.

"My division has the two in the middle," Phil said, his voice low, hard, intent. His four boats were ahead of the others now. They'd go in first. "We'll hold our fire until 25,000 klicks," he said. Maximum range on a pulse laser was 40,000 klicks. Twenty-five ought to punch a good-size hole.

Kris watched intently as the first four boats jitterbugged their way up to the line of battleships. Her board now showed the ships a fairly consistent pink. When the 5-inch twin lasers popped up to fire, they flared red, but when they dropped back behind their ice armor, most of that infrared signature vanished. Some of the incoming 944s were able to fix the turret position on the battleship's hull by spotting a bump or a mast. Something like that would let them triangulate on the turret. Most only saw a smooth expanse of ice. In those cases, the sensors either went looking for another major source of heat, or switched to another seeker. But the battleships had quit radiating most other signals as well. Most warheads just dug a hole in the ice.

A hundred-kilo warhead didn't dig much of a hole in four meters of ice. Some missiles did. Here and there, a 5-inch turret picked the wrong time to pop up and snap off a shot at one rocket . . . and drew the fatal attention of another. Or a search radar antenna stayed on too long and got slammed by a missile in terminal phase at just that moment.

And then there was the one missile that almost missed entirely . . . but clipped a rocket motor on the third battlewagon back from the flag. The warhead slammed into the huge bell-shaped rocket engine just where the electromagnetic coils were that kept the plasma demons under control. For a split second, tortured matter at 100 million degrees kelvin got loose.

It wasn't long, but in those brief moments, jets of raw energy ripped off another engine, smashed several electric generators, and might have done further damage if good damage control hadn't brought things under control. The battleship slowed in its deceleration, fell out of line, and quit firing.

It was at that moment that Phil's four boats rolled past, firing paired pulsed lasers at the wallowing ship and its sister. Kris measured the results. Fifteen lasers fired. Fourteen hit. Four paired hits slashed into the damaged ship.

And the battleship righted itself, started firing back, and kept right on decelerating.

"Damn," Phil growled through gritted teeth. "Twenty-five K and we might as well have thrown snowballs at them!" There was a pause as Phil's boat went through wild gyrations, but less fire was headed his way. "Our pulse lasers just don't pack enough punch to dent that belt."

"I hear you, Phil," Kris answered. "Division 2, we're

next. We'll go in closer. Nelly, what kind of really wild dance have you got for us?"

"Go to 6B on your mark, Kris."

"My mark is . . . now."

The 109 had been a mad hatter before. Now she was a crazy dervish, twisting, turning, never going in a straight line. Never going more than a few seconds before changing directions hard up, down, right, left. Forward, more missiles were mixed with Foxers as the 109 fought her way closer and closer to the second to the last ship in line.

"20,000 . . . 18,000 . . . 16,000. I'm at 15,000 klicks. Are you with me, 108?"

"Not yet, not yet. Almost. Now."

"Fire on mark. Now."

There was no sign that the four reasons for the 109's existence had been expended against a battleship, either on the bridge or, when Kris turned up the visuals, along the hide of the battleship. No . . .

Yes. There was a steaming gash aft, right about where Moose said the reactors were. Two long, steaming slashes.

But . . . no burn-through. No flaming wreckage.

Forward, Kris could hear Kami firing more rockets, as they shot past their target, but as for any apparent effect . . .

Nothing.

"This is Division 2, here. We turned armor to slush at 15,000 kilometers, but we didn't get burn-through. Repeat, 15,000 kilometers just doesn't cut it."

"Hear you," Chandra said. "Babs, you and the 104 go in to 10,000 klicks. See what that does. Heather and I are three, four thousand klicks behind you. We'll go closer if that doesn't work."

"You'll be all alone," Kris pointed out.

"I have Custer's incoming missiles pushing up my derriere. The thugs have to be paying as much attention to them as they are to me," Chandra said. Kris wondered if she believed it.

"Squadron 8, send some 944s back to support Division 3. All you can spare," Kris ordered. They had a second attack to make; they would need them. Right now, Chandra needed them, too.

From the bow of the 109 came the sound of more missiles launching out of their tubes.

The 104 and 111 boats flipped and cut, turned and twisted, as they made their final approach on the flagship. Behind them, missiles came at all six battleships. Some fire went for the missiles. Most went at the boats. Main battery now concentrated on Horatio just about to come in range with their supposed 14-inchers. The part of Squadron 8 that had completed their run had mostly been ignored. Now, as missiles came back from them, the battleships took them and their missiles under fire again.

It seemed like mighty thin help, but it was help. All the help they could give Division 3.

"Fifteen . . . Thirteen. Fire when I say . . . ten. Laser's fired . . . Nothing! Damn it! Nothing! What are these ships made of? Solid ice?"

"Maybe," Heather said. "Let's find out, Chandra."

"I have nothing better to do," the Navy mustang answered as if the wealthy debutante had invited her to go mall crawling.

"Think five thousand will do them?" Heather sounded as casual as if that might be the price of a dress.

"Easily. Nelly, do the numbers. Assume five meters of armor against two of our pulse lasers in close proximity. Two more close by."

"You could burn through four meters. Not five," Nelly said.

"Maybe we ramble a bit closer. Hey folks, keep those cards and letters coming."

"Yes, we need all the spare missiles you can afford."

"Back them up," Kris ordered.

"Div 2, you'll have to do it," Phil said. "We're out of position. Our missiles won't get there before it's over."

"Division 2 and 3, support Chandra and Heather," Kris ordered. Beside her, Tom's mouth was a hard line. She was depleting his boat.

"Do it, Kami," he ordered.

"On their way," came a cheerful voice.

"Eight thousand," Chandra called. "What's our mark?

In the background, almost forgotten, the song hit its refrain: *"How Many of Them Can We Make Die!"*

"That does it for me," Heather said, as cheerful as if she'd spotted a sale.

"Then we fire on *die*."

"Six thousand."

"How many of them can we make . . . die!"

"GEt those last two ships!" the Admiral shouted. "They're going to ram *Ravager*."

The Duty Lieutenant repeated the order. More missiles were inbound. Would this battle never end?

BEing belted in and at two g's kept Kris in her seat. Lasers were blowing missiles out of space all around the two attacking boats, Foxers were promising course changes to right, left, up, down, and taking laser hits, but not the two boats. They rolled over the second ship in line, firing simultaneously. At Heather and Chandra's cry of "die," their lasers lashed out through ice and steam and wreckage to slice into the stern of the battleship right at the reactors.

Heather aimed her two forward lasers for the same spot, her two aft ones for a different spot. And Chandra did the same. Four pulse lasers cut into one spot of ice. Four more cut into another spot just aft of that.

And nothing happened.

For a moment, that was how it looked.

Then one of the 5-inch lasers caught Heather's boat and pinned it, a second sliced through it and cut it in half. As the two ends fell apart, a missile from Custer impacted on the stern of Chandra's 105 boat.

"Oh no," went as a groan through the 109.

The 105 spun, but now she spun too slowly, too much to

a pattern. Five lasers caught her at once. She imploded like a star among them.

"No."

"Something's happening on the battlewagon," Moose said.

Kris tore her eyes away from the vanishing remains of her friends. The battleship leaked plasma from a new hole that was not an engine. Slowly, like an rhino trapped on ice, it accelerated into a spin. The main engines swiveled to correct the spin, but one of them was hanging off at an angle . . . and blowing plasma in fits and bursts. Then a second hole opened up further forward. A jet of hot plasma shot out, slicing chunks of ice off, hurling them into space. The huge ship spun and rolled and began to come apart.

Pieces flew in all directions. One, easily twice the size of the 109, shot across space to slam into the nose of the flagship. Others blew out toward the line of ships behind it.

"Her reactors are going unstable. She's going to blow," Moose said. First one reactor did, gouging a huge hole in the long stern of the warship, then another did, then, in a blinding flash, the two remaining ones went, flashing the entire ship into a radiant white ball of fire that quickly dissipated to sparkles and then darkness.

"Good God . . . have mercy," Tom prayed.

"On them," Penny added.

"And on us if we don't pay attention. Nelly, is the squadron still in full evasion?"

"Yes, Kris."

The ten surviving boats sped away from the battle line. The energy they'd put on the boats during their attack run in was already decelerating them quickly toward Wardhaven. They'd have to make major corrections to get themselves into a proper orbit, but those would wait until they were well out of 18-inch laser range. The battleships didn't seem interested in them, now. The incoming wave of missiles from Custer held their full attention. Most were being shot out of space. Many of the rest were just hitting ice. A few did damage on secondary batteries. There was another spectacular hit on an engine of the last ship in line, but damage control kept it from being anything but highly visual.

The attack of Squadron 8 was spent.

Worse, Kris felt wasted.

She'd given it everything she had. Everything her shipmates had. They'd tried everything.

Only two boats had succeeded.

It had cost Heather and Chandra their lives. For a moment the sight of Goran and the kids waiting on the pier for Mom to come home came at Kris. She willed it away.

Kris had ten more boats. The enemy had five more battleships. What price could she ask her shipmates to pay?

Could they destroy those monstrous battleships at any less cost?

The bridge was quiet as the enemy ships receded on the aft screen and Wardhaven grew on the forward one.

"I did it," the Admiral chortled, standing to tower over his battle board. "I beat them," he said, stabbing at the blips of the rapidly retreating patrol boats.

"You defeated them, sir," Saris agreed, also standing. "We took the best they had, and it just wasn't good enough."

"But what about that gun line?" the future governor said, keeping his seat but waving at the rest of the Wardhaven ships now retreating back out of laser range. "Aren't they a threat? Don't you have to blow them up?"

"They are nothing," the Admiral said, dismissing them with a wave of his hand. "The freighters throwing missiles aren't throwing any more, are they, Chief?"

"None behind this last wave, sir."

"Want to bet me the freighters have shot themselves dry? These last missiles are just there to draw our fire away from the patrol boats' attack," the Admiral said. "And these other boats, the ones that are trying to look like fast patrol boats. I'll bet you a month's pay they *are* Al Longknife's yacht, and a few of his wealthy friends' toys as well. Maybe some have 12-inch pulse lasers. What can they hope to do to us after those 18-inchers on the patrol boats failed? As for those 'battleships.' Chief, talk to me about how the reactors on those so-called battleships are fuzzy. You don't really have to. If they had real lasers on them, they'd have ducked in range while the patrol boats were charging in at us, got some shots off. No matter how old they were, how lousy they were, I'd have tried some shots then.

"They didn't shoot. They don't have anything to shoot. King Ray Longknife has spent too much time at masquerade balls if he thinks he can fool us with a few masks, some fancy feathers. Well, Longknife, sooner or later, the masks have to come off, the feathers, too, and then you're just left naked."

The Admiral stabbed a finger at the blips of the ships hurrying back out of range. "Those are nothing but feathers and glitter. The destroyers should have taken their chance to get in a shot when they had it. Cowards all," he spat.

"Lieutenant, order the ships to shoot down the last of the incoming missiles, then set a course for High Wardhaven. We will arrive right on schedule. Oh, and order all ships to stream their radiators. Let's get this heat off my ships. I want to be fully cooled when we make orbit. We are going to make things very hot on Wardhaven, and I don't want anything on my ships to delay us serving it up steaming and fast."

"Yes, sir."

The Admiral grinned at his Chief of Staff. It was good to know he could do the job he had promised his political masters he would do.

18

"**PF-109**, this is Tug 1040. Hold steady, now; I'll match with you."

"We have to hold steady, Tug 1040. Our tanks are dry," Tom admitted with a rueful shake of his head. They'd put whatever vector and energy on the boat it took to fight their way past the battleships. Only after they were out of laser range did they even start trying to reach for orbit. And it had taken all they had to get them close enough for a salvage tug to match.

But the tanks weren't all that was dry. Around Kris the crew sat at their stations in exhausted funks. They'd thrown everything in them at those battleships . . . and the battleships had thrown it back in their face.

Except for Heather and Chandra. They'd gotten their battlewagon. And they'd paid the full price.

Kris surveyed the 109's bridge crew; they were spent. They'd poured everything they had into that last charge. Their shipsuits were dripping, their faces were drawn from being slammed around at three times their normal weight.

Kris saw eyes dull with fatigue. Shoulders slumped. Did they have anything more to give?

Sometime during the reach for orbit, Tom had switched off the battle net and gone local, one loaded with a medley of traditional Irish tunes. They were quiet, kind of like Kris felt. One, about a minstrel boy, she liked. She was listening to it for the third time before she realized he died in the war. It wasn't just the rest of the crew. Her brain was mush!

"PF-109, Tug 1040 is matched to you. I've got salvage specialists, courtesy of Johanson Brothers Salvagers, ready to run a power line to you, so hold real steady now."

"We're holding steady, Tug 1040. Like we said, we couldn't change course if we had to."

"Understand, 109. We have reaction mass to transfer to you along with antimatter. We also picked up some more Foxers and, in case you're running low, twelve more of those 944 missiles you were tossing around back there."

Kris perked up. "Where'd you get those?"

"The factory's been running them up the beanstalk as fast as they could. This last batch arrived just as we were locking the hatches. We put twelve aboard each boat."

"How many boats?"

"Twelve," the tug skipper said softly.

"So two of your boats don't have a rendezvous."

"Turns out that way."

"But they have 944s and Foxers. Tom, you want them?"

"Aren't the 104 and 111 boats the lowest? They were closest to Heather and Chandra and did an awful lot of shooting."

"You'd have to be next."

"Give them first call," Tom said.

"I'll call and see who they can match orbits with," the tug skipper said. "Now my board says we have a good hookup for power. What's your board say?" Tom agreed. And a minute later they agreed that they had a good hookup for reaction mass as well. That left them looking at opening up the quarterdeck to space so the tug crew could start dropping off goodies.

"I'm thirsty," Chief Stan said, unbelting himself. "Anybody else here could use a drink?"

"Make mine Scotch, neat," Tom ordered.

"I'd kill for a Margarita," Penny said.

"I'll take a beer," Moose muttered.

"Me, too," Fintch put in through a shadow of her usually sunny smile.

"You're underage," the Chief growled.

"And didn't all of us age ten years this last week," she answered back in a perfect imitation of Tom's brogue.

Ignoring her performance, the Chief sailed aft. A few moments later, he popped back up from the mess area below the bridge and started throwing drink bulbs at the bridge crew. "Have a cold one," he ordered Fintch.

"Yes, Mother," the helmswoman answered, but she drank.

Kris took a sip of the fortified water . . . and then drained the whole liter bulb and called for a second. She hadn't realized she was so dehydrated until she got some water into her. Then again, a glance at her shipsuit showed it soaked through. That water had to come from somewhere.

"We drink this, and we're gonna have'ta pee," Penny warned.

"And in zero g." Fintch sighed. "You'd think in three, four hundred years some guy would have invented a decent zero-g toilet for a gal."

"Or a gal would have," Tom said.

"Quit changing the subject, Husband," Penny said.

"Warning, young man," Moose said, "when women are exercising their God-given right to complain about men, don't interrupt."

"Kris, what do we do now?" Tom asked.

"He interrupted you," Kris said to Penny.

"Worse, he brought up business. Think spacing him's too extreme?"

Fintch and Kris shook their heads.

"May I point out, I am the Captain of this boat, and unlike some ships the princess here has stolen, this one is an honest-to-God man-o'-war duly commissioned by a sovereign planet."

"I thought we were a pirate ship. Didn't you think we were a pirate ship?" Penny said, turning to Moose.

"Don't ask me, ma'am. I was just an innocent civilian, walking down the street, minding my own business, when I got shanghaied into something I know nothing about."

Penny patted his arm. "For someone knowing nothing about what you were doing, I was glad to have you doing it."

"You're welcome, ma'am."

Tom had that beautiful grin of his as he relaxed back into the captain's chair, watching the love of his life. Kris wished she could let this go on forever, let the crew crack jokes for at least another hour or three, but the clock on her board was counting down the time until they swung out from behind Wardhaven. They'd have to be ready for something by then. As much as she wanted to crawl under her bed, say it was time for someone else to step up and take their turn, she knew there was no one else in a position to do anything.

It was either her and her tiny band or no one.

Well, not exactly. This time, there was no use trying to fake anything. The hostiles had to have figured out that there were no battleships hounding their flanks. Next attack would be all-out. There was no tomorrow.

"Tom, could you switch us back to the main battle net? Put me through to everyone. We need to talk."

He pried his eyes away from Penny, took in a deep sigh and let it out, then tapped his board. The refrain of *"How Many of Them Can We Make Die!"* shot across the bridge. Below them, there was the clank of missiles being attached to the quarterdeck, courtesy of volunteers from the Milna Spelunking and Scavenger Hunt Club. Kris took a deep breath and mashed her commlink.

"Horatio, Custer, say your status."

"Horatio, here," came in Sandy's matter-of-fact voice.

"I got about a dozen skippers champing at the bit and threatening mutiny if you go charging off again and leave them behind."

"You got that right, honey," Luna cut in.

"But with the princess around," van Horn said dryly, "I thought mutiny was kind of the norm."

"But I prefer to lead them, not have somebody else cut in on my act." Kris tried to sound lighthearted. Maybe she did.

"Well you just get yourself ready to have one thrown your way if you do that again," Luna drawled.

"Custer, what's your status?"

"Lower than I'd like, but higher than I expected. Say 34 percent of what I started with. Enough for one hell of a last stand."

That was what it would have to be. One last stand. One all-out attack on the battlewagons as they came up on High Wardhaven station. Kris hunted for the right words as she keyed her mike.

"All right folks, this is what we came for. We're all going in together this time." There was a quiet cheer on net. Beside Kris, Fintch shook her head slowly as if to say, *They don't know what they're asking for.*

"The battlewagons are going to be slowed down to come alongside the station, make orbit to smash and batter Wardhaven. If we don't get them, the four reactors on those bastards are going to be powering up lasers to hack and slash Wardhaven to burning rubble. You want that for your families?"

"No," came back at Kris.

"You going to let them do that to your wives and husbands?"

"No," was almost a shout on net.

"Wish I had one," came from Fintch beside Kris.

"Get with the program." Tom grinned at her.

"I will, I will," the helmswoman promised. "Just offer me something I really want to fight for."

Kris lifted her finger off the mike. "They're gonna

shoot up the yacht club on High Wardhaven. No more racing skiffs."

"They gotta be stopped," the young woman growled.

"All right, troopers," Kris went on, back on net. "When
the time comes, Custer's gonna fire off every missile
they've got. Then we go in right behind them, every fast
patrol boat and destroyer, every armed yacht and runabout.
Anything that can fire or draw fire goes at them in one
charge.

"And this time, we hold our speed down, no wild charge,
'cause this time we ain't whizzing past them. Nelly will
give you evasion programs that let you dodge at one or two
g's. This time, Luna, you get to go gunning up close and
personal. If they try to dodge away from you, you chase
them down and shoot your lasers right up their engines."

"Up the kilt, I like that." The woman chortled.

"Their hide is too thick, so we don't aim for ice, we aim
for specific targets. They flash a laser turret, you burn it.
They raise an antenna, burn it.

"Now, if your 12-inch pulse lasers are anything like the
ones I've used, they have one setting. Shoot the works,"
Kris said.

"You got that right, honey," Luna drawled. "When'd
you ever work one of my holdout guns?"

"She stole a boat once with a set of them," Tom cut in.

"Tom, don't give away state secrets," Kris chided him,
but there were general chuckles on net.

"Anyway, when I had cause to use armed yacht lasers,
Nelly came up with a software patch that let me fire pulses
at half down to one-tenth power. Anyone interested in that
option?"

"You bet." "Yeah." And "Yes, please," came back at
Kris. Nelly sent the patch, and Kris waited while the yachts
loaded it.

"Hey, this really is nifty," Luna said. "If a troublesome
5-incher pops up, I can stomp it and still have something
left to shoot up the kilt of a battlewagon. Good going, kid!"

"Just remember, your 12-inch pulse lasers probably have a heat problem just like these battleships do. So you can't fire them too often before they'll overheat.

"But we can hit them," Luna growled. "We can shoot them hot, straight, and up so close that they can't dodge, they can't hide. They came to Wardhaven not expecting a fight. Well, we're going to show them the fight those cowards never expected."

That got cheers, even on the 109's bridge. For a moment, even Kris was cheering.

"Luna, you decoys better shuck those cocoons. Everyone, get it tightened down and dialed in. As soon as I bring Squadron 8 around to one hundred thousand klicks from those bastards, we all go in from both directions. See how they like that. Longknife out."

There were some more cheers on net. Kris let out a sigh; she must have found words that weren't too far off. She glanced at her board. An hour before the hostiles came to a halt at High Wardhaven. Forty-five minutes before Kris could intercept them.

Another long wait.

"109, Tug 1040, we've left our Father Frost gifts on your quarterdeck. You want to pressurize and get them? And, you want any of our folks to help you load them rockets?"

"Appreciate the offer," Tom answered, "but I don't want to have to bleed air again to let your folks leave, and I can't afford to take them with us. No extra high-g stations."

"Thought the princess said it would be low g this time."

"Two g is still rough when you're dodging like we'll be."

"Who's this Nelly, and how do I get an evasion program?"

Tom raised an eyebrow at Kris. She hit her commlink. "You're a tug, 1040. Your mission is rescue and salvage."

"Ma'am, a target's a target. Give them enough, and they're bound to miss the one they ought not to."

"Sure you aren't risking a mutiny?"

"Ma'am, looking around my bridge just now, talking to the folks out in suits, if I don't make this run in, I sus-

pect they'd leave me outside walking home, and do it
without me."

*Good Lord, where do we get these people? What has
Wardhaven done to deserve them? Father, you must be getting someone else's well-earned deserts.*

"Thank you, Tug 1040, your support is much appreciated."

"Not just me, ma'am. I don't think there's a hull out
here today that won't be in there with you."

"May God bless us all," Kris said, the unfamiliar bene-
diction borrowed from Tom. He smiled at its use and
blessed her with a wink.

"My folks are clear, you can pressurize now," the tug
skipper reported.

Tom did, and ordered all hands amidships to stow
stores. Kris, with nothing to do but bite her nails for half an
hour, dropped aft along with the rest. There was not one
but two antimatter containment boxes, ready to be mixed
with reaction mass and power the rocket motors of the 109.
And there were twelve long 944's cases lashed carefully to
the deck along with boxes holding four Foxers each.

Each missile and box of decoys got two crew members
to help guide them forward. While the two hundred kilo-
gram missiles might be weightless, they still had all their
mass, and the damage they could do . . . to themselves and
to the boat . . . was not something anyone wanted. Not
now. Not with the attack only minutes away. Now was no
time to have a wayward missile take out a comm unit as it
was passed up through the radio shack, or the sensor workstation on the bridge, or smash into a just-recharged laser
capacitor on its way to the rocket bay.

Each of the rockets was carefully handled. They had a
date with a battleship.

Loading the Foxers was easy; their canister was opened
and the rockets fed in. The 944s were longer and a problem. Each canister had to be freed from its launching tube,
then gently maneuvered to where it floated above the main

passageway where the missiles were coming up. Then the rocket had to be carefully slid from its traveling case into an empty canister slot.

"Do we just reload one canister?" The gunnery ensign asked.

There was a long pause. "I'd rather have six more in each," Tom answered. "One could hang up, get damaged. You know the saying. All your eggs in one basket."

The ensign nodded. "You heard the old man. Do it right. But do it fast." Kami and the gunner's mates went to work, doing it by their book, just as they'd practiced for, what, three days.

Kris left, not wanting to juggle elbows or add pressure.

Nelly was another matter; her computer had no elbows. "Have you gotten evasive schemes out to everyone who wants them?"

"They all want them."

"So I'm told."

"The salvage ships aren't even on a secure net. I've sent them tables of random numbers in code, and told them to jump from place to place in a random pattern, using one set of numbers to set up that pattern. Their pick. You know this has to meet every book in my database's definition of crazy."

"Yes, but it's also magnificent."

"I don't have a definition of magnificent."

"It's a human thing, Nelly."

"If I get out of this in one piece, I think I will begin to understand magnificent."

"So will we all."

Kris settled into her seat, pulled on her helmet, and tapped her commlink. "Sandy, how's it going? I've been busy doing housekeeping chores."

"Until a while ago, there was nothing to do but wind the clock, take out the cat, here, too. Unfortunately, I think our boy's getting smart. Five minutes ago, the battle squadron recovered their radiators, and they just put on a defensive spin."

"Oh damn," Kris muttered and turned to Penny.

* * *

"The *Avenger* reports she can not maintain a five-revolutions-per-minute rotation, sir," the Duty Lieutenant reported.

"Then tell him to fix what is wrong and do what I ordered," the Admiral snapped. He had taken the seat at the battle board that put his back to the spin now on the *Revenge*; the defensive maneuver did not bother him. It also did not bother the techs at the intel stations, since they also had their backs to it. Saris was side on to the spin. The future governor of Wardhaven had the biggest problem. He was in the chair across from the Admiral. Now he leaned forward as the spin tried to force him out of his chair.

"Is this damn whipping around really necessary?" the political appointee demanded.

"I suspect so, Mr. Governor," the Chief of Staff said.

"I would not like to guess wrong," the Admiral added.

"But you said you had beat them. You had won."

"I may have been premature," the Admiral muttered.

"They have nothing left to fight with."

"So it seemed an hour ago, but they do not act like that now, and I do not intend to assume anything where a Longknife is concerned, Mr. Governor. No, look at the board. The jackals are still nipping at our heels." He waved his hand at the forces hanging on his spaceward flank. The so-called battleships had, like snakes, shed their skin and now were smaller . . . and deadlier, if not in ability, certainly in intent.

"And now we have this." He pointed at the twenty plus targets coming up from a swing around Wardhaven.

"What are they?"

"They appear to be the survivors of the patrol boats that attacked us two hours ago."

"But patrol boats can only attack once. They have to go back to port. Refuel. Recharge. Even I know that," the governor said with a dismissive wave of his well-manicured hand.

"That is what they say on all the talk shows. Chief, talk to me about the ships coming up from Wardhaven."

"Ten are fast patrol boats, sir. They are not even bothering to mask themselves. The others are salvage tugs. All have oversize reactors for tow and salvage work. Right now, they're boosting right along with the patrol boats."

"Could the salvage tugs have passed a power line to the patrol boats, recharged their capacitors, Chief?"

The Chief coughed as if he'd swallowed a fish bone. "That's a bit above my pay grade, Admiral, but our fleet tugs do have the capacity to transfer major amounts of power to a ship in need."

"Your conclusion?" the Admiral said, eyeing Saris.

"That damn Ray Longknife figured out a way to get two attacks out of one squadron of fast patrol boats."

"I wouldn't put it past him," the Admiral growled. "And I do not intend to lose more of my battleships. We have five meters of armor. We will rotate our ships at five rpms, and we will make sure their pulse lasers only melt ice."

"What about those other ships?" The future governor suddenly sounded worried.

"Two of them are destroyers we actually have to worry about. But only two. Maybe a half dozen of those yachts have pulse lasers hiding under their brightwork. 12-inchers at best. This may be more of a fight than you were promised Governor, but rest assured, we will begin the bombardment of Wardhaven on time in"—he glanced over at a corner of his board—"thirty minutes."

19

Kris knew from her history books that attacks in the ancient world . . . twentieth century and earlier . . . were sometimes delayed for hours. She'd seen vids where actors had done a good job of showing the conflicted nature of officers and men . . . wanting to go forward and fight . . . afraid to go forward and die.

Kris and her crews may or may not have felt conflicted about their future, but delay was not an option. Orbital mechanics swung the battleships at High Wardhaven. Similar mechanics swung Kris's task force up from Wardhaven at them. Only a slight braking maneuver would send Horatio slicing down at them.

It was time.

"Sailors, my clock says we got five minutes," Kris said. "Chief, you got another one of those drinks for us?"

"I just might," he said, heading aft.

"Strange," Penny said, "I downed two of those and don't feel any urge to run for the head."

"We sweated it out," Kris said. Her own shipsuit was dark with dried perspiration, but either the life support

system was working overtime or they all stank so much it
was past notice. Strange what mattered at a time like this.

The Chief glided through, tossing liter bottles. "Last
communion," he said with a smile.

Tom caught the first one and raised it in salute. "As he
died to make us holy. Now we fight to keep us free."

Kris sipped her fortified water slowly, savoring the
taste. Maybe she was just enjoying the comfort of sharing
it with the others on the bridge. Last communion. Maybe
the Chief had hit something solid there. He passed through
again, collecting the empties. Tom turned to face his board,
eyed the battle forming up in front of him . . . and crossed
himself. "Into thy hands, Father, I commend my spirit," he
said softly.

Behind Kris, Penny was whispering the Twenty-third
Psalm, ". . . though I walk through the valley of the shadow
of death, I will fear no evil . . ." came a bit louder than the
rest. Beside Kris, Fintch was saying her Hail Mary over
and over, as fast as she could get the words out.

Kris swallowed hard. All her life, Father had taken his
family to church every Sunday. It was a photo op that was
not to be missed. But that photo op wasn't the comfort to
Kris just now that faith was to those around her. When this
was over, Kris intended to spend some time with Tom and
Penny, seeing what it was that made them want a priest
and a minister at their wedding, a prayer on their lips just
now.

But just now, orbital dynamics ruled their lives. Kris
mashed her commlink. "This is Light Brigade. Squadron 8
will be approaching the one hundred K boundary in sixty
seconds. Custer, you ready for your last stand?"

"Actually," van Horn said, "I was thinking of setting up
a lemonade stand and seeing if I could make a long-term
go of it."

"You sure couldn't make a joke of it," Sandy replied.

"Y'all both better be awful glad the Navy's keeping you
in ah day job," Luna drawled. "Thousands ah out ah work
comics and ya have ta try ya hand at it."

"Thirty seconds until we start the attack. Rockets on their way," van Horn reported.

"All right crews," Kris began, "every one of you is a volunteer. You knew coming into this that we were a pretty puny David and that those battlewagons were Goliath on steroids. Two of our fast patrol boats have shown that we can burn a battleship. But burning one doesn't come cheap.

"This time, we close with them. This time, we aim for the whites of their eyes. Hold your fire until they open up a gun turret to fire, then laser the turret while it's open. Their engines are vulnerable. They'll try to turn them away from you, so pair up with another, form threes and fours, and go for a battlewagon from every direction. They can't keep their stern turned away from all of you."

"You got that right," Luna said.

"And jink. Never go in a straight line for more than a second or two. You got to keep dodging constantly. Custer's gonna burn a lot more of their 5-inchers. We're going to take out more of them, but there's still going to be a hell of a lot of lasers coming at us."

"Dance, baby, dance, like you never done danced before," was Luna's answer to that.

"For our freedom. For your families. For Wardhaven. Let's go!" Kris shouted.

"For freedom. For families. For Wardhaven. For Princess Kris. Let's go," Luna shouted back. A second later, that was what echoed on net.

The 109 and twenty-one other boats crossed into 18-inch laser range. Above Kris, nineteen other boats followed the *Halsey* down into the danger zone. As they had before, they jinked up and down, right and left. For their very lives, they sped up and slowed down to no discernable pattern.

And the 18-inch lasers reached out for them.

"Admiral, Defense Central wants to know if you wish to change their priorities, sir," the Duty Lieutenant reported.

"I bet they do," the Admiral growled, but low. The standard doctrine called for the 18-inchers to take on anything within range for as long as they were in range. But the standard doctrine was developed by some dunderhead blissfully ignorant of the heat put out by the Whistler & Hardcastle, Limited, lasers provided to the fleet.

The Admiral was all too familiar with their heat problem.

He leaned into the spin of the *Revenge*. The 18-inchers would fill up the heat sinks quickly. Then, when the 5-inchers started their rapid fire, they'd lose efficiency very quickly.

What were the chances of winging one of those dancing hummingbirds with an 18-inch laser at 80, 90 K? What were the chances of taking them out at 30, 40 K with rapid 5-inch fire?

Certainly the main battery had contributed nothing the last time they'd tackled the fast patrol boats.

"Hold main battery fire."

"Hold main battery fire, aye, sir," the Duty Lieutenant repeated. "Defense Central has checked main battery fire."

"What!" the future governor of Wardhaven squawked. "You have them in your sights. Smash them."

"I will not waste my heat budget at this range. Governor, I promise not to tell you how to rape, pillage, and ravage unarmed civilians. Please don't jiggle my elbow while I'm handling the armed ones."

"I could have you relieved of your command."

"But right now might not be the best time to do it."

"Admiral, intel has cracked one of the transmissions from the Wardhaven fleet attacking us, sir. Some of the tugs do not have the strongest ciphers, and they are talking."

"And what are they saying?"

"They appear to be cheering Princess Kristine Longknife, sir. Intel thinks she may be the one leading the attack on us."

"That's impossible," the future governor huffed. "She was relieved of her command. She's disgraced."

"Maybe not as disgraced as someone had thought," the Chief of Staff muttered into his hand.

"So I face the little girl Longknife," the Admiral said thoughtfully. "Not bad. Not bad at all. Should I say, for a girl, Governor? For a girl who was relieved of her command? Sent home in disgrace to what, knit baby things? What did she have to draw on? A destroyer and a relic . . . and a dozen mosquitoes that were supposed to be demilitarized and put up for sale," the Admiral said, slamming his fist down on his board.

"And what, little girl, have you baked up for your Uncle Ralf? Freighters loaded with rockets. Yachts loaded with what I can only guess. So, little girl Longknife stands up and says she will fight me, and suddenly my battleships are facing not the fourteen we were told we might, but forty plus hulls charging hell for leather at us. Plus wave after wave of missiles intel never expected to see supporting a Navy attack." The Admiral shook his head and eyed his political master. Maskalyne's mouth hung open. Maybe it was the spin. Most likely it was the shock of seeing a Longknife held in respect.

"Mr. Governor, I wish I had half of what that little girl has. Here," he stabbed a finger at his head. "And here," now he stabbed at his heart. "Yes, I will defeat her because of what I have here." He stabbed at the dots on the battle board showing his ships. "But it would be nice to go into battle just once with people like she has racing to answer her call."

"Admiral, I should relieve you where you sit," the future governor snapped.

"But you won't, because I have a battle to win. Now, if you will please remain quiet, I must see about winning it."

Flag plot fell quiet. The first wave of incoming missiles began to strike.

"THEY have quit firing their big guns," Penny said. "They're still charged, but they aren't firing them."

"They've even retracted their ranging gear," Moose added.

"Hold your Foxers for closer range," Kris ordered on net. "If they aren't firing now, don't waste the decoys."

The ships still dodged and turned as they closed toward 5-inch range, but it was as if they were charging in slow motion. The 109 pitched and whirled, but the motion this time was almost gentle compared with the brutality of the first charge.

"We want to get within five thousand kilometers of the battleships and stay there," Kris reminded folks when a couple of runabouts dashed ahead of the rest. "Whatever energy you put on now, you'll have to be able to dump then."

So the boats charged in . . . slowly.

Squadron 8 still needed to close on the battleships first. Stan had the lead once again. "Division 1 is going for the second and third ships in line," he announced.

"Division 2 will take the last two," Kris ordered.

"I guess I get the flagship," Babs said.

"You're not alone," Sandy said. "The *Halsey* wants a big piece of that bastard." Now the chatter on net was ships sorting themselves out, pairing up, picking targets. Each battleship got two armed yachts and some runabouts. The *Cushing* begged off. "We can't get the old girl above one g, and she's not dodging so well. We'll come in late. Help where we can."

"We'll save some of the fun for you," Kris promised, but suddenly they were in 5-inch range, and the battleships opened up, and there was no time to talk. No time to do much more than hold her guts in and wait for the 109 to do its next erratic thing.

But there were answers to the battleships. Forward, Kami squeezed off 944s, adding them to the tag end of the cloud of missiles headed for the battle line. The *Halsey* added her own 5-inchers, taking shots at the flagship's antennas or 5-inch batteries when they popped up to fire at a missile or a boat. The battle was joined. Kris sat tight and watched the range drop from 40,000 to 30,000 to . . .

"I'm hit," came from Andy Gates on the 103.

"How bad?" Stan, his division leader, called back.

"Engine room. Losing power. I'm veering off, but I'll salvo all my missiles first."

"You do that, Andy. Take care."

"Hate to leave you folks."

"Go," Stan ordered his division mate.

Andy was lucky; he could limp out of the fight. Kris watched in horror as first one, then another runabout took direct hits and vanished. Kris mashed her commlink. "Runabouts, your maneuvering jets aren't good enough. Fall back. Slow down. Come in behind the yachts, or you won't come in at all."

"We can do it," one argued. But another one lit up in a pinprick of light, and the others slowed to fall behind the yachts.

Behind Kris, an old tug skipper announced a laser had opened his boat to space. Rather than abandon ship, they'd fight it in their salvage suits. A moment later, a second hit silenced him. Apparently, suited hands were not deft enough to fight a ship. Another tug trailed off to stand by Andy.

Ted Rockefeller's 102 boat took a hit. "They just winged me. We're still good. Besides, if I go, there won't be anyone left to go after that third battlewagon but a couple of Luna's nutty yachtsmen."

"I heard that," Luna said.

"So sue me," Ted shot back.

"Maybe I will if you don't get a big enough chunk of that battlewagon."

"I'll get a hunk of it. You just get yours."

"Hold your fire," Kris reminded them. Her range was down to 20,000 klicks. Over 20 percent of her boats were gone, and she had yet to ding a battleship. What was it going to take?

"**Hostiles** twenty thousand kilometers and closing," the Duty Lieutenant intoned. The Admiral eyed his charts.

They'd gotten a bare 20 percent of the attackers. His secondary batteries were tied up with the damn missiles. Dare he let the missiles have a free ride to concentrate on those damn patrol boats and the yachts?

Avenger staggered out of line, plasma blasting from an engine knocked askew by a rocket hit. Damn. They'd designed the battleships to handle big gun fights. Doctrine called for battle lines to turn their vulnerable engines away from laser fire and kinetic weapons. But doctrine was one thing; his orders were what ruled his life. Orders written on the assumption he would not have to fight his way into orbit.

Was it time to tear up his orders and fight this battle the way it needed to be fought? Was there any way he *could* fight it?

Sending in a battle line unescorted was a gross violation of doctrine. He should have had a squadron of cruisers and two of destroyers. But those were off demonstrating at Boynton because there just wasn't going to be any defenses left around Wardhaven.

Maybe there wouldn't have been, if it wasn't for you, little girl. Damn you Longknifes.

Eighteen thousand kilometers. If he ignored the missiles, they'd rape his sensors, leave him too blind to use his lasers. No, he had to defend against them. *So, we fight the missiles, then we fight the patrol boats.*

He glanced at his board. His secondary batteries were showing yellow. He was already pumping their coolant into his main belt coils to try to spread the heat, but they were firing so fast that they were heating up far beyond their specs. Well, he was pumping power from four reactors into those secondary batteries. They should be hot; hold out for just a bit more.

He had a major advantage. Pulse lasers were just that. They fired their energy off in one big pulse. Each of those fast patrol boats had four pulses. The yachts had two, maybe one pulse, then they were empty. And he had the armor to take a few pulses. No question about that.

"Lieutenant, advise Central Defense that the tugs are not to be ignored. They recharged the fast patrol boats once. I don't want that happening again."

"Understood, sir."

"Do we keep shooting the missiles?" Saris asked.

"Can't ignore them. If we do, they'll strip us blind and knock our engines to scrap metal. No, we have to keep knocking them down, then take on the ships behind the missiles. First one, then the others. You see something better, say so, and I'm sure our political master will relieve me with a smile," the admiral said with a toothy grin for the future governor.

"I see no better way to fight this, sir. We need support. Destroyers, cruisers of our own. We don't have them."

"My thoughts exactly," the Admiral said, eyeing his board. The 5-inchers were yellow and edging into the orange. Not good.

"Penny, Moose, what's happening on those battleships?" Kris asked as they crossed the 15 K line.

"They're hot and getting hotter," Penny said.

"Hot as a two-dollar pistol," Moose added. "They're gonna be slow reloading by the time we get down there among 'em."

"I like the sound of that," Tom said.

"I'm hit. I'm hit," the skipper of the 104 boat shouted. "I'm pulling out."

"To where?" Tom asked under his breath. A moment later, his question was answered as a second hit blew the patrol boat into a cloud of expanding gas.

"This close, there's no place to pull out to," Penny said.

"The 109 is going in, no matter what," Tom growled. "Dance, baby, dance." And the 109 whipped them around as it whirled into another turn. Now they fired Foxers, shooting out iron, aluminum, and white phosphorus a few hundred yards farther along their path, to convince tracking fire control systems that the boat was still on its course for a hair too long . . . to snap off a 5-inch laser blast at the decoy rather than the boat twisting away.

"Ten K," Kris muttered. Only five thousand more kilometers of taking this before they would start hitting back.

"Kris, you were always a better shot than me," Tom said, his voice urgent and low. "You want to take over shooting the 109, or do you think you need to observe and command?"

"It looks like it's every man for himself and the devil's offering no breaks. I don't want to sit here on my thumbs."

"Kris has weapons. I have the conn," Tom announced.

"Sink 'em all," Fintch said.

Kris took in the final situation as they closed, part commander's eye, part gunner. Her Division 2 had so far been lucky; they would hit the last two battleships in line with four fast patrol boats. The other divisions were all short; each battleship would get only one PF. Ungood. The yachts were coming in full strength, two per battleship, but there was hardly a runabout per hostile; they'd paid a high price. The *Halsey* was bearing down on the flagship with a bone in her teeth. She was also drawing more than her fair share of attention from the flag and the next two battleships in line.

So far, Sandy had been good. Or lucky. Kris prayed that luck would hold.

"Nelly, target the second to the last battleship. Pick two 5-inchers that should be opening up soon and the closest engine. Give each a 10 percent pulse as we cross the five K line."

"Target laid in."

Kris passed along what she'd done to the other ships and got "Aye aye," and "I *like* that," in response.

Everything done, Kris sat at her station. Around her, the 109 dodged and dipped. Kris ignored the now-familiar pounding as her body was slammed against the restraints. In the background the music played softly.

Close your mind to stress and pain,
Fight till You're No Longer Sane
Let not one damn cur pass by,

They were coming up on the line as the refrain came on. Around Kris, the bridge crew, the entire crew sang the words: *"How Many of Them Can We Make Die!"*

"Fire," Kris said softly.

From two dozen ships the pulse lasers reached out toward their tormentors, finally in range. They took on the 5-inch lasers, aimed for the vulnerable engines.

For a moment, the five battleships continued along their stately course. Then first one, then another, then all five began to dance off in different directions as the huge rocket bells that powered them, directed them, took hits and twisted in directions not ordered by Captains or navigators.

"Yes!" Tom shouted beside Kris.

"Don't go celebrating," Kris growled. "I just made the target harder to hit. Damn it all."

"But we hit it."

"Yes, we hit it." Kris pushed hard on her commlink. "Get in close now. Get in close and get them while they're trying to figure out which end is up."

"What the hell is going on?" the future governor of Wardhaven demanded as he was thrown against the restraints on his seat, then thrown half out of his chair.

"We seem to have taken a hit," the Admiral muttered.

"They fired off all their pulse lasers at once," his Chief of Staff said, "but they only winged us. We can handle this."

"But why would they waste a pulse on a 5-inch turret?" the Admiral mused, flexing his body with the bucking of the *Revenge*.

"They were desperate?"

"And they are still closing."

"They can't change course that fast this close?" the Chief of Staff suggested, but there was little force behind his words.

The Admiral frowned; there was something missing. Something he needed to know but had not been told. Had that Longknife girl pulled another trick out of her bag? The destroyer was commanded by a Santiago. Story was the Longknifes and Santiagos went way back. *Let's see what happens if we take a shot at killing that Santiago woman.* "The destroyer withheld its fire. Order *Revenge*, *Retribution*, and *Retaliation* to take it on with 18-inch fire as soon as they can steady on course."

"Aye, sir," said the Duty Lieutenant.

"CLOSE with the battleships," Kris ordered. "You can't do anything against their armor, so don't waste a full pulse unless you can fire right up their stern."

"Don't fire until you're looking up their kilt at their hairy balls," Luna chortled. "Come on, you damn chunk of ice. Quit jigging around and give me a peek."

Luna and two of her friends now hounded the third battleship in line; Kris kept an eye on the fourth one as Tom danced around it. His efforts to find a way in were hampered by the evasive program that seemed to only let them take one step closer before they dodged and dipped two steps back. But the evasion overrides kept the 5-inchers missing. That was the choice: stay in position for a good shot, or stay alive. No good options.

"Kris, the main battery on the battleships are activating."

"What could they be aiming for?" she asked no one.

"One just fired," Penny said. "It went for the *Halsey*!"

"Nelly, look for 18-inch turrets opening on the battleship. Give it a 20 percent pulse."

"Our battleship's not firing. It's the one up the line."

"Change target," Kris ordered even as Nelly was saying, "Changing target," and "Firing Laser One. 20 percent."

"Tell me how we did, Penny, Moose."

"Looks like you got that turret," Moose said. "Bad things are going on inside that ship. Really bad things."

Captain Luna was getting tired of this June-bugging around. She danced; her battleship did a jig right with her. Nobody stepped on anybody's toes. This was getting boring.

But the next battleship down, the one that belonged to Princess Kris, was not paying all that much attention to what went on around the next boat up. Paying real close attention to what Kris and those with her were doing, but not that much to what the boats hounding its buddy did.

"Seeing how the princess just poached on our boat," Luna muttered; she hit the override, squelched evasion, and swung her boat around just as that battleship presented her stern quarter.

Luna mashed the Fire button, sending twin 12-inch lasers up the rear of her target. For a second nothing happened; she frowned.

Beneath her, her boat bucked as a 5-inch laser cut into it. "Damn," Luna growled as she twisted the stick for evasion . . . nothing happened.

"Looks like we bought it, folks," Luna ordered. "Time to go," she said, reaching for the handle on her high-g station that would turn it into a life pod for a few hours.

But her boat still had power, and before it failed, she saw the most lovely sight as her target started to bubble, first at its stern, then amidships, holes opening in its ice as plasma shot out from reactors no longer contained.

"We done did it," Luna smiled. Then a 5-inch laser cut through her bridge.

There she goes," Tom said. "Luna got her."

"And they got Luna," Penny reported.

"Let's get that one," Kris said, switching targets to the next battleship up the line.

"We just got dinged," Tom reported. "Nothing we can't handle, but those damn 5-inchers are a pain."

"Nelly, take out a few secondaries on this one. 10 percent shots if you see a chance."

"Will do."

"Let me know if any more of those main turrets are powering up. How's the *Halsey* doing?"

"Not so good," Penny reported.

"Engineering, what can you give me?" Sandy asked.

"Not much, Skipper. They got our main feed line. I'm sucking reaction mass from the secondary line, and not much of it. 15 percent at max, ma'am."

"XO, you have the conn. Use what we've got to evade."

"Aye, ma'am."

"In a moment, I'm gonna ask you to hold her steady. You ready to do that?"

"If you're finally gonna off-load our pulse lasers at that bastard, you bet, ma'am," came back cheerfully.

"Sensors, talk to me. How's the flag doing at recharging his main battery?"

"They ought to be coming up real soon now."

"Pulse, you got a bead on them?"

"Dialed in, ma'am. At least, as dialed in as I can with us doing all this bouncing."

"Hold your horses. I'm about to give you a steady shot. You better make it worth our while." It would be a him *and* us situation. The *Halsey* would get one good shot at him. He would also get one good shot.

"We'll make him regret he ever came here, ma'am. Ever thought the *Halsey* would be a pushover."

"Make us proud."

"They're charged, ma'am."

"XO, one more dodge, then launch Foxers and hold steady."

"Bouncing now, ma'am. Steady now."

"Fire."

"All pulse lasers firing, ma'am."

The lights went dark in the *Halsey*'s CIC. "We're hit aft, ma'am. Engine room's off-line. Hit forward, ma'am. Bridge is off-line. So are lasers."

Then a laser cut through the CIC, and Sandy had just enough time to reach for the activation handle on her survival pod.

"The *Halsey*'s off net, Kris," Penny said softly.

"But they got the flag. It's really cooking," Tom reported.

Two more 18-inch turrets had taken hits while they were open, aiming for the *Halsey*. The battleship beside them was sparking into space. One of the yachts, freed from chasing the ship Luna had nailed, cut in to slice off two engines. Raw plasma shot into space . . . and for that moment, as the ship slowed in its evasions, Phil ducked the 106 boat in for a solid shot up its stern. He got it, but the next warship in line got a shot at Phil, and his boat shot away, out of control and spewing life pods as its plasma slowly ate it from the rear.

It was a melee of the worst order, with small boats going at the large ships like dogs against bears. The bears were hurting, three of the battleships were now vapor, but there were oh so many dogs down, too. "Tom, we've got to get the flag."

"I hear you. Fintch, move us up the line."

They danced into the fight around the middle surviving ship, dodged several shots from its 5-inchers, took out a turret that offered them a shot, and wound themselves into the battle royal around the flag just as the survivors of Kris's old Division 2 blew out the last battleship in line.

It cost them. Only one, the 108 boat, was still in good shape . . . and it was about drained dry. "Rendezvous with a tug that's close at hand if you can," Kris ordered. "Recharge."

"Kind of makes them a target," Tom said.

"It's up to the rest of you to keep that other battlewagon too busy to bother the 108," Kris said.

They piled in, but one yacht was immediately shot out, and the last runabout died as well. Still, the others hung at its neck, dogs gnawing at a bleeding bear. The bears were dying, but so many of the dogs were dying with them.

Kris dialed her commlink to a guard channel. "This is Princess Kristine Longknife, commanding forces defending Wardhaven, calling to those forces that have invaded our orbit and demanded our surrender. You are defeated. Only two of you survive. Are you prepared to surrender?"

"**Never,**" the possibly not future governor of Wardhaven said.

"You are still shooting at us," the Admiral said, waving the governor to silence. "Are you offering me a cease-fire?"

"Not unless you dump your reactors to space," came right back at him.

"Then how can I leave orbit?" he said, closed his commlink, and turned to the Duty Lieutenant. "Track this signal."

"Your ships are never leaving this orbit. You and your crews can arrange transportation on any number of liners out of here. Certainly the guy who sent you will pay your fare."

"We have her, sir!"

"Fire."

"**Kris**, you've talked long enough to triangulate on."

"Evade, Nelly," Kris ordered. "Fire at what shoots at us."

The 109 dropped out from under Kris, all lasers firing, but something was wrong. Even as a cheer went up on net, the hull of the 109 rang like a bell, then groaned as lights flickered.

Tom shouted, "No!" as the overhead bent above Kris and bowed. The skipper of the 109 launched himself from his seat. In the failing light, Kris was just able to see him hit the quick release on Penny's seat restraint, knock her from her station as the overhead reached down to meet the deck.

Then power failed, even auxiliary, and Kris was plunged into darkness. Beside her, Fintch gasped in pain. Somewhere others were screaming. And on her face Kris felt the wind of air racing out into the vacuum of space.

NELLY, SEAL THE HULL.

KRIS, I CAN ONLY MOVE THIS DUMB METAL ONCE, WHAT IF—

SEAL THE HULL NOW, OR WE'LL ALL BE DEAD.

HULL SEALED.

CAN YOU TURN ON SOME LIGHTS?

THE NET IS DOWN. I COULD ORDER THE RAW MOLECULES OF THE HULL, BUT I CAN NOT TALK TO ANYTHING SMARTER ON THIS TUB. Nelly sounded in a real huff.

Kris felt around. Nothing on her station responded. She reached for Fintch's station; it was knocked sideways. Kris found Fintch's hand; it was slippery. Blood? "Nelly, I could really use some light. A little hologram, please."

A tiny ball danced in front of Kris. It gave almost no light, just enough to see a bloodied hand protruding from the wreckage. Kris spotted an emergency light where the bulkhead should have been. It floated free now on wires. Kris had to fight free of her own seat; the release handle was bent double. Out, she worked her way, hand over hand, through the wreckage of the bridge to the unit. Its switch said it was on. She grabbed it by one handle and switched it off, then back on. Nothing. Holding it solidly in one hand, she hit it hard with the other.

She was blinded as the light came on.

Blinking, Kris looked around. The 109 must have been hit and folded double somewhere between the bridge and her weapons bay. Kris ignored the hanging gear and wires and looked for people. Penny was pushed up against the hull by the caved-in overhead. Where Penny's station had been, Kris saw . . . No!

She kicked off from the bulkhead and reached Tom in a second. His lopsided grin was there, but his chest disappeared under piping and power lines that belonged on the overhead, not down, crushing breath from him.

Kris checked for a pulse, for breath. For any sign of life. Nothing.

"I can't see," Penny whimpered softly between chattering teeth. "Is Tom okay?"

A glance over the wreckage showed Kris where it held Moose. Blood had quit spurting from his throat but hung in strange art about him and the wires of the station he had brought aboard such a short time before. Kris turned to the one person on the bridge who could benefit from first aid.

"Your leg looks broken. Does it hurt?" she asked Penny.

"I guess it does. I can't move it. I can't move much of anything. Could you move me where I could hold Tom's hand? I can't see him. I can't hear him. Is he hurt bad?"

Kris searched through all her years of glib political chat. "Tom's not in any pain," was what she finally said.

"I'm glad," Penny said softly, apparently not surprised at the answer. Then added, "I wonder why they haven't blown us out of space. Finished us off. They always gave the coup de grâce to the other ships they damaged."

"I hadn't noticed."

"I'm intel. I'm supposed to notice things like that."

"Then maybe we won," Kris said.

"I wish winning didn't hurt so much."

"Is there anyone there? Anyone who can help us?" Kris called. No one answered.

A forever time later, with the air tasting stale, there was noise along the outside of the hull. First a scraping, then a drilling. Finally there was fresher air.

And sound. "PF-109, this is Tug 1040 again. We're gonna put you in a salvage bubble before we try to open any of you up. Hold on tight. Can't be more than five minutes more. Trust me, the Johanson Brothers Salvagers are top-notch. They'll be with you in no time."

Kris couldn't get any answer through her dry throat. Past the ache that bound her chest in iron straps. It was as much as she could to lie carefully along Penny's mangled body as close as she dared, sharing what body warmth she could.

Kris tried to avoid the cheerful stare frozen on Tom's face. She had no answer for him any more than she'd been able to find one for poor Eddy. Why are you there . . . dead? Why am I here . . . alive?

It had been a while since Penny did anything but shiver.

"Hold on, gal, just a bit more," Kris whispered. "Tom wouldn't want you to give up this close to help. Hold on."

20

Kris lay facedown on her bed, listening to her breathing, the beating of her heart, the crinkling of her dress whites. Listening for anything . . . doing nothing.

The back of her ribbons bit into her flesh, but that sharp prickle was almost a friend. Not at all like the dry hurting that ate big chunks out of her heart and would not go away.

Tom's funeral had been beautiful.

Kris had never attended a Catholic funeral. Father didn't feel they were a good family photo op, so Kris had been spared the empty political eulogies. In something both poetic and ugly, the young priest who'd come all the way from Santa Maria for Tom's wedding was there to say his funeral Mass. No. The priest had been quick to point out this was a Mass of the Resurrection, a celebration of Tom's life and all their hope for the life to come. That was when Penny lost it.

Penny had struggled so hard to be the solid Navy widow, stiff upper lip and all, but the promise of life to come and the way the woman priest included Penny's own minister in this Celebration of Hope was too much. Maybe it would have been different if Penny's sight was still gone, but it was back, and the day was spring beautiful, the sky that horribly deep blue that seems to go on so far that you can almost see heaven. And fluffy white clouds, perfect for the angels themselves to perch on. And the saints, too, said the priest in her Irish brogue.

And someone found a piper to play "Amazing Grace" and "You'll No Come Home Again." And a bugler played taps.

And everyone cried. Everyone but Kris.

She stood, dry-eyed through it all, a good Longknife, watching yet another brave soldier who'd died for the Longknife legend go down into the grave. How many had Grampa Ray buried? Grampa Trouble? How many more would Kris bury if she followed the family trade? She dared not let herself feel for every one of them. Cry for every one of them. There'd be nothing left of herself if she did. Maybe she'd risk crying in private.

Only now she was alone, and her eyes were no more damp than a desert. It wasn't that she didn't feel. Good God, the pain in her chest was almost unbearable. But of tears nothing.

"You in there, Kris?" Jack called from the door.

"Go away."

"Thought I'd find you here. You voted yet?"

"No, and I don't intend to."

"Your dad won't be too happy about that."

"He can win or lose without me. He better."

There was a jiggling of the door handle. "Door's locked."

"I like it that way."

"Nelly, would you please unlock the door?"

"Yes, Jack."

"No, Nelly," but Jack had the door open already.

"Sorry, Kris." The door clicked back to locked.

"Fat good that does, Nelly. The horse is in and the barn's burned down."

"Sorry, Kris," Nelly repeated but she didn't sound at all

contrite. One more thing Kris needed to talk to Auntie Tru about fixing. Assuming even Tru could fix Nelly now.

"When was the last time you ate?" Jack asked, taking a chair at the foot of Kris's bed.

"Year or two ago," Kris guessed. "None of your business."

"Well, based upon early returns, your physical well-being just might become my business again, despite your refusing to vote for your dad."

"Maybe the party will choose a different Prime Minister?"

"In case you haven't noticed, the Longknife name has developed a new and rather special cachet. Not that you had anything to do with it."

Kris shook her head. "Hardly."

Jack shot her a frown. "Listen, seeing how I'm likely to be responsible for that body of yours again, and seeing how it's melting away to nothing, it seems to me that you ought to eat something. Now, you can walk out of here like a lady, or I can toss you over my shoulder like a sack of potatoes and carry you out. What's it gonna be?"

"All the way downstairs to the kitchen?" Kris said, measuring those strong arms and wondering how it would feel to be held by them for a few moments, even if it was only . . . But he was threatening to toss her over his shoulder, not carry her off in his arms. Nothing dignified or fun there. She rolled that image up, shut it away in a small lockbox she had for such . . . *very* small lockbox . . . and sat up in bed.

"Actually, I was thinking of a certain dive. A place where working folks like you and me might get a bite to eat and a drop to drink. Nothing private or special."

"Should I change?"

"Sailors eat free."

"Officers?"

"Well, they may have to pay. Don't know. Come on, let's go before all the greasy spoons are taken."

Kris let herself be cajoled out of her room and into Jack's car. He wasn't kidding when he said the place was a

dive. The Smugglers Roost was on the rougher side of
town, near the old shuttle port and close to the space elevator's industrial loading station. Jack parked across from it.
An unsightly thing, it filled the basement of an ancient
brick building. The steps down were broken and uneven.
The wooden floor was dark and worn by several hundred
years of workers' boots. The walls were hung with glowing
signs offering several kinds of beer on tap. Their light only
highlighted where raw bricks showed through chipped
plaster. Kris had been in college pubs that attempted this
ambiance. There was no attempt here; it was pure original.

As she took in the empty tables, she spotted several up
front occupied by huddled men and women in hard working clothes. It was the booth in the back that told her she'd
been had.

She whirled to leave and ran right into Jack. "You can't
go now."

"Watch me." But he had his hand on her arm, and it was
amazingly strong, and he was turning her around. She half
walked, half was pushed across the floor.

"Hi, Kris," King Ray said.

"Howdy, Lieutenant," Great-grampa Trouble put in. He
was in dress greens today, probably attending funerals for
Grampa Ray.

"Good to see you," Sandy said.

"Hello," Kris answered, voice flat.

"It that bad?" Ray said.

"Seems that way," Jack said, urging Kris into the booth
beside her Great-grampa Trouble, then pulling up a chair
for himself to blockade her from making a hasty exit. The
king wore a flannel shirt and slacks. Sandy was in cut-offs
for her leg cast. A tank top left room for her arm cast. They
fit right in.

"You doing the round of funerals?" Trouble asked.

"Tom today. The same priest that did his wedding last
week did his funeral today."

Both men shook their heads and took a long pull on
their beers. "Bloody shame, that," Trouble said.

"Beautiful funeral," Jack said.

"There's no such thing as a beautiful funeral for a twenty-three-year-old man," Ray said softly.

"No, sir," Kris agreed.

"You drinking what the rest of these decrepit wrecks are, Navy?" an old man in a checked shirt and jeans, gray ponytail half down to his thick black leather belt asked.

"Soda," Kris said.

He raised an eyebrow but wrote Kris's order and Jack's beer and left.

"Honey, I still think it was all the pills your mother was stuffing you full of," Trouble said.

"And not the brandy I was sneaking out of Father's liquor cabinet or the wine from Mother's supply. Sorry, Grampa, but I won't wake up a week from now and find out I drank my way past how many funerals?" she eyed Jack.

"A lot," he said.

"Chandra Singh's husband called me today, asked me if they'd found her body. The Sikhs are very particular about their funerals. I told him we were still hunting for the wreckage of the 105 boat. We'll keep hunting." Kris shook her head. "I have no idea what's going on up there in orbit. They pried us out of the 109 and shot us off to the hospital." Unconsciously, her hand went to the flaking bandage over her right eye. "I don't know what's going on up there."

"You're Squadron 8's Commodore; you should check in. Ask," Sandy said.

"No I'm not. Mandanti's the Commodore."

"By right of blood, by right of title, by right of name, I'm taking command," Jack intoned. "I was there."

"Yeah, when I stole his command."

"Looked more like you asked and he passed you the baton," Sandy said, "with my hearty support."

Kris blinked. "I didn't give you much choice."

"That mess we were in didn't give anyone much choice," Ray growled at his beer. "I was so busy trying to be evenhanded with this dumb troglodyte who'd just

ousted my grandson that I ended up bending over and kiss-
ing my own ass."

He shook his head ruefully. "Your brother, Honovi,
dropped by yesterday, had a long talk with me. We'll have
to change the way Wardhaven handles temporary governments. With a smart boy like that in the family, maybe
there is hope for us."

The king took a long pull on his beer, then fixed Kris
with a firm eye. "Kris, when people like me screw up,
dumping hot potatoes on people like you, battles like you
ended up fighting, we got two choices. We can eat our
heart, day by day, bite by bite. Or we can accept that what
we did was what looked like a good idea at that moment.
Was what had to be done just then. In the case of me and
your old man, we just about blew the whole ball game for
Wardhaven.

"But you saved our necks. You rallied some damn fine
people to step up to a near-impossible job. The best
dropped what they were doing and came running." He
paused, seemed to lose himself gazing off past Kris's head.
"Why is it always the best we lose?"

Trouble cleared his throat. Ray blinked twice and went
on. "You and they did what had to be done. Some of you
survived, despite the odds. Some didn't. There's nothing
right or fair about it. Your Tommy had more choice, I hear,
than most. He chose for his wife to live."

Grampa Ray shifted in his seat. "Now you're sitting
where all of us have sat. Stuck among the survivors. For
now. Tomorrow, there will be another dustup somewhere.
There's always another crisis somewhere. So you can
crawl into a corner, eat your heart out and die, or order
something to eat and stay with the rest of us living."

"Such encouraging words from your very own great-
grandfather," Sandy said. "How can you but choose to go
on?"

Trouble slapped Kris on the back. "What do you want to
eat?"

Kris ordered a hamburger when the drinks arrived. The

barkeep left the drinks and a vid controller. "Thought the likes of you might want to know what's going on out there."

"I was kind of hoping to ignore it," Ray said as he hit the selector switch and the beer ad switched to news.

"So, with the critical information I passed along to the Wardhaven Flagship, plus my own right-on analysis of the threat against us," Adorable Dora was saying to the camera, "our forces launched their assault on these unidentified attackers."

Jack exploded with a very bad word, then went on, still steaming, "Like hell she did. She was hiding in the run-about's bathroom, clutching two life pods. I don't know how she planned on using both, but she had two survival pods, one in each hand."

"I thought you were far enough behind us that you weren't in any danger," Kris said.

"We were, but don't tell that to Adorable Dora. And don't tell me that she saw any of the fight. She was in the bathroom, with the door locked. Glad the rest of us didn't need to go."

Ray hit the channel switch again. "From such things are the history books written. So Kris, you had poor Jack following two steps behind you and you didn't even need him."

"Couldn't tell what might have happened while we were behind Milna. Had to have a relay boat. Unfortunately, I picked Dora's boat, and she insisted on riding along. Doesn't Jack deserve a Wound Medal?" Kris joked. Then she remembered the price others had paid for their medal and felt sick at her stomach.

"A Wound Medal and a Meritorious Service Cross," Grampa Trouble jumped in. "Plus we need something for heroic displays of self-control under combat conditions. After all, he didn't throttle that reporter. How about instituting the Ray Cross."

"How about a Right Cross." Ray waved a fist at his friend.

"Stop there," Sandy said. "That's Winston Spencer, of the AP, my newsie. Let's hear his story."

The screen showed a man with a cast on his left arm. "At this point the *Halsey* had closed to within five thousand kilometers of the enemy flagship. She was hurting, but still fighting and hadn't fired her ten pulse lasers. Captain Santiago was looking for a good shot, but with the battleship now bouncing around as well as the destroyer, that just wasn't happening."

His picture vanished to show a view of tiny ship images dodging and jinking their way through black space.

"I was in the Combat Information Center, the ship's command hub," the reporter's voice went on so calmly, so matter-of-factly, "when the skipper risked taking her ship out of its evasion maneuvers to get that good shot. Before she could get back into evasions, the *Halsey* was hammered, and we lost all power, but I've constructed what happened next from other sources after they brought us survivors out of the wreck of the *Halsey*."

Sandy fidgeted with her own casts and eyed the floor.

"We know the enemy flagship was in bad shape, hurting from the *Halsey*'s attack and many others. At this point, Princess Kris Longknife, the acting Commodore of Fast Patrol Boat Squadron 8 called to offer the intruders a chance to surrender."

Kris sat up straight.

"That's how you're going into the history books, kitten," Grampa Trouble whispered.

"While negotiating, the enemy apparently tracked the signal and, while still talking surrender, fired off a blast at our flagship. Lieutenant Tom Lien, the skipper of PF-109, in which Princess Kris was riding, was watching for just this. He had his helmswoman, 3/c Mary Fintch, dodge away while he fired back at the battleship. Meanwhile, the ancient destroyer *Cushing,* under Commander Mandanti, called back from retirement, managed to limp into range and fired off their six pulse lasers. Or maybe three. I'm still trying to find out how many of them actually worked. That was all it took. The enemy flagship blew up even as PF-109 was heavily damaged. Lieutenant Lien, 3/c Fintch, and several others aboard the 109 boat are among the heroes who paid the full measure to save Wardhaven from this unprovoked attack."

"Where do we find such people?" Kris asked no one.

"We don't find them," King Ray said slowly. "They find us. They step forward when we need them. I don't know what we do to deserve them." He paused. "And God help us if we dam up that special well from which they come when we need them so desperately."

None at the table could add to that.

On-screen, the reporter struggled with the question topmost on everyone's mind. "Where did those ships come from?"

"There are no survivors from any of them. A check among the larger chunks of wreckage shows their survival pods were defective. We've recovered bodies in them, but being in them didn't help the crew. Now, Todd, as someone who spent several hours in one, awaiting rescue from the CIC of the *Halsey,* let me tell you, they are very simple and easy to operate.

"The Navy complains about using the lowest bidder," the anchorman said. "Sounds like someone used an even lower bidder."

"It does sound like that. Meanwhile, the Navy is going over what wreckage they can to identify who made it. However, I'm told that they aren't optimistic that it will tell them much. Designs have been shared across the Society of Humanity for eighty years. Items from one planet are used in other planets' products and built into other planets' finished ships. Whoever did this didn't want to be known, and now it seems that dead men will tell no tales."

"Hmm. Well, thank you for sharing your harrowing voyage, the last voyage, so it seems, of the good ship *Halsey.*"

"I shared it with a lot of good men and women. The best we have, Todd. I hope we never forget that or forget them."

"And now, at five minutes before the hour, we'd better update you on the election returns."

"Let's don't and say we did," Ray said, and flipped the channel. Ten flips later, he put it back on the beer sign.

"What are you grumping about?" came from behind Kris. "It looks like my vacation is gonna be canceled on account of election results." So saying, General Mac Mc-Morrison, the former chairman of the Joint Staff, slipped into the seat beside Ray.

Kris started to jump to attention, something hard to do with a table in front of her. Especially with the barkeep trying to slap a plate of hamburger and fries in front of her and another one in front of Jack.

"Relax, Commodore," Mac said.

"I'm sorry about that Commodore thing," Kris said.

"I'm not," Mac said. "Somebody had to rally the troops. I couldn't. My resignation had been requested, and I was on terminal leave. Admiral Pennypacker had always wanted my job in the worst way. I just didn't know how badly. He came out of retirement to take it and did just about the worst job anyone has ever done of it." Mac shook his head.

"Well, if you're retiring," Trouble started, "I've got this chicken ranch up in the foothills of the North Range. Hardly ever visited. Perfect place; your wife will love it. Ruth does. Keeps asking me when we're going to retire to it."

"Don't be too quick to sell off that old place," King Ray muttered. "This mess has got me thinking I need reps on every planet, watching them closer than I can. Maybe doing a better job. How'd you like to be Duke Trouble of Wardhaven?"

Trouble made a rude sound, but Kris noticed he didn't say no. Was poor Grampa Trouble ready to let a Longknife draft him into another rough job? Did Grampa Ray need help that bad?

Mac shook his head. "I hate to get between you two old war buddies, but Trouble, I don't think I'm in the market for a retirement business. I got a call a half hour back from this young Lieutenant's father. Seems he thinks his party is going to win the election, and he might be moving back into Government House. Wants me to take my old job running Wardhaven's military. Expand the fleet some more."

"How are the farmers going to take to that?" Kris asked.

"Farm coalition is one of the stronger movers on that. Seems someone passed around the farm policy that they have on Greenfeld. Not a nice one. What you grow, you sell to the government at the price the government sets."

"Why the Greenfeld farm policy?" Sandy asked.

"Well, while that guy you were listening to might be towing the official line that we don't know where those ships came from, there're an awful lot of folks who are hearing through the grapevine that a lot of that stuff has a distinctly Greenfeld flair to it."

"We find some Whistler & Hardcastle lasers?" Ray asked.

"Chunks of them."

"Father intend to do anything about that?" Kris asked.

Mac worried his lower lip. "Do you really want to be in the Navy of ninety planets that's fighting eighty planets?"

Kris took a drink of her soda. The thought of a long war between two evenly balanced and powerful alliances made her shiver. "Not really, but, blast it, I don't want to do nothing. If we do, won't the Peterwalds just come back?"

"The JO has a point," Trouble said.

"A good one." Mac nodded.

"I understand the threatening fleet has withdrawn from Boynton," King Ray said.

"Slipped away real fast once Kris nailed our attackers," Mac agreed. "Boynton is officially applying for membership in your union, Ray. Moving real fast now. I understand they and six other planets out that way are all coming in together."

"And Kris has Hikila ready to come in," Ray mused, swirling his beer and studying the bubbles. "Three other planets out that way will follow them in. Once the word gets out that Henry Peterwald tried for Wardhaven . . . and fell on his face . . . there ought to be several more planets joining, too."

"So we grow," Trouble said. "Grow faster than Greenfeld. And maybe, over time, cut out a few of their worlds."

Sandy raised her glass in salute, left-handed. The others joined her.

Kris frowned. "That's a lot of territory to defend."

"Boynton's asking us for the specs on the fast patrol boats," Mac said. "I intend to send them."

Kris opened her mouth. "But," Mac went on, raising a hand to silence Kris, "we're changing the design. Make 'em out of smart metal. With smart hulls and upgraded computers so they can repair themselves when they take hits, fill in battle damage."

"If we had . . ." Kris said softly.

Mac cut her off. "I just read the full salvage report on the 109. You think I came over here just to jabber with these old farts? Young woman, your having that fancy computer of yours seal the 109's hull saved the lives of the three survivors forward, and at least four of the crew aft who had their survival pods damaged in the fight. If you'd waited five seconds to analyze things, you'd all have been breathing vacuum. You made a snap decision, and it was the right decision.

"As for the three on the bridge, they were dead before the lights went out, crushed when the 109 bent in the middle. There was nothing you could have done to save them. You can hear what I'm saying to you, or not, but it won't change anything."

Mac shook his head. "Even if I hadn't let the damn bean counters talk me into having the experimental squadron made out of that damn semi–smart metal. Even if that brassy computer of yours had been ready to start ordering the metal around as soon as you took the hit, we would have lost five good men and women on the 109." His voice slowed, went low. "You were good, but nobody's that good, and those battleships were big honking mothers."

"Big honking mothers with lots and lots of guns," Sandy said, resting a hand on Kris's arm.

"I couldn't save Tommy," Kris said, her eyes rimming with moisture.

"Didn't you see before they evacuated you?" Mac asked.

"See what?"

"The skipper's station wasn't damaged at all."

"Huh?"

"If Tom had stayed in his seat, he wouldn't have been scratched."

"Oh my God," Kris said, the tears starting to flow. "Penny's going to be . . ." Kris said. The tears were coming heavy now. Softly. She shivered as something left her.

"He died saving her," Grampa Trouble whispered, putting his arm around Kris and holding her while she wept for the first time since she'd come out of the 109. She gave herself over to sobs that came from deep inside her and shook her to her foundation.

Sandy reached out to rest a hand on her shoulder. Jack added one on her back. Kris let her racking grief out to be shared among her friends, to swirl over all of them and slowly wash away.

As she came up for air, Jack loaned her his handkerchief. Kris righted herself, but she couldn't miss the way Grampa Trouble was eyeing Ray across the table.

The man of legends was looking very old, with his chin settled on his chest. His words, when they came, were hushed and wrapped around sobs. "I told Rita I should lead the diversion. She told me I had to stay back with the main force. She could take care of that distraction. She distracted them good. Good thing, too, 'cause there were a hell of a lot more Iteeche bastards than we ever thought there could be."

Ray shivered, shook his head, reached for his beer and took a long swallow. "And when we'd won, it was as if her task force had just vanished. Vanished."

"And he would have drowned himself in ten barrels of

beer if I hadn't pulled him out," Trouble said softly. "Ray, am I gonna have to pull you out tonight?"

"No, not tonight, but someone's gonna have to spend some time with Penny, helping her accept that she's condemned to live."

"I'll be there," Kris promised. And with that it came to her why it was that Longknifes and Santiagos stood so often together. Those who died sealed those who lived into a pact for life. She thought of Penny with understanding growing in her eyes. The destroyer skipper nodded and raised her glass in salute to the new knowledge.

Kris sighed. Grampa Ray was right. She could eat her heart in small bites every day, or she could put her heart into living every day that came her way. She could decide later . . . or she could make the call now and save herself a lot of wasted motion. Lose it now or suck it up. Let Tom's death, all their deaths, become a black hole that ripped her apart. Or find the strength she needed. That Penny needed. That a lot of them needed.

You weren't a Longknife just because you did what had to be done on the day it was demanded of you. No, Longknifes did what had to be done the next day and the next. They kept putting one foot in front of the other day after day, for themselves, and for those they led . . . until habit turned to purpose.

So . . . if she was going to keep going, and take others with her, she needed a job. What could a beaten-down old mutineer, deserter, once relieved of command, junior officer do these days. Kris found a smile creeping up on her.

"General, it seems to me that fast patrol boats don't take much of a crew, can be built real fast and cheap and, at least if you listen to what's being said on the talk shows, they seem to really be able to do a job on battleships."

"If someone's dumb enough to send them in without destroyers and cruisers," Sandy muttered. "Bunch of political plumbers."

"We don't need to let that get on the talk shows," Mac said.

"So," Kris went on, "if a lot of planets suddenly ordered a lot of fast patrol boats for their close-in defense, it sounds to me like they'll also need some training on how to use them. Now, I could be wrong on this, but if Wardhaven were to offer not only the boats, but say, the training assistance of one former acting Commodore Princess Kristine Longknife and associates of the famed Squadron 8, might they jump at the offer?"

"And might some folks we won't mention think them a bit more dangerous than they really are?" Trouble grinned wickedly.

Ray sighed. "Smoke and mirrors."

"The lies that some people live by." Sandy sighed.

"If they're dumb enough to let you do it, why not lead them around by their noses?" Mac said. "Besides, I was kind of wondering what to do with you next. I'm running out of jobs I could dredge up for you, Kris. Kind of poetic the condemned woman choosing her last waltz."

"And with any luck, it will get me away from Wardhaven and out of your hair. Father's hair. King Ray's hair. Maybe far enough away for some folks to forget I've been in their hair."

Sandy shook her head. Jack and Trouble joined in. "No chance of that," they agreed in unison.

About the Author

Mike Shepherd grew up Navy. It taught him early about change and the chain of command. He's worked as a bartender and cabdriver, personnel adviser and labor negotiator. Now retired from building databases about the endangered critters of the Pacific Northwest, he's looking forward to some serious writing.

Mike lives in Vancouver, Washington, with his wife, Ellen, and her mother. He enjoys reading, writing, watching grandchildren for story ideas, and upgrading his computer—all are never ending.

Oh, and working on Kris's next book, *Kris Longknife: Audacious.*

You may reach him at Mike_Shepherd@comcast.net.